Bound for Murder

**Center Point
Large Print**

**This Large Print Book carries the
Seal of Approval of N.A.V.H.**

Bound for Murder

LAURA CHILDS

Center Point Publishing
Thorndike, Maine

This Center Point Large Print edition
is published in the year 2005 by arrangement with
The Berkley Publishing Group, a division of
Penguin Group (USA) Inc.

Copyright © 2004 by Gerry Schmitt.

The text of this Large Print edition is unabridged. In other
aspects, this book may vary from the original edition. Printed in
Thailand. Set in 16-point Times New Roman type.

ISBN 1-58547-619-6

Library of Congress Cataloging-in-Publication Data

Childs, Laura.
    Bound for murder / Laura Childs.--Center Point large print ed.
    p. cm.
    ISBN 1-58547-619-6 (lib. bdg. : alk. paper)
    1. Women detectives--Louisiana--New Orleans--Fiction. 2. New Orleans (La.)--Fiction.
3. Scrapbooks--Fiction. 4. Large type books. I. Title.

PS3603.H56B68 2005
813'.6--dc22

                                                                    2005001149

Bound for Murder

Acknowledgments

Heartfelt thank-yous to my agent, Sam Pinkus; to Gary, for giving me an office at Mill City Marketing/Survey Value; to my husband, Bob, for his continued support; to the many scrapbook shops that carry my books and invite me in for book signings; to the tea shops that also carry my books and generously promote them via "scrapbook teas" (what fun!); to all the marvelous book sellers who not only stock my books, but recommend them to customers; and to all the wonderful writers, reviewers, web masters, crafts columnists, and editors who have been so kind and generous with their words.

This book is dedicated to my dear friend,
Diane,
whom I finally reconnected with after almost 30 years.

Chapter 1

AUNTED?" cried Carmela Bertrand as she and her friend Ava Grieux trundled their packages down a narrow hallway where sagging floorboards creaked and lamps with beaded shades cast a faint pinkish glow. "I don't recall Quigg ever mentioning that Bon Tiempe was haunted." With tall, narrow doors at every twist and turn and canted baroque mirrors that tossed back gilded reflections, the hallway felt more like a funhouse maze.

Putting her shoulder to the door at the far end of the hallway, Carmela nudged it open and the two of them stepped into a small, tastefully furnished business office that had been shoe-horned in where a butler's pantry had once existed. Back when Bon Tiempe Restaurant had been a private New Orleans home.

Ava Grieux's expressive brown eyes gave a languid sweep of the small office, taking in the slightly Gothic decor, the Tiffany lamp strewn with dancing dragon-flies, and the moss-green velvet settee pushed up against one wall. The opposite wall was dominated by an antique roll-top desk with a laptop computer sitting atop it.

"*Feels* haunted," said Ava, hunching her shawl-draped shoulders in a hopeful gesture.

Carmela uttered a soft laugh as she set her box of place cards down on a small marble-topped table, then grabbed the box containing the floral arrangement that

Ava, her best friend and female confidante, had been carrying. "Haunted by ghosts of customers past, maybe," Carmela told her, placing the oversized box on the desk. "Before Quigg turned this old Bywater mansion into a hoity-toity restaurant it was a costume shop." Quigg Brevard was the rather dashing proprietor of the fabulously successful Bon Tiempe. A bit of a bon vivant, Quigg was also a man who found Carmela most enchanting, much to her consternation. Because fortunately or unfortunately for Carmela, she was already married. To Shamus Allan Meechum, professional cad, sweet talker, and the youngest of the Crescent City Bank Meechums.

Although Carmela and Shamus were most definitely separated—physically, spiritually, and in all manner of opinion concerning the commonly held definition of matrimonial harmony—they'd simply never gotten around to making their separation formal and legal. Even for a banker, Shamus wasn't all that keen on formal and legal.

"Mmn," said Ava, surveying her wavering image in yet another antique mirror and obviously liking what she saw. "Lots of so-called costumers in New Orleans." Ava poufed her mass of auburn hair and pulled the front of her cocktail dress down to reveal a tad more of her luscious décolletage. Then, like a lazy, languid cat, Ava eased herself down onto the velvet settee, allowing Carmela an unobstructed view of the amber-tinted glass.

Carmela stared straight ahead as though confronting

the lens of a camera. Not unlike she'd done for her fourth grade class picture when, geeky-looking and skinny, she'd probably taken the worst picture of her life.

Now the image that stared back at her was quite different. Mid-twenties, pretty veering toward stunning, Carmela possessed a unique blend of kinetic energy and quiet confidence. Her looks were further enhanced by her glowing, almost luminous complexion. Her lovely oval face was loosely framed by streaked blond hair. And many thought her grayish-blue eyes strikingly similar in color to the flat glint of the Gulf of Mexico.

That's me? Carmela asked herself, always surprised by her now-comely image. Then, suddenly startled, she frowned and peered into the mirror for a closer look. As she studied her image, she realized that the silvering or mercury or whatever you called that shiny stuff on the back of the mirror had either flaked off or been improperly redone. So a faint double image was reflected. A *ghost* image. Carmela gave a slight shiver. *Maybe Ava's premonition wasn't so far-fetched after all.*

Ava dug eagerly into the box Carmela had brought along. "I haven't seen your place card designs yet, *cher,*" she said, carefully pulling out a stack of deckled paper cards and studying them.

"Honey, that's because my design isn't *done* yet," Carmela told her, letting loose a mighty sigh. "I ordered ribbon six weeks ago and it only just showed up on my doorstep late this afternoon!" Carmela pulled two spools of peach-colored ribbon from her purse and held them out for Ava's inspection.

"Personalized ribbon," said Ava, narrowing her eyes. "Perfect."

Carmela was the proprietor of Memory Mine, a small scrapbooking shop tucked away on Governor Nicholls Street in the French Quarter. Besides helping her customers create pluperfect scrapbook pages that showcased their precious photos, her talents also shone forth when it came to designing keepsake boxes, party invitations, and personalized albums.

Reaching into her bag again, Carmela produced a small gold snipping scissors. She spun out one of the spools of ribbon until she had a twelve-inch piece on which sparkled the gold-embossed words *Wren & Jamie*. Giving a quick snip, Carmela passed the twist of ribbon over to Ava.

"This is gonna be great," said Ava, studying the ribbon. "I love the script or type font or whatever you call it."

"I could order some for your shop," said Carmela, raising one skeptical eyebrow. Ava owned the Juju Voodoo and Souvenir Shop over on Esplanade Avenue. Voodoo being a thriving cottage industry in New Orleans, Ava's tiny shop was redolent with the heady scents of sandalwood incense, musk oil, and flickering vanilla candles. With its enchanting stock of love charms and tiny silk bags filled with "secret" herb mixtures (mixtures that Ava confided were better suited to seasoning a turkey) the little shop catered shamelessly to tourists who flocked to the French Quarter searching for an authentic voodoo experience.

Ava giggled at the thought of personalized ribbon for her shop. "I think my shop's a little trippy for something this classy." She eyed the twelve-inch hanks of peach ribbon Carmela kept snipping and handing over to her. "So what do you want me to do?" she drawled. "Just twine this stuff through the holes ya'll punched?"

Carmela nodded. "Thread it through and I'll finish up with some neat little bows and judicious trimming." The place cards Carmela had designed for tonight were truly miniature works of art. Four-by-six-inch pieces of floral card stock served as the canvas. Upon this, Carmela had created a mini collage, incorporating tiny Renaissance-style images of angels, pressed flowers, gold heart charms, and the guest's names printed on peach-colored vellum. She'd used a crinkle cutter to create a deckled edge at the bottom of each card. The personalized ribbon threaded through the top would be the final loving touch.

As Carmela worked, she glanced at her watch nervously. She knew the guests were probably arriving right now. And even though they were being hustled into the party room to mix, mingle, and enjoy cocktails and finger food, she still needed to get the place cards on the tables ASAP. After all, Gabby was counting on her. Big time.

As if reading Carmela's mind, Ava glanced up and smiled. "Is Gabby pretty excited about Wren's wedding?" she asked, her nimble fingers continuing to weave ribbon through the punched holes in the place cards.

"Gabby's ecstatic," confirmed Carmela. "She doesn't have any brothers or sisters, and Wren is her absolute favorite cousin."

"It was sweet of you to help with all the arrangements," murmured Ava, trying to keep up with Carmela, who was tying bows and trimming ribbon like a true scrapbook and craft pro.

"It's the least I can do," murmured Carmela. Ever since she'd opened Memory Mine, Gabby Mercer-Morris had served as her highly capable assistant and enthusiastic instructor of scrapbook classes. In fact, the place cards that Carmela and Ava were laboring over right now were a kind of by-product of Gabby's creativity.

Gabby was a paper freak of the first magnitude. She adored the myriad of paper designs they carried for scrapbooking, and positively swooned over the special vellums, mulberry papers, Japanese washi papers, flax and jute fiber papers, and parchment papers they also carried. And, although it had been Carmela's idea to offer their Paper Moon class, an introduction to the amazingly diverse world of paper, it was Gabby who'd hatched the idea for card-making classes. Classes that filled up immediately and taught eager scrapbookers how to apply the same stamping, embossing, and dry brush techniques they'd learned in scrapbooking to create highly personalized greeting

16

cards, thank-you cards, and even place cards.

Now Gabby's cousin, Wren West, was marrying Jamie Redmond this coming Saturday. And Carmela, with a little help from Ava, was doing her utmost to make tonight's pre-wedding gala an elegant and memorable occasion.

The place cards finished, Carmela let out a low whistle as she lifted the centerpiece Ava had designed from its tissue paper nest inside a cardboard box.

Ava glanced at Carmela. "What?" she asked, anxiously. "It's okay, isn't it?"

"Okay?" exclaimed Carmela. "This is spectacular." Time had run out for Carmela today, so she'd sent out a plea to Ava. And Ava, overachiever and dear friend that she was, had gladly responded. Besides owning a voodoo shop and freelancing as a custom mask maker, Ava was also a rather fine floral designer. For the big pre-wedding bash tonight, she'd created a floral arrangement using pink ruffle azaleas, foxglove, Louisiana peppermint camellias, and ferns, accented with sprigs of bleeding hearts and set in a cream-colored French crock.

"Twarn't nothin'," replied Ava, plucking at the sprigs of bleeding hearts to straighten them. But she was pleased just the same to receive Carmela's compliment.

Twenty minutes later the party was in full swing.

"Interesting crowd," commented Ava, as she sipped a dirty martini, her favorite drink du jour. "I've already been hit on four times."

"Good night for you?" asked Carmela.

Ava shook back her frowzled mane and considered the question. "A little slow," she admitted. Tall and sinewy, with the carriage of a New York runway model, Ava was zipped into a slithery gold dress that most definitely showed off her generous assets. Once crowned Miss Teen Sparkle of Mobile, Alabama, Ava had never abandoned the regal bearing as befitted a Southern beauty queen.

"Give it a few minutes," said Carmela, as the party swirled noisily around them. "Things should pick up." It was a good-sized crowd—exactly sixty people according to the guest list—that had turned out to celebrate the much anticipated wedding of Wren and Jamie. Most were friends of the groom, Jamie Redmond, who'd grown up just south of New Orleans in the little town of Boothville and then moved the seventy or so miles north to attend Tulane University. Wren, Jamie's fiancée and Gabby's first cousin, had moved to New Orleans from Chicago just over a year ago.

"Evenin' pretty ladies," drawled a male voice behind them.

"Hello," said Ava, arching a single eyebrow and turning to appraise their admirer.

"I bet you're Carmela," said the man, a tall, good-looking fellow with dark wavy hair and a pencil mustache. He was clutching a glass of bourbon and weaving slightly.

"I'm Ava, *this* is Carmela," said Ava, setting him straight.

"Blaine Taylor," said the man playfully, leaning in close. "But ya'll can call me B.T."

"You're Jamie's software partner," exclaimed Carmela. She'd heard all about Blaine Taylor from Gabby. Blaine was supposedly a bigtime real estate investor as well as former Tulane classmate of Jamie's. Although he didn't look it at the moment, Blaine was also a fairly savvy businessman and had teamed up with Jamie to help investigate potential markets for a software program Jamie had designed.

"Neutron," said Blaine, blowing soft, boozy breath into Carmela's ear.

"Pardon?" she said.

"Neutered?" asked Ava. "*That* doesn't sound good."

Blaine Taylor looked hurt. "Not neutered, *Neutron*," he said, lurching toward Ava and, in the process, sloshing half his drink on the Aubusson carpet. "Oops," he said, a silly smile flitting across his handsome face.

"I see you've made the acquaintance of my erstwhile partner," said Jamie Redmond, suddenly materializing at Carmela's elbow. Tall and elegantly slim, with a fair complexion, pale-blue eyes, and ginger-colored hair, Jamie appeared slightly embarrassed by his friend's behavior. "Has B.T. been boring you with tales of our software project?" he asked the two women.

"Mostly he's just been weaving and sloshing," commented Ava, still eyeing Blaine. "So we're kind of reserving judgment."

"What exactly *is* Neutron?" asked Carmela, turning her attention to Jamie.

"It's pretty neat," Jamie responded eagerly. "Neutron is a software program that helps detect bugs and bombs in newly written code."

"Oh," said Ava, suddenly disinterested. "Computer stuff."

"Wait a minute," said Blaine, holding up one finger. "This is cutting-edge stuff!"

"As you can see," said Jamie, making a self-deprecating gesture at the well-worn tweed jacket he wore, "I'm the tweedy, nerdish member of the team. And Blaine's the showy 'suit' side. Very buttoned up." He smiled enthusiastically at the two women. "Would you believe it? Blaine's already got us pow-wowing with a couple heavy-hitter high-tech companies! Both have expressed interest in either licensing or possibly even buying Neutron outright."

"For *big* money," Blaine blurted out, a silly, satisfied grin pasted across his face. "That is, if I can get this self-styled *dilettante* to seriously agree to sell." Blaine spat out the word *dilettante* like he was referring to cattle manure.

Jamie put a hand on Blaine's shoulder to steady him. "I have to admit, as a self-made real estate mogul, Blaine has opened a lot of doors for us."

"You're in real estate?" said Ava, perking up. Here was something a girl could understand and appreciate. Serious, tangible assets.

Blaine bobbed his head eagerly, delighted at Ava's

sudden interest. "I'm a private investor," he told her. His words came out *private inveshtur.*

"Honey, you and I should get better acquainted," said Ava, gently pulling Blaine away. "Tell me," she said as they strolled toward the hors d'oeuvre table, "do you hold *lots* of real estate yourself? Or do you mostly just buy and sell it for a tidy profit? Like playing Monopoly?"

Jamie chuckled as they watched Ava and Blaine wander off together.

"Like a lamb to the slaughter," said Carmela. "She'll have a P & L statement from him by evening's end."

"Blaine's a big boy," laughed Jamie. "He'll be fine. His only problem is he *does* like to party. At Tulane, Blaine was an absolute hellion. President of some ultra-secret group called the Phlegethon Society, although I think it was more about drinking than anything else."

"Ava means well, too," said Carmela. "But the prospect of your wedding this Saturday evening has her *altar ego* all in knots. Ava was positive she'd be married and divorced by now."

Jamie smiled at Carmela's little joke.

"With all this talk of selling your software program," continued Carmela, "what's going to happen to your cozy little bookstore?" Jamie owned a bookstore over on Toulouse Street, not far from Carmela's scrapbook shop. He specialized in secondhand books, maps, old engravings, and the occasional rare or antique book.

"*Possibly* selling my software program," said Jamie.

"It still needs a bit of fine-tuning. As for the bookstore, I think it might finally be turning a profit."

Carmela nodded knowingly. Although everyone thought owning a shop in the French Quarter guaranteed huge rewards, a lot of proprietors were lucky to eke out a modest living.

"Hey, you two!" cried Gabby, as she rushed over with her cousin Wren in tow.

Jamie wrapped his arms around his bride-to-be and planted a kiss on Wren's forehead. Wren, a petite blond with big blue eyes and short wispy hair, smiled up at him in complete adoration. In her cream-colored wrap dress and citrine chandelier earrings, she looked like anything but a wren.

"Who knew this bookish fellow was also a software genius," said Carmela, smiling as the two of them embraced. *Why,* she wondered, *can't Shamus and I communicate like that? Bear hugs, longing gazes, lots of sexual tension.*

"Genius? No way!" protested Jamie. "I was merely born with a love for the printed word as well as the digital. The luck of the draw."

"And a talent for choosing the right girl, too," said Gabby, obviously pleased at the fine catch her cousin had made. She put a hand on Carmela's arm and lowered her voice. "Your place cards are gorgeous," she said. "Thank you."

"My pleasure," said Carmela. She'd put them out earlier according to Wren and Gabby's seating chart.

Gabby laid a hand across her heart and ducked her

head. "You've done so much, Carmela," she said, her dark eyes filled with gratitude. "Designing the wedding invitations, the place cards tonight, helping Wren and Jamie with tons of arrangements . . ."

"How can we possibly thank you?" bubbled Wren.

"Just have a lovely wedding Saturday night and live happily ever after," said Carmela. *After all,* she decided, *isn't that what wedded bliss is really all about? Is* hopefully *all about?*

Carmela smiled at Jamie as he listened attentively to Wren and Gabby chit-chat back and forth. She decided that Jamie seemed like a nice enough guy, acted like a nice enough guy. Of course, the true test lay ahead. Could Jamie Redmond, this good looking, dripping-with-charm bookseller, put away his bachelor habits? Could he slip his old ways into his sock drawer without a single twinge of regret and settle down to a nice, long monogamous relationship?

Carmela shook her head to clear it. Of course he could. What was she thinking? It was Shamus, *her* husband, who'd been unable to succumb to a full-time commitment. Shamus, her adorable husband who swore he loved her, but still craved freedom. Who claimed they were soul mates, yet continued to sling barbed arrows into her heart. Ava had lectured her sternly about proceeding full steam ahead on a divorce, and she was probably right. Still . . .

Gazing across the crowded room, Carmela caught sight of Quigg Brevard, the owner of Bon Tiempe. Darkly handsome and oh-so-suave, Quigg made no bones about the fact that he was interested in Carmela.

But am I interested in him? she wondered. *Yes. And No. Yes, because Quigg is charming and courtly and talks a good game about honesty and relationships. And no, because somewhere, in the dark recess of my aching heart, I still believe Shamus and I might find our way back to each other.*

"Honey," said Ava, coming up behind her, "that man is about as subtle as a Zubaz track suit."

"You're talking about Blaine Taylor?" asked Carmela, slightly amused by Ava's apparent discomfiture. "Old B.T.?"

"We shall henceforth refer to him as Mr. Calamari," snapped Ava. "The man is a veritable *octopus*. Had his grabby little hands all over my sweet little bod. Didn't wait for an invitation or nothin'." Ava smoothed her dress, managing to look both pleased and outraged. "Can't say I care for a man who doesn't wait for my say-so."

"You don't think your come-hither dress and spring-loaded bra aren't the next best thing to an engraved invitation?" asked Carmela. Dressed in her skin-tight gold dress, Ava had caught the roving eye of nearly every man in the joint.

Ava grinned widely. "Sure, I dress to advertise my assets. But what's a girl supposed to do? Skulk around like a *nun?* Wear skirts below her knees?"

Carmela had to choke back a chuckle. For Ava Grieux, whose bursting clothes closet looked like something a drag queen would kill for, there was no middle ground. Dress like a meek Carmelite or boldly strut your stuff. That was it.

Ava nudged Carmela as her eyes roamed the room. "Monsieur restaurateur is gazing your way," she said in a coy voice.

Carmela glanced over toward Quigg Brevard again. Even though he was deep in conversation with one of his high-hatted chefs, he was indeed looking in her direction. Smiling at her, in fact. Carmela waggled her fingers at Quigg in greeting and he waggled fingers back.

"Now *that's* the man you should be involved with," whispered Ava. "A drop-dead gorgeous guy who could sweep you off your feet, maybe even start a rip-roaring scandal or two. Stop you from pining away over silly old Shamus Meechum."

"I'm not pining," said Carmela. "I'm getting on beautifully with my life. It's exceedingly busy. Hectic, in fact."

"You seem to be confusing your thriving business at Memory Mine with your rather dreary personal life," said Ava. "Tell me, what did you do last Friday evening?"

"Nothing," said Carmela, wincing. She had cleaned her refrigerator, a sputtering, vintage Norge that only an unscrupulous landlord would dare stick in a rental unit.

"Aha," said Ava, sounding victorious. "And Saturday evening?"

"Stayed home," muttered Carmela, not liking the gist

of this conversation one bit. Truth be known, Saturday night had been a total black hole. Sinking into the abyss of boredom, she'd alphabetized her spice rack.

Ava planted hands on slim hips and stared pointedly at Carmela. "You stayed *home,*" she said in an accusing tone. "With Boo." Boo was Carmela's little dog. A Chinese Shar-Pei.

"Boo is extremely good company," argued Carmela, trying to score a few points. Boo had proved useful at disposing of some stinky, slightly moldy cheese, but had been completely indifferent when presented with the spice rack project.

"Boo doggy is sweet and utterly adorable," agreed Ava. "Unfortunately, she is somewhat lacking in the conversation department. Carmela, you need a man who'll take you out and show you a good time. Jump-start your heart again."

"Jump-start my heart," repeated Carmela. This she wasn't so sure of. Although Ava's enthusiastic pitch did carry a certain appeal.

"That's right, girl," continued Ava in an upbeat, manic manner that seemed to veer between spirited cheerleader and hectoring, lecturing evangelist. "Your poor emotions have been lying dormant for months. Ever since—"

"I know, I know," countered Carmela. "You don't have to say it." *Ever since Shamus slipped into his boogie shoes and disappeared out the back door,* thought Carmela. *Ever since he tromped all over my poor heart, the rat.*

"Take a look around," urged Ava. "What do you see?"

"Ava . . ." pleaded Carmela. This was getting entirely too personal. Even for best friends.

"No, I mean it," insisted Ava.

Carmela surveyed the crowd of friends and well-wishers. Many were people she recognized from around town. Some were folks from the Garden District, the upscale part of town where she'd lived with Shamus before the demise of their so-called marriage. Before Shamus's big sister, Glory Meechum, had so rudely tossed her out of the family home. Other guests she recognized from the French Quarter. Shop owners, long-time denizens of charming courtyard apartments, a couple restaurant owners. And what they all seemed to have in common, what Ava had most certainly been driving at, was that certain sparkle in their eye, a light-hearted *joie de vivre* in their attitude.

"They're people having fun," Carmela grudgingly admitted.

"Not just fun, Carmela. They're having a damn *laugh riot!*" exclaimed Ava. "Honey, this is New Orleans . . . the Big Easy. We're the city that care forgot. The poster child for bad behavior! Our war cry is *Laissez les bon temps rouler*. Let the good times roll!"

"Point well taken," said Carmela. "I hereby resolve to have way more fun."

Ava let loose an unlady-like snort. "I don't believe you."

"No, really," persisted Carmela. "I'm going to march over to the bar right now and order a drink."

"Well, hallelujah," said Ava, brightening considerably. "That's a start. Whatcha gonna have, *cher?*"

"Maybe a hurricane," said Carmela. The hurricane was a marvelous concoction of fruit juice and rum that had been invented in New Orleans back in the thirties. Necessity being the mother of invention, the hurricane had come about because an overzealous bar owner had ordered one too many cases of rum and hurricane lamp-shaped glasses.

"You go, girl," urged Ava as Carmela sped off toward the bar. "And please! Smile pretty at all the nice men!"

"You look way too serious," a low voice whispered in her ear.

Carmela spun on her barstool to find Quigg Brevard gazing at her. "Why does everyone insist on telling me I'm having a rotten time?" she hissed.

Quigg stared at her as though she were a fragile porcelain angel that had suddenly morphed into a demonic Chuckie doll. "My, we sound cranky tonight," he said, deadpan.

Carmela managed a sheepish smile. "Yeah . . . well . . . sorry. I didn't mean to jump down your throat."

Quigg waved a hand. "Don't apologize. Your feelings are your feelings. And you, my dear Carmela, unlike many people in my circle of acquaintances, have the unique ability to vent your emotions honestly. And with great verbal flair, I might add." He peered at her closely. "I find that unusual in a woman."

"Are you kidding?" responded Carmela, studying his impossibly white Chicklet teeth and noticing the tiny gleam of gel in his hair. "If you listen closely enough, most women let you know *exactly* what's on their mind."

"Okaaay," said Quigg, obviously enjoying this discussion. "Are you implying that men are the ones who are emotionally dishonest?"

"No," said Carmela, "absolutely not. I think men are a remarkable species. Very up-front about what they want."

Quigg smiled ruefully. "I'm probably gonna regret this, but what *is* it you think men are up-front about?"

"Power and sex," said Carmela. "But not necessarily in that order."

"Whew," said Quigg, "you don't pull any punches, do you?"

The bartender slid Carmela's drink toward her. "I try not to," she said. *Now* she felt more like her old self. She took a sip of her drink. "Mmm, good. Strong."

Quigg Brevard fixed her with a rakish grin. "Bon Tiempe aims to please."

"Listen," said Carmela, "I didn't mean to get so . . ." she searched for the right word ". . . *visceral* about things. I'm going through kind of a weird phase right now." She didn't bother mentioning that she'd been going through the same weird phase since she was fourteen. Maybe thirteen.

"No problem," said Quigg. "Like I said, I find your

openness extremely refreshing."

Carmela took another sip of her drink, thinking: *Quigg wouldn't be a bad catch. He's handsome, has a good sense of humor, and the man's a gourmet chef. Maybe Ava's right. There could be some merit to exploring relationship options while enjoying a properly prepared soufflé.*

"Bon Tiempe looks enchanting tonight," Carmela told him, suddenly struck by the mellow feel of the Old World bar. Or maybe it was the smoothness of the ninety-proof rum.

"Lots of drawbacks to running a restaurant housed in a crumbling old mansion," said Quigg, "to say nothing of the madness that goes on in our kitchen. But our atmosphere seems to draw customers in like a magnet. Besides your group tonight we've got another forty or so dinner guests and bar patrons."

Indeed, Bon Tiempe dripped with Old World elegance. Antique chandeliers sparkled overhead, oil paintings crackled with age hung on brocade-covered walls, crushed velvet draperies with golden tassels sectioned off different parts of the restaurant to create cozy, private dining nooks. Throw in the cypress wood paneling and sagging floors, and the overall effect was refined and genteel, tinged with a hint of decadence. A perfect reflection of New Orleans in general.

Quigg glanced at his watch. "I'm gonna check with the kitchen in a couple minutes. Tell 'em to start plating the prime rib."

Three weeks ago, when Carmela, Gabby, and Wren

met with Quigg to plan tonight's menu, they had settled on prime rib with ginger peach chutney, bell peppers stuffed with rice and shrimp, and citrus salad. For dessert, Quigg's dessert chef was whipping up a sinfully rich Mississippi mud cake with brandy sauce.

"I'd better get busy and grab the centerpiece for the head table," declared Carmela. "It's a surprise for Wren, so we've been keeping it under wraps in your office."

"Go grab it," Quigg said enthusiastically, while behind them loud *clinks* sounded with a gaggle of guests raising their champagne flutes in a boisterous toast.

"Here's to our beautiful bride and groom," boomed an exuberant voice.

Carmela and Quigg glanced over their shoulders at a red-faced reveler, a beefy man decked out in an expensive-looking pearl-gray suit and showy tartan tie.

"Dunbar DesLauriers," muttered Quigg. "I better tell the kitchen to hold the brandy sauce for that one."

Carmela slipped off her barstool. "I really am going to fetch those flowers."

Moving quickly from the bar into the dining room, she stopped to admire the tables draped in white linen and sparkling with stemmed glassware and silver chargers. White tapers flickered enticingly, tiny silver place card holders held her cards.

Gorgeous, Carmela thought to herself. *A beautiful pre-nuptial dinner, lovingly planned right down to the last detail.*

31

"To Wren and Jamie," came another excited voice.

Carmela heard a faint spatter of applause as she stepped briskly down the hallway. She scooted past the coat check, twisted to the right past the dark little nook with the telephone booth, then jogged left and down to the end of the hallway.

Nudging open the door to Quigg's office, Carmela stopped abruptly in her tracks. Someone had doused the lights so only the eerie green glow from the laptop computer shone in the room.

Then, slowly, as she stood there getting her bearings, Carmela became aware of the presence of someone else. Someone sprawled on the green velvet settee where, just an hour earlier, Ava had reclined in languid splendor.

Some poor soul had too much to drink, was Carmela's first thought. Tiptoeing across the room, she made her way to the roll-top desk where the center-piece of azaleas, foxglove, and bleeding hearts sat.

But the position of the body on the settee, a funny *something* about the room, made Carmela hesitate.

Is that Blaine? she wondered. *Did the hail and hearty party animal finally veer from merely tipsy into full-fledged blotto?*

Hesitantly, Carmela's fingers tugged the metal chain of the Tiffany lamp. But its forty-watt bulb barely illuminated the amber and purple dragonflies that danced about the lampshade.

Even though the room was mostly still in shadows, Carmela's eyes landed on a tweed jacket laying in a puddle on the floor. And she recognized it instantly.

That's Jamie's jacket. Jamie's asleep on the settee!

Carmela frowned and took a step closer. It *was* Jamie who was just laying there, scrunched forward on his side, arms thrown carelessly over his head. She wondered if Jamie had fallen ill. Worried that maybe he wasn't used to drinking at all. Because Jamie, poor fellow, hadn't even stirred when she'd turned on the light.

Puzzling over what to do, Carmela decided the best thing was to give him a gentle nudge. Wake Jamie up. It would be infinitely better to share an embarrassed laugh with him now than let the poor guy sleep through dinner. A dinner that was in his and Wren's honor!

Carmela placed a hand on Jamie's shoulder.

Should I really rouse him? she wondered. And a little voice inside answered back, *Of course you should wake him up. Don't be a dim wit.*

Carmela shook Jamie.

Nothing. Poor guy was dead to the world.

Carmela shook him again, harder this time, and was rewarded when Jamie began to slowly roll over. But her expectation of a drowsy awakening suddenly turned to horror as Jamie rolled off the settee and dropped to the floor with a heavy *thud!*

Holy shit! What did I do to him?

Hastily retreating to the doorway, Carmela searched frantically for a light switch. Her fingers skittered across the switch plate, then finally found purchase. Overhead light suddenly flooded the room.

Ohmygod!

Jamie Redmond, mild-mannered bookseller and fiancé of Wren West, lay sprawled face down on the floor, a butcher knife jammed in his shoulder. His blue and white pinstripe shirt, that had probably been neat and crisp when he put it on, was now soaked a terrible dark red.

Unable to catch her breath for a moment, Carmela gaped at the hideous tableau. The protruding knife with the dark wood handle. The glut of blood seeping across the floor. The dark, wet stain on the green velvet settee.

Footsteps sounded behind Carmela as she leaned forward to feel for a pulse.

Nothing. Not a tick. Oh Lord!

"Carmela?" came Quigg's worried voice. "Everyone's about seated. They're waiting for Jamie. They're waiting for *you*," he added.

Carmela whirled about to face him. A lump in her throat the size of a Buick made her words tumble out in a hoarse croak. "Someone's attacked Jamie!" she cried.

"Good Lord!" exclaimed Quigg, catching sight of the fallen man. Quigg threw himself to his knees, did the same quick search for a pulse. Then, shaken at not finding any sign of life, leapt to his feet, whipped his cell phone from his pocket, and punched in 911.

Feeling sick to her stomach, Carmela stepped out of the room as Quigg screamed frantically into the phone. Demanding the police, an ambulance, an EMS team.

"Carmela?" called Ava's soft voice from down the

34

hallway. "What the hell's going on?" Ava was catching snatches of Quigg's frantic conversation.

Carmela caught Ava by the shoulders and halted her before she got too close. "It's Jamie," she said, her voice shaking.

"What?" Ava asked nervously, trying to peek past Carmela. "That boy didn't get cold feet, did he?"

With a stricken look, Carmela stepped aside, allowing Ava to see for herself. Quigg was still on his cell phone, his voice rising in intensity as he spoke with the 911 operator.

"Oh my god!" bellowed Ava when she saw Jamie's body. "He's *dead?*"

Still in shock, Carmela simply nodded. "I think so. No pulse."

Ava pushed a mass of hair off her forehead. "Jeez," she said, looking stunned. "What the hell are we gonna tell Wren?"

Carmela stared in horror at the unreal scenario. One minute Jamie had been alive and laughing and filled with hope. Now he was laying on the floor, a kitchen knife protruding from his shoulder, his fingernails already starting to turn blue. Carmela shook her head in disbelief. *What could have happened? Who could have done this?*

She tried to push her fear aside and concentrate on the here and now. Outside, sirens shrilled as police cars raced toward Bon Tiempe, and Carmela knew that in two more minutes they'd all be standing behind yellow police tape.

Focus, Carmela admonished herself. *Stay cool. For Wren's sake. And Gabby's.*

Carmela crept back into the office, Ava closely shadowing her. *Try to find a clue as to what happened,* she prodded herself. *Look around. Think!*

"Why would anyone . . . ?" began Ava, but Carmela interrupted her.

"What's that on the table?" Carmela asked in a whisper. "Those marks?"

Ava squinted at the small marble table nestled next to the blood-soaked settee. "More blood," she said, sounding horrified.

Carmela took another tentative step in. "Looks like Jamie tried to . . ."

"Mother Mary," breathed Ava, suddenly catching on.

Footsteps thundered in the hallway and Carmela knew a wall of people was poised to descend upon them. "Look," she said, in whispered excitement. "I think Jamie tried to write a message with his own blood!"

Chapter 2

THE women who were crowded around the craft table in the back of Memory Mine the next morning all exuded the expectant air of baby birds. Mouths open, eyes bright, every muscle straining to catch the retelling of the strange and sordid details of the night before.

Carmela and Gabby had both arrived at the shop

promptly at 9:00 AM this Thursday morning, even though they'd been up until well past midnight, talking with police and being interviewed by two detectives. Shortly after they'd hung the hand-lettered *Open* sign in the shop window, their "regulars" had come tumbling in. Worried, nervous, and rabid for details.

Baby Fontaine, the fifty-ish, pixie-like Garden District socialite, whose manners were superseded only by her good humor, had been the first to arrive. Byrle Coopersmith came in on her heels. And Tandy Bliss had tumbled in shortly thereafter, toting her oversized scrapbooking bag. Skinny with a cap of tight red curls, Tandy was a fanatical scrapbooker and a woman not known for mincing words. As Byrle had once remarked of Tandy, "She never met a subject she couldn't comment on."

Bony elbows propped on the table, chin cupped in her hands, Tandy was demanding more answers than either Carmela or Gabby could provide.

"But you saw the weapon," Tandy was saying. "So you must know *something*." Wren being Gabby's cousin, she had popped into the scrapbook shop frequently over the past few months, so Baby, Byrle, and Tandy had all come to know her fairly well. Plus, Gabby had continually regaled them with details of Wren's upcoming nuptials.

Gabby shivered. "Carmela was the one who saw everything. She and Ava stumbled upon poor Jamie's body." She held a hanky to her nose and sniffled.

"How grisly," murmured Baby. "Was it really a butcher knife?"

"Afraid so," said Carmela, wondering if she'd ever be able to exorcise that terrible image from her mind. Worse yet, would she ever be able to return to Bon Tiempe without thinking about their gleaming racks of sharpened knives?

"And this happened in Bon Tiempe's business office?" said Tandy, still trying to get the picture clear in her mind.

"In Quigg's office, yes," Carmela said slowly.

"You're sure nobody else was around?" queried Baby. "There were no witnesses who came forth?" It seemed inconceivable to her that a killer had slipped into an upscale restaurant, murdered this well-liked, mild-mannered groom, then disappeared without a trace. Baby was married to Del Fontaine, one of New Orleans's top attorneys, and, in her mind, there *had* to be a witness. There was *always* a witness. Even if you had to pay them.

"Quigg's office is tucked way back," said Carmela, feeling like she was almost offering an apology. "Behind the kitchen." She held a new stencil in her hand, a somewhat intricate design of what could pass for a Garden District home, but she hadn't shown it to anyone yet, so distressed was she. "The office, the hallway, the telephone nook, the coat check area . . . it's all kind of a rat's maze back there."

"Lots of doors in that hallway," piped up Tandy. "Darwin took me to dinner there one night and I got lost just trying to find the ladies' room. Thought I'd have to take a whiz in the potted palm."

"So what's going to happen now?" asked Byrle. "I mean, I know the police are investigating, but what about the . . ." Her voice trailed off.

"The wedding," said Gabby, in a somber tone. "I'm going to start phoning all the guests."

"Oh no!" the women exclaimed with collective dismay.

"Well, someone has to," said Gabby, a trifle defensively. "You certainly can't expect poor Wren to make those calls. It would break her heart."

"Of course we don't, sweetie," said Baby. "It just sounds like such an awful, sad task. You're very brave to take it on."

"I'm tougher than I look," said Gabby. And she was. At barely twenty-three, with dark hair, dark eyes, pale skin, and a penchant for sweater twin sets, Gabby came across as the sorority girl–type. Demure, sweet, extremely well-mannered. But there was flint beneath that polished exterior. Real fortitude when it was needed.

Tandy shook her head, still turning the whole situation over in her mind. She had read the *Times-Picayune*, scanned the TV stations for coverage, and called everyone she knew, trying to ferret out details. "Jamie Redmond's murder made front page news in the *Times-Picayune*," she said, as if everyone hadn't already seen the terrible headlines.

"The media adores bad news," commented Byrle.

"Somethin' good happens, they turn a cold shoulder. But a nasty murder or a family tragedy, they eat it up."

"It's about selling papers and garnering ratings," said Carmela who, besides being a realist, had once worked as a graphic artist at the *Times-Picayune*. "They're a business. You can't completely blame them."

"Spoken like a true Republican," muttered Tandy.

Carmela assured Gabby that it was fine to use her office and to take all the time she needed for her calls. And a grateful Gabby did exactly that, barricading herself inside Carmela's cluttered little cubby hole, tearfully whispering into the phone amidst a jumble of rubber stamps, paper samples, and scrapbook supply catalogs.

Hovering at the front of the store, Carmela waited on customers while she put together a new display featuring Asian-inspired stickers and charms. She was proud of Memory Mine, the little scrapbook shop she'd built on her own. And she loved how it had turned out. The brick walls held floor-to-ceiling brass wire racks filled with thousands of sheets of colorful scrapbook paper. She had one of the best selections of albums in all of New Orleans, and her flat files were filled with elegant, textural, handmade papers laced with linen, hemp, ivy leaves, and banana fibers. Her store had become a meeting ground, a place where friends could come and spend a few hours, roll up their sleeves, and be wildly creative while they enjoyed wonderful camaraderie, too.

Glancing toward the back of the store, Carmela saw that Baby, Tandy, and Byrle were slowly unearthing their photos, albums, paper, rubber stamps, and stencils and were starting to begin work on their scrapbook pages.

Good, she thought. *Hopefully we can enjoy business as usual. Sort of.*

Even though they'd all gone round and round on the details of Jamie Redmond's murder, there was one thing Carmela hadn't discussed with anyone besides Ava. The strange, squiggly symbols that seemed to be scrawled in Jamie's own blood. The message that had looked like "INA." Or maybe "INE." Or "INAE." She wasn't sure which it was, since, if they were letters at all, they were shaky and not very well defined.

The detective she'd talked with last night, a Detective Jimmy Rawlings, hadn't been terribly impressed with her hot theory that Jamie had scrawled out a final message. He'd yawned into his cup of coffee and copied the symbols down in his little spiral notebook. *Told* her he'd try to check them out. But she still had the impression that Detective Rawlings saw the marks as a kind of random by-product of the victim thrashing around. In other words, he hadn't seen any meaning in them at all.

Maybe so, thought Carmela. *But what if Jamie Redmond had known his attacker? What if, after being stabbed, Jamie had realized he was mortally wounded? So, painfully, carefully, he scuffed out those marks using his own blood.*

Because there were no witnesses, Jamie Redmond had to be his own witness. He had to leave a clue for the living.

It was an unsettling thought for Carmela. Yet one that was highly intriguing. So when Gabby took a break to run out and grab cups of chicory coffee for everyone, Carmela slipped into her back office and grabbed a pen and paper. She scrawled the letters down as best she remembered them and came up with a couple dozen ways to complete them.

INATE? I NEED? INACTIVE? INERTIA? Good heavens. Just what was it Jamie had been trying to convey?

But Carmela was either extremely tired or her neurons just weren't firing all that well today. Because nothing seemed to gel.

As Carmela sat puzzling over her scrawled symbols, the phone rang. Instinctively, she reached for it and answered with a not-so-chipper: *Memory Mine. Can I help you?*

"Carmela."

It was Quigg, who, for some reason, jump-started every phone conversation with a throaty, meaningful growl. In this case, it was actually kind of nice. Interesting, anyway.

"How you doin'?" Quigg asked. "You okay?"

Carmela gazed toward the back of her store where everyone was buzzing away at the big table they'd dubbed Craft Central.

Am I okay? Not really.

"Yeah, I guess so," she lied.

"What a *disaster,*" exclaimed Quigg, obviously referring to last night. "To have a customer murdered right in my own restaurant! Unsettling, truly unsettling. The police figure it was probably a robbery gone bad. Kids or maybe a junky who slipped in through the kitchen and was searching for the office safe."

"Is there a safe in the office?" asked Carmela.

"No," said Quigg. "But that's something only *I'd* know."

"People could slip past your staff?" she questioned. "In the kitchen?" This seemed totally implausible to Carmela.

"Oh, yeah," said Quigg. "Easy. Pick your area. Kitchen, prep area, pantry, or cooler. Cripes, it's always bedlam back there, and most restaurants have huge turnovers so there's always some new guy lurking about."

Damn, thought Carmela.

"That poor woman," said Quigg, obviously referring to Wren. "I felt so helpless. She seemed inconsolable. If only there was something I could have done!"

"Refunding the money was a nice gesture," said Carmela. Quigg had been so upset last night, he'd written a check on the spot, refunding all the money for the bar tab and dinner. Carmela had the check in her handbag.

"It was nothing," said Quigg, who sounded anguished. "I just wish we could have gotten to Jamie

43

Redmond sooner. Maybe the outcome would have been different."

"Maybe," said Carmela. "You did a lot, though. You were very take-charge."

"The police kept my entire staff until three o'clock this morning. Three bus boys and my damn *sous*-chef put in for overtime, can you believe it?"

She did, and told him so.

"On the plus side," continued Quigg, not sounding one bit happy, "business is suddenly booming."

"You've got to be kidding," said Carmela.

"I never kid about business, dawlin'. It seems everyone and his brother-in-law is burning with curiosity. I guess they want to enjoy a cup of *court bouillon* and bask in the midst of a real-life crime scene." Quigg pronounced it *coo-bee-yon,* which was, of course, the New Orleans pronunciation for that type of spicy fish stew. "Forensics a la carte," continued Quigg. "Sick, no?"

"Sick yes," murmured Carmela, knowing full well that the average citizen seemed utterly fascinated with crime scenes and forensic evidence these days. Case in point, just take a gander at what was being spewed out on TV.

"You've got to keep in mind," said Quigg, "that this is fairly typical for New Orleans. I mean, we're the Roswell, New Mexico, of the macabre. We've got more voodoo shops, ghost tours, haunted buildings, above ground cemeteries, and amateur vampires per capita than any other place in the world!"

"Good point," agreed Carmela. Visitors to the French Quarter were forever wandering into her shop and asking if there were any haunted houses or hotels in the area. Lately she'd been sending them down the street to Amour's Restaurant, a so-so brasserie that had been particularly snippy and pretentious to Gabby and her when they'd tried to order take-away.

"Listen," said Quigg, "I don't know if this is the right time to tell you this, but I'm opening a new restaurant in a couple months. Already leased space over on Bienville Street in a building that used to be an art gallery. Gonna call the place Mumbo Gumbo. Any chance I could talk you into designing the menus? I want the typography and overall look to have a kind of jumbled scrapbook feel."

"Sounds like something I could handle," replied Carmela. She'd turned him down on designing the new menus for Bon Tiempe and he'd ended up with heavy leather menus and old English type so ponderous looking it rivaled the Magna Carta. *So maybe, yeah.*

Carmela set the receiver back in its cradle just as Gabby came scuttling through the front door, carrying a cardboard tray filled with steaming cups of *cafe au lait*. She trundled the coffee back to the big square table and began passing out cups while everyone murmured thank-yous.

"Got one for you, too, Carmela," Gabby called.

"Be right there," said Carmela. She grabbed her paper filled with symbols and shoved it into the bottom drawer. She didn't want Gabby to know what she'd been up to. After all, the symbols or words or whatever they were could be nothing at all.

Jumping up, Carmela was eager to accept the little cardboard cup from Gabby. But as she held out her hand, she also stared in amazement at the person pushing her way through the front door.

"Carmela?" said Gabby. At first she thought Carmela didn't want the coffee. Then, suddenly catching on, Gabby quickly turned and followed Carmela's surprised gaze.

"Wren?" cried Gabby, utterly stunned by her cousin's unexpected appearance at the little scrapbook shop. "What . . . what are you doing here?"

As if on cue, Baby, Tandy, and Byrle all swiveled their heads to stare at Wren West, who was hesitantly making her way toward them.

Gabby hurried to meet Wren halfway. "Why honey?" she asked. "What possessed you to come here today?"

Wren looked subdued yet nervous. "I was just over at Jamie's store, a couple blocks away," she explained. "And it was like I could feel his presence."

That was enough for Tandy. She leaped from her chair, bounded over to Wren, and swept her up in her skinny arms. "Oh honey," she urged, "come over here and sit with us. Take a load off."

"You should be at home," murmured Baby, as Tandy hurriedly made room for Wren at their table. "You poor thing."

Like mother hens, they began clucking and cooing over Wren, offering their sympathy, their best wishes, and their assistance, should she need it.

"I really think you should just go home," worried Gabby.

Wren shook her head, looking miserable. "That's Jamie's place, too," she said.

"Oh my," said Tandy, looking perplexed.

"Blaine said he'd help me figure out what to do about the property," said Wren, sipping at the *cafe au lait* Carmela had given her.

Tandy's brows shot up in a question mark.

"Blaine Taylor," explained Carmela. "He was Jamie's business partner. Jamie invented a software program and Blaine was helping him market it."

"I didn't know Jamie had another business besides the bookstore," said Baby. "How nice."

"Ya'll are treating me like one of those poor sick kids they send to Disneyworld," said Wren. "Please don't."

"My sincere condolences," said Byrle, reaching over and gently touching Wren's sleeve. "Have you thought about funeral arrangements yet? I know we'd all like to attend."

Wren bit her bottom lip and shook her head. This was obviously a painful subject for her to talk about. "Not really," she said. "Jamie didn't attend one particular church or anything, so I guess I'm just going to have him cremated."

"Cremation is very dignified," said Baby, looking a trifle askance that there didn't seem to be a formal service looming on the horizon.

"Then what?" asked Tandy, handing Wren a Kleenex. "Maybe just have a private burial?"

Wren accepted the Kleenex and gave a defeated shrug. "I don't know. Maybe . . . lay him to rest with his parents?"

"They've both passed on?" asked Byrle.

Wren nodded and daubed at her eyes. "Oh yeah, long time now. Almost fifteen years. Jamie was adopted, and his parents were older." Wren was grasping the Kleenex with both hands now, twisting and turning it like a lifeline. "I mean, Jamie was just six or seven when he came to live with them, and they were both in their mid-forties by then."

"They lived here?" asked Baby, who was always interested in all aspects of parentage and lineage.

"No," said Wren. "Jamie grew up down in Boothville, where his dad ran a small printing shop. His parents were both killed in a car crash, and he doesn't have any other relatives." Wren blinked furiously. "You know, my parents are both dead, too. We called ourselves the two orphans," she told them, tears welling in her eyes.

"Where are Jamie's parents buried, honey?" asked Baby in her gentlest voice.

Wren's lower lip quivered and giant tears slid down her cheeks. "I have no idea!"

Chapter 3

GOLD charms tumbled onto the table as Carmela gripped open a little cellophane package. Wren, who'd been sitting at Tandy's elbow for the past hour or so, watching her create a page to showcase her granddaughter's birthday party, looked over with interest. Baby and Byrle had gone off to run errands, but Tandy, determined to add an overlay of sparkling confetti, soldiered on.

"What are those for?" asked Wren.

The wire cords that felt like they'd been stretched tight around Carmela's heart loosened a notch. Wren seemed to have gotten hold of her initial grief, the hard grief that psychologists say can be horribly debilitating. After this morning's tearful revelation that Wren had no idea where Jamie's parents were buried, Carmela had stepped in and offered to help. Born and bred in the New Orleans area, Carmela knew her way around fairly well. She also understood that a few well-placed phone calls could sometimes short-circuit the ponderous bureaucratic system that seemed to run rampant in Louisiana's cities and parishes.

"I put my foot in the glue again and volunteered to make two scrapbooks for Gilt Trip," Carmela told Wren.

Gilt Trip was the brainchild of a group of wealthy, good-hearted Garden District ladies who wanted to help raise funds for a new crisis nursery at a women's shelter. They'd decided that every year three or four of them would select an interior designer to completely renovate one room in their home. Once completed, these newly refurbished and hopefully splendiferous rooms would be thrown open to the public for their amazement, enjoyment, and possible envy. Hence the name Gilt Trip.

Tickets would be sold, of course, at ten dollars a pop and all money raised would be donated to the crisis nursery.

As a former Garden District resident, Carmela had been asked to create a scrapbook that highlighted the redone music room at the Lonsdale home. The scrapbook was supposed to showcase the step-by-step transformation of the room and include a few touchy-feely items like wallpaper samples, drapery fabric, and paint chips. It was also supposed to feature selling points about the interior designer and crafts people who completed all the glitzy renovations.

Carmela thought the cause highly worthwhile and the project not too difficult, so she'd gladly said yes. But somewhere along the line, a scrapbook-making volunteer had dropped away and Carmela's one scrapbook project had suddenly morphed into two scrapbooks. Now Carmela knew she really had to hustle to complete both books in time for the start of Gilt Trip next week.

"What I did," said Carmela by way of explanation to Wren, "was create my own album cover."

"Pretty," said Wren, admiring the deep plum-colored

velvet that Carmela had stretched over and glued to what had been an ordinary brown vinyl album.

"Then, to sort of set the stage, I'm going to add this free-form piece of gold paper," said Carmela. "You see? I just tore away the edges until I had a sort of circle."

"Then you added that smaller piece of wine-colored organza on top of it," said Wren, watching Carmela work.

"Right," said Carmela. "Those are the redone music room's primary colors. Plum and wine, very deep and rich looking."

"I've made little boxes that were decorated and dimensional," said Wren, "but I've never tried my hand at something like this."

"It's really not that different," said Carmela. "You just build up a few layers until you have a rich, tactile piece."

"So now what?" asked Wren.

Carmela picked up a two-by-three-inch piece of sheet music that had been torn into another free-form design. "Now I glue this on top, but slightly off center."

"Neat," said Wren.

"And for the *piece de resistance,* I'll daub a little blue and green paint onto these gold charms to give them some instant age. Then I'll string them on gold wire and anchor them on top of everything." The charms Carmela had selected were a violin, a baby grand piano, and a treble clef, motifs very much in keeping with the theme of the redone music room.

And now, thought Carmela, *if Margot Butler would just stop by with the before and after photos, I'd really be in business.*

"Carmela," called Gabby from where she was perched on a high stool behind the front counter. "Could you come up here a minute?"

"Sure," said Carmela, sliding the album and charms over toward Wren. "You'd be doing me a big favor if you fastened those charms on," she told Wren.

"You trust me?" asked Wren, blinking.

"Absolutely," said Carmela, thinking *This girl needs some TLC and a lot of confidence-building to boot.*

"Carmela," said Gabby in a low voice, "I've been thinking."

"About . . ." said Carmela, although she had an inkling of what might be on Gabby's mind.

"About poor Jamie, of course," said Gabby, her face reflecting her anguish. "Do you really believe that story the police seem to be proposing of a burglary gone awry? That it was completely random?"

"Not sure," said Carmela. The police, the two detectives, and the crime scene team had seemed awfully hasty in their assessment. Then again, they had loads of experience in this arena. She remembered a news story from not too long ago about how a gang of kids sent an old rusty bicycle crashing through the windshield of a car at a stoplight, then murdered the two passengers for a take of less than twenty dollars. So . . .

yeah, it was possible. Anything was possible.

"On the other hand," said Carmela, "Baby wangled that little write-up in the *Times-Picayune*. So anyone who had it in for Jamie would have known where to find him last night."

"True," said Gabby, furrowing her brow. "I hadn't thought about that." She was silent for a moment. "But do you *really* think a man like Jamie Redmond had an emeny? He sold books, for goodness sake. And old maps."

"Maybe there's a lot of money in that," said Carmela. "Or there's more to Jamie than meets the eye."

"Maybe," said Gabby, sounding unconvinced. "But if the assault on Jamie *wasn't* random . . ." She gazed at Carmela with a growing look of horror.

"Then it could have been someone who was a guest last night," finished Carmela. "Yes, I have considered that."

"You have? Really?" asked Gabby. She seemed relieved. "I thought maybe I just had a suspicious nature."

"You don't," Carmela told her. "I'm usually the one who starts babbling conspiracy theory."

Gabby continued to look worried. "What do you think we should do?"

Carmela thought for a minute. "A couple of things," she said finally. "One, let's take a good, hard look at the guest list."

"That's right," breathed Gabby, "we've still got a copy. Because you did the place cards." She put a hand to her heart. "Wouldn't it be *awful* if one of Wren and Jamie's guests wished them harm?"

If one of them had, thought Carmela, *they'd certainly been successful.* But she didn't share that unhappy thought with Gabby.

"And I'm thinking about making a phone call to a certain friend," continued Carmela.

"Would this be a certain Lieutenant Edgar Babcock?" Gabby asked. Lieutenant Babcock had helped them with a sticky situation a few months earlier.

"It would," said Carmela. "But, like I said, I'm still thinking about it. We should probably see how the police investigation proceeds before we interfere too much. See what the police come up with." She stared at Gabby. "But please, give me your word you won't breathe a hint to anyone that I'm going to do a little snooping. Especially to Wren."

"Agreed," said Gabby. She moved her hand to Carmela's shoulder. "What a friend you are," she said as tears sparkled in the corners of her eyes.

The bell over the front door suddenly tinkled.

"Car-*mel*-a," called a somewhat strident voice as Margot Butler, one of New Orleans's most edgy and outspoken interior designers, exploded into their shop. Dressed head-to-toe in black, Margot was rail-thin with large brown eyes and an upturned nose that gave her a slightly snippy air.

Gabby quickly swiped at her eyes. "Margot. Hello." Margot had taken one of Gabby's classes last spring on the pretense of learning all about card making and rubber stamping. Unfortunately, she'd been surreptitiously trolling for new design customers and had proved to be somewhat disruptive.

"Hello Gabby," said Margot, immediately dismissing her and focusing instead on Carmela. She dug into the red messenger bag she had slung across her skinny form and pulled out a bright yellow packet, obviously a pack of photos. "Lookie what I brought you," she sang out.

"For the scrapbooks?" asked Carmela. "Thank goodness."

"For *one* of them anyway," replied Margot, handing the packet over to Carmela. Digging in her bag again, Margot came up with a Chanel lipstick. Clicking open the shiny black case, she swiveled the lipstick up and applied it to lips that looked like they might be collagen-enhanced. Carmela noticed that Margot's lipstick was the exact same shade as her spiffy messenger bag, which looked very designerish and expensive and seemed to be made from some type of reptile skin.

"Just the photos for the Lonsdale house?" asked Carmela. "The music room?"

Margot nodded. "The dining room at the DesLauriers home isn't finished yet." She said it casually, as though they both had all the time in the world.

"You know, Margot," said Carmela, somewhat sternly, "Gilt Trip begins a week from today. And these are *custom* scrapbooks."

"Yeah," answered Margot. "And they're gonna add *beaucoup* credibility to all the decorated rooms. Plus, we were able to negotiate better prices with the vendors and crafts people, since they're going to be showcased in the book, too. That's what I call smart marketing."

"There isn't going to be *any* marketing if I don't get photos and materials," said Carmela in a firm voice. She tapped her foot to show her impatience. "What's the holdup?" she asked.

Margot frowned. "We're creating an entirely new room, Carmela. Genius can't be rushed."

But I can? thought Carmela. *What a crock.*

"We're awfully busy in the store," said Gabby, leaping to Carmela's defense. "If we don't have all the materials by Monday, I'm not sure we can promise anything." She smiled sweetly at Margot.

Carmela could have kissed Gabby. Usually mild-mannered and demure, this was an entirely new side to Gabby. She wondered where this newfound moxie had come from. *Does adversity really make us stronger? Oh, yes it does. I'm sure it does.*

Margot pursed her lips. "I'll see what I can do, Gabby," she said in a terse voice.

"So you'll stay in touch, let us know?" Gabby pressed her.

Margot dug in her bag, then tossed one of her business cards at Gabby. "Or you can try to reach me," she said, spinning on her boot heels and charging out the door.

"Woof," said Carmela. "*She's* hot and bothered."

"No kidding," said Gabby. "I just hated the way she was treating you. Like hired help."

"Are you kidding?" said Carmela. "I bet that woman doesn't treat her hired help like hired help."

"What do you think?" asked Wren once Carmela had made her way back to the craft table.

"Terrific." Wren had attached the charms and, as an added touch, curled the top and bottom of the music scrap, then gilded the edges. Now it looked like an old-fashioned piece of sheet music.

Wren gazed up at Carmela. "Can I come back tomorrow?" she asked in a small voice.

Carmela leaned down and put her arms around her. "Of course you can, honey."

"Why don't we make some of those bibelot boxes," suggested Tandy. She seemed to be wiping tears from her eyes as well. "Wren was telling me about a bibelot box she made that's very dimensional and decorated. We did keepsake boxes here once, but they were mostly decoupaged."

"I made my bibelot box for Jamie," said Wren. "I could bring it in and show everyone," she said hopefully.

"Sounds like a wonderful idea," said Carmela, wondering how on earth she was going to investigate a murder, get her scrapbooks done, prepare for the upcoming Scrap Fest, and suddenly run a class on bibelot boxes.

"Then it's settled," declared Tandy. "I'll call Baby and Byrle and maybe CeCe Goodwin, too. Tell 'em the agenda. I just know they'll all want to come!"

Chapter 4

THE French Quarter at night is a rare experience. Sultry, sexy, and seductive, it is a place where the residential and the commercial co-exist in a fairly easy truce. Street musicians, sketch artists, and horse-drawn carriages ply narrow cobblestone streets lit by soft, glowing gaslights. Blocks of raucous bars, strip joints, and music clubs, especially along Bourbon Street, come alive with neon bling-bling as carousing visitors stagger from one bar to the other, clutching their ubiquitous *geaux* cups.

The French Quarter yields pockets of unbelievable charm and beauty, as well. Hidden courtyard gardens, elegant Old World hotels, and esteemed restaurants such as Antoine's, the oldest restaurant in America, rub shoulders with posh antique shops brimming with oil paintings, family silver, and the *crème de la crème* of estate jewelry.

Heartsick after she and Shamus had broken up, finally deciding to settle down in a place of her own, Carmela had turned to her friend Ava Grieux for help. And as luck would have it, there was a little apartment available behind Ava's shop in the tiny, picturesque courtyard with the burbling fountain.

Carmela pounced. The apartment had everything she wanted. Cozy atmosphere, affordable price, and, as they say in real estate, location, location, location.

Inside, of course, the place had been a total disaster.

Carmela had to dig deep in her bank of creativity karma to come up with a solution. But dig she did, and now her little apartment exuded a lovely Belle Époque sort of charm. Carmela knocked down crumbling plaster to reveal three original brick interior walls. She painted the one remaining wall a deep, satisfying red to match the jumble of bougainvilleas in her courtyard. And, thanks to a fairly profitable first and second quarter, her early thrift shop finds had recently been replaced with honest-to-goodness real furniture. A gigantic leather chair and matching ottoman that was the exact color of worn buckskin. A marble-topped coffee table. And a fainting couch.

Carmela's walls displayed an ornate, gilded mirror, old etchings of the New Orleans waterfront during the antebellum period, and a piece of wrought iron, probably from some long ago French Quarter balcony, that now served as a bookshelf for her collection of antique children's books.

Imbued with all these loving touches, Carmela's apartment now looked like home, felt like home, was home.

Ducking through the tunnel-like confines of the *porte cochere* to enter her secluded courtyard, Carmela was suddenly aware of just how bone-tired she really was. She'd stayed at Memory Mine till almost six-thirty tonight, trying to get a few pages done on the first Gilt Trip scrapbook. Then she'd stopped at Mason's Market to pick up a few groceries. Potatoes, green onion, cheddar cheese—ingredients for a potato-cheddar soup. Now the clock was edging toward seven-thirty, and the thin January sunlight had long since departed.

Shifting her bag of groceries to the other arm, Carmela dug for her key and hastily jammed it into the lock.

The front door was half open when Carmela froze. There were low voices. Coming from inside her apartment.

Somebody's in there? Boo let somebody in? Must have. Either that or Boo has suddenly become a big fan of Wheel of Fortune.

"Awright," Carmela called out with far greater bravado than she felt. "I've got a gun and it's pointed right at your stupid head."

"No, it's not dawlin'," came a deep male voice. "You're not even close."

Shit, thought Carmela, instantly recognizing the voice. *It's Shamus. Shamus is in my apartment. Why didn't I sprinkle holy water on the doorsill and hang a garland of garlic over the doorway when I had the chance? Ward off the evil jinx of my estranged husband.*

Carmela flipped the light on. Shamus was lounging in her newly acquired leather chair peering at the TV. Boo, curled up on the ottoman at his feet, threw her a sleepy, guilty glance.

"Nice going, Boo," said Carmela. Ambling in, she plunked the groceries down on her small dining table, vowing *not* to invite Shamus to stay for dinner. "Once again you've managed to flunk Watchdog 101."

Like a furry croissant, Boo curled up tighter and feigned sleep.

The leather chair creaked as Shamus shifted his full attention to Carmela.

He was still drop-dead handsome, she decided. Tall, six-feet-two, with a lanky, sinewy body and curly brown hair. But his most insidious traits were dark, flashing eyes and a devilishly charming smile. *Satan, get thee behind me,* Carmela silently commanded.

Yet, like a stupid, silly zombie, she kept moving toward him. *What is wrong with me?* she wondered. *Sure can't be love, because love's supposed to feel good.*

A plush postal worker dog toy with a goofy face and detachable mail sack lay next to Boo. Shamus had brought her a toy.

Nice. Now he's even trying to buy Boo's affections.

Boo had chewed a corner on one of Carmela's Big Little Books last week and she still had mixed feelings about encouraging her dog to freely enjoy a chaw.

"You've still got a key," Carmela said in a flat tone. Their relationship always seemed to be in flux, so keys were constantly being offered, rejected, or hurled back and forth.

Shamus offered his best boyish look of concern, but made no motion to dig said key out of his pants pocket. "You want it back? I've still got one to your shop, too."

Carmela combed her fingers through her hair, thinking. She came up with nothing on the keys, but decided her "do" might be getting a trifle shaggy and that she probably needed to pay a fast visit to Mr. Montrose Chineal at the Looking Glass Salon. Except the last time she'd waltzed in and asked Mr. Montrose to cut it shorter, he'd left her looking strangely like an artichoke.

"No. Yes," said Carmela finally responding. She sat down on the edge of the ottoman next to Boo and let loose a deep sigh. "I don't know."

The fact of the matter was, Shamus had become an enigma to Carmela. He was the man who'd captured her heart, charmed her silly, and begged her to marry him. He was Garden District society, she was Metaire working class. But they'd clicked. In that magical, comfortable way that instantly tells you it's right.

She'd been intrigued by his manners, mildly impressed that he could navigate his way through a French wine list, and awe-struck that she—little old Carmela Bertrand—had seemingly grabbed this tiger by the tail.

Shamus, in turn, had been wildly smitten and declared her to be amazingly creative as well as the most divine creature he'd ever laid eyes on.

Their courtship had been whirlwind, the wedding ceremony a tableau of shocked relatives (on both sides). And their honeymoon, spent in one of the suites at the Oak Alley Plantation, had been filled with great sex and unbelievable tenderness.

Then all hell broke loose.

Oh, Shamus hadn't stayed out late drinking, hadn't

been unfaithful, hadn't been unkind or physically brutish in any way. He'd just . . . changed. Grew quieter, more somber, more unhappy.

Until one day he just left.

She'd likened it to a big cat who'd been caged. A chimera who'd been tamed.

And if I really believe all that hooey, I'm a bigger fool than I thought! mused Carmela.

Reality check? He's an immature cad. A grass-is-greener kind of guy. If Shamus really wanted this marriage to work, he'd make it work. Because Shamus generally gets what he wants.

"I take it you heard about last night?" Carmela asked Shamus, her tone weary.

He nodded. "I'm just back from a trip out to New Iberia to look at some property, but the break-in and murder are still big stuff on tonight's news. Channel Eight, Channel Four, some sketchy stuff on Six. That's why I came over." Shamus put a hand on Carmela's shoulder. "Lean back," he urged.

Warnings exploded in Carmela's head, but she was too tired to heed them. Instead, she leaned back against Shamus. Absorbed his warmth, savored his strength, and snuggled her tired head against the curve of his shoulder. He felt reassuring, infinitely strong, and achingly familiar.

"Tell me," he said. "Some of it was on the news, but I want to hear it in your words."

And so Carmela told him, her voice breaking more than once. About Wren and Jamie. All the planning

63

they'd put in. About how the much-anticipated party at Bon Tiempe had ended up as a crime scene with harsh black and yellow tape stretched everywhere.

"How's Gabby doing?" Shamus asked when she'd finished.

"Upset about her cousin, but hanging in there. She came to work today."

"That's a positive," said Shamus.

Carmela raised an eyebrow. This from a man who'd deserted his post at the Crescent City Bank and stayed away almost six months, pleading the Gauguin precedent?

"And Wren?" Shamus asked. "I don't really know her, but I'm pretty sure I met her once when I stopped at Jamie's bookstore to look for a Faulkner first edition. She worked there, didn't she?"

Carmela nodded. "She's shell-shocked, but I think she'll eventually work her way out of it."

"That's good," said Shamus. "Time heals."

"So they say," said Carmela, looking at him sideways.

Shamus sat for a long moment, then cleared his throat self-consciously. "So what's the deal? Are you seeing that restaurant guy?"

Well, that came out of left field, Carmela decided.

"Quigg Brevard?" she replied. "No. Not really." She'd sat next to Quigg at a dinner party and had gone to dinner at his restaurant a few times, but that wasn't technically *seeing* him, was it?

"Good," declared Shamus. "I don't like him. I don't

like him one bit. The man favors European suits and slicks on too much hair gel."

Okay, thought Carmela, *let's add those items to the column labeled Things Shamus Dislikes. A column that seems to expand exponentially with each passing day.*

Carmela picked up the plush postal worker toy Shamus had given Boo. The mailman had a glib smile and a newly shredded belly.

"She already ripped the squeaker out," said Shamus, a silly grin on his face. "Took her thirty seconds flat. It was like watching a crazed surgeon perform open-heart surgery."

"The postman always squeaks twice," muttered Carmela.

Shamus's grin expanded across his handsome face and, inside, Carmela felt a twinge of deep longing.

That was one thing Carmela still adored about Shamus. His sense of humor and whimsy. His quick laughter.

He was also an easy mark, she smirked to herself. Shamus could be taking a slug of Coca-Cola and if she laid a zany one-liner on him quick enough . . . presto . . . he'd hiccup and laugh and Coke would suddenly froth from his nose. It was one of those weird, gross, secret things they did to each other. Try to make Coke spew from each other's noses.

"Listen, babe," said Shamus, suddenly looking intense. "We gotta get together real soon and talk."

Carmela lifted her head and studied him. *We do?* she thought, her heart suddenly stalling a beat. *Really?*

Does this mean Shamus finally wants to sit down and talk about us? About our marriage?

"We do?" she finally said. Her mouth felt like it was stuffed with cotton, her palms seemed suddenly damp.

Shamus assumed his serious mortgage banker look. The look that said *We're not convinced your financial underpinnings are quite up to snuff.* "Absolutely," he responded. "The sooner the better."

"And we're going to discuss . . ." she said, trying to lead him.

"The photo show," he said, a bright smile on his face. "We've got a good shot here to have a joint show. I've got my portfolio all pulled together, now it's your turn to get it in gear. You've dragged your feet long enough, honey. We can't keep stringing the Click! Gallery along forever!"

As fast as it had flipped over, Carmela's heart thudded inside her chest. *The photo show. The stupid photo show is his big, fat burning issue.*

Carmela had done some fashion photography for a ritzy day spa by the name of Spa Diva. Clark Berthume, the owner of Click!, had seen her moody black-and-white shots and offered her a show. In a gesture borne out of guilt and graciousness, Carmela had asked Shamus to be part of it. He'd been dabbling in photography for a couple years now and was actually quite talented.

And here I thought that maybe, just maybe, Shamus wanted to talk about us, fumed Carmela. *About our marriage. Or total lack thereof.*

Carmela launched herself out of the chair and headed for the kitchen.

"Carmela," called Shamus. "Something wrong?"

"Nothing," she called. *Nothing that a really nasty divorce lawyer can't fix.*

Chapter 5

W REN," exclaimed Tandy. "I can't believe you really came in again." Scrapbook bags slung across her slight shoulders like a pack animal, Tandy chugged her way to the battered table at the back of the store.

Wren, who was sitting next to Gabby, helping her sort out packages of stencils, ducked her head shyly. "This is the only place I feel safe," she said in a quiet voice.

"Where do you live?"

"In Jamie's house," said Wren.

Tandy slid a pair of red half-glasses onto her bony nose and peered quizzically at Wren. "And where might that be?"

"Big old house over on Julia Street," said Wren. "I think it used to be a girl's school or convent or something."

"Good grief," responded Tandy. "Please tell me you're not referring to the old Benedictine convent. I didn't think that place was even habitable. Certainly not for *people,* anyway."

Gabby immediately dove to her cousin's defense.

"Jamie bought that place eight months ago and was working very hard to renovate it. You'd be surprised, Tandy, it's really quite updated and livable now."

"Just livable or comfy livable?" asked Tandy, looking skeptical.

"Jamie got a special grant from the Preservation Foundation," explained Wren.

"So it *had* been scheduled for the wrecking ball," said Tandy. "I thought so."

"He got a special grant?" asked Carmela, her ears suddenly perking up. She'd been camped nearby in her office, paging through a slew of vendor catalogs, getting ready to place an order for rubber stamps. There were some wonderful new ones available—antique engravings of botanical prints, carriage lanterns, ornate pillars, even French bistro tables. They had a slight Courier & Ives look, without being too New Englandy.

"You ask about the grant like it might be a problem," Wren said to Carmela. "Is it?"

"I honestly don't know," she said, emerging from her office.

"But you've got that worried look on your face," said Gabby, suddenly nervous.

"Sorry," said Carmela.

"And you know about grants and things," persisted Gabby. "You've served on committees."

"Arts committees and a Concert in the Parks committee a couple years ago," said Carmela. "Never anything to do with architectural preservation or renovation." She remembered that particular home on Julia

Street as one that had been used as a Benedictine convent for just a few years. Mostly it was a big stone building that had been in a state of disrepair since time immemorial.

"You think the Preservation Foundation is going to want their money back if the work wasn't completed?" asked Gabby.

"No idea," said Carmela, sincerely regretting she'd raised the question.

But Wren was suddenly galvanized by what she perceived as a new threat. "You think I'll get kicked out?" she cried. "It's my home. The only place I've got!"

"Honey," said Carmela, "do you know if the mortgage is in your name, too, or just Jamie's?"

Tears oozed from Wren's eyes. "Not sure. I know I signed *something*."

"Well," said Carmela, "I just happen to have an acquaintance in banking who'd probably be willing to do a little pro bono investigating."

Put that good-for-nothing Shamus to work, she thought to herself. *Although, if the grant had been awarded to Jamie, it might put Wren in a difficult, disputed position. To say nothing of the ownership of the home.*

Gabby gathered together the stencils Wren had sorted. "You look tired," she told her cousin.

"I didn't sleep very well last night," said Wren. "I kept hearing weird noises."

"Those big old homes are awfully creaky," said Tandy. "Or maybe it's just plain haunted."

"Please don't say that," cried Wren. "I'm terrified as it is to stay there all by myself."

"What if I came over and stayed with you tonight?" asked Gabby.

"Would you really?" said Wren, brightening. "That'd be great."

"We could . . ." began Gabby, then stopped abruptly. "Darn. I can't. Stuart's taking his sales managers and their wives out for dinner tonight. He for sure wants me to go along." Stuart Mercer-Morris, Gabby's husband, was the self-proclaimed Toyota King of New Orleans. In fact, Stuart proudly bragged that he owned dealerships in all four parishes that made up the New Orleans metro area: Orleans, Jefferson, St. Bernard, and St. Tammany.

As Carmela watched Wren's face fall, she thought: *It's Friday, and once again, loser that I am, I don't have a date. Or even a semblance of a plan for tonight.*

"Wren," she said. "How about if I came over and stayed with you?"

"Would you really?" squealed Wren. "That'd be great!" The girl did sound delighted.

Maybe I'll even invite Ava, decided Carmela. *Try to get an impromptu slumber party going. Maybe do a quick check of Jamie's home office and see if we can find any papers. See if he put his property in Wren's name, too.*

"Holy smokes," said Gabby, scrambling to her feet. "I've got to get our 'make and takes' ready for Scrap Fest tomorrow." Scrap Fest was a one-day scrapbook event sponsored by a local scrapbook club. Memory Mine was going to have a booth there along with quite a few other vendors. Scrap Fest would also be sponsoring scrapbook classes as well as an all-night crop.

"Aren't you happy you don't have to man the booth by yourself?" Carmela asked Tandy. Since Wren and Jamie's wedding had been scheduled for tomorrow evening, Tandy had volunteered to set up and work at Memory Mine's booth. Now, with no wedding to attend, plans had changed bigtime, and both Carmela and Gabby would be going to Scrap Fest.

"Actually," said Tandy, "I was kind of looking forward to working the booth. Hearkens back to my old retail days when I worked at the jewelry counter in Woolworth's."

"Then don't change your plans on our account," said Carmela. "You're always welcome to hang with us."

"Thanks," said Tandy. "Maybe I will."

The little bibelot box Wren had brought in proved to be the hit of the morning. It was a stunning little oblong box, painted a midnight blue and embellished with swirls of gold peacock feather designs and decorated with keys that had been painted antique gold. In the center of the lid was a large, sparkling crystal.

"The feather designs look like they were done in gold leaf," marveled Baby. She and Byrle had shown up some fifteen minutes ago. Her daughter, Dawn, and another friend, Sissy Wilkerson, had come along as well.

71

"It's really just gold paint," said Wren, pleased that everyone was oohing and ahing over her handiwork. "And the keys were just keys that Jamie had laying around."

"Still, you're *very* creative," said Baby.

Wren, not used to being the center of all this attention, gazed around the table at all the eager faces. "Ya'll are so sweet," she said, her voice catching.

Tandy waved a hand. "You're in the sisterhood now, honey. Which means we take care of our own."

"Okay, Carmela," demanded Byrle in a joking tone. "Show us how we can make some of these so-called bibelot boxes. And what exactly does bibelot mean, anyway?"

"A bibelot is like a bauble or trinket," said Carmela, setting a half dozen empty Altoid tins and three empty Camembert cheese boxes on the table.

Surprised, the women just stared at them.

Finally Byrle spoke up. "You've got to be kidding," she said, puzzled by the strange items Carmela had just dropped before them. Carmela had played tricks on them in the past, and Byrle wasn't exactly sure what was going on.

"Do we collectively have bad breath?" joked Tandy. She reached for one of the Altoid tins and flipped it open.

"It's empty," said Carmela, "all the mints long gone. But . . . once you choose a special theme, then do some painting and decorating, these rather ordinary little boxes are going to be transformed into precious little gems. In other words, bibelot boxes. Smaller than keepsake boxes, but just perfect for stashing a special locket or favorite pair of earrings."

"Now I get it," said Byrle, suddenly enchanted with the notion of turning the utilitarian red and white tin she held in her hands into a thing of beauty. "By the way, the one Wren did is stunning."

"Show us what to do," urged Tandy, settling her glasses on her nose and leaning forward eagerly. That was the thing about Tandy. She might have a sharp tongue, but she was always game for something new.

"First things first," said Carmela. "Select a box."

Hands darted into the middle of the table as each woman grabbed a box.

"I'm going to take this Altoid tin and guide you through a few steps rather quickly," said Carmela. "Then you can take your time, think about what you want to do, and create your own unique design."

"Sounds good," said Baby.

"Paint," said Carmela, unsnapping the lids on a couple jars of acrylic paint. "First I'm going to sponge on some blue, purple, gold, and copper pearlescent paint."

The ladies watched as Carmela deftly sponged on the paint, making the sides of the tin a trifle more bluish and adding a more dramatic hint of purple and copper on the lid.

"While that dries, I'm going to take three small squares of frayed brown burlap and daub them with purple and copper paint."

"Wow," said Baby's daughter, Dawn. "You made them look like antiqued screens or something. Now what? You glue them on?"

Carmela nodded. "And once those three painted squares are attached, I'll glue on a gold aspen leaf, a small gold bee charm, and a small sprig of faux fruit. In this case, frosted purple pears."

"It sure won't resemble an Altoid tin once you're finished," said Tandy. "It really will be a jewel of a box."

"Complete with four crystal beads at each corner for legs," said Carmela. "But don't just copy what I've done, really let your imagination soar. Think about using mosaic tiles or embossing powder. Or even creating a tortoiseshell look."

"Love it," declared Tandy. She had completed more than a dozen scrapbooks and was adept at all the various tricks and tools available to scrappers and crafters.

Carmela hung around the back table for another fifteen minutes or so, offering words of encouragement and giving a few small creative hints. Then she made her way to the front of the store where Gabby was packing up, getting everything ready for tomorrow's Scrap Fest.

"How's it going?" asked Carmela. Actually, she could pretty much see how it was going. Gabby had assembled several large cardboard boxes and was sifting through store merchandise, determining what should be brought along so it could be displayed in their booth tomorrow.

"Do we want to take these stencils?" asked Gabby, holding some up.

"The new ones, yes," said Carmela, gazing about her shop, wishing they could take along the metal racks that were filled with all their wonderful new papers.

"How about this rack of charms and tags?" she asked.

"Ditto," said Carmela.

"And the scissors," murmured Gabby.

"Gotta have those," agreed Carmela.

Gabby turned toward Carmela with a wry grin on her face. "Why don't we just transport the entire store!"

"Great idea," said Carmela. "Beam me up, Scotty!"

An hour later the women at the back table had made remarkable progress with their bibelot boxes. Tandy had covered her box with paisley paper, added a layer of gold mesh, then decorated the whole thing with squiggles of copper wire that had stations of pearlized gold and copper beads. Baby had painted her old Camembert cheese box to resemble Chinese red lacquer, then added a Chinese coin charm, gold tassel, and a tiny matching red tag stamped in gold with Chinese characters. Byrle and the other two girls were all going with romantic themes, incorporating bits of hand-colored photos trimmed to resemble stamps and emblems, mesh ribbon, embossed paper, silk flowers, and dragonfly charms.

"Wow, is that ever cute," said Gabby, looking at Byrle's bibelot box. "Very mauve."

"I'm making mauve my signature color this season," joked Byrle.

"You look like you're all done in," said Wren, glancing up at Gabby, who was still buzzing about the shop. Wren had been content to huddle at the craft table, watching and enjoying as the women created their personal bibelot boxes.

"I'm kind of brain dead," admitted Gabby. "It's tough trying to figure out the merchandise mix. What to take, what to leave behind."

"But you figured it out," interjected Carmela. "That's what counts."

"All I have to do now is tape the boxes closed," replied Gabby. "And therein lies my problem. We have roll after roll of masking tape, invisible tape, and double-stick tape, but, alas, no strapping tape."

"I'll run out and grab some," volunteered Carmela. "When the messenger service arrives to pick this stuff up, we want our boxes to be secure."

"Okay," said Gabby, content to stay and mind the store.

But as Carmela slipped out the front door, ready to head off toward Bultman's Drug Store, where she was pretty sure she'd find a good supply of packing materials, she encountered what seemed like an immovable object on her front sidewalk. A large man.

She tried to duck around him, but he side-stepped to block her.

"Hey there," said the man, definitely capturing her attention. He tucked his chin down and fixed her with a smile. A good show of teeth, she noted. But not much warmth.

"Do I know you?" Carmela asked. Somehow she had the feeling this little meeting wasn't exactly a chance encounter. That this man might have been *lingering* outside her shop.

"I'm looking for Wren West," said the man, staring at Carmela with pale, watery-blue eyes. "I was just over at Biblios Booksellers and the darn place is locked up tighter 'n a drum. Figured she might be here."

"How would you figure that?" asked Carmela, curious about this man who seemed to act so casual yet projected an aura of tension.

"I'm Dunbar DesLauriers," he said, pulling himself up to his full height and puffing out his chest.

Dunbar DesLauriers. The name rang a bell. Carmela stared at him for a second, then her brain suddenly made the connection. This was the same man who'd been wearing the tartan tie at Wren and Jamie's ill-fated prenuptial dinner two nights ago. The one who had been swaggering about, making the drunken toast.

"As a collector of rare books, I was Jamie Redmond's best customer," Dunbar drawled.

Carmela stared at him, slightly amused by his pomposity. *He wasn't just one of Jamie's customers, he'd been his* best *customer*.

Dunbar DesLauriers swiveled his oversized head and peered in the front window of Memory Mine. Past the display of spiral-bound journals and calligraphy pens, past the poster that advertised their tag-making class. "She's in there, isn't she?" he said in a low voice.

"Yes, she is," said Carmela, picking up a vibe she didn't much like and suddenly not wanting Wren to be disturbed by this strange, somewhat boorish man. "But she's still very upset. I think we need to respect her privacy." *What I really mean is* you *need to respect her privacy.*

"I'm sorry to hear that," said Dunbar, a touch of hardness coming into his eyes. "About her being so upset, that is. I really wanted to speak with Miss West. Make her a business proposition."

"A business proposition?" asked Carmela. *What is all this about?*

"Yes," said Dunbar, rocking back on his heels. "I was going to offer to buy the inventory. Take the whole mess off her hands."

Carmela stared at him. By *whole mess* he obviously meant Jamie's bookstore.

"I wouldn't exactly call Jamie's bookstore a mess," said Carmela, beginning to get her hackles up at this strangely self-important man. Last time she'd ventured into Jamie's store, it had been a charming mish-mash of old wooden bookshelves stuffed with leatherbound books, Oriental carpets on uneven wood-planked floors, antique oak flat files spilling over with old maps, and cozy stuffed chairs tucked into corners. The feeling was similar to being in your grandma's attic. Familiar and warm, a place where you could curl up and read undisturbed for a while. And with classical

78

music perpetually wafting through the air, Biblios Booksellers had seemed a most intriguing shop. Very Old World and charming.

"This probably isn't the time or the place for discussing business deals," said Carmela. Her words came out a little firmer than she'd intended and Dunbar cocked his head at her, registering disapproval.

Could this boorish fellow really have been a friend of Jamie's? Carmela wondered. *Then again, he had been an invited guest at their dinner.*

Dunbar DesLauriers seemed to consider Carmela's words for a while, then he bent forward and gave her a sly wink. "You really should tell that poor girl to sell to me, you know." Dunbar's voice was like butter. "She'd listen to you. She trusts you and that cousin of hers." He paused. "Rest assured, you'd be giving her solid business advice," he said, punctuating his words with another aggravating wink.

Carmela gazed at Dunbar DesLauriers, not liking his condescending attitude one bit, wondering exactly what his game was. "Think so?" she asked.

Dunbar DesLauriers curled his upper lip and sucked air in through his front teeth. "Oh sure," he said, looking extremely pleased with himself.

Carmela could feel her anger rising, could almost picture a cartoon thermometer where the mercury rose up, up, steadily up, then suddenly exploded off the top. She *really* didn't like the subtle pressure Dunbar DesLauriers seemed to be exerting. So why, she wondered, was he exerting this pressure? Why did he suddenly want to buy Jamie's bookstore, lock, stock, and barrel? What was going on? Was he just a businessman used to getting his way? Was there some rare book in Jamie's inventory that Dunbar wanted for his personal collection? Or did he just get off on bullying women? Hmm.

In Carmela's experience there was only one way to deal with a bully. Put 'em on the defensive.

"You know," she said, starting to regret her words even as they tumbled out. "You were probably the last person to be seen with Jamie Redmond on Wednesday night."

The smarmy smile disappeared from Dunbar's lined face in about two seconds flat.

His brows shot up in displeasure, his face suddenly took on the ominous hue of an Heirloom Tomato. "If I didn't know you better, Ms. Bertrand," he sputtered, "I'd say you were veering dangerously close to slander."

"You *don't* know me at all, Mr. DesLauriers," replied Carmela. "But if you did, you'd know I don't veer. I pretty much set a direct course. Now kindly leave us in peace. And if you have any more business proposals to make, perhaps you'd best send them via an intermediary. In other words, have your lawyer talk to Wren's lawyer."

And with that, Carmela took off down the street, leaving Dunbar DesLauriers fuming in her wake.

Chapter 6

BLUESY notes drifted out from the Copper Club and hung in the night air on Girod Street. Around the corner on Camp Street, coffee house musicians cranked out their own version of swamp pop, a riotous feel-good blend of rock, Cajun, and country.

In the area once known as the Warehouse District, a proliferation of blues clubs, art galleries, recording studios, and coffee houses had popped up like errant mushrooms, replacing old sugar refineries, tobacco factories, and cotton presses. Red brick row houses that were in disrepair were suddenly deemed highly desirable, and this once-industrial, working-class neighborhood that rubs shoulders with the Central Business District was reborn as the Arts District.

Jamie Redmond had been in the process of restoring a large, rather austere-looking limestone building on Julia Street. Looking more church-like than residential, it had originally been built as a home then used as a convent for a short period of time.

The interior was dominated by high ceilings, original slate floors, cypress paneling, and a small first floor rotunda that served as a sort of central hub with the various rooms radiating off from it.

Carmela, Ava, Wren, and Boo lounged in what had been Jamie's at-home library. The battered leather couches were comfortably slouchy, a fire crackled cheerily, but the faces the three women wore were a little grim.

As would be expected, Wren was still stunned and deeply disturbed by her fiancé's murder just two days ago. Carmela was troubled by her somewhat bizarre encounter with Dunbar DesLauriers earlier this afternoon. And Ava was pretending to be upset that tonight's date with a legislator from St. Tammany Parish had been canceled. She'd told Carmela and Wren that she'd been counting on a spectacular dinner at NOLA, Emeril Lagasse's famed five-star restaurant in the French Quarter.

"Ava," said Carmela, knowing her friend was trying her darndest to make Wren smile, "the man was *married,* for heaven's sake. You can't count that as a *date.* I think that's technically an affair."

Ava waved a hand distractedly. "Honey, how else am I gonna enjoy the company of a husband unless I borrow somebody else's?"

"You weren't really going to go out with a married man, were you?" asked Wren.

"Sure I was," grinned Ava. "It was going to be kind of a test drive."

"You're trying to cheer me up," said Wren, managing a half smile.

"Is it workin'?" asked Ava, peering at her speculatively.

"Some," admitted Wren.

"Well, good," replied Ava, reaching for a handful of popcorn. "Because I'd stand on my head and whistle

Dixie if I thought it'd make you feel any better."

"You're so sweet," said Wren. "Both of you." She was sitting cross-legged on the floor in her pajamas, sipping a cup of hot cocoa. Ava had kindly offered to make dirty martinis for everyone, but Wren hadn't been feeling up to it. And Carmela didn't think the two of them should be merrily imbibing when Wren felt so miserable. It just wasn't appropriate.

"Do the police have any ideas at all?" asked Ava. She'd brought her pajamas along, as well. A black satin negligee with a touch of marabou at the plunging neckline. Not exactly slumber party attire. Then again, she'd pointed out to Carmela that the gown *was* a sedate black.

"The police are still going over the guest list," Carmela responded. "Apparently trying to run down leads."

"I didn't think there were any leads," said Ava. "The story in this morning's *Times-Picayune* said the police were . . . and I quote . . . 'baffled.' "

"Maybe we shouldn't talk about this," said Carmela, seeing Wren fidget uncomfortably. She seemed to have gone downhill since this afternoon when she was at Memory Mine. Wren had appeared tired and sad then, but was still functioning. Now she looked extremely depressed, almost despondent.

"No," said Wren, in a tired voice. "I *want* to talk about it. The man I was supposed to marry tomorrow evening, the man I planned to spend the rest of my life with, was killed. Murdered. And nobody seems to have any answers."

"Honey," said Ava, "I'm sure the homicide detectives are busting their buns trying to solve this case. They've probably interviewed every guest and kitchen staffer. Even the folks who just dropped by Bon Tiempe for a quick drink at the bar."

"But they're not getting anywhere," said Wren. "I talked to Detective Rawlings earlier this evening and he said they had a short list of suspects but still nothing conclusive." She gazed at Carmela, her face etched with sorrow. "I wish we could do something," she murmured. "I know Gabby talked to you about looking into a few things. You are, aren't you? I mean I *hope* you are."

Carmela gave a tentative nod. "Did she tell you?"

"No," said Wren, "I figured it out by myself. You're . . . just that sort of person. Smart and naturally resourceful."

Carmela smiled at Wren's assessment of her. She'd promised Wren earlier today that she'd try to find out where Jamie's parents were buried. And even though Gabby had talked about going over the guest list, Carmela hadn't intended to do anything much beyond the scope of a little cemetery snooping. Now Wren seemed to be asking if she'd help *investigate* Jamie's murder!

"Wren, I don't pretend to possess any real investigative skills . . ." Carmela began.

"That's not what I hear," said Wren quickly. Her face sagged, but her eyes burned bright. She glanced over at

Ava, who threw her an encouraging look. A look that said *Go ahead and ask her*.

"Ava, you didn't," said Carmela. *Of course she had.*

"Face it, sugar, you're a natural," said Ava with enthusiasm. "You pulled old Shamus's butt out of the glue last year. And then your clever thinking helped Tandy out, too." Ava flashed a wide smile, her Miss Teen Sparkle Pageant smile. "We were all *real* proud of you for that."

Carmela shook her head slowly. "Nice try, Ava, but it's not going to work. Those cases were different. Everything just sort of fell into my lap."

"So we'll try to hand you this one on a silver platter," said Ava.

Carmela threw Wren an imploring look. "What has she been telling you?" Clearly Ava had been huckstering her investigative skills.

"That you're smart and feisty and don't take crap from anyone," said Wren.

"I also mentioned you've got a natural built-in bullshit detector, too," added Ava. "Which sure comes in handy."

"There's no way . . ." began Carmela. "I mean, I wouldn't have a clue where to start." She stopped abruptly, seeing the effect her words had on Wren.

A tear slid silently down Wren's cheek, a shudder passed through her body. "I certainly understand if you don't want to get involved," said Wren softly. "I truly do." She reached for a hanky and daubed at her eyes. Boo raised her head, gazed mournfully at Wren, and let loose a deep sigh, as if in sympathy.

Carmela stared at Wren and her heart went out to her. She knew what it was like to lose someone. She'd lost her father in a barge accident on the Mississippi when she was still a little girl. She'd lost Shamus. He hadn't died, of course, but his love for her had seemingly evaporated into thin air. And that had been awful. Losing a fiancé as Wren just had . . . Carmela couldn't imagine what kind of gut-wrenching pain the girl must be in.

"Wren," said Carmela cautiously, "what if we just batted a few ideas around? You let me ask a few questions, do a little cautious snooping. I'm not promising anything, but maybe something could turn up." She glanced at Ava and shrugged. "You never know." *Oh dear, why can't I leave well enough alone?*

Wren threw Carmela a hopeful look. "I'd be ever so grateful."

Ava reached over and patted Carmela on the knee. "I knew you'd want to dig in and help, *cher*."

"Okay then," said Carmela, turning her full attention to Wren. "You've been interviewed by the police, correct?"

"Twice," said Wren. "Two nights ago, the night of Jamie's murder, and then most of yesterday afternoon."

"What kinds of questions did they ask you?" asked Carmela.

Wren bit her lip and thought for a moment. "They asked if I knew anyone who might be angry or upset

86

with Jamie. You know . . . family, friends, business acquaintances, old enemies, old girlfriends."

"Ghosts from the past," murmured Ava.

Carmela gave Wren an encouraging look. "And were you able to give them any names?"

Wren shook her head slowly. "Not a one. The thing of it is, everyone *loved* Jamie. He was a terrific person. An all-around good guy."

"I don't want to sound harsh," said Carmela, "or like a traitor to Jamie's memory; but are you positive he never mentioned anything about his past? Something that might have seemed strange or a little bit off?"

"Not that I recall," said Wren. "Then again, he didn't talk much about it."

"What about his family?" Carmela knew that in a murder investigation the first thing police did was take a good hard look at family members.

"He didn't have any blood relatives that he knew about," said Wren. "Remember? Jamie was adopted."

"Hmm," said Carmela. "Do you know if Jamie was ever able to reconnect with his birth parents?"

"I'm almost positive he didn't," said Wren.

"Okay," said Carmela, "how about business partners or investors?"

"The only business partner he had was Blaine Taylor. And that was just for the software thing. Neutron." She took a sip of cocoa. "Blaine's been wonderful. Very solicitous and helpful."

"Think hard, Wren," Carmela pressed. "What about old rivals, a problem in the past, maybe an old enemy?

Did he ever mention anything like that? Even in passing? Or maybe in jest?"

"Not really," said Wren. "Like I said, people loved Jamie. He sold *books* for crying out loud!" She looked upset that she was unable to dredge something up. "Sorry," she said contritely.

"He must have been involved in *some* kind of dispute," said Ava. "I mean, half the people I know, people who are really dear friends, drive me nuts *once in a while*." She glanced over at Carmela. "Not you, honey."

"Thanks a lot," said Carmela. Drawing her knees up to her chin, she stared into the crackling fire, wondering if there was some way they could get more of a handle on this. *People didn't just sneak into fancy restaurants and murder a groom at his pre-nuptial dinner just for sport, did they? No. Someone had to have a motive. Someone had to be angry, jealous, looking for money, or out for revenge. Those always seemed to be the main motives for murder. At least on TV anyway.*

"Wren," said Carmela suddenly. "Does Jamie have a home office?"

Wren nodded. "Sure, next room over. What used to be the chapel back when this place was a convent. There are still a couple statues in there, in fact."

While Boo remained sprawled on the couch, the three of them trooped into the rotunda and across to Jamie's office.

"Spooky," said Ava, as Wren flipped on the light.

"Looks like Ozzie Osbourne decorated the place."

Jamie's office had indeed been a former chapel. A circular stained glass window served as backdrop for a large wooden desk that sat where a small altar had probably stood. A computer on a stand was canted to the left of it. On either side of the stained glass window were small recessed niches with old plaster statues tucked into them. Bookcases lined the side walls. Light fixtures in the shape of electrified candles threw their illumination upward to highlight cove ceilings with peeling paint.

"Jamie thought this place exuded a very Gothic feel," explained Wren. "So he never made any changes."

"Maybe he couldn't make any," said Carmela.

"What do you mean?" asked Ava. She pulled a leatherbound book from a shelf, blew dust from the top of it, then slid it back onto the shelf.

"Jamie received some sort of historic preservation grant from the city," Carmela explained. "Perhaps it stipulated that he had to leave some things as is. Not update them."

"Could be," said Wren. She reached out and tentatively touched one of the almost-ruined statues, an undetermined saint with socketless eyes who valiantly clutched a crucifix. "I've always found this room a little weird, myself. But Jamie said it appealed to him, reminded him of his parents." Wren paused. "Whatever *that* was supposed to mean."

"Maybe they were religious," said Ava.

"Maybe," shrugged Wren.

"I had an aunt who had loads of statues and stuff like this," Ava continued. "She even belonged to the St. Christopher Auto Club, although she hadn't driven her Chevy Bel Air in years. Just left it parked in the garage."

Carmela gazed around the office that was indeed rather Gothic in spirit. She wondered if the words Jamie had tried to scrawl in his own blood had any connection to all this. Had he been Catholic? Did he know Latin? She frowned. Maybe. Maybe not. Nothing seemed to come together.

"Have you looked through Jamie's desk?" asked Carmela, eyeing the scarred wooden desk with its array of drawers. She knew that, sooner or later, Wren would have to bite the bullet and search Jamie's papers. After all, who knew if Jamie had owned this house outright or still carried a mortgage on it? Same for his bookstore. Carmela knew that if they could find mortgage papers, a will, or even the name and address of Jamie's lawyer, they'd be miles ahead.

But Wren hung back. "You look," she urged Carmela. "I know I should, but I feel funny. It's still too soon."

"You're sure?" asked Carmela. "You don't mind me pawing through Jamie's desk?"

Ava knelt down next to Carmela. "Come on, let's have a look. I can't believe we're gonna find anything particularly shocking."

"Agreed," said Carmela. "So you take the left set of

drawers, I'll take the right."

"And I'll get to Scotland before you," joked Ava.

Ten minutes later, one of their burning questions had been answered. It turned out that Jamie did have a little bit of equity in the house on Julia Street. He'd put ten thousand dollars down on it, made about four years' worth of mortgage payments, and then refinanced it. It looked like he now owed a balance of approximately one hundred thousand dollars to the bank. Crescent City Bank to be exact. And he *had* added Wren's name to the title. So, whatever else happened, boom, bust, or bear market, Wren would always have a place to live as long as she kept making payments on that mortgage. Or, if she decided she didn't want to live there, couldn't face the memories, it was at least hers to sell and still realize a small profit.

They could find nothing to do with Jamie's business, however. No lease, tax records, or inventory sheets. Carmela figured that information must either be on Jamie's computer or stashed at the bookstore. That issue, however, wasn't quite as pressing. Obviously Jamie owned his inventory of books and maps. And, like every other shopkeeper in the French Quarter, he probably had a landlord that collected rent every month.

"Should we check the computer?" asked Carmela.

"Go ahead," said Wren.

Carmela sat down and clicked open the hard drive. A quick perusal showed that pretty much everything there pertained to Jamie's software program, Neutron.

Carmela wondered if the program existed only there, on that computer, or if it was backed up somewhere on CD or zip drive or existed on the Internet in the form of a beta site. She also wondered who owned Neutron. Was it Jamie's program and Blaine Taylor was helping sell it for a piece of the action? Or did both men own an equal share? Frowning, she found a blank CD, stuck it into the computer, and made a backup copy of Jamie's Neutron files. *This is another issue we'll have to sort out sooner or later,* she decided.

As far as clues pertaining to Jamie's background, or any long-forgotten relatives, or even something that alluded to a murky past, there didn't seem to be any-thing. They found household bills, invoices from trades people who'd done work in rehabbing the house, electric bills, records of sewer and water assess-ments, and credit card receipts. But that was it.

Carmela also didn't find anything that had to do with Jamie's family. She knew Wren was counting on her to find out exactly where Jamie's parents were buried, so Jamie could be laid to rest along side them. And she'd been keeping a keen eye out for death certificates, burial information, or even a deed to a cemetery plot, but nothing had materialized so far.

"Except for the mortgage information, we've got zip," said Wren. She was obviously relieved she wasn't going to be kicked out onto the street, but disappointed that nothing else had surfaced.

"What about photos?" asked Ava. "We haven't peeked through any of these yet." She held a stack of photo envelopes, most of them bright yellow and looking fairly recent. A couple cream-colored envelopes at the bottom of her stack looked like they might be a little older.

"Let's scoot back across the hall and take a look," suggested Carmela.

"These are from the Literary Festival last year," said Wren. "Jamie was on one of the panels." She smiled wistfully. "The one about Mark Twain. He *loved* Mark Twain."

"What about that other packet?" asked Ava. She had given Wren a couple photo packets to look through. She was nosing through the rest of them.

"And these were taken the last time Jamie had an open house at the bookstore," said Wren, shuffling through the photos.

"Y'all are so *academic*," drawled Ava. "My photos are usually of crazy relatives and such. You know, my brothers and cousins with their souped-up Chevys and aunts with big hair who wear rhinestone cat-eye glasses."

"Sounds like the *Dukes of Hazzard*," said Carmela.

"You're not far off, sugar," replied Ava.

"Here's something," said Wren, digging into another envelope.

"What?" asked Carmela.

"A bunch of black-and-white photos," said Wren. She frowned. "I've never seen these before. I wonder . . ."

Carmela leaned over and took a look. They were

black-and-white photos of what appeared to be an old homestead. A white wood frame house, part of a small barn in the background, what looked like swampland off in the distance. *Could this be the place where Jamie grew up?* Carmela wondered. *Is this his parents' home?*

"Where did you say Jamie was from?" Carmela asked.

"Boothville," said Wren.

"Did he ever take you down there?" asked Carmela.

"Nope," said Wren. "And Jamie didn't talk much about it either. I wonder . . . are the photos dated?"

Carmela flipped one over. "Ten slash eighty-four. October, nineteen eighty-four."

"Mmm," said Wren, studying the photo. "This could be his parents' place. Wonder why he never bothered showing me this stuff."

"Hard to tell with people," murmured Carmela. "Some folks are just more private than others. They need to keep things to themselves."

Sitting across from them, Ava had been quiet for some time.

"Did you find something, Ava?" asked Wren.

"Uh . . . ah . . . no," said Ava. She had a smile pasted on her face, but her eyes darted from side to side.

A warning bell sounded in Carmela's head. Ava was rarely at a loss for words. She had obviously found something fairly sensitive.

"What is it?" asked Wren, curious that Ava wasn't being more forthcoming.

"Just more old photos," said Ava, trying to feign an offhand manner. "From before you guys were engaged." She slid the stack of color photos back in the envelope.

"Can I see?" asked Wren, holding out a hand.

Ava glanced up and met Carmela's eyes. And Carmela had a pretty good idea at that moment what Ava had stumbled upon.

"You don't really need to . . ." began Ava, sounding apologetic.

"But I do," insisted Wren.

Wordlessly, Ava handed Wren the envelope of photos.

Wren pulled the photos out, one by one, studying each shiny image carefully. When she got to about the sixth one, she stared at it for at least a full minute. Then the photo toppled from her hand and landed face down on the carpet. And Wren stood up and abruptly left the room.

You could have heard a pin drop as Carmela and Ava gazed at each other in shocked silence. Then Carmela reached down and plucked the photo from where it lay on the carpet.

Ava edged in closer as Carmela flipped it over. Together they stared at the shocker photo.

His arm draped possesively around a young woman, Jamie was gazing at her with what could only be called unabashed love. The woman wore a dazzling smile on her face and a large, sparkling diamond on her third finger, left hand.

"Can you believe this?" breathed Ava. "Jamie must have been engaged once before! Poor Wren. This ain't exactly what she needs right now. A ghost from Jamie's past."

Carmela stared at the photo, stunned. It wasn't the photo of the deliriously happy couple that took her breath away and made her heart pound a timpani drum solo. It was the smiling woman. Because this was no ghost from the distant past. This woman was very real and very much among the living.

Margot Butler.

Wearing a major bling-bling ring.

Jamie Redmond had once been engaged to Margot Butler.

Carmela grimaced at the thought. Margot Butler, the chatty, pushy, in-your-face interior designer who'd popped by Memory Mine just yesterday afternoon. Who *had* to know that her former fiancé had been stabbed to death the night before, but hadn't uttered a peep, hadn't seemed the least bit concerned.

Margot Butler, who'd have to be brain dead not to notice Wren sitting at the back table.

So just what the hell is going on? Carmela wondered. *Because whatever Margot's game is, it's very strange indeed.*

Chapter 7

Y OU really know her?" cried Wren. Her sad eyes searched the faces of Carmela and Ava.

"*I* never met the little hussy," said Ava in her most righteous tone. "But Carmela knows her."

Carmela gave a silent nod. They'd finally coaxed Wren back into the library, and this time Ava *had* mixed up a batch of dirty martinis. Now they each sipped one.

"Jamie was engaged to someone else," said Wren, an incredulous look on her face. "Before me." She seemed to be in a mild state of shock.

"It certainly looks that way," said Carmela. She took a tiny sip of her martini. *Strong. Good. Wren probably needs a strong drink right about now. We all do.*

"I don't think this should change the way you feel about Jamie one bit," said Ava. "After all, this was *before*. It's ancient history. Everyone has previous relationships. God knows, *I've* had my share of previous relationships."

Carmela had to smile. Ava'd had more than her fair share of previous relationships.

"I understand all that," said Wren, "and the rational part of my brain tells me I should be okay with it. But my heart tells me Jamie deliberately hid something from me. That's the part that hurts like hell. It means . . . it means he lied." Wren practically whispered the last part of her sentence.

"Not technically a lie," said Carmela, "more a sin of omission."

"But a sin just the same," insisted Wren.

"Maybe that's why Jamie put his office in the old chapel," offered Ava. "Maybe he was praying for forgiveness." Ava, having been raised a Catholic, prayed often for forgiveness.

"You think so?" asked Wren, brightening some.

"Sure," cooed Ava. "Or maybe he was trying to summon up the courage to tell you," Ava continued. "To come clean."

"Now I'll never know," murmured Wren.

Carmela put a hand on Wren's slim shoulder. "But you *do* know. You know that Jamie loved you. Loved you so much he put the house in your name. And please remember, Jamie didn't go through with his marriage to Margot Butler. He was planning to marry *you*. You've got to hold that truth sacred."

Ava drained her glass and stood up. "Anybody want another one?" she asked.

"I do," said Wren.

"Then I'm gonna put the sausage and cheese and stuff I brought along out on a plate, too," said Ava. "We can have ourselves a little oinkfest."

"I'm stunned," said Wren, turning to Carmela. "There's a lot about Jamie I didn't know."

Carmela peered at Wren. Her eyes looked clear, she was holding her head up again, and she'd stopped daubing at her eyes with a tissue. She looked like she might have possibly rejoined the living. On the other hand, maybe the dirty martinis Ava had whipped up had finally taken the edge off.

"Agreed," said Carmela. "But you look better. More composed."

"This is going to sound weird, but I *feel* better," said Wren. "I mean, I'm still utterly heartbroken, this was the man I loved, after all. But it feels like I'm getting a handle on things."

"Good," said Carmela.

"For one thing, I'm mad," said Wren.

Carmela threw her a quizzical look. "You're mad?"

"Hopping mad," declared Wren. "And I want revenge for Jamie's death."

"Revenge isn't always a positive thing," Carmela said cautiously. *Was this really Wren talking or was it the martini?*

"Okay then, how about justice?" said Wren. "I want justice."

Wren's desire for justice seemed like a very logical and rational emotion, Carmela decided.

"And you will help me, won't you?" asked Wren. "Gabby bragged that you can do anything once you put your mind to it. So did Ava."

Carmela reached over and clasped one of Wren's hands as she heard a whisper of movement out in the rotunda. "I'll try," she said. "I'll give it my best shot." She looked up, expecting to see Ava, but saw only shadows.

"Thank you, Carmela," said Wren. "I know you're not that much older than I am, but I feel like you've become my mentor. Or maybe my fairy godmother. Not the old-fashioned kind who grants silly wishes, but the smart *today* one. The one who watches over you and gives good advice."

Ava appeared in the doorway, laden with a large silver tray. Wedges of bright yellow cheese, rounds of sliced sausage, and stacks of crackers were piled on it.

"Who's ready for some . . ." Ava's words suddenly died in her throat. Eyes round as saucers, blood draining rapidly from her face, she gaped at the floor. "Holy shit!" she suddenly shrieked. "Watch out! Get back!"

"What?" cried Wren, looking around wildly. "What?"

Just as the silver tray crashed to the floor, just as crackers, cheese bits, and sausage rounds exploded everywhere, Carmela caught a flash of gray-brown scales as something raced across the Oriental carpet then slithered under the sofa.

"Snake!" came Ava's blood-curdling cry. "Snake!"

Like Lot's wife turned to salt, Wren froze on the sofa. In full-blown panic mode herself, Carmela noted that Boo had jerked awake and let loose a series of panicked barks.

No, Boo! thought Carmela. *Please don't get brave on me!*

Carmela wrapped a hand around Wren's arm just below her elbow and squeezed tightly. With her other hand she got a firm grip on Boo's collar, ready to haul the dog along with her. "On my count, we make a dash," she told Wren harshly, her jaw clenched, her voice hoarse. "One, two, three, NOW!" She jerked Wren's arm and Boo's collar, pulling them both up.

A twinge of pain flickered across Wren's face, then they were bounding gazelle-like across the room and out into the rotunda to join a terrified Ava. From there it was a mad dash to the front door, feet and paws clattering on slate, voices raised in alarm, as they scrambled down the limestone steps.

And rushed headlong into . . . the arms of Blaine Taylor!

"You!" screamed Carmela, freaked out for a second time in the space of about five seconds.

"What's wrong?" yelled Blaine. He seemed as stunned as they were to have run smack dab into them on the sidewalk like this. "Did someone break in? Is everyone okay?"

"Snake!" screamed Wren. She wasn't having any trouble vocalizing now. People coming out of the bar a half a block away looked over in alarm.

"Ava!" screamed Carmela, suddenly realizing her friend wasn't with them.

Carmela spun on her heel and dashed back up the steps.

"No!" screamed Wren, trying to keep Boo from following. "Don't go back in there!"

But Ava was pushing her way out the heavy door. "I'm here. I'm okay," she was gibbering. "I just had to grab my purse in the hallway . . . get my cell phone!"

"Sweet mother of pearl," exclaimed Blaine. "Are you ladies okay?"

"Hell no," snarled Ava. "There's a friggin' snake in there!"

"What!" said Blaine. He took a step back, peered at the house as though the unwelcome reptile was about to come hurtling out at him. "Are you serious?"

"You heard me," said Ava. "Some idiot tossed a cottonmouth into the house."

"A cottonmouth?" said Blaine, still sounding incredulous and trying not to stare at Ava in her negligee.

"We don't know somebody tossed it in," said Carmela. "It could have just been there. It's an old house. Who knows what the hell lives down in the cellar." She knelt down and gently massaged Boo's head, trying to calm the little dog down.

"She's right," said Blaine. "These old places can house any number of varmints. Rodents, snakes . . ."

"Please!" shrilled Ava. "Do us all a favor and kindly skip the rundown!"

"Okay, okay," said Blaine Taylor, slipping an arm around Wren's waist. "Everybody just calm down, okay?"

"By the way," said Carmela, who had pulled herself together and was gazing at Blaine Taylor, noticing that the man seemed to relish his role as the great calmer-downer. "What were you doing out here on the sidewalk?"

"Just dropping by to see how Wren was doing," he said in a sincere tone. "I was worried about her."

"Kind of late, isn't it?" asked Carmela.

"Is it?" asked Blaine, glancing at this watch. "Jeez. After nine. Wow. The thing of it is, I was working at my office and was headed home." He smiled again at Carmela. "I live over on Harmony Street, so I usually take Tchoupitoulas. Just a hop away."

"Uh huh," said Carmela. The coincidence bothered her, but this probably wasn't the time to make an issue of it.

"What are we going to do about the snake?" demanded Ava. "Bribe it to leave? Get it into the witness protection program?" There was a tinge of hysteria in her voice.

Blaine pulled off his jacket, removed the cell phone from the pocket, then draped his jacket around Ava's almost-bare shoulders. "I'm gonna call somebody," he told them. "There's a company called Critter Gitters. Their guys come right to your house and take care of unwanted varmints. They had to come to my place once to retrieve an opossum that got stuck in the chimney."

"Are you serious?" said Ava, seeming to finally calm down. "There's really a company called Critter Gitters?"

"Looks like," said Carmela, as Blaine called information, waited a couple seconds, then was connected to the critter-gitting people. They milled about on the sidewalk for a minute or two, listening as Blaine described the problem, then he clicked off his phone.

"They can be here in thirty minutes," he told them.

"You know where the thing is?"

"Hell, yes," said Ava. "Under the sofa. Probably eating our cheese and sausage."

"I don't want you staying here tonight," Blaine said to Wren.

"I don't think I could," responded Wren.

"She can come back to my place," offered Ava, who lived above the voodoo shop and across the courtyard from Carmela. "I've got one of those inflatable beds. You just pull the ripcord and the thing balloons up in about six seconds flat. Sweetmomma Pam ordered it off the TV last time she was in town." Sweetmomma Pam was Ava's granny, a feisty old gal who was addicted to infomercials and the shopping channels. Last they'd heard, Sweetmomma Pam had discovered eBay.

"And you're going to wait here?" Carmela asked Blaine.

Blaine nodded. "I don't mind. I'll have 'em check out the whole house." He stared pointedly at Wren. "Of course, it ain't cheap."

"Just do it," said Carmela.

Blaine nodded. "Right. You never can tell what burrowed in during the hot summer months, then decided to snuggle in and take up residence now that it's cooler. But if there are any more unwelcome guests, I know these guys will find 'em."

"Good," breathed Wren. "Great."

"So you'll call us with an *all-clear* in the morning?" asked Ava.

"You got it," said Blaine. "No problem."

But there were problems. Lots of strange coincidences and unanswered questions. And it was a long time before Carmela was able to drift off to sleep that night. Swirling images kept sparking her brain. The image of Jamie Redmond felled by a butcher knife seemed indelibly burned in her brain.

And she was haunted by other questions, too. Could Margot Butler have been angry at Jamie because he'd broken off their engagement? Why did the bull-in-a-china shop Dunbar DesLauriers suddenly have a burning desire to buy Jamie's complete inventory of books? And just what the hell was Blaine Taylor doing outside Wren's house on Julia Street at nine o'clock at night?

Answers? She didn't have any yet. But she would. God help her, she would.

Chapter 8

THE meeting rooms at the Le Meridien New Orleans pulsed with activity. Dozens of Scrap Fest workshops were underway, demonstrating such scrapping techniques as writing with wire, paper layering, stitching on scrapbook pages, and glitter dusting. Various scrapbook pages were being scrutinized and judged for originality and technique, and more than one competitive finalist bit her nails in anticipation of receiving a coveted purple ribbon.

In the main ballroom, exhibitor booths, most of them manned by manufacturers and suppliers, displayed the very latest in rubber stamps, cutting tools, albums, archival and scrapbook paper, templates, toppers, borders, and punch art.

It was, quite frankly, a scrapbookers heaven. And Carmela and Gabby were reveling in the excitement of it all. Scrapbook clubs from all over Louisiana, as well as Mississippi and Alabama, had descended upon this first-ever Scrap Fest. Manufacturers and suppliers had arrived with their newest and neatest products, which meant that Carmela and Gabby were not only busy manning their own booth, they also were buzzing around, snapping up the latest products to stock in Memory Mine.

"Did you see the new rubber stamps from Kinetic Creations?" asked Gabby breathlessly. She had just returned from a whirlwind tour around the convention floor and looked exhilarated but slightly discombobulated.

Carmela nodded as she rang up customers two at a time. "I already ordered the entire Romance and Renaissance series," she said. "The stamps are absolutely gorgeous."

"Have Baby, Byrle, and Tandy shown up yet?" asked Gabby, looking around.

"Baby and Byrle stuck their heads in the booth for a moment and then disappeared," said Carmela. "They're out making the rounds. And Tandy was just . . ." She glanced around, slightly perplexed. "Well she's here *somewhere*."

"Here I am," screeched Tandy, pushing her way through the crowd and flashing a wide, slightly toothy grin. "I didn't forget. My nimble fingers are poised and ready to dig in."

Carmela checked her watch. In about two minutes, Gabby and Tandy were scheduled to preside over a "make and take." This was a special hands-on demo at their booth where customers could sit down at the craft table and actually work on a project. In this case it was to be a scrapbooky-looking bookmark. Because seats were offered on a first-come basis, customers had already settled onto most of the folding chairs and now stared up at them expectantly.

Noting this, Gabby hurried to the head of the table to deliver a friendly welcome and quick introduction. Tandy hastily gathered up pre-cut paper, strands of fiber, and glue sticks for the actual "make" part.

Carmela knew she could breathe easy for a while; once Gabby started her demo, most of the booth traffic would gather round the table to watch.

"Okay," said Gabby, as Tandy passed out card stock cut into bookmark-sized strips, "we're going to start by stamping a series of designs."

Carmela slid onto a tall stool and relaxed. From where she was perched she could keep an eye on their paper assortment, their rack of watercolor brush markers, and their huge display of faux finishes, embossing powders, ribbons, and tags.

"I thought I'd find you here," said a voice at her elbow.

A smile was instantly on Carmela's face, even though she didn't immediately recognize the stocky, somewhat forceful-looking woman who'd suddenly materialized beside her.

"You're Carmela, aren't you?" asked the woman.

Carmela nodded. "Yes, I . . ."

"Pamela DesLauriers," cut in the woman, extending her hand in a no-nonsense manner. "Dunbar's better half."

Good lord, thought Carmela. *The woman's a virtual clone of her overbearing husband. Right down to the florid complexion and tartan scarf wrapped around her neck.*

"How can I help you?" Carmela asked pleasantly, slipping off the stool to face Pamela DesLauriers.

Pamela responded by dangling a large manila envelope in Carmela's face. "Knock knock," Pamela said, wobbling her head in a slightly ditzy manner. "*You're* doing the scrapbooks for Gilt Trip?" With her expectant, crowing manner, yet slightly condescending gaze, Pamela looked like a cross between a cockateil and a Chinese lap dog.

"And *you're* the owner of Happy Halls," responded a surprised Carmela. "How wonderful." *Crap,* Carmela thought to herself. *This is my other scrapbook project. Why do I suddenly have the feeling things are getting a little too complicated? I've been tapped to do a scrapbook for the wife of the man who's making moves on Jamie's bookstore. And,* she reminded herself, *who was present the night Jamie was murdered.*

"Margot Butler assured me you'd do a wonderful job," gushed Pamela. "Of course, *she's* the designer extraordinaire. Who else could come up with the concept of mixing damask and tulle? The woman's got a brilliant eye. So iconic, so forward thinking."

"I've heard wonderful things about Margot's work," Carmela responded brightly, even as her mind flashed on the photo of Margot and Jamie that they'd stumbled upon last night.

"But back to the scrapbook," said Pamela. "I wanted to bring the photos and fabric materials by personally so I could point out a few key concepts to you." One chubby hand dug into the envelope as Pamela stared at Carmela with hard dark eyes and pencil-thin eyebrows raised in a question mark. "Do you mind?"

"Heavens, no," said Carmela, wondering if the smile on her face looked as forced as it felt.

Pamela DesLauriers wasted no time in spreading out her photos, wallpaper pieces, and fabric swatches on top of Carmela's vellum samples.

"You see," said Pamela, fingering one of the photos. "This was the dining room *before*. Elegant, certainly, but perhaps lacking a certain transcendency."

"Mmn," said Carmela, not about to tell Pamela DesLauriers that her dining room looked pretty much like a dining room and that she had no idea what it was supposed to transcend.

"But *voila*," exclaimed Pamela grandly, pointing to the photograph that was, obviously, the *after* photo. "Look what I have now! Calls to mind the grand salon of an Italian villa, don't you think?"

Carmela studied the photograph. It showed the same dining room, now with earth-toned faux finishing on the walls, a Mediterranean-style chandelier, and a sweep of gold damask drapery at the window. Pretty, but certainly nothing that would get the Medici family in a twist. "Great," said Carmela. "I've got some nifty twelve-by-twelve paper that will pick up that same faux finished feel. Should make a perfect background."

"I just knew you'd benefit from my input," said Pamela, obviously pleased. "Of course, I'll want to see your concepts before the scrapbook is finalized. Before you glue it or fuse it or whatever it is you people do."

"We're on a pretty tight schedule," said Carmela slowly. "I'm not sure that's possible." *And I am doing this as a Gilt Trip volunteer, not your personal employee.*

"Of course it's possible, dear," insisted Pamela in a saccharine tone. "Just give me a jingle and I'll run down to your shop for a quick look-see." Pamela swiveled her head, glancing around. "Is Gabby's little cousin here today?" she asked.

"Wren is back at Memory Mine," said Carmela. "She offered to watch the shop while Gabby and I worked here at Scrap Fest."

"Such a dear, sweet girl," said Pamela. "I know Dunbar always found her so helpful when he stopped by Biblios."

"That sounds precisely like Wren," said Carmela,

wondering just what this was leading up to.

"You know," said Pamela, "Dunbar has his heart set on buying Jamie's collection of antique books." She cocked her head and dangly earrings swung from her lobes, grazing her plump cheeks.

Bingo, thought Carmela. *This is what Pamela is leading up to.*

"I'm not sure the books are for sale," said Carmela. "I'm not sure anything's for sale." She knew that if Jamie had also put the bookshop in Wren's name, Wren might decide to keep it and run it. Biblios Booksellers was a viable business, after all. Wren might not feel like putting her heart into it right now, but things could certainly change. Wren had worked there for the past six months, so she already knew the ropes and was well-versed in the realm of antique books.

Pamela laughed out loud at Carmela's words, however. "Honey," she gushed, "the one thing I've learned is that *everything* has a price."

"I'm not so sure about that," cautioned Carmela. *Why is it rich folks always think everything has a price?* she wondered. *When the things that really matter—family, friends, tradition, loyalty—are clearly priceless.*

"But *I* am," responded Pamela. "Besides, I can't imagine that a bunch of dusty old books would fetch all that much money."

"Depends on what they've been appraised at," responded Carmela, thinking this might be the perfect project for Jekyl Hardy, her float-builder friend who was also a licensed art and antiques appraiser.

Pamela waved a chubby hand dismissively. "Honey, when Dunbar puts an offer on the table, people generally accept."

Pamela DesLauriers's visit left a bad taste in Carmela's mouth. So after checking Gabby and Tandy's progress with the demo, Carmela pulled out her cell phone and called Memory Mine. She'd been quite willing to close the store, but Wren had volunteered to work there and keep it open. Carmela said okay, partly because she didn't think it would be terribly busy—all the truly manic scrapbookers would be here at Scrap Fest—and partly because it gave Wren something to do. Helped keep her mind off the fact that today was supposed to have been her wedding day.

Wren answered on the first ring. "Memory Mine. How can we help?"

"You're not busy," said Carmela.

"Oh, but we were," said Wren, instantly recognizing Carmela's voice. "Business has been good. We had a real rush maybe thirty minutes ago. Well . . . *you* had a rush."

"The possessive *we* is just fine," said Carmela, "because you are part of the family."

"So you keep telling me," said Wren. "Thank you. That means a lot to me."

Carmela hesitated. "You've been fielding calls okay? No problems?" She wondered if Dunbar DesLauriers had possibly tracked Wren down and dared to pester her.

"No problems," said Wren. "A fellow by the name of Clark Berthume called for you. From the Click! Gallery."

Oh oh. "Did he leave a message?" asked Carmela.

"He said he was trying to fix a schedule for the gallery's upcoming shows and he wanted to know when you were going to drop by with your portfolio." Wren paused. "Carmela, I didn't know you did photography, too. That's wonderful! You're a regular Renaissance woman!"

"No, I'm just a twenty-first century gal who's completely over-booked like everyone else," said Carmela. "But I'll try to give him a call." *Try to call him off,* thought Carmela.

"And Blaine Taylor dropped by earlier," added Wren. "He said the house received the all-clear. They caught the snake and, luckily, didn't find anything else wiggling around."

"Good," said Carmela, still a little shaken, as they probably all were, by last night's snake incident.

"Blaine said the Critter Gitter people told him this wasn't at all uncommon. Apparently, snakes and lizards and stuff are often found crawling through pipes and up from basements."

"Really," said Carmela. She'd lived in and around New Orleans all her life and never experienced anything quite like that. "I guess that helps put some perspective on it."

"I'm a little nervous about going home," said Wren, "but I have to face the ordeal sometime."

Poor Wren, thought Carmela, *has to face a lot of tough ordeals.*

"Oh, and I asked Blaine about the software thing," said Wren.

"What about the software thing?" asked Carmela.

"You know. Who owns Neutron Software."

"What did he tell you?" asked Carmela, hating herself for having such a suspicious nature.

"That he and Jamie had drawn up a tentative buy-sell agreement," said Wren, "based on book value of the business."

"Uh huh," said Carmela.

"But they also had a provision," continued Wren, "that should one partner die, proprietary rights automatically revert to the surviving partner."

"Is that a fact," said Carmela. *Interesting little codicil. And oh-so-convenient for Blaine.* "We should get a copy of that agreement and take a look at it," said Carmela. "Better yet, we should have a smart lawyer look at it."

"I don't know if Jamie had a lawyer," said Wren.

"Well," said Carmela, as a spatter of applause erupted from the table nearby and a dozen happy customers popped up with their completed bookmarks. "We're just gonna have to do some snooping. And then we'll find ourselves a good lawyer." *One who isn't tied to Blaine Taylor,* she added silently.

. . .

"Hot diggity," said Tandy to Carmela. "You sold a ton of rubber stamps and packages of that crinkley fiber."

"Thanks to the terrific demo you and Gabby did," said Carmela.

"Shoot, it was all Gabby's doing," said Tandy, waving a hand. "She's sweet but so persuasive. Even *I'm* gonna buy some of those new stamps. I mean, I *love* that heritage series."

"Tandy," said Carmela, "can you help Gabby with the booth for about ten minutes?"

"Sure 'nuf," said Tandy. "Whatcha gonna do? Take a spin around the hall again?"

"That's exactly what I'm going to do," declared Carmela. There was a new vendor who was selling templates for pop-ups and she wanted to place an order or at least grab one of their catalogs.

But twenty steps away from her booth Carmela ran smack dab into Margot Butler.

"How do, Carmela," drawled Margot. Looking very much the *avant-garde* interior designer, Margot was dressed in a slinky black blouse, black leather slacks, and dark green leather boots.

"Margot!" said Carmela, surprised. Fresh in her mind was the photograph of Jamie Redmond with his arm around Margot's waist, looking extremely amorous. And extremely engaged.

"Has Pamela dropped by yet?" asked Margot. "With the photos and such?"

"Maybe ten minutes ago," said Carmela.

"Drat," said Margot. "Looks like I missed her. Oh well . . ."

"Margot," said Carmela, wondering how to phrase her question.

Delicately or plunge right in?

Carmela decided she was definitely a plunge-right-in type. "Margot," said Carmela again, "I didn't realize you and Jamie Redmond had been engaged."

Margot didn't miss a beat. "Oh, yeah." She gave a dismissive shrug. "Jamie and I were quite the item for a while. But . . . well, things just didn't work out." She paused. "And now look what's happened. Pity."

"Are we talking ancient history, Margot?" asked Carmela, trying to keep her voice light.

But Margot was instantly suspicious. "Why are you asking, Carmela? What business is it of yours? And why this sudden inquisition?" she demanded. "You think *I* had something to do with Jamie's death?"

"We came across an old photo last night," explained Carmela. "At Wren's house. We were just surprised."

"Mnn," said Margot. "Did she see it? Wren?"

"Yes, she did," said Carmela.

Margot chewed at her lower lip. "I imagine it upset her."

"I think it might have," replied Carmela. *Is Margot enjoying this little exchange? Yes, I believe she is.*

"Too bad," said Margot. "But like I said, it's old news."

"You mentioned that," said Carmela. "But I'm still curious about timing. In other words, how long ago were you two an item?"

"Oh, let's see," said Margot, pretending to rack her brain. "Last year."

Last year! thought Carmela. Shamus had skipped out on her more than a year ago, and her wounds still hadn't healed. Hadn't even begun to heal. So, this was the question on the table—had Margot been carrying a torch for Jamie? Or worse yet, had she been nursing a nasty grudge? One that had stung and festered until she finally took matters into her own hands?

"You know," said Margot, "we're going to need those scrapbooks by next Wednesday at the latest. This is a very important fund raiser. A lot of people are counting on you."

"They'll be finished," said Carmela. "One way or the other, they'll be finished."

"You're such a pro, Carmela" murmured Margot as she edged away. "Well, toodles, dearie. See you later."

"Margot," said Carmela, just as the designer was about to dash off. "What kind of boots are you wearing? I mean the leather?"

Margot paused a few feet from Carmela and tipped a heel up to show her boots off. "Snakeskin," she purred. "Don't you just love 'em?"

Chapter 9

AVA brushed back her frizzled mass of auburn hair and leaned over her Eggs Benedict. "Weird," she murmured. "This Margot person really wore snakeskin boots?"

"Cross my heart and hope to die," said Carmela. "Let's hope she's either a confirmed fashionista or she's planning a guest appearance on the *Crocodile Hunter.*"

The two women were sitting on the broad front porch of the Columns Hotel. It was a magnificent structure originally designed by the architect Thomas Sully. In more recent years, giant Doric columns had been stuck onto the front to supposedly add charm and make the whole thing look even more like a Southern mansion.

As they nibbled at their Sunday brunch, Carmela had filled Ava in on some of the newer, stranger revelations. She'd related her encounter with the pushy Pamela DesLauriers who claimed husband Dunbar always got what he wanted. And she told Ava about Blaine Taylor's purported buy-sell agreement with Jamie Redmond. An agreement that didn't just give Blaine first dibs, but seemed to give him *carte blanche* to the entire Neutron computer program.

And then, of course, they'd rehashed their thoughts on Margot Butler with her broken-off engagement and snakeskin boots.

Ava had pretty much reserved comment until all of the strange news had been spilled out onto the table. Finally, she shook her head in amazement. "Honey, I hate to say it, but it sounds like any *one* of those folks might have had it in for Jamie Redmond."

Carmela nodded slowly. She, too, was gradually coming to that same conclusion.

"Dunbar and Blaine were *there* that evening at Bon Tiempe," said Ava, "so they'd be tops on my list."

"But don't forget," said Carmela. "Margot of the snakeskin boots knows her way around Bon Tiempe, too. I called Quigg last night and found out that Margot's design firm sold him some of the chandeliers. The small crystal ones hanging in the bar, I think."

"Don't you think it's strange that Blaine Taylor showed up just in the nick of time Friday night?" asked Ava. "That really bothers me."

Carmela sighed. "Me, too."

"Is Wren suspicious about any of this?" asked Ava. "I mean, she knows about Margot being engaged to Jamie, but what about the rest?"

"I don't think she's put anything together yet," said Carmela. "And I wasn't planning to fan any flames, either. She's got enough to worry about."

"You're a girl after my own heart," said Ava. "One who knows how to keep her lips properly zipped."

"Don't you think?" asked Carmela. She was torn between protecting Wren and sharing—or rather spilling—her suspicions.

"A little discretion is always the best policy," said Ava. "The question is, what are you going to do now?"

"Correction; what are *we* going to do," said Carmela.

Ava watched the waiter refill her champagne flute, then picked it up, swirling the elegant golden liquor to release the bubbles. Taking a delicate sip, she contemplated the wine. "Terrific," she finally proclaimed.

"Nothing like a dry finish to roll your tongue up like a window shade."

Every Sunday, the Columns Hotel hosted a lovely champagne brunch. However, the champagne they opted to serve was a domestic variety. Ava, claiming she was making a decided effort to expand her cosmic consciousness, had ordered a bottle of Perrier-Jouet, a rather fine French champagne. That's what the two women were drinking now. And Carmela, who was also intrigued by the burst of tiny dry bubbles inside her mouth, had to admit the extra thirty dollars was probably well worth it.

"What if," said Ava finally, "we called that nice detective and had a talk with him? The one that helped you out before. Edgar . . ."

"Babcock," said Carmela, finishing Ava's sentence. "Gabby and I talked about calling Lieutenant Babcock, but we really don't have any concrete evidence to present to him. And we're still pretty much going on hunches and theories."

Ava wrinkled her nose. "We need concrete evidence, huh? What about that photo of Margot and Jamie?"

"Doesn't prove she murdered the guy," said Carmela. "Just means she was in love with him. Or used to be in love with him."

"I wonder," said Ava. "I wonder which one of them broke it off. Margot or Jamie."

"Don't know," said Carmela. "And I don't think it's likely we're ever going to find out. Margot got very prickly when I asked a couple questions about her relationship with Jamie."

"Sounds like a lady with something to hide," said Ava.

Carmela shrugged. "Maybe. Or else she's embarrassed because she got dumped."

"The big D," said Ava. "It can be an ego-crusher."

And it can push some people over the edge, thought Carmela. She knew there was a reason an awful lot of killings were dubbed "crimes of passion."

"I wonder if Margot gave the ring back," mused Ava. "I mean, is there a set protocol on that? I can see where if a woman dumps a guy, she's morally obligated to return the ring." Ava took another sip of champagne, enlivened by her train of thought. "But if a guy dumped me? I don't think I'd be hopping up and down, eager to return my engagement ring like I was taking back a pair of bowling shoes or something. Especially if the ring was in the category of a two karat flawless, colorless stone. Say a marquis or princess cut."

"What would you do with it?" asked Carmela, as her cell phone burped inside her purse and she leaned down to retrieve it.

"Have it reset as a fancy pendant," said Ava promptly. She'd obviously given this careful thought.

"Hello," Carmela murmured into her phone.

"Carmela? It's Wren."

Carmela mouthed *Wren* to Ava, who nodded as if she'd almost expected Wren to call.

"What's wrong, honey?" asked Carmela. She thought Wren sounded slightly panicky.

"Dunbar DesLauriers just called and made an offer on the inventory at Biblios. What do I do now?"

"Do you want to sell?" asked Carmela. "Providing we find out you really do own the inventory?"

"I don't know," said Wren. "I haven't really thought about it, so I need some advice. You and Ava are the only business people I know."

Carmela put her hand over the receiver. "She says we're the only business people she knows," said Carmela.

"God help her," said Ava, rolling her eyes skyward.

"There's Stuart," suggested Carmela. Gabby's husband, Stuart, who owned a chain of car dealerships, was forever being lauded by one or another business club or chamber of commerce. He was knowledgeable, but all his honorary titles, plaques, and pins also tended to make him a bit pompous and overbearing.

A long silence spun out.

"Right," replied Wren finally, "there's Stuart."

"Okaaay," said Carmela. "Let's forget about old Stuart. What kind of advice do you need from me?"

"For one thing, I'm flat broke."

"Explain please," said Carmela.

"After I moved in with Jamie six months ago, I quit my job at the travel agency and was really just helping out at the bookstore."

"You worked there full-time, but didn't take a salary?" asked Carmela.

"Oh, she *does* need our help," said Ava in a low voice.

Wren's voice contained a hint of a quaver. "Yes," she answered. "Do you think I should have taken a salary?"

"There's no hard and fast rule, but . . . yeah, probably," said Carmela. She thought for a moment. "What we need to do is poke around and see if there's money left in the business checking account. If there is, that's your back salary."

"Wow," breathed Wren. "We can do that?"

"Sure we can," said Carmela. She didn't know the legalities involved, but figured she'd find a way. She usually did.

"That'd be just great," said Wren, sounding better already.

"Do you know where Jamie kept his checkbooks and ledgers and all that?" Carmela asked.

"Sure," said Wren, "but I never had anything to do with them. The most I ever did was make change for cash purchases or take credit cards. And even then, all I did was take an impression, fill in the numbers, and file the flimsy."

"Tell you what," said Carmela, "Ava and I are just about finished with brunch, so I'll meet you at Jamie's store in . . ." she glanced at her watch, "let's say an hour. We'll see what we can figure out."

"Is she okay?" asked Ava, after Carmela hung up.

"She sounded a little strung out," admitted Carmela. The two of them sat and watched a cluster of tourists amble up the front sidewalk, cameras poised. The Columns Hotel, with its beveled-glass front door, spectacular main staircase, and stained glass windows, had been used as a location by filmmaker Louis Malle when he'd shot scenes for the movie, *Pretty Baby*. Just like the *Cat People* house over at Chartres and Esplanade, tourists were forever flocking to this real-life location.

"Pardon me," said a young man in a flat Midwestern accent as he stepped onto the porch. "Can we take your picture?" He ducked his head, suddenly turning shy. "I mean, you girls are real Southern belles, aren't you?"

Inhaling deeply, Ava turned her megawatt smile on the handsome young man. "We sure are, sugar," she told him. "Best the South has to offer."

Chapter 10

Boo strutted along Dauphine Street, her Shar-Pei head held high, tail curled into a tight, furry doughnut, wrinkles jiggling gently. Carmela had dropped by her apartment earlier and changed into blue jeans and an *I Brake for Whales* T-shirt in anticipation of what would probably prove to be a dusty, dirty prowl. Boo had watched solemnly, her shiny bright eyes following Carmela's every move, hoping for an invitation. And Carmela had figured, *Why not?* Why not bring Boo along to Biblios Booksellers? Because, let's face it, the little dog had already been in half the shops in the French Quarter, and conducted herself quite properly, thank you very much. Except for that tiny little incident with Teddy Morton's Siamese. And who's counting *that!*

Lights were on and Wren was already moving around inside the bookstore when Carmela and Boo arrived.

"Knock knock," said Carmela, rattling the doorknob and peering through the frosted glass window on which *Biblios Booksellers, Rare and Antiquarian Books & Maps* had been painted in flowing gold script.

Wren came scampering to the door to let them in. She was also dressed in blue jeans and wore a chambray shirt knotted at her waist. "Hey there, Boo Boo," she called, reaching down to scratch Boo's tiny triangle ears. "Make yourself at home. There's a nice cozy sofa up in that half loft if you want." And Boo, ever grateful for an invitation to catch a snooze, scurried up the stairs to investigate.

"Have you started going through Jamie's records yet?" asked Carmela.

"No," said Wren. "I was waiting for you. I didn't know exactly what to look for, and you're . . . well, you've got business experience. So I thought I'd just sit tight."

Carmela gazed about the bookstore. Leatherbound volumes gleamed from tall wooden shelves and faded Aubusson carpets covered the floors. Cozy leather club chairs and worn velvet wing chairs were stuck wherever an impromptu seating area presented itself. To Carmela's right was a huge, ornate wooden flat file that boasted dozens of extra-wide drawers. That, she figured, was probably the repository for the antique maps. To her left, six narrow steps led to the loft where Boo was snuffling about; ten feet ahead and two steps down led to a small business area with a desk, file cabinets, and counters piled high with books.

"I love this place," said Carmela. Her dad, though he'd long since passed away, had instilled in her a deep and abiding love for books, and she had never lost that feeling. Books were her ticket to untold journeys, her storehouse of knowledge, her refuge. To this day, Carmela loved nothing better than to curl up with a good book and a steaming cup of tea.

Carmela's early love for books and short story collections had probably served as the impetus for her collection of antique children's books. After a dozen years of combing flea markets, bookstores, and antique shops, her collection now included three dozen early Nancy Drew books, the thick ones from the thirties where Nancy still drove a spiffy, red roadster; at least two dozen Big Little books; Albert Payson Terhune's entire *Lad, a Dog* series; and an early copy of L. Frank Baum's *The Wizard of Oz*.

"This is an amazing collection, isn't it?" said Wren. Now that she was back in the store and had a purpose, she seemed much more relaxed. Happy almost, to be among these tall, sagging bookshelves.

"Did you know that Jamie also did book binding and book conservation?" asked Wren. "Collectors from all over Louisiana would bring Jamie their precious but ailing books and he would repair the leather bindings. Or sometimes he'd completely re-bind them or just get pages unstuck. Then there were the people who'd discover old books that had been stored in attics or stuck in musty old trunks for decades. Jamie would treat the pages with archival preserving spray and try to undo the damage done by mildew, heat, mold, and insects."

Carmela nodded approvingly. She was no stranger herself to working with acid-free paper and archival spray. Old photographs were just as delicate as the pages of old books.

"I keep forgetting what an amazing inventory Jamie had," said Wren. "No wonder collectors from all over sent him letters and e-mails with their want lists."

"*Inventory* is the operative word," said Carmela. "If Dunbar DesLauriers really does want to buy the whole shebang, you've got to get a handle on what you really have here."

"I have an inventory list with Jamie's suggested prices," said Wren. "But that doesn't include the couple hundred books shelved in the rare book cases."

"That's a problem," said Carmela. "And, on a business note, we should regard this as a collection rather than just a store full of books. Collections always command higher prices." She thought about what she'd just said. "I suppose that's because someone has already invested considerable time and effort to bring like-minded pieces together and then categorize everything."

"What if I went on the Internet and tried to get prices on the books that aren't on the price list?" suggested Wren. "Some comparables."

"That's a terrific idea," enthused Carmela. "Then we'd have a ballpark idea of the value of the total inventory." She knew the more information they could give Jekyl Hardy, the easier his task would be to appraise the inventory. Or, if he couldn't do it, Jekyl would find someone who could.

They both looked around at books strewn and shelved everywhere. It suddenly seemed like a daunting task, even for a bookstore pro.

"Of course, I'm going to have to do some organizing first," amended Wren. She, too, seemed suddenly overwhelmed by putting a price tag on all this.

"First things first," said Carmela, realizing they were getting side-tracked. "Job one is we go through Jamie's business papers."

"Which ones?" asked Wren.

Carmela shrugged. "Bank statements, the building lease, payables and receivables, his partnership agreement with Blaine Taylor if we can find it. Hopefully a last will and testament," she said as Wren flinched. "Sorry."

"That's okay," said Wren.

Taking a deep breath, Carmela sat down at Jamie's desk and began to paw through his drawers and files. Jamie hadn't exactly subscribed to the organized desk theory, so Carmela had to sort through a lot of junk, too. Letters from book collectors, price lists, catalogs from other book dealers, invoices that had been marked "paid" but never filed. But in the second drawer, she began to unearth the beginnings of the mother lode, finding Jamie's business checkbook.

"Checkbook," said Carmela, laying the green plastic book atop the desk.

"You peek," said Wren. "I'm too nervous."

Carmela flipped through the pages. Jamie's commercial account for Biblios Booksellers wasn't all that different than a personal account. He used the same type of check register to keep track of deposits and the checks he'd written. Carmela figured he probably gave the checkbook to his bookkeeper or accountant and let them get quarterly information that way.

"Is there a balance?" asked Wren.

Carmela's eyes sought out the last number in the column. "Yes, there is," she said. "Sixteen thousand and change."

"Sixteen thousand *dollars?*" said Wren.

Carmela nodded.

"Is that good?" asked Wren.

"It is if the rent, heat, and light bills are paid," answered Carmela, scanning the check register. "And they seem to be. Through January in fact."

"So I've got some breathing room," said Wren.

"You've also got a salary," said Carmela. Her hands went to the adding machine that sat atop Jamie's desk. "Let's see. Forty hours a week times approximately twenty-five weeks is one thousand hours. Times . . . let's say twelve dollars an hour . . . that's twelve thousand dollars due to you, my dear." Carmela turned and looked at Wren. "Or do you want me to figure it at fifteen dollars an hour?"

Wren shook her head, "Twelve is fine."

"Okay then," said Carmela, "back to the search." She looked up at Wren. "If there's something else you want to do, go right ahead."

Wren thought for a few seconds. "Jamie kept an old four-drawer filing cabinet in the basement. What if I go down and look through that? See if there's anything worthwhile?"

"Go for it," said Carmela, as Wren walked to the back of the store and pulled open a door she hadn't noticed before. Wren flipped a switch, then disappeared down a steep set of wooden stairs.

Carmela could hear Wren clattering down the last few steps even as her fingers flicked over a bundle of statements from Kahlman-Douglas Certified Public Accountants. She pulled one out, took a quick look. *Good. Now we know who Jamie's CPA firm was. Gonna make things a whole lot easier.*

The middle drawer was stuffed with inventory lists. But they were all computer printouts, so obviously a master list existed on the Dell computer that sat on Jamie's desk.

It wasn't until Carmela pulled open the bottom drawer of Jamie's desk that she found what she was really looking for. The heart of the matter. Tucked in a light blue legal-sized envelope was Jamie Redmond's Last Will and Testament.

Should I read it? wondered Carmela. *Or give it to Wren? This is, after all, a very personal document.*

Then she figured, *The heck with it. I'm gonna go*

ahead and read it. That's why Wren asked me to come here in the first place.

The first few pages were fairly standard, probably boiler-plated by Jamie's attorney. The fifth page was the crux of the matter. The information they really needed to know.

Carmela closed all the desk drawers and did a fairly plausible job of straightening the desktop. Then she climbed the half-dozen narrow steps up to the loft to see what Boo was up to.

When Wren came upstairs some ten minutes later, clutching an armload of dusty file folders, she found Carmela stretched out next to Boo, looking serene, reading from Pablo Neruda's *Twenty Love Poems and a Song of Despair.*

Carmela closed the book and smiled up at Wren. "You own it," she told her.

"What!"

"The bookstore. All of this. It's yours. Jamie put it in your name, same as the house. Except this seems to be free and clear, whereas the house has a mortgage."

File folders slipped from Wren's arms and her knees seemed to grow weak. She crossed one leg over the other and slid to a sitting position on the carpet.

"You okay?" Carmela asked.

"I feel like I just woke up from a bad dream," said Wren. "All this time I've been thinking I had to hurry up and sell all this stuff in order to pay the bills. And that it would be a horrible, gut-wrenching experience. And now I find out that I own it." She gazed around with a startled look on her young face. "And you know what?"

Carmela raised one eyebrow.

"I'm glad," said Wren.

"Good for you," said Carmela. "Now you're showing real spunk."

Wren swiveled her head around, as though she were seeing the bookstore for the very first time. "There's just one problem," she said finally. "I'm terrible at this. Business stuff, I mean."

"Hey, don't sell yourself short," said Carmela. "Business can be fun."

Wren wrinkled her nose and snorted. "Fun? How can you even say that?"

"Don't get me wrong, running a business is a tremendous challenge," Carmela told her. "But it's a real character builder, too. Helps you discover what you're really made of. And, in a funny way, running a business helps you prioritize what's really important in your life."

"That wouldn't be a bad thing," admitted Wren. "But I really don't know any of the . . . what would you call them? Business fundamentals?"

"It's not that tricky," said Carmela. "In your case, you have a retail shop. So your business mission is to deliver a good product, a unique product, and make sure your customer enjoys a positive buying experience. That all relates to inventory and customer service."

"I think I can handle that," said Wren, glancing around.

"You also have to concentrate on sales and marketing," said Carmela. "You have to figure out who your audience is. Who your *market* is. Your target market."

"You mean I shouldn't advertise to everyone and his brother?" said Wren.

"Exactly," said Carmela. "In the case of this bookstore, I'd probably generate a few pieces of direct mail and target area book collectors."

"I think Jamie *did* have some kind of mailing list," said Wren, suddenly sounding hopeful.

"And I'd for sure go after the tourist market," said Carmela. "After all, you've got a fabulous location here in the French Quarter. Tons of people who are knowledgeable about antique collecting flock here every year. Chances are, a good portion of them collect antique books and maps, too."

"You make it sound like fun," said Wren.

"Business can be fun, once you get the hang of things," said Carmela. "The most important thing to remember is there are no hard and fast rules. Some of the best, most serendipitous business opportunities occur when you think outside the box."

Wren gazed around the dusty shop with a hopeful look on her face. "So you really think I could run this place? All by myself?"

"I think with a couple terrific employees you could definitely get Biblios Booksellers humming along," said Carmela.

"What kind of employees?"

"If this were my shop," said Carmela, "I might look for a retired college professor or somebody with a library background. Librarians are very smart cookies, you know. They'd bring organization to the business and lend credibility, too."

"What a good idea," enthused Wren.

"Sounds like you're seriously considering this," said Carmela.

"I am. Wow! I can believe I said that."

"What did you find in the basement?" asked Carmela, making a motion toward the file folders that lay on the carpet next to Wren.

"Not much. Old business records from, like, five years ago, a few old photos, and a bunch of other junk. Looks like letters and old news clippings."

"Let me see," said Carmela.

Wren handed Carmela one of the brown file folders. "These are very old photos," said Carmela, pawing gently through the contents. "Some of them look like they might even date back to the forties and fifties. And there are old negatives, too." She was suddenly formulating an idea. What if she took some of these old negatives and printed them in different ways? Maybe a photo montage effect combined with some of her own photos? Then she could colorize them on the computer or even hand-color them using some of the oil pens she had at Memory Mine.

Would something like that make a nice addition to her somewhat skimpy portfolio? Yeah. Maybe.

Better yet, would producing a few pieces like that get

Shamus off her back? And satisfy Clark Berthume from the Click! Gallery? Worth a shot. Definitely worth a shot.

"Mind if I take some of these home?" Carmela asked Wren.

"Be my guest," said Wren. "In fact, you can *have* them. I certainly don't know what I'd do with them."

"Except for this one," said Carmela, peering into another brown folder. "These look like they might be pictures of Jamie." She handed the folder to Wren, who immediately clutched it to her chest.

"I'm not going to sort through this right now," Wren told her. "But I am considering doing some sort of scrapbook in Jamie's memory."

"I think that's a lovely idea," said Carmela, smiling at Wren. The girl seemed to have definitely perked up. Maybe it was the knowledge that she now owned tangible assets. Maybe she was starting to work through her grief.

Boo suddenly let out a loud, wet snort. Startled, the dog sprang from the couch and spun around, ears perked, as if to ask, *Who on earth made such an undignified noise?*

"She woke herself up," said Wren suddenly convulsed with laughter.

"She does that a lot," said Carmela. Shar-Peis are soft-palette dogs, renowned for their prodigious sound effects.

Wren reached out and stroked Boo's velvety fur. "This is going to be a very tough decision. Now that

I'm back here, I do love the atmosphere. So cozy and welcoming. But I know I'll have some demons to work through, too, if I stay and keep the store going. I'm sure I'll be constantly jumping at shadows. Hoping against hope that Jamie's going to walk through that front door again."

"You'll need some time," admitted Carmela.

"But I don't have much time," said Wren. "Aren't business people always saying 'Time is money'? Well, there isn't a lot of money here. Especially since rent needs to eventually be paid. As well as heat, light, and all those other things you mentioned."

"Come work at Memory Mine for a while," said Carmela.

Wren stared at her, amazed. "What? Are you serious?"

"There's sixteen grand in the business checking account," said Carmela. "That should cover operating expenses for two, maybe three months. Buy you some time. Plus I could really use the help, since Mardi Gras is just around the corner. Besides our usual scrapbook customers and scrapbookers looking for unique gifts, we'll probably be inundated by people who want to create their own cards and party invitations."

"And you'd actually pay me?" said Wren.

"That's the general idea," said Carmela.

"Wow." Wren's face lit up.

"Is that a yes?" asked Carmela.

"Yes!" enthused Wren. She clambered to her knees, leaned forward, and threw her arms around Carmela, giving her a huge bear hug.

Woof!

"Hugs all around!" cried Wren as Boo pounced happily at Wren and, in the process, knocked over a half-filled cup of coffee that must have been tucked beneath the sofa. "Just wait until I get back to Gabby's," declared Wren. "She'll be thrilled to hear we'll all be working together!"

Carmela dug in her purse for a tissue to mop the spilled coffee. "She sure will," she replied, her smile suddenly frozen on her face. *Please tell me why this coffee smells so fresh?* she asked herself. *Has someone been in this store very recently? Like late last night or earlier today?*

Oh dear. And please don't tell me it could be the same someone who snuck down the hallway at Bon Tiempe and wielded that nasty butcher knife! That would be very bad, indeed!

Chapter 11

CLOUDS of pink and blue swirled overhead in a colorful wind-swept sky. The late afternoon sun, glinting orange, threw an extra scrim of light on the Caribbean colors of the French Quarter buildings as Carmela and Boo walked slowly home. The familiar *clip clop* from one of the horse-drawn carriages echoed down the block, a low mournful *toot* sounded from some tugboat anchored over on the Mississippi.

Carmela had been tossing around the notion that

someone might have been poking around Biblios Booksellers not long before she and Wren had shown up today. But now, as she sped along, she'd almost succeeded in talking herself *out* of her paranoia.

Probably it was an old cup of coffee, right? That someone had carried in last week. Probably no one has been stretched out on that old sofa in the bookstore's loft.

"Hey there, Boo," said Carmela. "You didn't catch any kind of scent, did you? Someone who might have been sitting on that sofa just before you?"

Boo shook her head and kept chugging along.

A young couple standing in a doorway, locked in a heated embrace, paused for a few seconds to stare as Carmela walked by.

Yeah, I talk to dogs. Because sometimes dogs are the only creatures who truly listen.

Turning into her courtyard, Carmela glanced up at the gracefully arched second story bow window that overlooked the fountain. Ava's apartment was up there. And usually a light burned bright. But right now her place was still dark.

"She probably went out on a date," Carmela told Boo. "She didn't *mention* anything about it, but I bet that's what she's doing. Having a fun date." Carmela unlocked the door to her apartment, nudged it open with her foot so Boo could scramble in. "In fact, that's where I would be, if I wasn't so socially impaired."

Boo immediately sped toward the kitchen, where she parked herself and proceeded to stare intently at the doggy cookie jar that held her dry kibbles.

"Isn't is a little early?" Carmela asked her. "Wouldn't you rather dine fashionably late?" It wasn't quite five. If Boo had her way she'd be eating supper at two in the afternoon.

Boo continued to stare at the jar as if she could levitate the lid, Uri Geller–style.

"Okay, you win," Carmela told her.

She fed a delighted Boo, plopping a spoonful of yogurt on top of the dry kibbles, then changed into a comfy velour track suit that Ava had given her for her birthday. The track suit didn't exactly carry a fancy designer label, but Ava had assured her it was probably made in one of the same overseas sweatshop that did the Juicy Couture or J.Lo line.

Then Carmela settled in at her dining room table. She finally had a chance to breathe. No major distractions seemed to loom on the horizon, so she was determined to take the plunge and see what could be done about putting her photos in order. The ones Shamus had been so hot and bothered about. The ones that were supposed to go to Click! Gallery to help determine if she and Shamus were really going to have a joint photo show.

Carmela still wasn't completely positive she even wanted her photographs in a show. It wasn't that she was shy about people seeing her work. After all, people looked at her scrapbook pages every day. In her shop, her front display window, and even on her website. It was just that photography was one of her favorite hobbies. Something she could do with her heart instead of her head. And once you turned that hobby into a vocation, treated it more like a business, you really had to start thinking consciously about it. And then it wasn't quite so pure and joyful anymore.

Carmela had just hoisted her black oversized portfolio onto the table when the phone rang. Casting her eyes toward the heavens, she prayed it wasn't anything major.

It was Shamus. So, of course it was major.

"Meet me for dinner," he said, his invitation sounding peppy, just this side of manic.

Carmela stared at the photos spread out before her. She was determined to get through this. "Can't," she told him. "I'm in the middle of something." *Besides, what's the point?* she wanted to say, but didn't.

"I bet you're planning to go out for dinner tonight, aren't you?" said Shamus, taking her refusal as a challenge. "Let me guess. It's that sleazy restaurateur. That Quigg person. Did I guess right? Are you going to slither off to his restaurant and let him ply you with wine and truffles?"

"No," Carmela said, although she had to admit Shamus's little restaurant fantasy sounded pretty damn good. Preferable, certainly, to poking through a bunch of black-and-white photos that she was struggling to get excited about.

"What are you in the middle of?" he asked. Shamus had never been big on subtlety. Or privacy for that matter.

"If you must know," said Carmela, "I'm working on my photos."

"For the show?" exclaimed Shamus. "The one at Click!?"

"You got it," said Carmela, casting a discerning eye at a black-and-white shot of a Mississippi river boat. Not bad, but not stunning either. Maybe a six on a scale of one to ten.

"Good girl," commended Shamus. He'd suddenly revised his tone to bubbly and enthusiastic. "This could be a very big step for us, Carmela. Very major."

"Mnn," said Carmela, noncommittally. Shamus was definitely way more into this show than she would ever be.

But Shamus babbled on. "I don't think I told you this, but Glory liked two of my photos so well that she hung them in the bank lobby. The ones of that Creole-style townhouse on Royal Street. Anyway, I understand they're garnering rave reviews."

"Rave reviews," said Carmela. Shamus was beginning to seriously get on her nerves. "Rave reviews from people who come in to grab twenty bucks from the ATM. Those are pretty high accolades, Shamus. Sounds like you're one step away from having a big show in a fancy New York gallery."

"You're just jealous," said Shamus, sounding hurt.

"Actually, I'm not," said Carmela. "In fact, I'd be delighted if you did this show all by yourself."

"We had a deal, Carmela," said Shamus. Now there was an edge to his voice. He was definitely giving her

141

the Shamus Meechum Seal of Disapproval. "You said we'd do this *together.* You can't just pull out now."

"Why not?" said Carmela. "You pulled out of our marriage." *Oh oh, now I've veered into that old territory again. Oh, shame on me.*

"Totally different situation, Carmela. You know that."

Carmela sighed. "Okay, Shamus, cards on the table. I can't quit, but you can? Where's the fairness in that?" She knew she was being petty, knew she was beating a dead horse, but she couldn't stop. Anger and frustration still burned inside her like a molten ball.

"This is hopeless," fumed Shamus. "Utterly hopeless."

I'm afraid you're right, thought Carmela.

Silence hung between them for a few beats, then Shamus finally said. "So you're going to drop by Click! when?"

"I don't know," said Carmela, who by now had completely lost interest in perusing her photos. "Maybe next Tuesday," she lied. "Wednesday at the latest."

"Good," said Shamus. "Glad to hear it." He seemed to have blanked out their snarling, sniping go-round of ten seconds ago.

Wonderful, thought Carmela. *Shamus is having a senior moment.*

"Be sure to let me know how it goes," urged Shamus. "In fact, call me the minute you're finished."

"Right," said Carmela, knowing she wouldn't. She hung up the phone, stared down at the table. *Crapola.*

Any iota of enthusiasm she'd had for this project had just flown right out the window.

So now what?

Carmela exhaled slowly, stared across the room at the chair where her purse and the brown file folders from Jamie's store sat. Maybe take a look through those, she decided. They were one thing she could follow up on.

But after thumbing through the files for a few minutes, Carmela didn't find anything that was particularly interesting. Or enlightening.

Most of the photos were similar to the ones she'd looked at the other night. Black-and-white shots of what had to be Jamie's old homestead down near Boothville. There were a few variations on the same theme, but nothing that knocked her out.

No, these aren't going to work even if I hand-color them. Not thematic enough. Oh well.

There were a few old news clippings tucked in among the photos, too. Most were from the *Boothville Courier* and dealt with high school sports team wins. A baseball conference championship, a football win, a wresting match.

It looked like Jamie might have been a frustrated scrapbooker, Carmela decided. But then again, lots of people were. They amassed huge amounts of photos, clippings, programs, and letters, but never quite made it to the next logical step, that being scrapbooking, journaling, or creating genealogy albums. Because they never found a logical way to chronicle their jumbled collection of photos and moments, they were never able to fully enjoy them.

Carmela was about to stuff everything back in the folder and fix something to eat, when one of the clippings caught her eye.

A faded news clipping with the headline *Bogus Creek Boys Await Sentencing.*

Bogus Creek Boys? The name had a funny, colorful ring to it. Old fashioned. Like the bank robbers who populated the American landscape during the twenties and thirties. Bonnie and Clyde. The Al Karpis Gang. Ma Barker and Al Capone.

So who were these Bogus Creek Boys? she wondered. *And why had Jamie Redmond elected to save this particular clipping?*

Carmela scanned down the narrow column, quickly absorbing the gist of the story. A ring of counterfeiters had set up shop near Boothville. In fact, they'd operated out of an abandoned camp house on the banks of Bogus Creek. Hence the moniker, Bogus Creek Boys. They'd been apprehended by a savvy local sheriff, but no printing plates had been recovered.

However, it was the final paragraph that riveted Carmela's attention and caused a sharp intake of breath.

It said, *T.L. Walker and J. Redmond, two members of the counterfeiting gang, are slated for sentencing this Thursday.*

Carmela stared at the clipping in her hands.

J. Redmond. Jamie Redmond? Jamie had been one of the Bogus Creek Boys? Good lord!

Carefully setting the snippet of paper on the table, Carmela tapped it gently with her index finger, as though trying to ascertain if the article were truly genuine.

Jamie Redmond a convicted criminal? A criminal who'd actually served time? Carmela pursed her lips, thinking.

Or was this article about his father? Hadn't his father owned a little printing shop? Sure he had.

She turned the article over, looking for a date. There was nothing that lent a clue as to whether the article was ten years old or twenty-five years old.

So Jamie, or Jamie's father, had a shady past. She wondered if that's why Jamie had been so closed-mouthed about his life in Boothville. And Carmela also wondered if this strange link to a sordid past might hold an important clue as to why Jamie Redmond had been murdered.

Did one of the Bogus Creek Boys get out of prison and come back to target him? Had Jamie or his father plea-bargained? Enough so there might still be anger and bad blood at work?

Worse yet, could someone have been blackmailing Jamie? Extracting money from him in exchange for remaining quiet about his past?

Could it have been Blaine? Or Dunbar DesLauriers? Had Jamie finally cried *enough?* And been murdered because of it?

Had Margot Butler broken off her engagement because she learned of Jamie's past?

Unanswered questions were piling up faster than broken beads and empty *geaux* cups after a Mardi Gras parade.

Carmela stood up, wandered into her kitchen, and plucked the lid off her cookie jar. She stood there nibbling one of her homemade Big Easy chocolate chip peanut butter cookies. She usually loved them, but tonight she didn't seem to be getting her usual kick. Tonight she was just too upset.

Chapter 12

"THESE pumpkin muffins are heavenly," raved Tandy as she helped herself to a second plump muffin drizzled with cream cheese frosting. "Is this your recipe, Carmela?"

"My momma's," said Carmela, as she sorted through one of her drawers of oversized sheets of paper. Last night, after her unsettling conversation with Shamus and her discovery of the news clipping about Jamie Redmond, she had whipped up a batch of pumpkin muffins to bring to Memory Mine. Baking was one of Carmela's sure-fire ways to let off steam. Short of actually throttling someone to death.

"Well, I want your momma's recipe," declared Tandy. "I swear, I could probably get Darwin to balance on a rubber ball and bark like a seal if I dangled one of these muffins in front of him." Darwin, Tandy's husband of many years, was known for his incurable sweet tooth.

"If I let Stuart barely breathe the aroma from these muffins," said Gabby, "he'd probably go into insulin shock. How much sugar does your recipe call for, anyway?" she asked, taking a nibble.

"Quite a bit," admitted Carmela, glancing about her shop. For a Monday morning, Memory Mine was already pleasantly crowded. Gabby and Wren had shown up for work promptly at 9:00 AM, and Baby and Tandy had arrived some twenty minutes later. Baby was bound and determined to turn out her first batch of Mardi Gras party invitations, and Tandy had decided she wanted to make a second bibelot box for one of her daughters-in-law.

Six more customers had since wandered into Memory Mine and, wicker baskets in hand, were happily browsing the racks of paper and displays of albums, glitter glue, scissors, and oil pens as they tossed various scrapbooking must-haves into their baskets.

Carmela was delighted that Wren had seemingly jumped, feet first, into her new role at Memory Mine. In fact, when one of the customers inquired about scrapbook borders, Wren had quickly produced a book of border designs as well as several of their new adhesive-backed borders. And when another lady asked about embossed paper, Wren was immediately able to pull out a half-dozen samples.

Watching Wren work so diligently, Carmela felt

anguished, knowing she'd ultimately have to share her discovery of Jamie's sordid past with her. She had to tell Wren what she'd found because it was the honest thing to do. But she certainly wasn't relishing the task.

"She's good, isn't she?" whispered Gabby. She had noticed Carmela watching Wren.

Carmela nodded. "Wren's a natural. Like you."

Gabby thought for a moment. "But I'm here because I'm a scrapbook fanatic. Whereas Wren seems to genuinely love working with people."

Carmela playfully raised an eyebrow. "And you don't?"

"It's not that," Gabby hastened to explain. "It's simply that Wren seems to connect with them on a completely different level."

"I know what you mean," said Carmela. "We understand scrapbooking and rubber stamping backwards and forwards, but Wren seems to sense what customers need and knows when they could use a little help or encouragement." She paused. "Or maybe not so much help as a gentle *nudge*. I don't know how to explain it any better."

"You just did," said Gabby.

"Has Wren told you anything about Dunbar DesLauriers's offer?" asked Carmela.

Gabby nodded. "Just that he offered to take the inventory off her hands. Nothing about price or anything like that."

"I think Dunbar figures he can toss out any number he feels like and she'll leap at it," said Carmela.

"That's the problem with really wealthy people. They're so focused on money that they think everyone else is, too."

"Well," said Gabby, "Wren was sure tickled that you took so much time with her yesterday, prowling through that old bookstore and giving her real-life business advice. For that I thank you, too. There aren't a lot of female entrepreneurs around, in case you hadn't noticed. Not many role models."

"But more than there used to be," said Carmela. "Which I take as a very positive sign."

Gabby slid her velvet headband forward, shook her hair, then replaced the headband. "Do you really think Wren could run Biblios Booksellers?" she asked. "I thought for sure she'd be hot to unload it, but now she's talking about maybe giving it a shot. Possibly re-opening the place sometime in March."

"She could probably handle it," said Carmela. "She'll need help, of course, but there are lots of good people out there."

Gabby smiled, aware that Carmela had just paid her another compliment. "So you don't think she should just sell everything—lock, stock, and barrel? That's what Stuart advised, you know."

"That's Stuart," said Carmela. "No offense, but he's a little hide-bound when it comes to women and business."

"A little!" exclaimed Gabby. "He wasn't all that keen about me working here. I think if Stuart were actually able to execute his master-of-the-universe plan, he'd have me staying home all day wearing a perfect little pink suit and a string of pearls, cultivating roses, and learning how to bake the perfect soufflé."

"Hey," said Carmela. "At least the guy has good taste and he cares."

"Good point," said Gabby, watching Wren ring up a customer at the front counter.

"When it comes to either selling or keeping the bookstore, she'll make the right decision," said Carmela, reaching for the telephone as it let off an insistent ring. "She'll figure it out." Carmela put the phone to her ear. "Good morning," she said. "Memory Mine Scrapbooking."

"Is Wren there?" asked a male caller.

Carmela watched as Wren handed a brown paper bag stuffed with scrapbook goodies over to her customer, then bid her good-bye. "She's with a customer right now," Carmela lied. She had just recognized the voice on the other end of the line. "Perhaps I could take a message?"

"Is this Carmela?"

"Yes, it is," she answered sweetly.

"Well, this is Blaine Taylor. And it's imperative I speak with her."

"Old B.T.," said Carmela. "How are you, anyway?"

"Fine, fine, but I—"

"I imagine you're pretty busy these days, anticipating all the money you're going to make selling Jamie's software program," said Carmela.

There was a stunned silence, then a burst of angry

static. "What are you talking about?" Blaine demanded.

"I'd love to see that so-called buy-sell agreement you and Jamie drew up," continued Carmela. "You don't have a copy handy, by any chance, do you?"

"That's absolutely none of your business!" cried Blaine. "You have nothing to do with this."

"Actually I'm making it my business," said Carmela. "Wren's asked for my help with a few loose ends. And guess what, pal? You're one of them."

Whether it was Carmela's casual reference to him as a loose end or her bemused yet aggressive stance, Blaine Taylor was suddenly furious.

"You're out of your league," he warned. "Don't even bother getting involved. This has nothing to do with you."

"Here's a grand idea," continued Carmela, not allowing his blustering to faze her. "Why don't you shoot a copy of that buy-sell agreement of yours over to the law firm of Leonard, Barstow, and Streeter," she said, naming one of the top law firms in New Orleans. "In fact, send it to the attention of Seth Barstow, Senior Partner."

"What?" said Blaine, his voice rising in a high squawk. "LBS is your counsel?" He sounded stunned.

Hooray. Score one for the good guys.

"Yup," said Carmela. "They sure are." Of course that particular law firm wasn't *exactly* her lawyer. But they *were* one of the law firms that did work for the chain of Crescent City Banks that Shamus's family owned.

151

And in her mind that was close enough for jazz. Plus, Leonard, Barstow, and Streeter had posh downtown offices and a reputation for pit-bull tenacity, so why not dangle them as a threat? Why not, indeed?

Blaine Taylor was still stuttering and stammering. "Perhaps we could work something out after all, Carmela. You know I don't want to see Wren completely—"

"Do you actually have the software program?" asked Carmela, interrupting him. "Do you have a copy of Neutron?"

"Well, no," stammered Blaine. "Not physically. Although Neutron exists as a *virtual* product." Blaine was still babbling.

Good, thought Carmela. *And it's also a smart thing I made a virtual copy of everything on Jamie's home computer. Just in case.*

"Talk to you later, Blaine," said Carmela. "Be sure to send a copy of that buy-sell to my attorney." She paused. "Or you can drop it by my shop."

"What was *that* about?" asked Gabby, eyeing Carmela suspiciously as she hung up the phone.

"Just that weirdo, Blaine Taylor," grumbled Carmela. "I swear that old boy is trying to pull a fast one on Wren."

Gabby's smile suddenly crumpled. "What?" she said, shock morphing into anger. "What is this, anyway? Let's see how badly we can bash Wren when she's down? First Dunbar DesLauriers wants to ram through a quick sale, now Blaine Taylor, who was *sup-*

posed to be Jamie's good friend, is trying to screw her. Why is this happening?"

Carmela grabbed Gabby by the arm and pulled her into her office. "Take it easy," she said. "Unfortunately for Wren, it's business as usual."

Carmela knew you couldn't compete in business these days without running up against a few nasty, nefarious people. And having your teeth kicked in a time or two. Getting blind-sided was a hard-learned lesson for many business owners. But it was almost a right of passage. Something you couldn't escape. And if you *did* stay under the radar, remain complacent, and play it safe—that seemed to be the kiss of death, too. As her daddy used to tell her, if you want to run with the big dogs, you gotta climb down off the porch.

But as Carmela was giving a whispered explanation to Gabby, Wren suddenly appeared in the doorway.

"You've got a visitor," Wren told Carmela.

Carmela glanced past Wren and her heart sank.

Glory.

Glory Meechum was Shamus's big sister and the senior vice president of the Crescent City Bank chain. She was also hell on wheels. As matriarch and self-appointed leader of the snarling Meechum clan, it was she who'd pinned the blame for Carmela and Shamus's break-up squarely on Carmela's head. Even though Shamus had been the instigator, the one who'd tossed his tightie-whities into his Samsonite jet pack, grabbed his Nikon cameras, and skedaddled to the family camp house in the Baritaria Bayou. Go figure.

This can't be good, thought Carmela as she strode out to meet Glory Meechum. *Glory never just pops in for a fun, impromptu visit. She's got to have something evil percolating in her strange brain.*

"Carmela," said Glory in a loud bray. "We need to talk." Standing a husky five-feet-ten in her splotchy print dress, with a helmet of gray hair and a countenance reminiscent of an Easter Island statue, Glory presented a formidable figure.

She wants to talk about me and Shamus again? Now what's the problem?

"Glory," said Carmela, deciding to grab the bull by the horns. "Why don't you direct whatever inquest you've decided to launch directly at Shamus. He's the one who's been acting like a bad boy in all of this." Carmela kept her voice even, being mindful not to appear challenging or threatening. Bad things happened when you challenged Glory.

"This isn't about Shamus," snapped Glory. "This is about *you.*"

"We've been through this before, Glory," sighed Carmela. "I'll be happy to grant Shamus a divorce. *He's* the one who keeps dragging his size elevens when it comes to putting the paperwork in motion."

Glory's face, already set in a frown, switched to a glower.

Ah, thought Carmela, *there's that famous Meechum Seal of Disapproval again. The family could almost copyright it.*

"Before you go off on a tangent," said Glory, "perhaps you'd give me a chance to speak my peace?"

"Fine, Glory," said Carmela. "What?"

Glory's eyes shifted toward the back of the store where Wren was doling out paper samples to Tandy. "I want you to instruct that girl to sell her collection of moldy old books to Dunbar DesLauriers."

"What!" said Carmela, stunned. Those were not the words she'd expected to come spewing out of Glory Meechum's mouth.

"I know Dunbar will give her a fair price," continued Glory in a naddering tone. "The girl could do a whole lot worse."

"Will you stop calling her *the girl?*" said Carmela. "And why on earth are you remotely concerned with what happens to Wren or Biblios Booksellers?" *Good grief, who's going to crawl out of the woodwork next to take a bash at poor Wren?*

"Not that it's any business of yours," said Glory. "But Dunbar DesLauriers is an extremely valuable customer at our bank. Which is why I'm willing to do almost anything in my power to keep the dear man happy."

"Uh huh," said Carmela, still stunned by this twist in the conversation.

Glory's unplucked eyebrows formed stormy arcs over hard, beady eyes. "I understand you've been giving the girl some *business* advice," she said.

"Wren," said Carmela. "Please say her name. Wren."

"Wren," snarled Glory.

"Thank you."

Glory slammed her sensible black handbag onto the counter and glared at Carmela. "You think you're a pretty tough cookie, don't you? Well let me give you a word of warning: Don't take me on. Because you'll lose, Carmela." She pronounced her name *Car-mel-la,* spitting out each syllable venomously hard.

"I wasn't aware this was a contest," said Carmela. *Just a contest of wills.*

"You've visited the bookstore, correct?" said Glory.

"Sure," said Carmela.

"And the girl . . . Wren . . . has expressed some interest in selling?"

"She's still deciding," said Carmela.

"Dunbar DesLauriers is prepared to pay seventy-five thousand dollars for the entire inventory," said Glory. "He'll write a check today, in fact."

"You realize," countered Carmela, "Wren hasn't had a chance to bring an appraiser in yet."

Glory shrugged. "A mere technicality in the face of such a generous offer." She rearranged her frown into a friendly grimace. "I can't impress upon you what a valuable customer Dunbar is. I see no reason to upset him with petty dickering."

"That's funny," said Carmela. "Because the only person I've seen upset so far is Wren. Everyone, and I do mean everyone, seems to think they can come cowboying in and strong-arm her."

"I certainly wouldn't do that," snapped Glory. She pulled a handkerchief from her bag and blew her nose into it, letting loose a good, loud honk.

"Of course you would," Carmela fired back. "You are."

Glory stuffed her hanky back into her purse, then rubbed her large hand, palm down, across the top of the counter. When she turned it over, she stared at it for almost a full minute, then wiped it hard against the side of her splotchy print nylon dress. *Wshst wsht.*

She's off her meds again, thought Carmela. Glory had been diagnosed with a mild obsessive-compulsive disorder and was supposed to be taking medicine to help control it.

Carmela let loose a deep sigh. "Tell Dunbar we'll get back to him, Glory."

"When?" demanded Glory, obviously intent on keeping the pressure on.

"I don't know," said Carmela. "Two or three weeks, maybe a month. Like I said, we'll get back to him."

Glory stared hard at Carmela and took a step closer to her. Closer than she'd ever come before, her anger overshadowing the OCD that always kept her a protective arm's length away from everyone. "There are *debts,*" Glory murmured, her eyes glinting like hard marbles. "Outstanding *loans* that Jamie Redmond incurred. All this must be taken into account."

"The debt you refer to is a mortgage," said Carmela.

"A mortgage with *my* bank," said Glory, her thin lips twitching upward slightly. "A variable-rate balloon mortgage that *I* control."

"Don't," said Carmela, holding a finger up. "Don't you dare threaten."

But nothing could wipe the smile of satisfaction from Glory's doughy face.

"Well *that* was good for business," remarked Gabby after Glory had finally stalked out, slamming the door behind her.

Carmela cringed. "Do you think everyone heard us?" They were standing at the front of the shop while most everyone else was grouped at the back.

Gabby shrugged. "Probably not. It was mostly your body language that gave away the tone of the argument. One petite bulldog . . . you. Up against one very large, immovable object . . . Glory."

"She's a fruitcake," admitted Carmela as she and Gabby walked slowly back toward the craft table where Baby, Tandy, and Wren were gathered, heads bent over their various projects.

"And you're a defender of the underdog," said Gabby, her eyes shining brightly. Then, without warning, she gave Carmela a quick hug. "Thank you," she told her.

Carmela nodded. It was flattering to be thought of as *Carmela, fearless defender of underdogs*. Even though her heart was beating like a fluttering dove.

And, of course, she *still* wasn't sure how to break the rather shocking news to Wren about the Bogus Creek Boys news clipping she'd stumbled across. Or tell her about Dunbar DesLauriers's seventy-five thousand dollar offer on the bookstore. Or tell her about Glory's nasty threat.

Gulp.

Carmela wiggled her shoulders to dispel the tension, sucked in a deep breath. She'd find a way. She always did.

Chapter 13

WHY did I think you were making party invitations?" Carmela asked Baby.

Baby swiveled in her chair and adjusted the Chanel scarf draped around her patrician neck. Her blue eyes looked mischievous, her short blond hair artfully tousled. "Because that's what I told you when I came in this morning. But, surprise surprise, things have changed."

"I guess," said Carmela, gazing over Baby's shoulder at a marvelous array of colorful tags.

The women had sent out for salads from the French Quarter Deli an hour or so ago. Now, the salads munched and the debris cleared away, Tandy and Baby were back at their projects, while Gabby and Wren buzzed about, kibitzing and unpacking boxes of newly arrived scrapbooking supplies.

And while Tandy had made great progress on her bibelot box, Baby was indeed working on an entirely different project.

"Your little tags are gorgeous," Wren told Baby. "But Carmela's right, we all thought you started out with invitations."

"You don't like my photo tags?" asked Baby.

Now Tandy jumped in. "Are you kidding, sweetie? They're *wonderful*." Tandy was always big on unabashed enthusiasm.

And Baby's photo tags were adorable. She had cut out individual faces from a number of color photos, then matted them with small bits of pebbled card stock so they looked like miniature portraits. Baby then sponge-dyed ink on large colorful tags to achieve a textured, marbleized surface, then mounted each "portrait" on one of the faux-finished tags.

"So now what?" asked Wren. "You're going to put the tags on a scrapbook page?"

"I could do that," said Baby. "But instead I'm going to make a front and back cover from this leather-looking paper, then bind all the tags together with a piece of silk ribbon twined with different fibers. So they become like pages in a book."

"You're creating a little memory book," said Wren, obviously charmed by the craft project. "Very clever."

"Wren," said Tandy. "Show me your bibelot box again, will you? I want to see how you affixed the legs."

Wren popped into Carmela's office to grab her bibelot box while everyone gathered to admire Tandy's handiwork.

Tandy had decoupaged a square tea tin with dark-red mulberry paper that had gold Japanese *kanji* writing on it. Then she had added several colorful postage stamps depicting Mount Fuji and cut-outs of Japanese family crests. Gold fish charms were glued on the sides of the box, and the top featured a lovely red tassel strung with pearls and Japanese blue and white beads.

"It's gorgeous," said Gabby. "Now I'm in the mood to make one."

"Can you believe it started out as an ordinary tea tin?" asked Baby. "Now it looks like something you'd see in one of those expensive gift shops down on Magazine Street."

"I think you should just add four more of those blue and white beads for feet," suggested Gabby. "Right on the corners. Like Wren did on hers."

"Here it is," said Wren, as she set her little bibelot box covered with keys in the middle of the table. "My mystery key box, as I like to call it."

Tandy slid her glasses onto her nose and peered at Wren's bibelot box carefully. "I wouldn't mind making one just like that. Lord knows, I've got a dusty jar filled with antique keys sitting on a shelf in my basement. There's probably still a key in there for my dad's old place over in Westwebo."

"Wren," said Carmela in a quiet voice, once things had settled down and everyone was busily working away. "A few things have come up that you need to know about. And some decisions need to be made."

Wren turned toward Carmela. "Tell me."

Carmela cleared her throat. "Ah . . . maybe it would be best if we went and sat in my office?"

"Do we have to?" asked Wren. "I feel like I'm definitely among friends here. In fact, I feel like I'm able

161

to draw strength from everyone's concern and support."

"It's just that one of the items we need to discuss is somewhat personal," pressed Carmela.

Wren shook her head. "I don't care. I can't tell you how much I love and trust this group of women."

"Aren't you sweet," said Tandy, reaching over to pat one of Wren's hands.

"*She's* the love," said Baby, threading a piece of silk ribbon through her photo tags.

"Okay, then," said Carmela, sitting down at the table and putting her hands flat. "There's good and bad news."

"Good news first," said Wren, taking a deep breath.

"Dunbar DesLauriers has put a cash offer on the table for Biblios Booksellers," said Carmela. She hoped this would be perceived as good news.

"Did he really?" exclaimed Gabby, suddenly excited. "How much?"

"Seventy-five thousand dollars," replied Carmela.

"Not bad," Tandy said. "That'd keep a girl in stickers and rubber stamps for a good long while."

Carmela bit her lower lip. "I have to admit seventy-five thousand dollars doesn't sound bad, but we don't really have a handle on the value of the rare book inventory." She looked over at Wren for confirmation.

"They're not all rare," offered Wren. "A lot of them are more like first editions."

"So a first edition would sell for . . . what?" asked

Gabby, obviously intrigued by Dunbar's offer. "What would be a ballpark figure?"

Wren shrugged. "Depends. A first edition of, say, *Mosquitoes* by William Faulkner might be three . . . maybe four hundred dollars."

"So Dunbar's offer sounds fair?" asked Carmela. "Maybe even a bit on the high side?"

"It could be," said Wren. "Again, I'd have to check the inventory price sheets that do exist. And maybe run an Internet search for comparables on the rarer books."

"Do we know if Dunbar DesLauriers knows what he's bidding on?" asked Baby. She'd been listening quietly, now she spoke up.

"What do you mean?" asked Wren.

"Dunbar DesLauriers is a rare book collector," said Baby. "He may be just as familiar with the inventory as Jamie was. Or even *more* familiar."

"You think he's trying to put one over on me?" asked Wren.

Baby shrugged. "Don't know." Baby was no stranger to the competitive world of collecting. Her husband, Del, had amassed a spectacular collection of antique Japanese swords. And Baby herself collected miniature oil paintings and antique jewelry.

"I assume there's some play in Dunbar's number," said Carmela. "I see his offer of seventy-five thousand dollars as more of a *suggested* retail price."

"I like the way you think," said Tandy. "Although seventy-five thousand does sound good."

"Unfortunately," said Carmela. "Nothing's ever easy.

There's more to this deal than just a straight ahead offer of cash."

Gabby looked at her sharply. "What do you mean?"

Carmela sighed. "There's also an implied threat," she told them.

"Concerning what?" asked Wren.

"Your mortgage. The mortgage on the house on Julia Street," said Carmela.

"The *mortgage?*" said Wren, clearly puzzled. "But Jamie put the house in my name, too, right? So all I have to do is make the monthly payments and I'm okay?" She stared at Carmela. "Right?"

"Well, not exactly," said Carmela. "It seems that the mortgage Jamie has with Crescent City Bank . . . the mortgage *you* now have . . . is an adjustable-rate balloon mortgage."

"Is that why Glory Meechum came storming in here earlier?" asked Baby. "With her underwear all in a twist?"

Carmela nodded. "She claims Dunbar DesLauriers is one of her best customers. That she'd do anything to keep him happy."

"I'll bet," muttered Baby. Glory lived two blocks from Baby in the Garden District, and there was no love lost between the two women. When Glory had been the chairman of their Garden Club's Spring Rose Show, she'd accused Baby of bringing in ringers. Roses that hadn't actually been grown in Baby's garden. Which had been an outright lie, of course. And an accusation that *still* aggravated Baby.

"A balloon mortgage," repeated Wren. She wrinkled her nose. "What a funny name. What is it? What does it mean?"

Carmela took a deep breath. "Basically, it means your monthly payment has nowhere to go but up and that the entire balance is probably due in a matter of months."

"Are you serious?" cried Wren. "You mean I could lose the house!"

"That possibility does seem to exist," said Carmela, hating the fact that she had to break this news to Wren. "Unless, of course, you get busy and pay the mortgage off."

"With the profit I make from selling Biblios Booksellers," said Wren. She crossed her arms and hugged herself tightly. "This feels suspiciously like a trap."

"It sure does," agreed Gabby.

"A catch-22," added Tandy.

"But legal, just the same," said Carmela. She hated to be the one hard-ass in the bunch, but the mortgage *was* completely aboveboard. It may not have been a smart choice on Jamie's part, but it was legal just the same.

"Well, this has been quite a day," declared Wren, looking forlorn.

"Wait," said Carmela, "it's not over." She slid the news clipping across the table.

"What's this?" said Wren.

"I'm afraid it's even more disturbing news," said Carmela. *Who am I kidding? It's beyond disturbing.*

It's downright crappy.

Gabby sped around the table so she could read over Wren's shoulder.

"Good lord!" said Wren, when she'd finished the article. Her face was white, her hands were shaking. She slid the article over to Tandy and Baby, who quickly scanned it.

"Oh, my goodness!" declared Baby. She looked over at Wren with pity on her face. "This is quite a shocker."

"When does it end?" stammered Wren. "I thought finding out that Jamie was once engaged to Margot Butler was a terrible shock."

Baby and Tandy quickly exchanged glances. "He was?" asked Tandy. "Wow."

"Now I find out Jamie was a convicted felon!" continued Wren in an agonized voice. "Which is even worse!"

"Don't jump to conclusions yet," warned Carmela. "This could be about Jamie's father."

"No," said Wren. "I'm sure it's about Jamie. That's why he was always so closed-mouthed about his past." She leaned forward, rocking back and forth in her chair as though the pain were almost too much to bear. "I feel awful," she murmured. "Ashamed, almost."

"It's not *your* fault," said Gabby, patting Wren on the shoulder.

"Please don't feel bad," said Tandy. "Try to look on the bright side. Lots of perfectly lovely people have done jail time."

Baby swiveled in her chair, aghast. "Are you

166

serious? Name one."

Tandy thought for a moment. "Leona Helmsley."

"Leona Helmsley was dubbed the *Queen of Mean,*" snorted Baby. "I don't think her poor ex-employees would characterize her as a lovely person at all."

Tandy pursed her lips. "Well, she certainly *seemed* kind of sweet when Suzanne Pleshette played her in the made-for-TV movie."

"Look," said Gabby, "could we please not dwell on this? What's done is done. Even if Jamie served time in jail, he'd put it behind him by the time he met Wren. He paid his debt to society, as they say."

"She's right," murmured Tandy. "Jamie was a lovely person."

"I think for now we have to focus on the positive," continued Gabby. "Keep Jamie's memory sacred and continue in our quest to find his parents' final resting place." She gazed pointedly at Carmela.

I know, I know, thought Carmela. *I was supposed to make a few calls, try to figure out where Jamie's parents are buried, and I still haven't gotten around to it.*

"That's for sure," said Wren, shaking her head, not knowing what to think. "I'm having Jamie cremated, and I still don't know what to do with his ashes."

"When Jamie is finally at rest," murmured Baby, "maybe Wren will rest a little easier, too."

"That's a lovely thought," said Wren. "Thank you."

Gabby gazed at Carmela. "When were you going to look into that grave site thing?"

"Ava and I are gonna take a drive down to Boothville

tomorrow," said Carmela. This was going to come as big news to Ava. Of course, it was also big news to Carmela. Until she'd just blurted it out, a trip down to Boothville hadn't been in her forecast. *Oh well.*

"I'm going to light a few candles tonight," said Gabby. "And say a little prayer that everything will work out okay." Gabby took great comfort in lighting the colorful vigil lights that were prevalent in French Quarter shops. Her favorites were Saint Cecilia and Saint Ann.

"Amen," said Tandy, as she inked a rubber stamp and slammed it down hard on a piece of craft paper.

When Margot Butler walked in the door at four o'clock, Carmela was thankful Wren had gone home early. She didn't think Wren could deal with seeing Margot in person, knowing the woman had once been engaged to Jamie.

And Wren just might start mulling over the possibility that Margot could be a possible suspect in Jamie's murder. Because I sure am.

Today Margot was bouncy and vivacious, filled with energy and big ideas.

"Pamela DesLauriers is absolutely *thrilled* that you're working on her Gilt Trip scrapbook," Margot enthused.

Carmela, who hadn't had a free moment to even think about the scrapbook, just smiled.

"But some enhancements have been made," said Margot. "In Pamela's dining room. In fact, the photos she dropped off simply don't do it justice."

"What are you suggesting, Margot?" asked Carmela. Margot was kicking up a lot of dust, but they didn't seem to be getting anywhere.

"Could you . . . *would you* . . . stop by in person?" begged Margot. "It would mean so much to us."

"You're re-taking photos?" asked Carmela. Margot was still being resolutely obtuse.

Margot suddenly looked unhappy. "Yes, I suppose we're going to have to do that. Although a re-shoot is simply not in the budget . . ." She shrugged. "I'm not sure *how* we're going to pull that rabbit out of a hat."

"Maybe I could re-take a couple photos," suggested Carmela. It suddenly seemed like a good idea to get inside the DesLauriers home. Maybe take a look to see what kind of book collection Dunbar really had?

"Good heavens, Carmela!" exclaimed Margot. "What a spectacularly brilliant idea! You're a photographer?"

"I've been known to snap a picture or two," said Carmela.

"Tomorrow," said Margot. "You must come tomorrow, then."

"No," said Carmela. "That won't work. I've got to take a quick trip out of town. But I can come on Wednesday. Thursday at the latest."

Margot's bony little hand suddenly gripped Carmela's arm hard. "It's gonna be tight, but I love the idea!"

Carmela had to turn away so Margot couldn't see her

amused expression. As long as Margot was getting her way she was sweet as pie. And when she didn't get her way? Well, Carmela had seen *that* side to Margot, too. She wondered if Jamie had also seen that side.

Is that why Jamie broke off the engagement? Carmela wondered. *And Margot, strange little lady that she was, had become totally enraged?*

If Margot couldn't have Jamie, was she crazy enough to make it so that no one could have him?

Carmela shook her head as Margot skittered out the front door, then she headed back to see if Tandy and Baby needed any help finishing up their projects.

"Did you ever notice how much Margot likes snakes?" piped up Baby. "She always seems to be wearing snakeskin shoes or carrying a snakeskin bag."

"Well, heavens to Betsy," shot Tandy. "Look what she named her company."

Carmela, Gabby, and Baby mouthed a collective, "What?"

"Fer de Lance," replied Tandy. When they all continued to stare at her, she set her hot glue gun down and stared at them. "Well for goodness sake," said Tandy, her tight curls bobbing. "A fer de lance is a snake!"

Chapter 14

THE oil pens were put away, the mulberry paper returned to the flat files, the day's receipts tallied and scribbled in the little black ledger Carmela kept to assure herself Memory Mine was indeed a viable business.

And now Carmela was going to follow through on an idea she'd hatched earlier this afternoon.

Just before Wren had left for the day, Carmela had asked for the key to Biblios Booksellers. Wren, of course, had immediately turned it over to her. Which meant Carmela could now pay a second visit to the dusty little bookstore over on Toulouse Street to see if she could unearth anything else that might shed a little light on Jamie Redmond's past. And on his tragic demise.

Clues. Let's call 'em what they really are. They're clues.

But even the most well-intentioned plans are generally fraught with a few problems. Because once Carmela arrived at the store, she realized *her* problem was going to be tiptoeing down the creaky flight of stairs into that musty old cellar.

Standing in the middle of the bookstore, listening to the quiet, she gazed at towering cases of books. Then she slowly let her eyes slide toward the cellar door.

Spiders and mousies and bugs, oh my!

It wasn't that she was *afraid* of these things. Good heavens, no. She was merely . . . well, let's call it apprehensive.

Buck up, girl. You've never backed off from anything in your life!

Carmela walked over to the cellar door, her footsteps echoing in the empty store, half wishing she'd strong-armed Wren to coming back here with her. Putting a hand on the doorknob, she gave a good, firm yank. The door creaked back on its hinges and the smell of mildew and dust immediately assaulted her nose.

Whew. Not exactly eau de magnolia, is it?

Fumbling for the light switch, Carmela flipped it on. She was rewarded with a dim glow at the bottom of the stairs. Slowly, carefully, she headed down the creaky stairs toward the faint puddle of light, one hand gripping the flimsy wooden railing. It wouldn't pay to take a tumble here.

At the bottom of the stairs, Carmela paused. The basement or old root cellar or ancient torture chamber, or whatever it had been, was small. A lot smaller than she'd imagined it would be. The ceiling was low and oppressive, a tangle of furry cobweb-coated beams, and the floor was packed earth. Up against one wall, looking strangely like a log jam, was a ceiling-high jumble of broken bookcases. An old sink, dirty and rusted, hung from another wall. A dusty four-drawer metal file case stood poised in front of her.

This must be where Wren got the file folders with the photos and clippings.

Fighting an urge to sneeze, Carmela slid the top drawer open. Empty. She wasn't surprised. Its former contents were probably the very same files that were stashed at her apartment. Sliding the drawer closed, she heard a faint skittering in the corner.

Mousies? Yeah, probably.

She slid the second and third drawers open. The

second drawer was empty, the third drawer was filled with old office supplies. Tape that probably wouldn't stick anymore, an old stapler, a couple jars of hardened White-Out, an ancient tube of glue.

Carmela moved on to the bottom drawer, but it was stuck tight.

Which means Wren probably didn't check this drawer. Should I? I can try, anyway.

The grubby-looking sink hanging from the wall was dripping a steady *drip drip drip* that annoyed Carmela, grating on her nerves.

I'm gonna get this done with and get the heck out of here.

Steeling her shoulders, grasping the handle with both hands, Carmela gave a might yank. Nothing. Searching around the basement, she finally found a wooden box that had a pile of rusty tools in it.

Good. Maybe there's something here.

She passed on the saw, the hammer, and the broken pliers. But decided the rusty screwdriver just might do the trick.

Carmela went back to the file case, wedged the screwdriver into the edge of the drawer, and put as much muscle behind it as she could.

Creak. The drawer popped out a quarter inch.

Repositioning the screwdriver, Carmela dug it in deeper and tried to leverage it with all her might.

A high-pitched *creak* dropped to a low *groan* as the drawer slid grudgingly open.

Success!

Carmela peered in. A single brown file folder lay in the bottom of the drawer. With one quick motion, she grabbed it, executed a fast spin, and bounded back up the stairs.

Enough of this creepy place!

Back upstairs, Carmela found that the sun had just gone down. And the frosted windows, the ones that always made the place seem so warm and cozy when sunlight filtered through them, now lent a dark, spooky feel.

Hmm, does Wren really want to run this place all by her lonesome?

But Carmela knew where she could find a cozy spot to take a look at the file she'd just retrieved. Climbing the half-dozen stairs to the little loft, she plopped down on the sagging couch. The same couch she'd sprawled on yesterday with Boo.

Feeling old wire springs shift beneath her, Carmela flipped open the file folder and perused its contents.

More photos. Black-and-white photos mingled with a few color Polaroids. But these photos all had a collegiate feel to them. Guys partying, drinking beer, posturing with their arms slung about each other's shoulders.

Boy's bonding, thought Carmela. Maybe from Jamie's earlier days at Tulane?

A phrase Shamus used to toss around bubbled up in Carmela's mind. *Shit-faced.* That's what Shamus had called partying. Only it wasn't really partying at all, but getting drunk. Binge drinking. An epidemic, apparently, on today's college campuses.

Squinting in the dim light, Carmela quickly sifted through the rest of the photos until she came to a thick glob of papers. Here were more photos and papers, but they were all hopelessly stuck together. Pulling at one corner, she immediately tore a piece off. Oops. Not good. This was obviously going to require some careful work on her part. But nothing that she could do now.

Lost in thought, Carmela stared at the jumble of pillows sitting at her feet. Casually, mindlessly, she contemplated the nubby kilim fabric, with its Oriental design and colors of muted blue, green, and purple. And then she suddenly blinked hard.

Why are these pillows piled on the floor?

She stared at them quizzically, knowing something wasn't quite right. Felt a jittery "What's wrong with this picture?" vibe suddenly run through her.

Then, sudden comprehension kicked in. And Carmela scrambled to her feet. Some time between late yesterday afternoon and right now, someone had been in the store!

How did she know that for sure? Because whoever this mysterious visitor had been, he or she had removed the cushions and piled them on the floor.

Who? The same person who'd left a half a cup of coffee there yesterday? Yipes!

She knew it hadn't been Wren who moved the pillows, because Wren had been working at Memory Mine all day. Could it have been Blaine Taylor?

175

Searching for something that belonged to Jamie? Something that he desperately needed to find?

Or could it have been Dunbar DesLauriers? As a long-time customer, Dunbar DesLauriers might have known if Jamie had hidden a key somewhere. On a nail out back or under one of the back steps. If it had been Dunbar, maybe he'd come back to check on one of the precious antique books he wanted to buy.

But did that even make sense? wondered Carmela. *If there were two or three books Dunbar specifically wanted, wouldn't he just steal them?*

Carmela gazed around. It was possible Dunbar had already stolen them. Maybe his big fat offer of seventy-five grand was just his version of a clever smoke screen.

And what about Margot Butler? Carmela wondered if she had a key to the bookstore. Or if Margot had visited the bookstore right before she'd dropped by Memory Mine earlier. Would that have accounted for her manic mood?

Carmela shivered. Margot's snake fetish scared the bejeebers out of her. In Louisiana, snakes were generally given a wide berth.

Scrtch scrtch.

A sudden scratching at the front door startled Carmela.

Now what's going on?

Putting a hand to her chest to calm her beating heart, Carmela realized someone was at the door. Probably a customer, wondering if the bookstore was open.

Carmela descended the few steps and hurried over to the front door where a dark shadow moved on the other side of the frosted window pane.

She pulled the door open, ready to tell whoever it was that the store was closed until further notice, and got the surprise of her life when the unexpected visitor turned out to be Shamus!

"Shamus!" she cried. "You scared me to death!"

Shamus looked totally unapologetic. "Sorry. Didn't mean to."

"How did you know I was here?" she asked. She wasn't sure if she was still angry at him or secretly relieved that he'd turned up like the proverbial bad penny. She'd been talking herself into a pretty good case of the willies.

Shamus shrugged. "When I stopped by the store and you weren't there, I just put two and two together."

"Did Glory send you?" Carmela asked, wary now. "Are you here because of her?" *There's an old adage that warns against shooting the messenger, but I could certainly make an exception in this case.*

Shamus squinted at her. "What are you, loony or something? I'm here because of you."

"Yeah right," said Carmela.

"Are you going to let me in?" he asked, pushing his way through the open door.

Carmela shrugged and retreated deeper into the store. Amazingly, the place didn't seem nearly so gloomy or frightening now. Funny how another warm body can make things feel a whole lot safer.

"Call Glory off, Shamus," said Carmela. "She's been acting very badly. Threatening Wren and making wild assumptions."

"It's just business," said Shamus. "That's how Glory is. She takes everything very seriously." He shook his head, assuming a look of bemused befuddlement. "You have no idea how tough banking is these days, Carmela. People think you've got millions to spread around when actually you're dealing with extremely narrow margins. Banking has become a very demanding business. We're constantly being pushed to our limits."

Carmela folded her arms and threw him a wry glance. "Those pesky usury laws make it *so* hard to earn obscene profits these days, don't they Shamus?" She knew that Louisiana's banking laws were some of the most liberal in the country.

"Carmela," said Shamus. "A word of warning. Glory is dead serious about helping Dunbar DesLauriers get his way. If you have *any* influence with this young lady at all, I think you should advise her to sell. For gosh sakes, wake up and smell the red ink! Small businesses are collapsing all around us. This isn't the go-go nineties anymore. Times are lean. And from what I hear, Dunbar's offer is more than fair."

"Save the *strum und drang* for all the loan customers you give thumbs down to, Shamus," snarled Carmela. "And by the way, when did *you* suddenly evolve into a wise old business sage? You watch maybe thirty minutes of CNN at best and catch a few installments of

Lou Dobbs and you think you're a whiz kid. Well you're not, Shamus. Take some advice from someone who's really *in* business. Climb down from your high horse and into the trenches. See what it's *really* like."

Shamus bristled and took a step forward just as a ball of brown and white fur shot through the door and swirled wildly about his knees.

"Holy shit!" shrieked Carmela. "What's that?"

"A dog," said Shamus, suddenly back in nonchalant mode.

Carmela peered at the creature who had, in fact, stopped swirling and was now sitting rather complacently beside Shamus. "I can *see* it's a dog," she huffed. "What's it doing here?"

"It kind of followed me."

"Followed you? Why would it do that?"

"Because I'm lovable?" proposed Shamus.

Carmela ignored his remark. "Followed you for how long?"

"The last few blocks," said Shamus.

"And you just *let* it?" said Carmela, a critical tone creeping into her voice. "Jeez Shamus, the poor thing probably belongs to someone. You probably lured it away from its neighborhood. From its home."

"No, I don't think so," said Shamus. "See, Poobah isn't even wearing a collar."

"Then how do you know the dog's name is Poobah?" asked Carmela, starting to get exasperated.

"Because I named him," said Shamus, looking pleased.

"You named him Poobah," said Carmela. *Obviously, Glory wasn't the only fruitcake in the family.*

Shamus reached down and rubbed the dog under its chin. "You're a good boy, aren't you, Poobah?" he crooned. "You're kind of a scratch-and-dent guy, but you've got a big heart."

Tail thumping like crazy, Poobah snuggled up against Shamus. Carmela rolled her eyes skyward.

"Bet you're hungry, too," said Shamus. He cast a meaningful gaze at Carmela. "This dog needs a decent meal."

"Take him to the Humane Society," advised Carmela. "I'm sure they'll be more than happy to feed him. Probably even help locate his owner. This dog could have an ID chip imbedded under his skin somewhere, you never know."

"I don't think so," said Shamus slowly. "He's clearly a stray." Shamus squinted at Carmela. "What if he stayed with you for a couple days?"

"No," said Carmela, always amazed by Shamus's extraordinary chutzpah. "No way. Take him home with *you.*"

Shamus grimaced. "Can't. I'm staying with Glory right now. That sublet over by Audubon Park didn't work out."

In what struck Carmela as a bizarre coincidence, Shamus and the dog both seemed to be gazing at her with the same sad, befuddled looks on their faces.

Same limpid brown eyes, too. Damn.

"Glory doesn't like dogs," continued Shamus. "But

you do. In fact, you're the best person I know with dogs. You're kind . . . tender-hearted. Animals just naturally respond to you. They *love* you."

"What if he's got fleas?" asked Carmela, looking askance at Poobah. The poor guy really did look as though he'd logged some serious time on the mean streets of New Orleans. His fur was matted, one ear looked like it was partially ripped off. Her heart went out to him. "Boo could catch fleas from him," Carmela continued, trying to resist the little stray's charms.

Trying to resist Shamus's.

"I'll bet he's just fine," said Shamus.

"Boo is extremely fastidious," said Carmela. "It would just kill her if she got creepy-crawly fleas."

"Jeez, Carmela," laughed Shamus. "It's not like we're talking about a sexually transmitted disease or something. It's a few lousy fleas!"

"Still . . ." said Carmela.

"Tell you what," said Shamus. "I'll run out and buy a flea collar."

"And if Poobah lays claim to my furniture and *I* get fleas . . . ?"

"I'll buy two collars."

"Shamus . . ." said Carmela, a warning note sounding in her voice. "This is really a terrible idea."

"No, it's not," enthused Shamus. "It's a wonderful idea. This is a terrific little dog. A diamond in the rough. Plus, we'd be giving the poor fella a home."

"*We'd* be giving it a home?" said Carmela. She

stared at Shamus. "No. *We're* not doing anything of the sort."

"Pleeease," he cajoled. "Everybody deserves a second chance."

Carmela stared at Poobah. The little dog gazed mournfully back at her, then cocked his head as if to say, *Well, what about it? Like the song says, Should I stay or should I go?*

"Good lord," cried Carmela, throwing her hands helplessly in the air. "I'm a sucker . . . a pushover . . . a patsy!"

"You're a love," said Shamus, slipping an arm around her waist and pulling her toward him.

"Promise me you'll run an ad," said Carmela, savoring the way his body felt pressed up against her. "In the lost and found section of the *Times-Picayune.* Promise me you'll try to find this guy's owner."

"Of course I will," said Shamus. "You know I will. Have I ever let you down?"

Oh boy, thought Carmela. *Time to tattoo the word STUPID across my forehead in capital letters.*

Chapter 15

I WOKE up and looked in the mirror this morning," began Ava as she climbed into Carmela's Mercedes, "and was utterly shocked to see how awful my lips looked." She pulled down the passenger-side visor and squinted into that mirror. "Look," she cried unhappily. "My lips used to be all plump and full and now they're thin and wrinkled. I'm gettin' *turtle* lips!"

"No way," said Carmela, laughing. "Your lips and every other body part are still utterly gorgeous. In fact, you're the last person in the world who'd ever have to think about getting collagen injections or Botox or whatever the procedure *du jour* happens to be." Ava, who was not yet thirty, was drop-dead beautiful. No lines or crows feet had dared insinuate themselves on her face, and her lips were decidedly lush.

"You really think so?" queried Ava. "I still have my looks? To say nothing of my lips?"

"You're fine," Carmela assured her. "Now will you please fasten your seat belt so we can get going?"

"That's funny," said Ava. She was still squinting in the mirror and happened to catch the reflection of Boo and Poobah perched on the tiny shelf that served as a rudimentary back seat in Carmela's Mercedes. "Last time I looked you just had the one dog. Now I'm seeing two dogs squished into your back seat."

"Hey," said Carmela, popping the car into gear and squealing away from the curb. "Last time *I* looked I had one dog."

"Uh-oh, sounds like you found yourself some trouble with a capital T," said Ava as they shot down Barracks Street. "What happened?"

"Shamus happened," said Carmela.

Ava rolled her eyes. "Don't tell me . . ."

"Long story short," said Carmela, "Poobah's a stray. Shamus found him. Or claims he did, anyway."

"Let me guess," said Ava, quickly sensing the gist of

the story. "Shamus felt sorry for the dog, but in typical Shamus style he foisted the little mutt off on you. Jeez, Carmela, you're not gonna *keep* him, are you?"

"Of course not," said Carmela, wondering if Ava meant Shamus or the dog. And wondering, also, how to extricate herself from yet another Shamus-induced mess. Shamus obviously adored the poor stray, and Boo, the little traitor, had promptly adopted Poobah as her long-lost little brother.

"What's the dog's name?" asked Ava, scrunching around to get a better look at him.

"Poobah," answered Carmela. Upon hearing his name, Poobah was suddenly at full attention, tail wagging, nose quivering, brown eyes shining eagerly.

"Well, he's kinda cute," said Ava. "I like that furry, Muppet look. Except for that one ear that looks like it's about to fall off. Makes his head look all crooked and goofy."

Poobah, delighted to be the center of conversation, eagerly stuck his head over the back seat and licked Ava on the ear.

"Hey, watch it, fresh guy," she warned. "Those are very expensive chandelier earrings you're nuzzling!"

"You got new earrings?" asked Carmela.

Ava tossed her head and her oversized earrings twinkled and danced, catching the light provocatively. "Twelve ninety-nine at WalMart," Ava told Carmela in a conspiratorial tone. "And believe me, honey, with romantic music and soft lighting, you can't tell the difference between these babies and the fancy schmancy

Fred Leighton baubles Nicole Kidman wears on the red carpet."

"Works for me," said Carmela, whose jewelry budget these days was just as tight as Ava's.

"So where are we headed again?" asked Ava. They had entered Plaquemines Parish a while back and just passed through Port Sulfur, one of the small towns strung along Highway 23.

"Boothville," said Carmela. For the last ten miles or so she'd regaled Ava with her recent discoveries involving Jamie Redmond, as well as all the various and sundry players who'd had walk-on parts in Jamie's life and whom she now deemed as suspects. In other words, Margot, Dunbar, and Blaine.

"You got weird things going on, suspects up the wazoo, and you still want to go lookin' for the graves of Jamie's folks?" asked Ava.

"Of course I do," said Carmela. "Wren had Jamie cremated, and she'd like to put him someplace."

"I suppose," said Ava. "But I know lots of folks who keep their loved ones close by instead of stickin' 'em in some grave or marble mausoleum."

"Kindly explain what you mean by 'close by,'" said Carmela.

"My Aunt Eulalie keeps her dear departed husband, Edgar, in a Chinese ginger jar on her night stand," explained Ava. "Says it makes her feel like he's still with her. Except now he doesn't snore or hog the remote control. And this fella I used to work with,

Carlos? He's got his mother's ashes in a coffee can under the sink. Says he's going to plant her next spring when he puts in new rose bushes."

"A double planting," said Carmela.

"Something like that," replied Ava, peering in the mirror again. "You know, *cher*," she said, frowning, then poking at the tiny wrinkle that formed between her eyes. "That blue car's been on our tail for the last few miles."

Mildly curious, Carmela glanced in her rearview mirror. "This is the only decent highway going south," she said. "He's probably headed down to Pilottown or the Delta Wildlife Refuge."

"Mn," said Ava, settling back. "Probably."

There was no sign of a blue car when they pulled into a roadside cafe for a bite of lunch.

"Big Eye Louie's," said Ava, as tires crunched across gravel. "Place looks awful."

"Doesn't it?" agreed Carmela. Big Eye Louie's was a battered, one-story wooden building that could have benefited greatly from a coat of paint. An overhang of rusty corrugated tin stuck out from just below the roof line to shield the front door and the large windows to either side of it.

"Which means we might just get ourselves a decent bowl of gumbo," Ava added gleefully.

"Or jambalaya," said Carmela. She was passionate about the rice-based dish that often featured spicy andouille sausage.

"Dogs okay in the car?" asked Ava.

186

But Carmela had already left the driver's-side window partially cracked and was making tracks for the front door of Big Eye Louie's.

Once inside, the roadside cafe was everything they expected it to be. Smoky, fairly crowded, hideously decorated. Men with red-and-white checked napkins tucked into their shirt fronts labored over steaming bowls of gumbo. Neon beer signs lent a crazy Times Square feel. Loud zydeco music pulsed from the jukebox. Stuffed possums, alligators, and fish hung overhead. The wooden walls were a veritable rogue's gallery of photos, sports pennants, team jerseys, and trophies. A big-screen TV dominated the back wall of the bar.

"The prototypical sports bar," murmured Ava. "Designed for the sporting gent with a lust for life and an urge to blast away at small animals."

They walked up to the bar where a tall, lean man with curly red hair and a handlebar mustache was briskly wiping glasses. "Help you?" he asked.

"Are you Big Eye Louie?" asked Ava.

"Might be," smiled the man, whose two front teeth were rimmed in gold. "You ladies interested in lunch?" He gave the bar in front of him a neat swipe with his rag, then quickly snapped down two paper place mats and fresh red-and-white checkered napkins. "We got turtle soup today—'the other white meat.' And it's on special."

"Is it really turtle?" asked Carmela. "Or alligator?" She knew that most turtle soups in Louisiana restaurants and cafes contained a good bit of alligator meat. There were over one hundred alligator farms in southern Louisiana, and alligator meat was big business.

The red handlebar mustache twitched faintly. "There's some of that in there, too," he allowed.

"You got gumbo?" Ava asked.

The bartender nodded. "Chef's partial to crawfish and a bit of okra."

"Good enough," said Ava as the two women slid onto barstools. "But I want a bowl, not just a cup."

Carmela opted for the hybrid turtle-alligator soup and they both ordered Dixie longnecks.

"We didn't miss the turn off for Boothville, did we?" Carmela asked, once big steaming bowls had been set in front of them.

"Another mile down," said the bartender. He smiled and slid a plate of hush puppies between them. "Compliments of the house."

Their respective lunches were steamy, hearty, and spicy. And Carmela and Ava soon fell into what Carmela called "the N'awlins feeding frenzy." In other words, the food was so good and hot and spicy that it actually prompted you to eat faster. Whatever the logic behind Carmela's feeding frenzy theory, they both finished their lunches in record time.

"My lips are on fire," remarked Ava. "They feel all puffy."

"That's good, right?" smiled Carmela.

"Yeah," said Ava, poking at one with a manicured

finger. "I guess so. I never thought of cayenne and Tabasco as natural lip plumpers, but if they do the trick—great!"

Carmela paid the bill, leaving three single dollar bills on the bar. "You ever hear of a family by the name of Redmond who lived around these parts?" she asked the bartender, after he'd carefully folded the bills, tapped them on the bar in recognition, then slipped them into a glass jar that had a hand-lettered TIPS sign pasted on it.

The man thought for a moment. "Sounds familiar." He nodded toward the wall filled with framed photos. "Seems to me there was one or another Redmond who played football. You might check them pictures over yonder."

Carmela slipped off her barstool and walked over to the wall. She stood there a moment, studying the various photos. There were pictures of guys playing football, guys playing softball, guys hunting, guys fishing, guys cleaning fish.

Louisiana. Sportsman's paradise.

Carmela was halfway through the sportsman's rogue's gallery when she found what she was looking for. A photo of one of Boothville High School's football teams.

And there was Jamie Redmond, in a somewhat younger incarnation, staring back at her.

"I think this is him," she called over to Ava.

"Yeah?" Ava slid off the barstool and sauntered across the room. Her mass of auburn hair, lithe sinewy figure, denim mini skirt, and leather jacket were almost too much for the men still sitting at tables.

They stared, gaped, and ogled.

In the silence that spun out, one man snapped the head off a crawfish and sucked the spicy juice. Loudly.

A chorus of *ooohs* rose from the table where he was sitting.

Ava tossed her head nonchalantly. "You *wish*," she sang out.

Which touched off a hearty spattering of applause for Ava.

"Time to go," announced Carmela. She hustled back to the bar, grabbing her denim jacket off the back of the stool.

"You ladies care for a slice of homemade bread pudding with brandy sauce?" offered the bartender, grinning stupidly at Ava. "It'd be compliments of the house."

Ava reached up and fingered a stuffed catfish that dangled overhead. "Thanks," she told him, "but I'm stuffed, too."

The bartender shook his head and grinned at her. "You're a real pistol, aren't you? Why don't y'all come back Saturday night? We got a live zydeco band that cranks up about nine o'clock." He winked at Ava. "We'd show you a real good time."

"Thanks," she said as they headed out the door. "Maybe we will."

"Now wasn't that an amusing little interlude," said Carmela. She pulled the car door open, caught the two dogs by their collars as they struggled to make a break for it, and unceremoniously stuffed them back in. "Vastly entertaining. And such scintillating conversation. With Noel Coward–type *bon mots*."

"Oh you," laughed Ava. "They're just good old boys havin' fun."

"Maybe a little too much fun, if you ask me."

They stopped at the local library looking for information. An elderly gent with faded blue eyes and a "Friends of the Library" pin in the lapel of a too-large, slightly frayed blue suit, carefully informed them that the "regular librarians" were still out for lunch.

"What I'm after is a little information," Carmela told him.

He smiled at her politely.

"There was a man named Redmond who used to run a small printing shop in these parts," she began. "I know he and his wife passed on a while ago, but I'm trying to find out where they're buried. Or perhaps where they once lived." She pulled out a black-and-white photo. "I think this was their house."

The old man pursed his lips and nodded slightly as he glanced at the photo. "I remember the family," he said in a soft voice. "Baptists, I believe." He reached for a pencil and a piece of paper and slowly began sketching a rudimentary map. "You'd want to look for them in this particular cemetery," he told her. With great precision he drew a criss-cross of streets, then placed an X in one area of the map.

"And the homestead?" said Carmela. "I understand the family lived out of town a ways. On Fordoche Road."

The old man bent over his map again. "Turn here," he told her, tapping his pencil. "Lidville Street to Fordoche. Then follow Fordoche, maybe ten miles out."

"You knew them?" Carmela asked. "The Redmonds?"

He gave a faint nod. Carmela couldn't figure out if the old man was trying to cover up for his forgetfulness or was just covering up.

"Anything you can tell me about them?" she asked. "About the family?"

The old man closed his eyes slowly and Carmela was reminded of an old turtle. "Don't like to speak ill of anyone," he told her as he slid his homemade map across the scarred counter to her.

"What was that all about?" asked Ava, once they were back in the car.

"I have no idea," said Carmela.

"Seemed like he wanted to say more, but was too polite," said Ava.

"Seemed to me he was being awfully careful," replied Carmela.

Chapter 16

THE cemetery was, no pun intended, a dead end. There was no marble gravestone with the name Redmond carved into it, no family marker, no caretaker nearby to query.

They had split into two teams—Carmela with Poobah on a leash, and Ava with Boo—and walked the rows of tombstones for the better part of an hour. But they'd found nothing. The results were disappointing, to say the least.

"At least the dogs got to stretch their legs," said Ava, noticing the glum expression on Carmela's face.

"Us, too," said Carmela.

"We goin' to the house, then?" asked Ava. They had gravitated to a large memorial commemorating all the veterans who'd fought in this country's wars, both foreign and domestic. "That is, if the house is still there."

"We've come all this way," said Carmela. "It'd be a shame to quit now."

Bumping down Fordoche Road, following the map the old man at the library had sketched, Carmela was struck by the raw beauty of the area. On either side of what seemed more like a dike built to keep the bayou at bay than a road were great expanses of brackish water, punctuated by mangrove trees and towering, bald cypress. This was the realm of egrets, herons, ibis, and cormorants. Where the American alligator was most at home, too. The one also dubbed the Mississippi alligator, pike-headed alligator, or just "gator." Whatever the moniker, this contemporary cousin of the dinosaur garnered a good share of respect.

"It's kinda spooky," said Ava. Poobah had wormed his way from the back seat into the front and was now firmly ensconced in Ava's lap. Boo, happy to have the entire back seat to herself, looked on approvingly.

"I truly do love it down here," said Carmela. "Lots of folks get all fidgety and nervous about bayous. They find them haunting and dangerous. But I think they're incredibly beautiful and mysterious."

"Everything's so soggy," said Ava, peering out the window. "I guess I'm more of a dry land gal."

"Are you kidding?" said Carmela. "Of the three hundred sixty-something square miles that make up greater New Orleans, half of that is water."

"Good heavens," exclaimed Ava. "Half? That much, really? Well, I still prefer the dryer things in life. Dry land, dry martinis . . ." She thought for a few seconds. "Dry cleaning."

The sun peeped out from behind high puffy clouds and suddenly illuminated the entire bayou. Greens became brighter and more intense, water riffled by breezes suddenly sparkled like jewels, tendrils of Spanish moss swung gently. Two large heron, both with heroic wingspans, swooped gracefully in front of the car, then settled near a stand of swamp grass.

"Gonna be a nice day after all," said Carmela, feeling upbeat. She had a good feeling about this little trip. She felt sure they'd obtain some sort of resolution. Or new information, at the very least.

Jamie Redmond's home was instantly recognizable from the photographs Carmela had brought along. Though not quite as rustic as a traditional bayou camp house, the two-story building still had that same hunkered down, home-sawed look. Only now, of course, the place was deserted and half falling down.

The front door hung on a single hinge, the little overhang that had sheltered it had tumbled down. Every window pane was broken or gone. Exterior paint had long since been eaten away by heat and unbelievable humidity, beaten away by rain. Pared down to bare wood, the house was a not unattractive silvered gray.

Carmela wondered who owned this property now. Was the title still in Jamie Redmond's name? Or had someone purchased it years ago and maybe just used the land for hunting and fishing? She decided that was something else she might have to look into.

"This is very creepy," said Ava. "Kinda like that old farmhouse in *The Texas Chainsaw Massacre.*" She rolled her eyes, ever the devotee of horror flicks. "And you know what happened *there,*" she added.

"This isn't Texas and I'll venture to say nobody's fired up a chainsaw around here in years," said Carmela.

"The place does seem a tad overgrown," commented Ava.

Ava's words were a complete understatement. Perched on the edge of a pond, the out-buildings were practically shrouded in kudzu. Mangroves had taken over where the yard had been.

"Look-it," said Ava as they finally climbed out of the car. "Alligators."

Way out in the middle of the pond, a half-dozen little rough humps stuck up out of the water. To the untrained eye they looked like half-sunken logs. Or rocks. But Carmela and Ava knew better. Those were the tell-tale backs of alligators.

Once hunted to the point of endangerment, alligators had made a nice recovery. The hunting season in Louisiana was now just one month long, the month of September. And many commercial alligator farms were required to return up to seventeen percent of their juvenile alligators back to the wild. So the snaggle-toothed *lagato* enjoyed a robust population.

"They won't bother us," said Carmela, "as long as we're active and moving around. But we'll keep the dogs in the car just to be safe."

"So what do you want to do?" asked Ava. "Just snoop? Check the place out and see what we can see?"

"Sounds like a plan to me," said Carmela. "What if I looked inside the house and you took a stroll around the out-buildings?"

"Sure," said Ava. "But be careful. That old place looks like a stiff breeze could bring it crashing down around you."

"Don't worry," said Carmela, heading for the main house. "I'll tread lightly."

Ducking under fallen boards, Carmela clambered over the front porch and stepped through what was left of the front door.

"Hello," she called out, even though she knew no one was there.

Gazing around, Carmela's first impression was that the place looked like a *Wizard of Oz* house. A house that had been ripped from its foundation, spun around inside an F-6 tornado a few hundred times, then slammed back down to earth. Broken furniture lay everywhere, old pictures hung catty-wampus on walls, plaster had crumbled off to reveal lath board and, in some places, interior wiring.

Ava's right. This place is spooky and looks like it could collapse at any moment.

Glass crunched underfoot as Carmela moved through what must have been the front room, the parlor, and into the kitchen.

There wasn't much left. Wooden cupboards had long since been torn from the walls and pitched outside. Carmela could see what was left of them lying in the overgrown backyard. Twisted black wires, the old connections for an oven that no longer existed, poked from the wall. A sink, rusty and dirty and piled with dust-coated dishes, was the only thing left.

What happened here? wondered Carmela. *When the Redmonds died, was this house rented out to tenants who just let it go? Or was it put on the housing market where it just languished?*

The notion of a house that had once hummed with people and their things, had once been cozy and secure, and then had fallen into utter disrepair, was depressing. Someone had probably hung curtains here once. Had lovingly prepared meals. Had mopped floors and polished wood. Had read books, played music, sang their child to sleep.

Carmela wandered back toward the parlor and carefully made her way up a narrow flight of steps. The upstairs was small and in slightly better condition. Two small bedrooms, a bathroom, and a storage closet occupied this floor. Peeking into one of the bedrooms, Carmela was startled to see what looked like an old sleeping bag.

Or is it just a pile of rags?

She tiptoed in. Well, it was *something*. Maybe a dirty old comforter that had been scrunched up.

Has someone been sleeping up here?

It was certainly possible. And the notion of someone hiding out here gave her a serious case of the creeps.

Time to go. Check around outside, see if I can find a family plot or something.

Descending the stairs, she heard a noise, a faint scuttle, on the front porch.

Ava?

Bending low as she ducked through the front door, trying to avoid shattered wood and splinters, Carmela was intent on making a fast exit. But as she began to straighten up, her head ran smack dab into a very hard, immovable object. *Whack!*

The blow rocked Carmela's entire being and sent her crumpling to her knees. Still wondering what had happened, not comprehending that she'd just been hit, Carmela uttered a lone groan as she struggled to her feet. She took three, maybe four stumbling steps and then she was falling, falling, falling and the lights winked out.

Minutes later, she was aware of warm sunshine on

her face and a buzzing, a terrible reeling in her head. But to move, to actually move, would require an act of sheer heroism.

Ava, where are you? Help me. Something happened. I whacked my head or somebody whacked it for me.

Slowly, like a diver coming up for air, Carmela began to regain consciousness. Struggling mightily, Carmela pushed herself up on one arm. Sunlight glinted off the nearby pond. A gentle breeze riffled her hair. And the alligators, the humpy bumpy alligators that had been way out in the middle of the pond, seemed strangely closer.

Alligators? Are they really there or am I just seeing things? Oh, lord, my head aches.

Carmela closed her eyes and fell back. The pounding in her head was making her almost physically ill, and she had to suck in air quickly to avoid getting dry heaves.

She lay there panting for a few minutes until she was finally able to get a grip on things. But when Carmela finally opened her eyes a second time, they were immediately drawn to the alligators. The humps of their backs were more defined, eyes and snouts protruded just above the surface of the water. They had definitely moved in closer! And this time Carmela understood that they were very, very real!

Got to get out of here! Got to haul ass!

Carmela knew she had to move, but her brain still kept going fuzzy. She could clearly hear Boo and probably Poobah barking off in the background somewhere, but the synapses still weren't firing properly.

Then she was aware of footsteps nearby and a sharp cry of alarm. And warm hands quickly encircling her shoulders.

Ava. Dear, dear Ava.

"Get up!" screamed Ava. "Now! Those damn gators have got you in their sites!" She grabbed one of Carmela's arms and tugged hard. "Holy shit, Carmela, they've moved in at least fifty feet! I think they're still coming!"

Carmela fought for consciousness even as she struggled to her feet. Ava charged a few steps forward, cartwheeling her arms and letting out whoops and hoots that would have been worthy of one of Jean Lafitte's pirates.

"Heeyoo! Get away, gators! Shoo, you ugly buggers!"

The alligators seemed to hesitate a moment, trying to decide what to do. Then they slowly slid backwards in the water, their powerful feet and tails acting as silent-running reverse motors. In the alligator universe, anything taller and larger than they were wasn't usually worth the tussle.

Ava came circling back to help Carmela. "Did you fall?" she babbled. "Did you hit your head?"

"Not sure," said Carmela, tentatively. "Somebody could've whacked me one."

"I thought I heard a car," said Ava. "I was walking down this path through the woods 'cause I thought it might lead to a family plot or something. Anyway, I heard it and I thought you might be leaving! I got panicky!"

"I heard someone outside," said Carmela, "and thought it was you!"

"I *knew* that blue car was following us," Ava fumed. "I had a bad *feeling*. Damn, if it turns out to be that weird Margot person, I'm gonna kick her skinny butt from here to next Tuesday."

"What if it was Dunbar? Or Blaine?" asked Carmela. Ava was still pulling her and half carrying her toward the car.

"One thing you should know about me," said Ava fiercely. "I'm an equal opportunity ass-kicker." She looked at Carmela closely and her eyes suddenly teared up. "You're really hurt, aren't you?"

"Don't know," said Carmela, still struggling to walk on her own. Ava let go and Carmela tottered a few steps, stopped, then reached a hand up to gingerly touch the back of her head. She winced. There was an enormous bump that felt like it was growing rapidly larger with each passing second.

"Do you need stitches?" Ava asked as she led Carmela to an old tree stump and eased her down into a sitting position. "Ooh, jeez. It looks like you got bonked pretty hard," she said as she gently parted Carmela's hair.

"It hurts like hell," groaned Carmela, trying to pull away.

"Shush," said Ava. "Keep still and let me take a look."

Carmela finally held still and let Ava inspect her aching head.

"No gash or nothin', *cher*," said Ava. "But you've got a bump the size of a golf ball. You're gonna have a killer headache."

"I already do," said Carmela.

"We better stop and get a can of Coke."

"I don't think I could swallow a drop," protested Carmela. "I still feel woozy and sick to my stomach."

"Not to drink," said Ava, helping Carmela back up and over toward the passenger side of the car. "To hold against your poor little head."

Chapter 17

THREE squares of melted chocolate formed a rich, dark puddle in the bottom of the sauce pan, as Ava stirred in water, watched the mixture thicken and bubble, then whisked in the rest of her ingredients. When the hot chocolate concoction was perfect, Ava poured a frothy serving into a large ceramic mug and carried it in to Carmela, who was holed up in the bathroom taking an extended hot shower.

"I'm gonna set this on the counter here," Ava told her as she stepped into the warm, steamed-up bathroom.

Carmela's head poked out from behind the shower curtain and billows of steam poured out. "Set what?"

"This cup of bubbling brown sugar hot chocolate," Ava told her.

"What?" squawked Carmela. "You told me you

couldn't cook! You told me you never cooked!"

"Making hot chocolate doesn't qualify as cooking," said Ava, squinting at the fogged-up mirror. "It's more like whipping up a little comfort." She paused. "Do I look like I'm gettin' a pimple? Sure I am! I had a teeny little bump this morning and now it's glowing like a tiki torch!"

"Your face looks fine," said Carmela as she reached out, grabbed the mug, and took a sip. The hot chocolate was rich and creamy and redolent with brown sugar. Even with her hair streaming down in wet tendrils and her face sans makeup, Carmela suddenly looked like she was in seventh heaven. "This is delicious!" she exclaimed.

"Of course it is," said Ava. "But I have to tell you, I pretty much follow Sweetmomma Pam's recipe. So it's really her creation, not mine."

"Whatever magic you worked, it's fantastic," said Carmela.

Pulling open the door to Carmela's medicine cabinet, Ava rummaged around and eventually came up with a bottle of Motrin. "No witch hazel or nothin' for my face, huh? Too bad." She snapped the cap off the Motrin and shook out one of the orange tablets into her hand. "Take this," she instructed Carmela as she held the tablet out to the shower curtain.

Carmela's hand came out and grabbed the tablet. She popped it into her mouth and took a follow-up sip of cocoa. "This drink is so *good*," she declared again.

"Good is when we get that nasty bump on your head

knocked down a little more," said Ava. "I sure hope your poor brain didn't get all jiggled around inside your skull."

Ducking back under the shower spray, Carmela said: "My brain's been jiggled for years. Why else would I have married Shamus Allan Meechum?"

"Good point," said Ava. "And don't stay in there too long. Looks like your wallpaper's starting to peel. Which could be a serendipitous thing, since you haven't done a lick of decorating for almost two whole months."

Ten minutes later, Carmela emerged from her bathroom wrapped in a white terry cloth bathrobe and smelling of lavender soap. She looked scrubbed, rested, and considerably more relaxed. "Something smells good," she said.

"That something is dinner," Ava told her.

"Now I know I've died and gone to heaven," said Carmela, plopping down at the table where Ava had arranged two place settings and a small array of twinkling votive candles.

"Now don't go gettin' all moony on me," warned Ava. "Because I didn't fix much. Just a little soup."

"You made soup?" Ava never made anything. She either chugged a can of Slim Fast, grabbed takeout, or ate in a restaurant. There was no in between. Certainly no actual *cooking*.

"Pull yourself together and take a closer look at me," said Ava. "Do I look like a fat little Italian granny? Hell no. It's *canned* soup, Carmela. Minestrone. So don't make a big thing of it, okay?"

Carmela smiled. "Okay. But it sure smells good."

"That's because I added a few spices along with some grated cheese and a splash of red wine. Oh, and I ran across the courtyard to my place and grabbed a few extra ingredients. So we're also having bruschetta."

"I love bruschetta," said Carmela as Ava ladled out soup.

"So do those dogs," said Ava.

"Oh, the dogs!" said Carmela, about to jump up. "I didn't feed the dogs!"

"Already taken care of," said Ava. "I gave 'em some of those kibble bits and they went face down like a couple of professional chow hounds."

"That's 'cause they are," said Carmela. A stock broker friend of Carmela's had once told her that one of the stepping stones to wealth was to never own anything that needed to be fed. And now she had *two* dogs slopping around in her kitchen. Oh well.

Over steaming bowls of minestrone soup and crusty slabs of bruschetta, Carmela and Ava rehashed the afternoon.

"What do you think really happened out there, *cher?*" asked Ava. "Did you just smack your head on one of those tumbled-down timbers or did somebody club you? Somebody who thought you might be gettin' in the way. Doing a little too much investigating."

Carmela nibbled at her bruschetta. It was garlicy and cheesey and smothered with bits of chopped tomato drizzled with olive oil. Fantastic.

"That blue car that you saw earlier," said Carmela. "Who drives a blue car?"

"Aha," said Ava. "Told you so. I thought some yahoo was following us."

"The question is, which yahoo and why?" said Carmela.

"Don't know," said Ava. "But it sure looks like somebody might have been checkin' us out. Trying to figure out what we were doing. Or, if we really want to stretch the bounds of paranoia, trying to *stop* us."

"Maybe," said Carmela. She took another bite of bruschetta, wiped a dribble of olive oil from her chin. "But try this on for size. What if somebody was *looking* for something out there?" Still fresh in Carmela's mind was the nagging feeling that someone had been prowling about Biblios Booksellers yesterday. Looking for something there, too.

"Do you think it was the same somebody who wanted us out of Jamie's house last Friday night?" asked Ava. "When that damn snake just happened to make a guest appearance?"

"Maybe," replied Carmela.

"So . . . this person," said Ava, "and I'd have to say he or she is a very *dangerous* person . . . what are they looking for?"

"Search me," said Carmela. "But it feels like I'm starting to get a slightly clearer picture of what's going on."

"Then kindly tell me what's going on," said Ava.

"Because nothing's clear as far as I'm concerned."

"What if Jamie Redmond had something very valuable in his possession?" proposed Carmela.

Ava considered this. "Like what?"

"Don't know," said Carmela. "But it must be something valuable enough to kill for."

Ava frowned. "Whatever it is, they obviously *didn't* get it when they killed Jamie."

"Let me show you something," said Carmela. She got up from the table, found the file with the photos and news clipping about the Bogus Creek Boys, then handed it over to Ava. "Take a look at this."

Ava quickly scanned the clipping. "Right," she said. "You mentioned some of this before. Kind of a shocker for Wren, huh?"

"She was stunned," said Carmela.

"So . . . what are you thinking?" asked Ava. "You think Jamie's got money stashed away somewhere? Counterfeit money?"

"The thought had crossed my mind," said Carmela. "His family was in the printing business."

"And someone knows about this money," said Ava, catching on. "And is looking for it."

"What else could it be?" asked Carmela.

"I have no idea," said Ava. "But now the actions of certain suspects start to make a little more sense."

"Explain," said Carmela, gesturing with her fingers.

"Well, you told me that Dunbar DesLauriers was hot to trot about buying the bookstore from Wren. Why would that be?"

"Because he thinks there's a pile of counterfeit money stashed inside?" answered Carmela.

"Bingo," said Ava. "Cold cash, hot moola, the mother lode."

"But Blaine Taylor doesn't come off looking completely innocent in all this either," said Carmela. "He was Jamie's business partner in Neutron Software and he's the one who's been oh-so-solicitous to Wren. Offering to help her wherever he can."

"Right," said Ava. "Trying to get close to her. Or close to Jamie's stash, if there is one. Plus, Blaine just happened to pop up right after the snake incident."

"But if this mythical funny money is so important to Blaine, why is he trying to cut Wren out of the Neutron sale, if there ends up being a sale?" asked Carmela. "Doesn't that just draw the wrong kind of attention to him?"

Ava shrugged. "I have no idea. Maybe Dunbar and Blaine are in cahoots."

"Doesn't feel right," said Carmela. She sat there thinking, as rain began to patter down on the roof. "Rats. It's starting to rain."

"It's been threatening to for the last hour," said Ava. She leaned forward, flipped her hair forward, then straightened up and let it settle about her shoulders, suddenly looking like a beauty in a Pre-Raphaelite painting. "What about this Margot Butler? You're the one who thought she was acting so kooky."

"She was . . . is," said Carmela. "Then again, Margot may just be a genuine kook."

"It's not like New Orleans is immune to people with personality disorders," said Ava. "In fact, sometimes I think we're a big fat magnet for them."

"Amen," said Carmela, thinking immediately of Shamus and his nutty family. They were about as dysfunctional as any group could hope to be.

Ava tapped a fingernail against the file folder Carmela had given her. "This is pretty interesting stuff."

"There's more," said Carmela. "I went back to Biblios last night and unearthed another file folder. I just haven't gotten around to looking at everything yet. The contents were in pretty tough shape. All gunked together because of mildew and water damage."

"Well," said Ava. "*You're* supposed to be the expert when it comes to paper restoration and photo conservation, aren't you?" She jumped up to clear the table. "So let's get busy and see what little tricks you can work to remedy the situation."

"Okay," said Carmela, jumping up, too, and heading for the kitchen.

"I'll clear," said Ava as Carmela pulled open the freezer door. "Got a hankering for ice cream, do you?"

"No," said Carmela. "This is where I put the contents of that folder."

"You're kidding," said Ava. "You froze it for safe keeping? Is that kind of like hiding your diamonds in the icebox?"

"Not quite," said Carmela. She pulled out a square tray that held an inch-thick pile of photos and papers.

"Freezing wet paper makes it a lot easier to separate."

"Do tell," said Ava, intrigued. "You certainly come up with the darndest things." She followed Carmela to the table, then sat down and watched as Carmela slid a thin steak knife into the top of the pile and pried very gently. Like magic, the top few papers released themselves from the bottom pile.

"Amazing," said Ava. "I would have steamed everything."

"Steaming paper just makes it wet and gloppy," said Carmela. "And it can actually cause paper to disintegrate. But freezing dries papers out. The moisture turns into ice crystals so everything can be easily separated. Well, *sort of* separated." She inserted her knife and pried another few papers loose.

"Now what?" asked Ava.

"Now we separate them again and try to dry them," said Carmela.

The two women worked diligently for several minutes until finally they had a half-dozen photos and five pieces of paper spread out on the dining room table.

"This one's still folded in half," Ava told her, plucking at it with her fingertips.

"Are you always this impatient?" asked Carmela.

"Always," said Ava. "I'm an instant gratification kind of gal. I like instant coffee, minute rice, and pop-top pudding. When I want something, I want it *now*."

"Then take the bone folder and try and work it in there," Carmela instructed. "If you can get it open, I'll hit it with a shot of archival spray."

"It's working!" exclaimed Ava as she worked the bone folder in and loosened the folded paper. Then, ever so gently, she flipped it open.

"Well done," said Carmela as she went over to the sink to rinse her hands.

Sitting at the table, head bent low over the still-wet piece of paper, Ava studied the sheet intently. "It's a news story," Ava told her.

"From the *Times-Picayune*?"

"Not sure," replied Ava. "There's no newspaper masthead or anything like that."

"What's it about?" asked Carmela.

Ava was hurriedly scanning the story. "Some party that apparently got out of hand."

"Uh huh," said Carmela. Nothing weird there. Lots of parties in New Orleans got out of hand. Especially during Mardi Gras.

"Uh-oh. Guess who's the star of this little article," said Ava, with a note of triumph in her voice.

"Surprise me," said Carmela. Although she didn't think she would be.

"Blaine Taylor," chortled Ava. "Apparently, as a result of rowdy goings-on, old B.T. was arraigned on charges of assault and battery."

Carmela came around to the table and stood next to Ava, drying her hands. "So Blaine Taylor's a regular bad boy, too."

"Looks like," said Ava. "Do you think that's why he and Jamie ended up as business partners in that computer software thing?"

Carmela frowned. Interesting thought. Perhaps theirs *was* a case of two bad boys finding each other. Two rotten eggs who'd connected on a visceral level and then just naturally sought each other out on a business level.

"It's a thought," Carmela told her. "On the other hand, Blaine's bad boy escapades might help explain why he was trying to claim Neutron Software as his own."

"You mean Blaine's a cheat and a jerk and his true character is just shining through?"

"Something like that," said Carmela.

"Do you think Blaine Taylor could have been one of the Bogus Creek Boys?" asked Ava.

"He wasn't mentioned in the article," said Carmela.

"Maybe the authorities just didn't catch him," said Ava. "Or Blaine was what you'd call a silent partner."

"Maybe," allowed Carmela. "Maybe."

Two hours later, a slew of unanswered questions still buzzed like angry bees inside Carmela's head. Ava had cleaned up the kitchen, then slipped out the door and dashed across the courtyard as Carmela drifted off to sleep in her leather chair. Around 9:00 PM Carmela woke up feeling groggy and sore and more than a little discombobulated. Rain was still drumming down on the roof and there was the rumble of thunder off in the distance.

Struggling out of the chair, Carmela padded into the kitchen, figuring a glass of water and another Motrin might be in order. Ava had put the bottle on the kitchen counter so she'd have easy access to it. Plus, she needed to climb into bed, where she could get some proper rest and log some serious REM time.

As Carmela waited for the water to get cold, which always seemed to take an eternity, she noted that Boo and Poobah were snuggled together, muzzle to muzzle, on Boo's comfy L.L. Bean bed. She hoped Boo wasn't getting too attached to the little guy, because there was no way he was going to stay.

Boo attached? What am I thinking? Shamus is the one who's ga-ga over the little stray. But, naturally, I'm the one who's taking care of little Poobah. Or, better yet, I'm the one who was taken in.

Carmela swallowed her pill, downed half a glass of water, and headed for the bedroom. As she passed the dining room table, a spill of light from the kitchen cast a faint glow, causing her eyes to be naturally drawn there. Drawn toward the articles that had been laid out to dry.

Carmela hesitated. *Had Blaine Taylor been one of the Bogus Creek Boys?* she wondered. No, she didn't think so.

She didn't think Blaine was completely innocent. But was he a murderer? A cold-blooded killer?

Not enough to go on yet. Not enough evidence to make any sort of accusation stick.

The tips of her fingers hovered above the photos and articles that lay there. One photo of Jamie that they'd found—maybe even his graduation picture, since he was neatly dressed in a suit and tie—caught at her heart. He looked so young, so eager, so innocent.

Almost like he had the night of the pre-nuptial dinner, Carmela decided. The night he was murdered. When he'd looked happy and eager to start a new life with Wren. And very much in love.

A sudden crack of thunder and bright flash of lightning caused Carmela to jump.

Yeeow! That's positively cataclysmic!

Feeling foolish, knowing it was just positive and negative charges cast off from the storm's roiling clouds, Carmela glanced out the window, wondering if Ava had been shaken by nature's heroic display, too.

But what she saw silhouetted in the window rocked her back on her heels!

What the . . . ?

Three more pulses of lightning strobed in rapid succession.

It can't be!

Racing to the window, Carmela pressed her face to the glass and peered into the courtyard. Because just for a flash, just for an instant, she thought she'd seen Jamie Redmond's face at her window!

But I couldn't have, could I?

Nervously, Carmela scanned the dark courtyard, but it was empty. Just rain pounding down on flagstones, pots of drooping bougainvilleas, and a fountain that bubbled furiously even as it filled to capacity.

Pulling herself away from the window, shaking from the tiny shot of adrenaline that had insinuated itself into her nervous system, Carmela told herself she'd seen some kind of optical illusion.

Of course it was. Don't be silly. Don't get all weird.

Had to be her retina picking up the image of Jamie from the photo, then projecting it in her brain. So it caused the *illusion* of seeing him silhouetted in the window.

Just my eyes playing tricks on me.

After all, there was no other logical explanation.

But even after Carmela crawled into bed and settled under her down comforter, it was a good long time before sleep came to carry her away.

Chapter 18

Y OU didn't find anything?" asked Gabby. The rainstorm had continued through the night and into the morning, burbling down drain pipes, swirling in gutters and storm sewers, and, in general, snarling up city traffic. Which seemed to set the tone for the day.

Carmela shook her head. "Nothing. Sorry." She debated telling Gabby about the conk on the head she'd received, but decided not to. Things were getting decidedly stranger and there was no reason to panic her.

"And you for sure checked the Boothville Cemetery?" Gabby asked.

"Ava and I walked every row," Carmela assured her, "and found nothing."

Gabby drummed her fingertips on the front counter

and gazed toward the back of the store where Wren was showing a customer how to use a template to create a miniature shopping bag. "What are you going to tell Wren?"

"That we tried," replied Carmela. "Which we did. Truly." Carmela sighed. She felt like she'd let Gabby down. She hadn't meant to, of course. It was just that the Redmonds must be buried somewhere else.

"Thank you, Carmela," said Gabby finally. "You took a day off work to do this and here I am being a sourpuss. Sorry."

"No problem," said Carmela, although she appreciated the apology.

"And with this rain pouring down, I can't imagine we're going to be busy today." Gabby shook her head. "There's enough coming down out there to turn Canal Street into a real canal."

"Actually," said Carmela, "I could use a catch-up day."

"Scrapbooks for Gilt Trip?" asked Gabby. She knew that Carmela's life was perpetually over-booked.

Carmela nodded. "Even though you backed Margot off on the deadline, I still have to get them done."

"Today's the deadline," said Gabby.

Carmela shrugged. "I know. But tomorrow's going to have to do."

"Carmela," said Wren as Carmela drifted toward the back of the store. "Can I talk to you?"

Carmela held up a finger. "Hang on a minute, will you?" She wanted to check in with Lieutenant Edgar

Babcock. He was her conduit in the New Orleans Police Department, and she wanted to see if they were any closer to naming a suspect or perhaps even making an arrest.

They weren't.

Lieutenant Babcock was sympathetic, courteous, and sincere, all the things Boy Scouts are supposed to be, but he also seemed profoundly down when it came to talking about the case.

"Nothing," he said in a tone that made no bones about the fact that he was disheartened. Not with Carmela. But with the lack of progress.

"We thought for sure you'd be hot on the trail of *someone* by now," said Carmela. She didn't want to come down too hard on Lieutenant Babcock or his colleagues. Criticism and negative pronouncements had a way of discouraging people.

"Jimmy . . . Detective Rawlings . . . and the other officers have gone back and talked to the kitchen employees a half-dozen times," Lieutenant Babcock told her. "And they all tell the same story: Bon Tiempe was a madhouse that night. There were new people being trained in, a *saucier* got fired, several late deliveries were made."

"Your people checked on these deliveries?" asked Carmela.

"Sure did. As I recall, one was from Vincent's Wine Shop, another from Le Fleur; a florist shop, I'd guess. And the third was . . . ah, I'd have to check the case file."

"But nothing," said Carmela. "Nothing out of the ordinary."

"Oh, there's gotta be something," said Lieutenant Babcock. "Or, rather, some*one*. It's just that nobody's pinned him down yet."

"What about the murder weapon?" asked Carmela. It had, after all, been a kitchen knife. Which would seem to indicate a weapon of convenience, grabbed from a drawer or a knife rack in Bon Tiempe's sprawling kitchen.

"We're still looking at that," said Lieutenant Babcock.

Carmela debated telling Lieutenant Babcock about her trip down to Boothville yesterday. About the blue car that had seemed to follow them. And the nasty conk on the head she'd received. But she didn't want Lieutenant Babcock coming down hard on her. Telling her to stay the hell out of the investigation. She was too far in and wanted to see this through to the end. For her own sake as well as Gabby's and Wren's.

"Say," said Lieutenant Babcock, "your friend is still around, right?"

Carmela knew he was referring to Ava. "You mean Ava?"

"That's the one." A silence spun out. "Do you happen to know if she's seeing anyone?"

What to tell him? Ava dated a lot.

"I don't believe she's seeing any *one person* in particular," said Carmela. There. That answer was technically correct.

"Think she'd go out with me?" asked Lieutenant Babcock.

"Why don't you give her a call and find out?" said Carmela. And then, because she thought her answer might sound a trifle flip, she added: "I'm sure she'd love to go out with you."

"Okay, then," said Lieutenant Babcock. "Thanks."

"You'll let us know," said Carmela. "The minute you have something?"

"Count on it," Lieutenant Babcock assured her.

Hanging up the phone, Carmela stared down at the photos and fabric scraps that were sitting on her desk. All stuff to go into the Happy Halls scrapbook for Pamela and Dunbar DesLauriers. She didn't have much of a stomach for completing the scrapbook right now. But a promise was a promise and the Gilt Trip promotion *was* a fund raiser for the crisis nursery. So . . . she knew it was best to get on with things and focus on the end result, which was a very positive thing. And *not* worry about Margot Butler and her petty posturings. Or Pamela Dunbar and her delusions of grandeur. Still, it was difficult. And maddening, too.

Carmela's phone gave off a single ring and she snatched it up.

"Memory Mine. This is Carmela."

"Good morning," came a carefully modulated voice. "This is Ross Pitot at the Selby Pitot Funeral Home."

"Oh," said Carmela. She *really* wasn't expecting this call.

"Is Miss Wren West available?"

"She's here," said Carmela, "but she's with a customer." This time Wren really was with a customer.

"Perhaps I could call back," said Ross Pitot. "If there's a time . . ."

"This is about Jamie, right?" said Carmela. She paused. "Jamie Redmond. You handled the cremation?"

"That's correct," said Ross Pitot. "And you are . . ."

"I'm Carmela Bertrand. I'm a friend of Wren's. I know the police released Jamie's body a couple days ago, so I'm assuming you have since handled the . . . ah . . . cremation and that Jamie's ashes are ready to be picked up."

"Yes ma'am," said Ross Pitot in a somber voice. "That's exactly why I was calling. The cremains are ready for whatever final disposition Miss West has in mind."

Cremains. What a strange, made-up word, thought Carmela. *Almost clinical sounding. But very final, too.*

"Wren . . . Miss West . . . is still a little upset," said Carmela. "Obviously. But we will be by to pick up the . . . cremains." Carmela grimaced. "I assume there's no immediate rush?"

"Good heavens, no," Ross Pitot assured her. "No hurry at all. Mr. Redmond's cremains are really quite fine here. Tell Miss West to take her time. No problem."

"Thank you," said Carmela. "I'll relay that to her." *I just have to work up my nerve first.*

But Wren seemed to know.

"That was a call about Jamie, wasn't it?" she asked Carmela. Wren was pulling out sheets of sports-themed paper for Tandy and had a stack of photos on the table next to her. "I was going to work on that scrapbook about him," she explained to Carmela, indicating some of the photos of Jamie they'd found at his house. "Over the lunch hour."

"Do it now," said Carmela, suddenly flashing on the image she saw—or thought she saw—in her window last night. *My eyes were just playing tricks on me,* she told herself.

"Are you sure?" said Wren. Carmela didn't seem to be listening, so she said, "Carmela?"

Carmela suddenly snapped out of her strange reverie. "We're not particularly busy," she told Wren. "And you and Gabby did a phenomenal amount of straightening up yesterday, so . . . go ahead." She glanced at the stack of photos with the portrait of Jamie sitting on top. "We just got some new leatherette albums in. One of those might work nicely for what you've got in mind."

Wren gave her a shy smile. "Thank you. And hopefully you'll give me a few pointers, too." She paused. "That call *was* about Jamie, wasn't it? I kind of overheard some of it. I guess his ashes are ready."

Carmela nodded slowly. "You're right, they are. But the fellow at Selby Pitot said there was no hurry."

Wren chewed her lip. "I want to apologize for sending you and Ava on such a wild goose chase yesterday. For some reason, I was sure his parents were buried down in Boothville."

"Not a problem," said Carmela. "I'm just sorry Ava and I didn't find anything." Carmela surreptitiously rubbed the bump on the back of her head. She hadn't found anything, but trouble seemed to have found them.

"Well, if there's no hurry . . ." said Wren. Again Carmela had a strange faraway look in her eyes. But then she was smiling and back to her usual self.

"Don't worry," Carmela told her. "We'll find his parents' grave. It's only a matter of time."

"Good lord," said Tandy, sliding her red cheaters onto her bony nose. "You've completely covered that page with the most marvelous chintz fabric. I've never seen you do that before."

"That's because I've never done it before," admitted Carmela. "But this is one of the scrapbooks for Gilt Trip, so I really wanted to make a bold design statement."

"You certainly did," said Tandy. "In fact, the end result is pretty fabulous."

"Actually, this isn't quite finished," said Carmela. "I'm about ready to zip down the street to Gossamer & Grosgrain and borrow one of their sewing machines for a few minutes." Gossamer & Grosgrain was the premier fabric and needlecraft shop in the French Quarter. They specialized in elegant silks, damasks, organzas, and satins. And they carried an exemplary array of Venetian point lace and duchesse lace.

"You're going to stitch . . . what?" asked Tandy. Tandy was big on details. In fact, Tandy *demanded* details.

"The whole page," replied Carmela. "I want to create lines of stitchery that will outline each photo."

"Whoa," said Gabby, suddenly interested. "Neat idea. But I thought you weren't going to beat your brains out over this scrapbook. Especially since Margot strong-armed you."

"She didn't beat her brains out," spoke up Wren in a soft voice. "Carmela's pouring her heart into it. Big difference." She flashed a faint, almost triumphant smile at Tandy and Gabby. "Did you really think she wouldn't?"

"I guess not," said Gabby. "Carmela pretty much throws herself wholeheartedly into everything she does."

Don't I wish, thought Carmela. *Don't I wish.*

Chapter 19

THE proverbial bull in a china shop was posturing smack dab in the middle of Memory Mine when Carmela returned from her visit to Gossamer & Grosgrain.

Dunbar DesLauriers, arms akimbo and voice in the dangerous decibel range, had seemingly reduced Wren to tears. And Tandy, all skinny one hundred and seven pounds of her, was advancing on Dunbar like an avenging angel.

"What the hell is going on?" Carmela demanded at the top of her voice as she came flying through the front door. Her profane and thunderous approach was designed to startle Dunbar, not upset the others. Unfortunately, it seemed to have the reverse effect.

Dunbar shook his head and rolled his eyes upon seeing her. "Finally!" he cried in a petulant tone. "Someone with a little common *sense*."

Tandy continued to advance on Dunbar. "Shoo," she told him, flapping her skinny arms at him as though she were trying to oust a flock of disobedient chickens. "Get out. We don't want your kind around here. All you do is bring trouble!"

"Carmela!" demanded Dunbar. "Tell them it's a *business* deal. That it isn't personal, just business. It's the way things are *done*."

Where have I heard that before? Oh, yeah, in the movie. The Godfather. *And always right before they wacked some poor sucker.*

Dropping her newly stitched scrapbook pages onto the counter, Carmela approached the pleading Dunbar. "What are you talking about?" she asked. Then she glanced past Dunbar at Tandy, Gabby, and Wren and extended her hands in what she hoped was a calming gesture. "Let me sort this out," she told them.

"He's an *ass*hole," sniffed Tandy, retreating a few steps and savoring the impact of her words. Reveling in her succinct characterization of Dunbar, Tandy made her pronouncement again: "A total asshole."

"Carmela," pleaded Dunbar, obviously not used to

having women ridicule him to such an extent.

"Talk," Carmela ordered, once the three women had retreated all the way to the back craft table.

But Dunbar DesLauriers was still wound up and blustering mightily. "Business," he declared again. He shook his head and his jowls sloshed furiously. "Simply business," he repeated, but his voice resonated with heated anger.

"Why don't you tell me about this little business deal that's got everyone so worked up," said Carmela. A nasty feeling had taken root in the pit of her stomach, but Carmela wasn't about to show any weakness in front of Dunbar DesLauriers.

Never let 'em see you sweat.

Amazingly, she'd learned that valuable lesson from Shamus's sister, Glory.

"I assure you," said Dunbar, whipping out a piece of paper and smacking it down hard on the front counter, "this is all quite legal. All aboveboard."

It had been Carmela's experience that whenever someone went to great lengths to explain how legal and aboveboard something was, it meant they were set to screw you royally.

"What's this, Dunbar?" she asked, snatching up the document and scanning it. "Talk to me. Tell me what's going on."

"Glory sold me the paper," spat out Dunbar DesLauriers. He was fighting to stay in control now. Angry and completely pissed off, he seemed poised to strike, just like the proverbial scorpion.

225

"The paper on what?" demanded Carmela. The nasty feeling in her stomach was spreading way too fast for comfort.

"Twenty ten Julia Street," said Dunbar. He sounded angry but suddenly looked slyly pleased. Like an errant little boy who'd just pulled one off.

"On Wren's house," said Carmela. *Oh crap.*

"On the house Crescent City Bank *owned,*" said Dunbar. "If you recall, they held the title."

"And now you do," said Carmela. She was seething inside. This was just the kind of dirty, underhanded trick she expected from someone like Dunbar DesLauriers. "I'm sure you're very proud of yourself," she told him.

Dunbar chose to ignore Carmela's biting sarcasm. "I explained to Miss West that we could execute a simple trade," said Dunbar. "A business deal of sorts. The paper on her house for the contents of Biblios Booksellers." Dunbar paused and smiled then, looking all the world like a friendly but ravenous barracuda. "Once she has this paper," he added, "the residence is hers. Free and clear."

"Free and clear," said Carmela, the words almost catching in her throat. "Wrong, pal. Free and clear is when you do the deal *above*board."

"It *is* aboveboard," countered Dunbar.

"You are a despicable weasel," snapped Carmela. "So don't try to take the moral high ground with me. You couldn't just bide your time and maybe do this with a little grace and good faith? For goodness sakes, Wren might have even *sold* the bookstore to you if you'd let her do it in her own good time and of her own free will. But, no, you've got to come cowboying in here with your conniving ways and dirty tricks. It's probably more *fun* that way, though, isn't it?" Snatching up the piece of paper, Carmela crumpled it into a ball and hurled it at him. "Get out!" she ordered. "Tandy was right. You *are* an asshole."

A spattering of applause erupted from the back of the room as Carmela's ranting came to a rapid conclusion. Chest heaving, face slightly pink, she'd suddenly run out of words.

Dunbar DesLauriers bent swiftly and snatched up the crumpled paper from the floor. He thrust it toward her in a threatening gesture. "This is *legal,*" he hissed. "I can call this paper in tomorrow if I want to!"

"Get out!" ordered Carmela.

And with that, Dunbar DesLauriers spun on his heels and caromed out the front door.

"I'm cooked," said Wren. "Now I don't have any choice." She sat at the table, looking dazed. Gabby and Tandy sat on either side of her, looking supportively morose.

"You're not cooked," said Carmela, still trying to catch her breath after her retaliatory outburst. She was striding around the store, trying to dispel the jittery feeling that had built up inside her from too much adrenaline. Way too much adrenaline. *That's my second hit in the span of twenty-four hours,* she told herself. *Sure hope I don't go into cardiac arrest or something.*

"What if Dunbar wants to call in the loan?" asked Wren, looking dispirited.

"I don't know how much you guys know about real estate foreclosures," said Carmela, "but I used to listen to Shamus endlessly grump and groan about foreclosures. And from the way he carried on about the unfairness of the process, I know it takes a good two or three months. Minimum."

Wren looked up hopefully. "Really? You're sure?"

Carmela nodded. "Yup. And that's after going to court. If you can even get a court date."

"That sounds *good*," quipped Tandy. "Buys her some time."

"Carmela's right," said Gabby. "Dunbar DesLauriers is a fool and a blowhard. Stuart held a CD on some property and when the tenants didn't make the payments, it took him forever to get it back. Almost six months, I think."

"Six months is even better," said Tandy. She patted Wren's hand. "See, sweetie, you've got plenty of time."

"So what were his histrionics really about?" asked Wren. "Was he just trying to *scare* me?"

"Probably," said Carmela. "Dunbar's a bully, clear and simple. And it's been my experience that bullies always lead with threats and tough talk."

"So what do we do now?" asked Gabby.

Carmela thought for a minute. "Why not call Dunbar's bluff?"

"How on earth can we do that?" asked Wren.

"Well," said Carmela, hastily working through her plan, "why don't you tell him you're going to finalize an inventory list. Make it sound very business-like, but also give him the impression we're knuckling under a bit."

"And our real agenda is . . . what?" asked Gabby.

"We'll ask Jekyl Hardy to do an appraisal on the more-collectible books," said Carmela. "Or, if he can't do it himself, he can recommend one of his friends who's a licensed appraiser."

"Okay," said Wren. "Then what?"

"Not sure," said Carmela. "Maybe you'll end up selling to him after all. Or maybe, in the process of putting a value on the business, you'll be able to walk into another bank and qualify for a mortgage on the house."

"Or a bridge loan for the business," suggested Gabby.

Wren sat quietly for a few moments, then a smile began to spread across her face. "You're right, Carmela," she said quietly. "Business can be fun."

"And it's especially fun," said Carmela, "when you're able to make a tasty profit or hopscotch the other guy!"

Another lesson learned from Glory, thought Carmela. And then she decided that there was no way Glory was going to get away scot-free in all of this.

No way. Glory played a major role in this little fiasco. Her business ethics are cheesy and underhanded at best. She sold the paper on Wren's house to Dunbar DesLauriers, and now she's going to pay the price.

"Carmela," said Gabby, "Quigg Brevard is on the phone."

"Mmn," said Carmela, darting into her office to take his call.

"Hey gorgeous," said Quigg when she picked up the phone. "Whatcha doing tonight?"

All thoughts of staying late to work on the Gilt Trip scrapbook flew out of Carmela's head at the sound of Quigg's voice. Here was a charming, interesting man who sounded like he actually wanted the pleasure of her company. On the other hand, she didn't want to sound *too* anxious.

"I've got some work to finish up," she told him.

"Survey says . . . *wrong*," answered Quigg. "I've got some Chilean sea bass that has your name on it."

"Imagine that," said Carmela. "All the way from Chile. And with my name on it."

"Dinner's at seven," Quigg told her. "And if you're really good, I'll pop the cork on a bottle of Laetitia Pinot Noir."

"How can I say no," said Carmela. *Besides, this gives me one more chance to snoop around Bon Tiempe. I don't expect to find any hot clues, but you never know. It's worth a shot.*

Chapter 20

WHAT the . . . ?"
Carmela's first thought when she walked into her apartment was that someone had ransacked the place. Broken in and scattered all the photos and papers she'd laid out so carefully last night.

Then she saw the tiny snippet of paper caught in Poobah's whisker.

Poobah. Oh no. I never pegged you for a chewer.

"Did you do this?" Carmela asked the little dog sharply. Poobah's tail thumped the floor even as his shoulders slumped and he looked evasively away.

"You're a very naughty dog," Carmela told him. Crouching down, she gathered up the mangled remains of the photos and shredded documents. She'd read somewhere that you were never supposed to reprimand a dog after the fact. That they weren't smart enough to put two and two together.

Yeah right. Then why is it dogs universally remember where the treats are kept, how to spell O-U-T, W-A-L-K, and about a hundred other words? And know precisely when you're going to walk through the door? Cripes, most dogs possess the I.Q. of a fourth grader.

"We're going to take you back to Shamus," Carmela told Poobah. "The nice man who found you. Because the cardinal rule around here is never, ever touch the papers and photos." She put her hands on her hips and

continued to lecture Poobah, who really did look peni-
tent. "You see, pal, I'm in the scrapbooking business.
And we really can't have you undermining any of my
handiwork. You understand?"

Poobah rolled his eyes nervously, as if to say *I didn't
mean to screw up so badly.* Boo, sensing this was a piv-
otal moment in canine commiseration, moved in to
make her appeal. Eyes bright, paws dancing, Boo
pranced in a tight circle around Carmela.

"Sorry, Boo, that's not going to work either. I'm
gonna feed you guys, then take a quick shower and
change clothes. While I do that, you two say your
doggy farewell's to each other, because Poobah's
going back with Shamus tonight. Shamus is in
banking, and they don't look as unkindly upon
shredded documents as I do."

I'm also gonna kill two birds with one stone,
Carmela decided. *When I swing by the Garden District
to drop Poobah off, I can say my piece to Glory
Meechum. Hoo yeah.*

Carmela nodded to herself, resolute in her mission.
Then she dashed off to dig in her closet for the perfect
pair of strappy sandals to go with her new black crepe
dress.

Six o'clock in the Garden District was a magical time
of night. Gaslights silhouetted stately oaks, and enormous Victorian, Greek-Revival, and French Gothic
homes glowed from within. High-ceilinged dining
rooms, quiet during the day, suddenly came to life

when candles were lit and crystal and silver laid out on damask linen.

Shamus's family had lived in the Garden District for well over fifty years, with various and sundry relatives occupying different homes. Carmela had, of course, lived here with Shamus until they'd split and Glory had driven her out. That former home was now occupied by a Meechum cousin, some poor unfortunate who'd been conscripted and was probably being groomed for an entry-level slot at one of the banks.

Carmela stood on Glory's wide, graceful verandah and pounded on the front door.

She'd already tried the doorbell three times and got no answer. Probably, Carmela decided, Glory was busy doing a little post-workday touch-up with the vacuum cleaner. Glory's diagnosis of a mild case of OCD meant she was forever cleaning, polishing, nit-picking, and, in general, searching for fly-specks in the pepper.

Suddenly, much to Carmela's surprise, the door flew open and there stood Glory, looking frumpy and frowsled in a splotchy print housedress. "Carmela." She frowned. "What are *you* doing here?"

"Hey there, Glory," said Carmela in hale-hearty greeting. She figured she'd start with a friendly opener, then move in for the kill once she'd gained entrance to Glory's inner sanctum.

But Glory was a tough nut to crack. For one thing, she'd noticed the dog hunkered down at Carmela's side.

"What's that?" she demanded.

"Dog," said Carmela. "Canine."

"You can't bring a dog in here!"

"Sure I can," said Carmela, struggling to maintain her upbeat, semi-friendly ruse. "In fact, it's Shamus's dog."

Glory suddenly looked stunned. "Shamus bought a dog?" The notion seemed inconceivable to her. "He'd never do that! He knows I deplore dog hair and dander. Makes me sneeze and go all itchy."

"Actually," said Carmela, beginning to relish the conversation, "Shamus *found* this dog. It was a stray."

"He *found* a dog?" muttered Glory. She gazed in unabashed horror at the little brown and white mutt at Carmela's side, as though he might be a carrier of the deadly Ebola virus.

"Can we come in?" asked Carmela, brushing past her.

"Absolutely not. Stay right where you are!" ordered Glory. But Carmela breezed on into the living room, definitely inner sanctum territory, then turned to confront Glory. Carmela didn't look quite so friendly now, and Glory, sensing conflict might be imminent, crossed her flabby arms across her broad chest.

"Thanks a lot for selling that mortgage paper to Dunbar," began Carmela. "Your little business deal really helped things along." Her voice dripped with sarcasm.

"It was perfectly legal," snorted Glory. "Standard business practice."

"No, Glory, it was perfectly awful," Carmela fired

back. "Wren's fiancé was murdered and all you can think about is keeping Dunbar DesLauriers fat and happy. I know customer loyalty and customer relationship management are hot buttons in business today, but I'm not sure your little stunt was the best way to put those principles into practice."

"It's a free country," said Glory. But her words didn't carry their normal dose of venom. Glory was clearly uncomfortable with Poobah in her house. She squirmed, flinched, and one eye seemed to be bouncing around all on its own.

"Right," said Carmela slowly. She knew the "free country" defense was another one of those lame, dumb-ass excuses that really meant *I'm gonna do whatever I want and you can't stop me.*

"Carmela. Glory. What the heck's going on?" Shamus was suddenly in the room with them.

Glory looked relieved. As though reinforcements had arrived just in the nick of time. "Good. You're home," said Glory, edging toward Shamus.

"I brought your dog," Carmela told Shamus.

Looking suddenly uncomfortable, Shamus chose to ignore both of them and focus on Poobah. "Hi, pup," he said, bending down to gently scratch behind the dog's ears.

"Are we quite finished?" asked Glory. She stared belligerently at Carmela. "Because I for one have better things to do than stand around listening to you belly-ache about business that doesn't concern you."

"Don't talk to Carmela like that," said Shamus.

"She's still my wife."

"*Humph,*" said Glory, scratching at her neck. "Not for long. If you two don't get divorce proceedings rolling, I'm going to step in and put one of my own lawyers to work. It's high time you . . ."

"Stay out of it," snapped Carmela.

"She's right," said Shamus. "We'll deal with it ourselves."

"In our own sweet time," said Carmela. *Good lord, what am I saying? Our own sweet time? Hasn't this thing dragged on long enough?*

"Mother of pearl!" thundered Glory.

Startled, both Carmela and Shamus jumped at the sound of her strident voice.

"What?" asked Shamus.

Eyes bugged out, looking completely aghast, Glory was leaning forward, pointing to a wet spot on the carpet. "Look! That hideous animal Carmela dragged in here has had an accident! In my *house!*"

"I don't think so, Glory," began Shamus. "Gus was in here earlier watering plants." Gus was Glory's gardener.

"Gus doesn't spill," spat Glory, itching furiously now. "He's not *allowed* to spill."

With a look of panic on his face, Shamus was suddenly back-pedaling like mad. "For cripe sakes, Glory, it's not that big a deal. The dog simply had an accident. A little tinky-poo on the carpet's not going to hurt anything."

Carmela stared at Shamus in utter amazement. First

of all, she'd never seen him this panicked, except for the few minutes right before their wedding ceremony. And second, and possibly most startling of all, she'd never ever heard Shamus spout baby talk before. It was extremely odd. And more than a little unnerving. Was this what she had to look forward to if they ever decided to grow old together? Shamus talking about his drinky-winky or his lunchy-munchy? It would be like being forced to endlessly watch the Teletubbies.

But Glory wasn't about to be put off by Shamus's suddenly regressive choice of words. "This carpet will have to be replaced," she barked. "It's probably soaked clear through to the foam padding."

"You might have to rip up the floorboards, too," Carmela added helpfully. "Or, at the very least, disinfect them."

Shamus threw her a disparaging glance. "Thanks a *lot!*"

"Don't mention it," Carmela told him sweetly. She was pleased to see that Glory seemed to have developed a full-fledged rash on her neck.

"Take your dog outside now!" Glory commanded Carmela.

"Sorry, but he's not my dog." Carmela tried to hand the leash off to Shamus, but he stood there stubbornly, hands held firmly at his sides.

"Sure he is," whined Shamus. "Poobah's *your* dog. You've been taking care of him."

"Nice try," said Carmela, now finding herself in a face-off with Shamus. "Your mewling and puling might have worked on me once, but not a second time. I'm immune, Shamus. I've found the antitoxin."

"Shamus!" snapped Glory. "If it's your animal, take the damn thing outside!" She pushed out her lower lip and glowered at Shamus like *he* was the one who'd wet the carpet.

Carmela fought to control her glee. Dealing with Glory was a lot more fun when she wasn't on the receiving end of that razor-sharp tongue.

Shamus grabbed the leash from Carmela's hands and headed for the door, Carmela following on his heels. They steamrolled through the doorway together like they were beginning some grand adventure. But Shamus wasn't finished with his petty grumblings.

"You've got to take Poobah home with you," he pleaded, once they hit the front porch.

"No can do," countered Carmela.

"Pleeease," said Shamus.

"Put a lid on it, will you?" snapped Carmela. She gazed down at Poobah, who was looking a little dazed and confused. *They weren't all going for a walk together? He had to stay in this strange house with the scary lady?*

"Look," said Carmela, "Poobah's a terrific little dog, okay? Maybe, if things were different, I could keep him. But . . . well, it's just not going to work out."

"If things were different," said Shamus, pouncing on her words. "What things?"

"Oh, I don't know," murmured Carmela. "Bigger

238

house, a fenced-in yard . . . just things."

"Us?" Shamus asked sharply. He was grasping Poobah's leash like it were a life line.

"Maybe," said Carmela. She was suddenly cautious about the direction this conversation was taking her. *Proceed carefully,* she told herself. *This is dangerous ground.*

"You know I love you," blurted out Shamus. "I always have."

Carmela felt like her head was spinning. Like she was imprisoned on a runaway tilt-a-whirl and the ride operator had wandered off somewhere. To have a smoke, or maybe never come back.

"Shamus, telling me you love me is not going to motivate me to keep Poobah." Carmela's words came out harsher than she'd intended and she inwardly cringed. *Great. Lash out and really hit the guy when he's down. Way to go.*

Shamus was peering at her closely now. "Are you going on a date tonight or something?" He'd obviously just noticed her black crepe dress.

"Why do you ask?" *Damn. I thought if I tossed this ratty old sweater on over it he wouldn't notice.*

"You're all dressed up," he said, his tone verging on accusatory. "Your hair looks really cute. And you're wearing makeup. Eye liner."

The one night Shamus suddenly decides to talk about us, I'm heading off to see another man. Could our timing be any more bizarre? Is this not the story of our entire life together?

Pulling her sweater tightly around her shoulders, Carmela stood on tiptoes and gave Shamus a kiss on his cheek. His skin felt smooth and cool and smelled faintly of spicy after-shave. "Good night, Shamus," she told him. "Good luck with Poobah."

Chapter 21

Q UIGG Brevard caught both of Carmela's hands in his as he greeted her at the front door. She'd left the ratty sweater in the car and freshened her lipstick, seeing as how it seemed to have worked its way off during her altercation with Glory.

"You look ravishing," Quigg growled. Snazzily turned out in a dark-blue suit with a starched white shirt and Chinese red tie, his fashion choice was highly complementary to his dark hair and olive complexion. It also served to make him look a little more handsome, a little more dangerous.

Carmela did what any normal woman would do under the circumstances. She blushed and stammered out a *thank you*.

"No, I mean it," Quigg told her, slipping an arm about her waist. "Your skin is glowing, your hair looks incredibly blond and fantastic, and I love the dramatic eye makeup."

What's with the comments about makeup? wondered Carmela. *First from Shamus and now Quigg. Do I normally not wear enough makeup? And here I thought I was single-handedly supporting the Chanel and Estee Lauder counters at Saks.*

"Thank you," Carmela murmured again. Quigg's compliments were a far cry from Shamus's almost accusatory remarks about her makeup and hair. But could she really buy into Mr. Oh-so-polished-restaurateur's words? Ah, that was the sixty-four-thousand-dollar question. Quigg Brevard talked a great game and fairly oozed charm, but was he really a one-woman, settling-down kind of guy? Maybe. Or maybe not. Carmela wasn't so sure she wanted to lay her beating heart out there on a silver platter to find out. Been there, done that, as they say. This time, if there was a *this time,* she was determined to proceed with extreme caution.

"This cozy spot right over here," said Quigg, as he hustled Carmela across the dining room, "has been reserved exclusively for *us.*"

A table for two, set with white linen, gold chargers, and a virtual hedge of red roses, sat right in front of the marble fireplace and the crackling fire that burned within. The coziest and very best seat in the house. The table that was *the* focal point of the restaurant. Where you could see everyone and they could see you.

Gulp, thought Carmela.

But slipping into her chair, she still couldn't help but be charmed. "You're sure this is just an impromptu little dinner?" Carmela asked him. It sure looked like Quigg had gone out of his way.

"Absolutely," he replied, flashing her a wicked grin.

"Worst table in the house. Can't give the darn thing away."

A waiter hustled over to fill Carmela's water glass, gently drape a damask napkin across her lap, deposit a basket of fresh-baked rolls and honey butter at her fingertips, and, in general, fuss over her.

"We'll start with the carpachio, Gerald," Quigg told him. "And bring the wine right away."

"Very good, sir," replied the waiter.

"No menu tonight," said Carmela. "You must have dinner all figured out."

"We can get you a menu if you prefer," Quigg told her. "But, as I mentioned on the phone, we have some superlative Chilean sea bass fillets that the chef is going to prepare with a barbecue glaze and side of mango salsa."

Carmela shook her head as she suddenly felt faint hunger pangs in her tummy. "Sounds heavenly." She sank back in her sumptuously upholstered chair, watching as Quigg and Gerald went through the wine ritual. Gerald opening and pouring, Quigg sniffing and swirling the contents of his glass.

One of the delights of seeing Quigg was that Carmela *didn't* have to order off the menu. He almost always had a spectacular dinner lined up. Sometimes he surprised her with an exotic appetizer of quail's eggs or *foie gras*. Sometimes it was as simple and basic as sliced beefsteak tomatoes with a slice of fresh mozzarella and drizzle of balsamic vinegar.

"The restaurant's packed tonight," she told him.

Indeed, every table in Bon Tiempe seemed to be occupied, and Carmela could see a line forming at the front door. Late arrivals waiting for a table or hopefuls praying for a cancellation.

Quigg shrugged. "It's been this way for the past week. Absolutely jam-packed."

"More curiosity seekers?" asked Carmela.

A dark eyebrow shot up. "I prefer to think my menu is the major draw," said Quigg. "But . . . yes, I think so." And then, because Quigg could tell that Carmela really wanted to talk about Jamie's tragic murder, he added: "Curiosity seekers. And amateur investigators, too."

She took a quick sip of wine, put her crystal goblet down. "What you really meant was amateur investigators like me."

Quigg grinned. "You try to look so innocent, but I know you can't resist getting involved."

Carmela's cheeks suddenly flushed with color. "We've all been pretty stunned by this," she told Quigg.

"By *we* you mean your little circle of scrapbookers," said Quigg.

"Well, yes," replied Carmela. "But most especially Wren and Gabby."

"I can't tell you how many times the police have been back here," said Quigg. "The detectives interviewed absolutely everyone who was here that night. Kitchen help, wait staff . . ."

"And nothing?" said Carmela.

Quigg gave a small shrug. "Apparently not. You've been in contact with the police, too. What do they say?"

"They're baffled."

Carmela hesitated as the waiter set small plates of carpachio in front of each of them. After he left, she continued.

"You trust all your employees?" she asked Quigg.

Quigg gave a rueful smile. "Hardly," he said. "Then again, I can't say I know them personally. I'm more concerned with their ability to whip up a French remoulade sauce, green tomato relish, or a pan of pecan biscuits than I am with their personal ethics, so I really only know the faces they present here. But lots of people do lead double lives."

"I know they do," she answered. *Case in point: Jamie Redmond seems to have led a bit of a double life himself.*

"How do you like the wine?" asked Quigg. "It's Laetitia Pinot Noir Estate."

"Absolutely superb," Carmela told him.

They were well through their Chilean sea bass and mango salsa before Quigg circled back to the subject of Jamie's murder.

"Do you still believe Jamie Redmond was trying to scrawl some sort of final message before he died?" Quigg asked her.

Carmela looked pensive. "Don't know," she told him.

"You sure thought so that night," said Quigg. "At least that's what you and Ava were chattering about."

"I know," said Carmela. "But the police pretty much blew that idea out of the water. So I guess I'm not convinced, either."

"It did seem a little far-fetched," allowed Quigg.

"Do you think . . ." Carmela began, then cleared her throat. "Do you think I could have a word with some of the people who were working in the kitchen that night?"

Quigg set his fork down and reached across the table to take her hand. "Carmela, the police really are doing their best. I think your heart is in the absolute right place, but there comes a time when you just have to trust people."

"You're right. I know." She extricated her hand gently, picked up her wine glass, took another sip. *Trusting people isn't something I've had a lot of luck with.*

"And while we're on the subject of hearts and trust," said Quigg, "I'd like to say a little something about us."

Carmela almost choked on her wine. *Us? Uh-oh, where is he going with this?*

"I'd like to see you, Carmela," began Quigg. "And I mean more than just an occasional dinner here at the restaurant. And more than just socially."

"Uh huh," she said, knowing she probably sounded like a supreme idiot. But Quigg's words had come out of left field, raining down on her like errant meteorites. *He wants to see me more. A lot more. I suppose it was coming, but it still feels like a bit of a shocker!*

Quigg continued to stare at her with great intensity. Until he lobbed the final bombshell. "But you're *married,* Carmela."

"Oh," she said. "That."

"Yes, that," said Quigg. He leaned forward, his voice dropping to a conspiratorial pitch. "Honey, this may be the Big Easy, but the flipside is that New Orleans is very much a God-fearing, church goin' city. In other words, people will eventually start to talk."

And disapprove, she thought. *People love to find something they can disapprove of. It always seems to warm their little hearts.*

Quigg suddenly looked puzzled. "You're getting that weird look on your face," he told her.

"Look? What look?" Carmela asked, innocently. Shamus always told her she got a petulant, mischievous look on her face whenever she was trying to worm her way out of something. He called it her petchevious look.

"It's a look that clearly broadcasts, *I don't give a damn,*" said Quigg. "But I can tell you right now, you should give a damn. Because *I* give a damn, Carmela. So I need to know, are you planning to get a divorce from Shamus Meechum or not?"

There it was. Out on the table. Right alongside the leftover sea bass, spatters of mango salsa, and the empty wine bottle.

Quigg wants to know if I'm getting a divorce, thought Carmela. *And isn't that a good question? I always assumed I was, but I just never seem to get around to the mechanics of it. So what does that really mean? That I'm purposely sabotaging my own divorce? That would make me a complete fruitcake.*

"This silence is lasting way too long for comfort," Quigg said finally.

"Sorry," said Carmela. "Really."

The busboy arrived suddenly to clear away dishes, and they sat quietly, sipping wine, gazing into the fire.

Now we look like we're married, thought Carmela. *Glum looks, zero communication. Isn't this great.*

Once the dishes had been whisked away, Gerald appeared at their table, carrying an enormous dessert tray. He tipped it down for Carmela to inspect, then he carefully and lovingly detailed each small plate filled with lemon truffle, fruit-topped brioche, bread pudding, praline pie, almond cake, and chocolate *gateau.*

The City That Care Forgot never forgets to eat dessert, thought Carmela.

"Have you made a choice yet?" Quigg asked her. His dark eyes stared intently at her across the sugary expanse of the dessert tray.

"No," Carmela told him. "But I will."

Chapter 22

Y OU'RE not coming in this morning?" said Gabby. "That means I'll be here all alone."

"Where's Wren?" asked Carmela. She was trying to watch the road, shift from second gear into third, juggle her cell phone, and navigate Prytania Street all at the same time.

"She went over to the bookstore," Gabby told her. "Apparently you talked to Jekyl Hardy about doing some sort of appraisal on those rare books?"

"I left a message on his answering machine last night," replied Carmela. "I never did talk to him."

"Well, Jekyl called here about twenty minutes ago and told Wren that if she could meet him at Biblios right away he could start on the appraisal. Apparently he had some free time."

"That's terrific," said Carmela. She pulled over to the curb, scanning the homes, reading house numbers.

"Carmela?" said Gabby. "You still there?"

"Sorry," said Carmela. "I'm bumbling around the Garden District trying to do six things at once."

"So you'll be in later?" asked Gabby.

"Yeah, but probably not until late morning. For some bizarre reason known only to myself, I promised Margot Butler I'd take a few more photos of the DesLauriers' newly decorated dining room," said Carmela.

"Ouch," said Gabby. "I guess you volunteered *before* Dunbar bought the paper on Wren's home and tried to call in the loan."

"You got that right," said Carmela.

"I take it you're there now? Traipsing about on eggshells?"

"Not quite," said Carmela. "I'm actually parked at the curb, staring at Casa DesLauriers."

"I thought they called it Happy Halls," chuckled Gabby.

"Please don't remind me," said Carmela.

"What are you going to do if Dunbar's home?" asked Gabby.

"Not sure," said Carmela. "Kick him in the shins? Toss sand in his face? I don't know, I haven't thought it through yet." *So what's new? I don't think a lot of things through.*

"You said Dunbar was just a big bully," said Gabby, "so maybe he got wind you were coming and took off. He's probably long gone."

"Let's hope so," said Carmela. "Facing Pamela DesLauriers is bad enough!"

But Pamela DesLauriers, dressed rather strangely in a salmon-colored harem pants outfit and dripping with pearls, couldn't have been sweeter as she greeted Carmela at the door of her palatial home.

"Carmela," purred Pamela. "Welcome. I've been so looking forward to your little visit."

You have, really? Then you're the only one. "Sorry I'm a little late. Is Margot here?"

"In the dining room working on a few finishing touches," said Pamela, rolling her eyes expressively. "What an amazing *artiste* that woman is. Always searching for the very best in color and form."

"Uh huh," said Carmela, deciding Pamela *had* to be quoting from Margot's brochure. Nobody really talked like that, did they?

The DesLauriers house was as spectacularly palatial on the inside as it was on the outside. But even though it was expensively furnished, the interior lacked a certain warmth.

It's got that direct-from-the-showroom feel, thought Carmela as she followed Pamela, lugging her scrapbooks, camera gear, and handbag, feeling like an overburdened pack animal. *It's like the furniture movers wheeled in a shitload of stuff, set it down, then took off. Nothing's technically incorrect, but the home just doesn't exude that genteel lived-in feel.*

"Here's our Carmela," announced Pamela in a sing-song voice as they arrived at the doorway to her newly refurbished dining room. Coming to an abrupt stop, Pamela cupped both hands together in front of her, then asked in a chirpy voice: "Would you like a cup of coffee? Or small pot of tea?"

"Tea would be nice," murmured Carmela.

"Hey there, Carmela," called Margot, hearing Pamela's announcement, but not bothering to turn around. Margot seemed agitated and lost in thought as she strode to and fro, pondering the placement of a pair of rococo-looking wall sconces that two of her assistants were struggling to hold up. "No, that's way too high," she finally told them. "Slide them down a bit. Everything must feel *accessible.*" Margot whirled and threw Carmela a bright smile. "You brought the Lonsdale scrapbook? Showcasing the music room?"

"I did," said Carmela, setting all her gear on the

250

dining room table. "It's all finished." Fact was, Carmela had put a final hour in on the scrapbook last night when she arrived home from Bon Tiempe. Now if she could just get *this* one finished.

Margot immediately grabbed the scrapbook from Carmela and squinted at the cover. "Love it," she declared, then began to page through it. "Good. Good. Good. Perfect," was her verdict. Snapping the scrapbook shut, Margot flashed Carmela another winning smile. "As you can see, we made a few last minute *changes* in the room."

Carmela glanced about. The dining room didn't look all that different from the original photos Pamela had delivered to her. "You sure have," said Carmela, pulling open her camera bag to grab her digital Nikon. "Everything looks great."

"For your first shot," said Margot, "the draperies. You see that lobed medallion design? It was inspired by an Italian Renaissance fabric."

"All righty," said Carmela, snapping away.

"Now step back and get a wide shot," commanded Margot, running a hand across the edge of the dining table. "This table is yew wood. Very rare."

They continued on like that, Margot pointing and explaining the *provenance* of every bit of furnishing, Carmela snapping away.

Once Margot's assistants got the wall sconces screwed firmly in, Carmela took a shot of those, too.

"I talked Carriage House Lighting into donating them," Margot told her in a conspiratorial whisper. "In exchange for being mentioned in the Gilt Trip scrapbook."

"How exactly will the scrapbooks be displayed?" asked Carmela.

"We'll put up the usual velvet ropes and lay down heavy rubber mats to shepherd in visitors," explained Margot. "And then at the end of the tour, we'll have a table set up with the scrapbook and all the brochures and sales sheets from the various vendors. That way, if anyone falls in love with draperies or carpets or wall coverings, they'll know exactly where to get them for their house."

"Gilt Trip isn't a bad way for you to troll for new business, either," remarked Carmela.

Margot gave a slow wink. "That's for sure."

When Carmela was finished taking pictures, Pamela suddenly appeared, a friendly wraith in harem pants. Somewhere along the line, though, the clanking pearls had disappeared.

"Would you like to see the rest of the house?" Pamela asked Carmela.

"That'd be great," Carmela told her. *I thought you'd never ask.*

Turned out, Dunbar *was* a serious book collector. While the living room was a testament to chintz and prints, the library was very clubby, with Oriental carpets, leather chairs, and wall-to-wall books.

"This is a great library," said Carmela, meaning it.

"Oh, silly old Dunbar and his precious books," said

Pamela, waving a hand. "He does so love to collect them."

"Looks like he has a fair amount of first editions," said Carmela scanning the shelves.

"I think he's got his heart set on acquiring quite a few more," said Pamela, giving her a meaningful gaze.

"You know, Pamela," said Carmela, "Dunbar is being awfully pushy about acquiring Biblios Booksellers."

"Honey, that's just Dunbar's way," replied Pamela. "He's just a hardheaded good old boy. He certainly doesn't mean to *offend.*"

"He's not exactly being subtle," said Carmela. "I know what he's doing is considered legal and aboveboard and just business. I've heard all the arguments. But he's just not being very honorable."

Pamela looked almost hurt. "Why on earth would anyone want to run a dusty old bookstore like that anyway? Especially when Dunbar is offering such a great deal."

A great deal, thought Carmela. *That's exactly what John Law, the Scottish financier, told thousands of wealthy Frenchmen as he was bilking them out of their money. His was the very first "swampland deal" in America. And it originated right here in Louisiana. Now Dunbar DesLauriers was doing his best to carry on a proud tradition. Wonderful!*

Chapter 23

W E were just about to order out for salads," called Baby as Carmela came flying through the front door of Memory Mine.

"Turkey and baby field greens for me," answered Carmela. "With citrus dressing."

"Got it," said Gabby, who stood poised with pencil and pad.

"Anybody else coming in?" asked Carmela as she dumped her gear on the front counter. "I mean of the regulars?"

"Tandy might drop by later," said Baby. "I think she wants to work on another bibelot box." She laughed. "Tandy's mad for those little things."

"They are pretty neat," admitted Carmela. She grabbed her purse and dug inside for her little Nikon. "I take it Wren's still at the bookstore?"

Gabby nodded. "Yup. She seemed excited, and I think it's good for her mental health to sort through all that stuff."

"It's also good business," said Carmela. "Now she'll know exactly what she has and be able to put a real value on the inventory."

"You're such a smart lady," said Baby. "Always thinking in terms of dollars and cents. Oh," she exclaimed, "what an adorable little camera."

"Isn't it slick?" said Carmela, holding it up.

"Where were you taking pictures?" asked Baby.

Carmela made a face. "Pamela DesLauriers's new dining room."

"Oh you poor thing," laughed Baby. "How'd it go? Is Pamela's house as underwhelming as I've heard?"

"It's not *terrible*," said Carmela slowly. "But it does have that mannered decorator feel. Like every little *tchochke* was placed just so. And her living room definitely looks like a chintz-and-prints factory exploded."

Baby gave a mock shudder.

"Was Dunbar there?" asked Gabby. She'd just phoned in their lunch orders and her ears perked up at Carmela and Baby's conversation.

"No physical sign of Dunbar," said Carmela. "But he was certainly present in spirit."

"I take it Pamela was acting as his little mouthpiece," said Gabby.

"You might say that," said Carmela. "She's under the impression that Dunbar is going out of his way to offer Wren a fantastic deal."

"But you don't think he is," said Baby. "You think he pitched her a lowball number."

Carmela shrugged. "To be honest, I have no earthly idea what constitutes a fair price. Which is why it's a good thing Wren and Jekyl are huddling at the bookstore today."

"She's been working on a scrapbook about Jamie," spoke up Gabby. Her eyes turned suddenly sad as she stared across the table at the neat little stack of photos Wren had left sitting there.

Baby followed Gabby's gaze. "Such a sweet girl," she murmured. "To tackle such a sad project."

By two o'clock, Carmela finally had a handle on the DesLauriers's Gilt Trip scrapbook. She'd sorted through her digital photos, selected a dozen or so, used Photoshop to do some judicious digital retouching, then printed her photos out on four-by-six and six-by-ten glossy photo paper.

"Too bad we're not getting paid for this," said Gabby, looking over her shoulder.

"Mn hm," said Carmela. She received lots of requests these days to design and create what they now referred to as "commercial" scrapbooks. She'd just designed one for a high-test realtor to showcase all the exceptional properties he'd sold in the past year. And she'd also created a really nifty smaller-sized scrapbook for a woman who guided walking tours through the French Quarter. That scrapbook had been almost collage-like in concept, with photos interspersed between short, fun quotes from satisfied clients.

"Hey, are you still going to design that Mumbo Gumbo menu?" Gabby asked. "For your friend, Quigg?"

Gabby's innocent question seemed to suddenly paralyze Carmela's brain.

My friend Quigg. Is that what he is? A friend? This man who wants to see me more than just socially. Who wants a commitment of sorts. Or, to put it more bluntly, a non-commitment on my part with Shamus.

What am I going to tell Shamus? What does my heart tell me?

No crystal ball, Magic Eight Ball, or tarot cards hold the answer. I'm going to have to figure that out by myself.

Carmela forced herself to tune in to Gabby, who was going on about an idea she had for Mumbo Gumbo's menu. Something about a five-panel booklet that opened up and a cover adorned with embellishments from Ava's voodoo shop.

"Anyway," said Gabby, "what do you think?"

Carmela, embarassed that she had no earthly idea what Gabby had been talking about, said, "I think you're on to something."

"Really?" said Gabby, sounding pleased. "Thanks."

"Hey, you two," called Tandy, who'd shown up about an hour ago. "Get out here and tell me if silver embossing ink is going to work on this gray frosted vellum."

"Yes," said Baby in a mock pout. "It isn't any fun hanging around here if you two are going to huddle in that little office all afternoon."

Grinning, firmly back in the here and now, Carmela carried her photos out to the craft table. "Sorry," she told them, although she knew they weren't really upset.

"Good heavens," exclaimed Tandy when she saw the photos of the DesLauriers's dining room. "Don't you have that last Gilt Trip scrapbook done yet?"

"Tandy!" said Baby, a cautionary note in her voice.

"Carmela's been ferociously *busy*."

"She sure has," added Gabby.

Tandy looked contrite. "My apologies, sweetie. I didn't mean to insinuate you were lazy. I just assumed you'd off-loaded that project by now."

"Tonight," sighed Carmela, spreading out a number of twelve-by-twelve sheets of creamy yellow-beige paper that had a Tuscan motif border. "I'm gonna whip through this baby and then Margot Butler's going to stop by here around five o'clock to pick it up. Then my last Gilt Trip scrapbook will be off-loaded, as you so elegantly put it!"

"Hey ya'll," called Ava as she popped through the back door. Carmela had given Ava a key so she could cut down the back alley.

In unison, Baby, Tandy, and Gabby sang out hearty hellos.

"What are *you* doing here?" asked Carmela. "I thought you had forty cases of saint candles to unpack!" Saint candles were tall jar candles with colorful images of saints either painted on the glass or printed on paper that was wrapped around the glass. They were popular items in French Quarter gift shops.

"Hey," said Ava. "We're workin' our way through the alphabet. Saint Anthony, Saint Bridget, Saint Cecilia . . . well, you get the idea."

"Be sure to save me a Saint Joseph," said Gabby, as she ducked into the office to answer the ringing phone.

"Hey, Ava," said Tandy. "Are you still dating that head chef?"

"You mean Chef Ricardo?" asked Ava.

"That's the one," said Tandy. "He works at Bon Tiempe, right? He should have a little inside information."

Ava shook her head. "He moved to Shreveport last month. Works at a place called Coconut Billie's. It sounds neighborhood, but it's real fancy."

"Too bad," said Tandy.

Ava shrugged. "He was a nice fella, but still kind of a fixer-upper."

"Good lord," said Baby. "He's a man, not a house!"

"I brought you somethin', *cher*," Ava told Carmela. She reached down and gently took Carmela's right hand.

Carmela felt something cool and metallic slither into it. *Jewelry?*

"I ordered this at the last gift show I attended and it just now arrived," said Ava.

"Oh my gosh!" exclaimed Carmela, examining her impromptu gift. "A charm bracelet!"

"Let's see," urged Baby.

Carmela held up a sparkling silver chain bracelet with tiny picture frames dangling from it.

"Little picture frames," said Tandy. "And they're empty! Oh, too cute!"

"Oh, it's a scrapbook charm bracelet," marveled Baby. "You put little photos in there, right?"

"That's the general idea," said Ava. She stood there

looking languid and lovely in her tight blue jeans and wrap-around brick-red sweater.

"I love it," said Carmela. "I've heard about these, but never got around to sourcing a vendor for them." She reached out and gave Ava a quick hug. "Thank you!"

"You know we're all going to want one," said Baby. She could barely take her eyes off the adorable charm bracelet.

" 'Course you do, sweetie," said Ava, reaching into the pockets of her sweater. "Which is why I ordered a half-dozen of them!" She tossed five more plastic packets, each containing a silver charm bracelet, onto the table.

"To die for!" exclaimed Baby, grabbing one immediately. "I can't wait to put my kids' photos in here."

"And grandkids," said Tandy, happily shredding the plastic to get to her bracelet. "You can never forget grandkids."

"Who was on the phone?" Carmela asked Gabby, once Ava had scampered off and Gabby had been presented with *her* very own charm bracelet.

"It was Wren," said Gabby, who suddenly seemed to be glowing with excitement. "And you'll never guess what she and Jekyl found at the bookstore!"

"Tell us," urged Baby, sensing good news.

"A signed first edition of John Steinbeck's *East of Eden* that Wren didn't even know they had!" exclaimed Gabby. "Isn't that great?"

"Terrific," said Carmela.

"I guess some of the first editions got mixed in with the other books," said Gabby. "So now they're hunting for more."

Tandy frowned and slid her glasses on top of her head. "What's something like that worth anyway? Ball park?"

Gabby looked proud. "Jekyl thought the Steinbeck might fetch as much as fifteen hundred dollars."

"That much?" said Tandy. "Very impressive."

"Wonderful," murmured Baby. "It's just like you said, Carmela. Now Wren can put a value on her inventory."

Margot came sashaying into Memory Mine promptly at five o'clock. Gazing around with mild curiosity, she noted that Carmela was the only one left. "Is it ready?" Margot asked without preamble.

Carmela, who'd been busting her buns to finish the DesLauriers's Gilt Trip scrapbook, wasn't one bit thrilled with Margot's attitude. The woman was rude, demanding, and projected an air of grand entitlement. *Maddening, truly maddening.*

"I hope," said Carmela, "that Gilt Trip succeeds in raising much-needed funds for the crisis nursery." *After all, most of the work, and not just my work, was done on donated time. And it would be a shame if the focus of the fund raiser shifted away from the very real needs of the crisis nursery and onto Margot's decorating and self-promotion skills.*

"You're such a worry wart, Carmela," chided

Margot. "The whole Gilt Trip event is going to be a huge success, you just wait and see."

"Let's hope so," said Carmela, handing over the final scrapbook to Margot.

"Interesting," said Margot, as she accepted the scrapbook. She frowned and knit her brows together as she studied the cover. "I'm surprised you chose a rather plain kraft paper cover for the album." Margot's words were just this side of accusatory.

"To better showcase the accent piece of wrought iron," exclaimed Carmela. She had run out to a nearby antique shop, done a fast forage through their scratch-and-dent room, and come up with a nice, flat snippet of antique wrought iron. It had been a snap to drill a couple grommets and attach the small curlicue wrought iron piece near the spine. "You see," continued Carmela, "the design is slightly reminiscent of your wall sconces."

"Hmm," said Margot, suddenly warming up to the concept. "You're right." She flipped open the book and began paging through it. "Your photos turned out rather well."

Carmela shrugged. "It's a point-and-click Nikon. Hard to go wrong."

"Still," said Margot, "the mood feels very painterly, and your prints are nice and sharp."

"Good printer," said Carmela. The new color printer *had* been a good investment on her part.

"Very understated," said Margot, continuing to peruse the scrapbook. "But also highly effective. The medium doesn't overshadow the message."

"Right," said Carmela, not exactly sure how to take that comment.

Snapping the book shut, Margot looked pleased. "Thanks, Carmela. Good job."

"You're welcome."

Margot tossed her black portfolio onto the table, unzipped all three sides, then carefully slid Carmela's scrapbook into it for safe transport. "What's this?" Margot asked casually, once she had everything all packed up.

Carmela grimaced. Wren had left her stack of photos sitting on the table alongside one of the Memory Mine coffee mugs. And, of course, Margot's sharp eyes had noticed them. "Just something Wren was working on," Carmela told her.

"A scrapbook on Jamie?" Margot's inquisitive fingers were suddenly riffling through the photos. "How touching."

Carmela decided Margot had to be the only person she knew who could murmur heartfelt words like *how touching* but convey a sense of not really meaning it.

"Well," Margot said, snatching her portfolio up and leaving the little stack of photos in complete disarray. "Life goes on, doesn't it." And then Margot's boot heels were clacking loudly across the wooden floor, and she quickly disappeared out the front door.

Carmela stared at the photos spread out on the table. Deep within her was a sense that Margot had been sublimely disrespectful. That Margot had pawed through

263

this stack of photographs that Wren had lovingly and carefully collected without any regard for feelings or circumstances.

Margot's a cold woman, thought Carmela. *Cold and distant. No wonder her relationship with Jamie ended. No wonder she gives me the creeps.*

Sliding into one of the chairs, Carmela slowly gathered the photos into a pile and began to carefully re-stack them. As she did so, one of the photos that had ended up on top of the jumbled pile caught her eye. A photo of a middle-aged couple standing in front of the very same house she and Ava had visited! Only in this old photo, the house wasn't nearly as dilapidated as it was now.

These have to be Jamie's adoptive parents. I think Wren said they were already in their late forties or early fifties when he came to live with them.

Her curiosity getting the best of her, Carmela continued to sift through the stack of the photos, studying them. Here was one of Jamie, looking skinny and young in a Tulane softball team jersey.

After his ball-playing days in high school Jamie must have joined the varsity team at Tulane.

Carmela studied the next photo. Here Jamie was posed on a wooden dock in front of what had to be a commercial shrimping boat, since it bore the intricate rigging and hoists that allowed wide, sweeping nets to be lowered from each side.

Hmm.

Flipping the two photos over, Carmela checked the

dates that were still faintly visible on the back.

Look at this. Here's Jamie at Tulane, and then, a week later, he's working on a shrimper in the Gulf. Jamie must have been a very industrious, highly motivated fellow to go from finals week right onto a shrimp boat. Then again, with his parents dead, the poor guy probably had to struggle to put himself through school.

The last photo in the stack caused a sharp intake of breath and raised the hair on the back of Carmela's neck.

"What the . . . !"

She stared at an old black-and-white photo that depicted a bizarre grouping of false limbs and crutches!

What on earth does this have to do with Jamie?

Carmela studied the photo, feeling unsettled and a little perplexed. Then, slowly, a distant memory tripped in her brain.

Wait a minute. I know this place, don't I?

She propped it up, resting it against the coffee mug.

It's the chapel at St. Roch!

The St. Roch Chapel was located in the St. Roch Cemetery, one of New Orleans's older cemeteries over on St. Roch and Derbigny Streets. Built to honor St. Roch, intercessor for the sick and victims of the plague, the cemetery had been constructed after the yellow fever epidemic of 1868 ravaged New Orleans. At one time, thousands of people had flocked to the St. Roch Chapel on All Soul's Day to pray for friends and relatives who were sick or in distress. A small side room adjacent to the chapel now contained the *objects curieux* that had been left in St. Roch Chapel. These strange objects included crutches, false limbs, glass eyeballs, plaster anatomical parts, and even medical supplies.

Carmela recalled that, long ago, her dad had taken her to St. Roch for a visit and she'd been terrified by what she'd seen. She had worried that the wooden limbs and glass eyes and strange orthopedic appliances would suddenly come to life, not unlike the dancing broomsticks in that Disney classic, *The Sorcerer's Apprentice.*

Carmela shivered. *Okay, I'm grown up now, and that stuff doesn't freak me out like it used to. But still, the question remains, why is this photo stuck in here with all the other photos of Jamie?*

Carmela let the question percolate in her brain.

Unless . . . this has something to do with Jamie's parents' graves? Could Jamie Redmond's parents be buried in St. Roch Cemetery?

She thought about this for a moment, warming up to the idea.

Yeah, maybe they are. If this photo came from Jamie's old photo collection, then there's an outside chance of it. The question is . . . has Wren seen this photo and possibly asked the same question?

Carmela dialed the number of Biblios Booksellers. It rang once . . . twice . . . three times. *Please be there.*

"Hello?" answered a tentative voice. It was Wren.

"Wren," said Carmela, "you're still there." *Good.*

"We're making a terrific progress," chortled Wren. "In fact, Jekyl just ran out to grab us a couple po-boys. We're going to make a major push and try to finish up tonight."

"Wonderful," said Carmela. She paused, unsure how to pose her question. "Wren, that stack of photos you left on the craft table? Have you had a chance to sort through all of them yet?"

"No," said Wren, sounding puzzled. "Is there some sort of problem?"

"Not at all," said Carmela, fighting to make her voice sound breezy and upbeat. "I was just going to tuck them in an envelope for safe keeping."

Wren hasn't seen the photo of St. Roch yet. Good. I don't want to get her hopes up and then disappoint her again. She's had so many disappointments already.

"You're so sweet, Carmela," said Wren. "But I've got a better idea. Why don't you just take the photos home with you and I'll drop by your place later to pick them up. Get all that stuff out of your hair. My photos, the bibelot box I left there. I have a feeling I'm going to be changing careers from scrapbook shop assistant to bookseller real soon."

"That's great, Wren, really great," said Carmela.

"Yeah, well. I guess I really love this place after all." Wren paused. "So you're heading home now?"

Carmela glanced at her watch. Five-fifteen. There was just time enough for a quick run over to St. Roch Cemetery.

"Pretty soon," answered Carmela, crossing her fingers at the little white lie.

"Well, see you later then," said Wren. "And thanks again for all your help."

Carmela hung up the phone and wandered back to the table to stare at the strange photo.

It wasn't much to go on. In fact, this photo taken in St. Roch Chapel might have nothing to do with where Jamie's parents were buried. On the other hand, Carmela knew there was only one way to find out. And if she *did* stumble upon their graves, then Wren and Gabby could finally arrange for Jamie's ashes to be buried along side them.

Lay Jamie to rest, lay Wren's mind to rest. Wouldn't that be nice for a change?

Carmela slipped into her suede jacket and hurried out the door. The sun was sinking fast and she had work to do.

Chapter 24

*T*his might be a bad idea, Carmela told herself as she pulled her car over to the curb. *A very bad idea.*

New Orleans's cities of the dead had always been considered dangerous territory after dark. Muggers, drug dealers, and all manner of unsavory characters came out at night to claim the spooky above-ground cemeteries as their turf. It was never a great surprise when the occasional tourist, curious but unsuspecting, wandered into one of these cemeteries and had his wallet stolen or ended up requiring a few stitches at a nearby emergency room.

The sun was a red orb sinking behind a screen of bare trees as Carmela pulled her jacket tight around her and stepped smartly through the wrought iron gates of St. Roch Cemetery. The evening was cold and turning colder, the dying shafts of light fading faster than she'd like.

Sundown's in about five minutes, Carmela told herself. *Once that happens, this little foray becomes awfully dicey.*

Gravel crunched beneath Carmela's feet as she hurried down the path to St. Roch Chapel. Mausoleums, vaults, family crypts, and tombstones loomed on either side of her, a spooky setting for an even spookier errand.

At the heavy double doors of St. Roch Chapel, Carmela's fingertips brushed rough wood and she wondered if the building was still unlocked. Then she put a shoulder to the ponderous doors and pushed. Slowly they creaked inward.

Candles flickered on the altar as Carmela hesitantly entered the dim chapel. Her footsteps echoed off the walls and vaulted ceiling, sounding hollow in the cold, still church.

Is there a caretaker around, I wonder?

"Hello," Carmela called out, her voice sounding shaky and shrill. "Anybody here?"

But there was only emptiness. And the moaning of the wind outside.

Slowly, feeling her way carefully in the dim light, Carmela approached the altar, stopping just short of the metal railing. She gazed up at the altar with its statue of St. Roch depicted as a plague victim, skin sores and all. Altar panels on either side illustrated his travels and service to other poor plague victims.

Carmela decided the first order of business was to check out the rather spooky side chapel.

Taking a deep breath, she ducked inside.

The objects adorning the small side chapel were just as strange and disquieting as she remembered. Only now there seemed to be an even more bizarre jumble of items. Leg braces with shoes still attached to them hung on the walls. There were false teeth, replicas of disembodied legs, arms, and hands, and even plaster casts of internal organs. Carmela stared at the strange collection, oddly fascinated. They reminded her of objects that might be found in an old Roman cata-comb. Except, of course, there weren't any actual skulls.

Okay, smarty. Now what? No clues are jumping out, nothing says X marks the spot.

Creeping back through the chapel, Carmela slipped back outside, trying to figure out her next move. Coming here had seemed like such a good idea at the time. Now she saw that she might have made a bit of a tactical error. It was dark and dangerous and she prob-ably wasn't going to experience any *aha!* moments stumbling around in the dark.

Still . . . she was here. And that photo had her

curiosity working at fever pitch. So maybe a quick peek *was* in order.

Carmela moved down a narrow path that led through a section of larger tombs and mausoleums. A few steps in, the hulking repositories for the dead seemed to lean in on her with a kind of menacing claustrophobia.

She recalled accounts from not so long ago of New Orleans cemeteries that had fallen into terrible disrepair. Tombs that had crumbled, caskets that had disintegrated and broken open to reveal remnants of bones and skulls. She hoped that wasn't the case at St. Roch Cemetery. Prayed there might be a caretaker *somewhere* on the premises.

With thoughts this wild, Carmela's imagination began to work overtime. And a nasty thought bubbled up in her brain.

Did Margot Butler also see the photo of St. Roch Chapel? Would the photo have meant something to her? Could she possibly have followed me?

Carmela cut left past a row of oven tombs, so named for their strange oven-like shape.

What am I doing here, anyway? This is pure craziness, sheer madness, she fretted. *I better get the hell out of here before they close the gates and lock me in for the night!*

Carmela stopped in her tracks to gather her wits and get her bearings. Glancing left, she saw a faint shaft of light from a street lamp illuminating several whitewashed tombs. She relaxed. A street lamp meant she was probably near the stations of the cross that stretched around the exterior wall of this place. Probably near one of the gates.

Correcting her course, Carmela walked another fifteen feet, glancing about hesitantly. And she suddenly halted dead in her tracks.

There, chiseled into a crumbling crypt that lay directly before her, were the words IN AETERNUM. She stared as something familiar sparked deep in her brain.

Oh my God, can that be the INAE that poor Jamie had tried to scrawl in his own blood? What does it mean? In eternity? Forever?

Hesitantly, nervously, Carmela approached the crypt. It was a good-sized crypt, probably built to hold two coffins, but the structure tilted back like it had settled unevenly over the years. A heavy wrought iron gate barred the way to an old wooden door.

Door. That means you can go inside. Gulp.

As Carmela reached out to touch the crypt, dry flakes of whitewash crumbled against her fingertips. Then her eyes widened in disbelief and she moved her hand across rough stone. Slowly, her fingers traced the name Redmond.

Oh no! This is where Jamie's parents are buried! Not down in Boothville.

Carmela pulled her hand back, wiped it against her slacks.

But why was this place so important to Jamie? Why did he try to scrawl these words in his own blood?

Her heart thudding like mad, a *swish swish* of blood

pounding in her ears, Carmela forced herself to think.

And suddenly, the feeling crept over her that something more important than Jamie's parents' remains was contained within this crypt.

Something's locked inside here! And it's got to be something very important. For the past week, strange forces have been at work. Possibly put into motion by someone who was trying to locate this very place!

Almost on their own, Carmela's hands reached up to grab the rusty lock that hung on the wrought iron gate.

It was fastened tight. She needed a key.

Carmela thought for a minute. She knew the caretaker probably had a key. But even if she found him and rousted him, there was no way he was just going to hand it over to her. Or even to Wren. In fact, it would probably take a court order to get inside.

As Carmela tugged at the cold metal in her hands, a single thought formed in her head.

What about the keys on Wren's bibelot box? She was very specific about Jamie giving them to her. Does one of those keys fit this padlock? Is there something inside here? Something besides Jamie's dear departed parents that Jamie had wanted to keep safe?

Like a woman possessed, Carmela hurried back to her car. She jumped in, feeling momentarily safe as she sat there thinking. She had the photos and the little bibelot box stashed right there in the back seat. Wren, after all, had asked her to bring those items home with her, so they could be picked up later.

Did she dare? Did she have the courage?

Suddenly, Carmela's cell phone sounded, filling the car's interior with its shrill ring, scaring her half to death.

She pawed for the phone in her bag and pressed the Receive button. "Hello?" she said shakily.

"Carmela?" came an urgent voice. "It's Shamus."

She pressed a hand to her chest, trying to still her fluttering heart. "Shamus? What do you want?"

"I have to talk to you!" Urgency filled his voice.

"Not now," Carmela told him. "I'm busy."

But Shamus was persistent. "It's very important. What are you doing right now?"

"Running an errand." *Am I ever!*

"Are you're still at your shop?" Shamus asked. "Are you at Memory Mine?"

"Uh . . . sure . . . maybe later. Listen Shamus, I'll give you a jingle later tonight, okay?"

"Carmela . . . wait! I have to talk to you! Please, I'm in my car and I could meet you in two shakes!"

But she'd already hung up.

After two wrong turns and a moment of sheer mind-blowing panic at what she was about to do, Carmela found her way back to the Redmond crypt.

A sliver of moon had emerged, adding a ghostly glimmer to the cemetery, as Carmela pried the first key off Wren's bibelot box. Taking a deep breath, she stuck the key into the lock. Of course it didn't fit.

Kneeling down, Carmela eyeballed the lock, trying to decide which key might work. Prying off a second key, Carmela stuck that in the lock. Still nothing.

Well this was a bad idea, she told herself. *So far all I've done is manage to ruin a perfectly good craft project.*

But she wasn't about to give up now. She'd come too far, taken too many risks.

Third one's the charm, right?

It was indeed. The key slipped into the padlock and, as Carmela gave it a good hard crank to the right, the rusty hasp fell open.

Holy smokes. I'm in.

She paused for a moment, then swung the wrought iron door outward. It made a loud creak, and she prayed no one had heard it. Putting a hand on the heavy wooden door, she tripped the outside latch, then pushed inward.

Dust and mustiness assaulted her nose.

Whew. I still can't believe I'm doing this.

Carmela had decided that her actions probably constituted breaking and entering, but maybe not quite to the letter of the law. She figured since she had the key in her possession, it gave her a sort of tacit permission. Sort of.

Carmela took two steps in. One. Two. She switched on the tiny Mag-lite she'd grabbed from her car's glove box and peered anxiously about.

A pair of coffins, encrusted with a half-inch of furry dust on top, were hunkered side by side.

Oh lord. This is beyond spooky. Now we're entering Twilight Zone *territory.*

Carmela knew she'd found Jamie's parents. But what else was she going to find? Why had Jamie attempted to scrawl a final message? Just what was in here?

Taking a couple more tentative steps, Carmela edged in slowly until she was facing both coffins. She shone the flashlight around. Between the two coffins, she could see a small trapdoor set in the back wall. Carmela shuddered. This was one of the old trapdoors that facilitated removal of bones. As the tradition went, once your dead relatives were finished decomposing and were down to just bare bones, those bones could be disposed of down the chute that led to a pit, or *caveau,* to make room for the tomb's next occupants. It was a strange custom, but one that had been in existence in New Orleans for almost two hundred years.

Interesting cultural and historical trivia, but it doesn't have anything to do with what I'm looking for.

The little Mag-lite, shone up and down the walls, revealed tangles of cobwebs, more dust. Carmela probed the corners of the crypt, too, but found nothing. And was about to give up, to chalk the night up to a very strange adventure, when her light caught an object on the floor.

Stepping closer to examine this strange lump, Carmela bent down and aimed the full force of her light on the strange object.

What on earth?

A dirty piece of leather seemed to be wrapped around some sort of box.

But what's inside? Please, don't let it be bones or

ashes or something funereal.

Tucking the flashlight into the crook of her arm, Carmela reached down and tentatively grabbed a rough edge of the dusty leather. She pulled hard, unwrapping as she tugged. There was a loud clank, and then the hunk of leather was dangling in her hand.

She grabbed for her light and shone it down. Metal engraved images stared back at her.

It took Carmela a few seconds before the realization hit her.

"Counterfeiting plates," she whispered aloud.

Sadness swept over her. This certainly seemed to confirm that Jamie Redmond had been one of the Bogus Creek Boys. And it probably wasn't a great leap of crime-solving logic to assume that one of his fellow gang members had come after him, looking for these very same plates, pressuring him hard for these plates. Probably, Jamie hadn't been so eager to give them up and, in the process, had sealed his fate.

How awful. And senseless.

Maybe now, Carmela decided, the police could pull some records and pick up a trail. But for now, she was going to leave everything just as she'd found it. Maybe wrap the plates back up and . . .

Carmela sensed a presence a split-second before she heard a raspy voice command: "I'll take those."

Stunned, caught completely off guard, Carmela whirled about, aiming the little Mag-lite toward the dark figure that loomed in the doorway of the musty mausoleum.

You could hear a pin drop when the light hit the man's face.

"You!" Carmela gasped. There, in the narrow doorway, holding a gun and blocking her exit, stood Jamie Redmond!

"Jamie?" Stunned beyond belief, Carmela's words were a terse whisper.

The man reached out and roughly wrenched the Mag-lite from Carmela's hand.

"Jamie . . . ?" she began again. *It couldn't be, could it? Unless I'm looking at a ghost!*

A low, menacing chuckle filled the dead air of the tomb. "Not quite," he told her.

"Then who . . . ?" began Carmela.

"You mean to say you've never heard of the ne'r-do-well brother?" came a low, sarcastic laugh. "Oh, how that family did love to hide their dirty little secrets!"

"Jamie's brother?" Carmela said, stunned. "I didn't know Jamie *had* a brother."

"And neither will anyone else," said the man, taking a step toward her. "I doubt if even the folks down in Boothville remember Jud Redmond, seeing as how I wasn't around all that much. Unfortunately for them, even though I was the older *frater,* I was also the proverbial bad seed. The one the dear old orphanage foisted off on the Redmonds as part of what you might call a *package* deal. Lucky me, I spent most of my formative years languishing in reform school over in Tallulah." Jud Redmond uttered a harsh laugh.

Carmela was stunned. *Oh my God. J. Redmond of the Bogus Creek Boys hadn't been Jamie Redmond at all. It was Jud Redmond. Poor Jamie was innocent!*

Jud Redmond pressed even closer to her and Carmela could feel the hair on her arms prickle.

"You have no idea what my life has been like," snarled Jud Redmond.

"Tell me," said Carmela, trying to buy time, trying to think. "I really want to know."

"Pollock Federal Prison," Jamie hissed. "Federal. Maximum security."

Carmela nodded. "But they let you out."

Jud just snorted. "Think I'd ever be able to live any semblance of a normal life? Think anyone would hire me? Would ever trust me?" He shook his head with anger. "Think I'd ever win me a pretty little fiancée?"

"I can't answer that," said Carmela, fighting to keep her voice even. "But you're probably going to dig yourself a deeper hole if you go back to counter-feiting." She glanced toward the doorway, wondering if she were quick enough, agile enough to dash by him. She didn't think so. Jud Redmond looked hulking but fast. Like a football player. Like someone who'd had plenty of time on his hands to pump iron.

Seeming to pick up her thoughts, Jud Redmond leaned in toward her. "I never imagined my brother would hide the printing plates here with the folks," he told Carmela in a mocking tone. "Snatching the plates before the Feds discovered them was the only good thing my brother did for me. The only time Jamie gave a rat's ass about me. His fast thinking got me a lighter sentence."

"So Jamie did try to help you," said Carmela, understanding Jamie's motivation, but knowing the law would've looked askance at his actions.

"Yeah, right," said Jud. "When I got out of prison two weeks ago Jamie offered to help me again. This time the boy genius wanted me to learn *computers*." Jud spat out the word. "He wanted me to assume a place among the nine-to-five drones. I told him I wanted one thing." Jud paused. "The plates. All he had to do was hand over the plates and I'd leave him alone. Disappear completely."

"He had to refuse," said Carmela. "Jamie didn't want you breaking the law again. Getting sent back to prison."

"He was a *stupid* man," said Jud angrily.

"He had everything going for him," said Carmela. "And you killed him."

"I didn't mean to," snapped Jud. "He just . . . *refused* to help. He was stubborn."

"Jamie cared for you," cried Carmela. "How could you have murdered him?"

For a split-second Jud Redmond's shoulders seemed to sag and his voice falter. "I was trying to scare him! Who knew the poor jerk was going to grab for the knife. We struggled . . . Jamie twisted the wrong way." Jud paused, more angry than ever now. "It was a stupid, foolish accident!"

"You won't get away with any of this," said Carmela

in a voice that sounded far braver than she felt.

Jud Redmond waggled a finger at her. "But I already have. Nobody knows about me, nobody remembers."

"We could go to the police, explain to them what happened. I'll go with you."

"No," said Jud. "That's not gonna happen." He bent forward quickly, gathering up the printing plates. "And unfortunately for you, you've been way too nosy for your own good."

"What are you talking about?" snapped Carmela.

"You made certain *inquiries,*" Jud told her, lashing out. "Even when you were warned, you didn't have the common sense to back off."

Carmela thought about the snake, the conk on the head, the face in her window. She recalled the coffee that had been left in the loft at Biblios Booksellers. Jud Redmond had been shadowing their every move, searching for the damned printing plates. In Jamie's house, at the old homestead, at the bookstore. And none of them had had the faintest idea.

"Putting it all together, are we?" taunted Jud. "Pity it's too little, too late."

Carmela rushed him then, launched herself at Jud Redmond with surprising speed and momentum. Fists flailing at his chest, Carmela brought one knee up sharply, connected hard, and was rewarded by Jud's shocked cry of pain and outrage. As he bent forward slightly, dropping the printing plates, she curled her fingers into claws and tore at his eyes.

Suddenly, her jaw exploded in pain and she was

flying backwards across the interior of the small tomb. She landed hard across one of the coffins.

"You bitch!" screamed Jud. "I'll kill you!"

Her back spasming with pain, Carmela scrambled to her feet and dodged around the coffin, putting it between her and Jud. *If I had a stick, a piece of metal, anything to help defend myself!* But there was nothing.

"Give me the key!" Jud commanded.

Throwing herself to her knees, Carmela dug in her pocket until she felt the cold metal.

"That's it, now hand it over." Jud Redmond was advancing on her.

In one swift motion, Carmela pulled out the key, shoved open the trapdoor in the wall, and tossed the key down. There was a faint metallic *clink,* and then it was gone.

"Not very smart, lady," snarled Jud. "You just sealed your fate." He backed toward the entrance to the crypt, picking up the plates as he went. "Better take some time to get acquainted with the folks," he taunted. "You're going to be their new roommate!"

"Don't you dare!" shrieked Carmela, real terror welling up inside her as she suddenly realized Jud's dark intentions.

"Nighty-night," came Jud's loathsome chuckle as he grabbed the wooden door and tugged it closed. "Enjoy your new home!"

Carmela let out a blood-curdling scream as the heavy wooden door swung shut with a terrible thud.

Chapter 25

ARMELA was pretty sure her jaw was broken. It not only throbbed like mad, it felt like it was on fire, too. And every time she moved her head, which was every time she screamed, another sharp pain at the back of her neck made her wince.

She'd been screaming for a good twenty minutes now. Standing in the pitch dark, hoping against hope that someone (the caretaker?) would stumble along and hear her through that thick door. But nothing had worked. Not even the muggers, who were *supposed* to populate the cemeteries, had heard her cries.

Now Carmela knew what she had to do.

Try to get that key. Oh lord, but I don't want to.

She wondered if she could do it, then decided she had to give it a shot. After all, she told herself, they're just bones. Ancestral bones.

Ancestral bones. Oh great.

Feeling her way along the floor, Carmela came to the trapdoor. It was a square piece of metal, maybe twelve by twelve inches, hinged at the top.

She laid down, feeling the damp and cold pierce her, hating that she was groveling among dust and mildew. Taking a deep breath, Carmela pushed the trapdoor open and stuck her arm down.

She felt only cold air. *No way. I can't reach.*

Carmela pulled her arm back, shaken. But knew she had to try again.

This time, she shucked her suede jacket off, the better to rid herself of any unnecessary bulk. Then she lay completely flat, head touching the hinged door, and shoved her hand down. This time, her fingertips grazed something hard and brittle. Carmela shuddered.

Bones? Have to be.

But still she couldn't reach.

Easing herself down on her left side, trying to ignore her aching back and jaw, Carmela thrust her right arm back through the trapdoor. Then, driving hard with her legs, she continued to push all the way through until her head and entire right shoulder were wedged inside the top of that terrible vault.

Reaching down, down, down, into the pit, she felt . . . bones. Smooth bones nestled in a pile of dust.

Stifling her revulsion, Carmela searched tentatively with her fingertips.

No . . . no . . . nothing . . . damn. Hey . . . wait a minute.

Carmela took another deep breath and tried to mash herself into the vault another inch or two. Then she forced her hand to dig where she thought her fingertips had felt something.

Trying to blank out the pain in her jaw, the revulsion in her stomach, thoughts of spiders in her hair, Carmela calmly and carefully felt for the key.

Fingers functioning like a hermit crab, scuttling carefully and methodically across the debris, she groped for that all-important treasure.

And, suddenly, there it was. Cool, metallic, infinitely

different in texture from the bone fragments she'd been fingering.

Carefully, gently, Carmela curled her thumb and index finger toward each other . . . and snagged the key!

Bringing her arm up carefully, then backing out of the hole with even greater care, Carmela clung tightly to her prize.

Success! Mission accomplished!

Pulling herself into sitting position, Carmela reached for her jacket and wiped her face off as best she could with one of the sleeves.

Then she slipped the jacket back on and edged toward the door.

Okay, she decided, *now that I've got the key, I've got to figure a way out of here.*

Ten minutes of examining the wooden door told her there was no way it could be opened from the inside. It didn't lock, but she recalled that it had a latch that only worked from the outside. Only if she got the door open could she get to the wrought iron gate beyond and use her key.

Maybe, she decided, if someone came along tomorrow, they'd hear her screams and get help. Maybe then she could slip her precious key under the door through what seemed to be a tiny gap between the bottom of the wooden door and the stone lintel.

But those were gigantic maybes, and it meant spending the night here. Entombed.

Carmela fought back tears.

Sliding to the floor, she rested her throbbing head against the door. She thought of Boo, who'd be wondering where she was, why she hadn't come home. Carmela thought of Ava, who'd probably call to say hi and figure she was out on a date. She thought about her cell phone that she'd left in her car. And Carmela thought of Shamus, whom she'd pretty much blown off and hung up on earlier. He'd had something important to tell her, but it hadn't been important to her. Then.

Carmela huddled there, thinking how her life had been so topsy-turvey in the past couple years. Marrying Shamus, starting the scrapbook store, separating from Shamus but still feeling a closeness with him.

Closing her eyes, Carmela willed herself to relax. If she was going to keep her wits about her and get through this, she had to somehow calm her still-fluttering heart and quell her anxious mind.

I need a mantra, Carmela decided. *A word I can focus on. Something that makes me happy, something that calms me.*

Scrapbooking.

That was it, she decided. Scrapbooking, made her happy. It released her creativity, drew dear friends together, dispelled tension, touched her soul.

Scrapbooking, she thought to herself. *Let me drift off, thinking about scrapbooking, meditating on the word* scrapbooking.

She tried to clear her mind, to focus on that one word.

Scrtch scrch.

Carmela's brows furrowed. *Not scrtch scrtch. Scrap-booking.*

Scrtch scrtch.

Carmela shook her head, worried that she was imagining sounds. Terrified that Jud had hit her harder than she'd initially thought, had maybe given her a concussion.

Then she heard it for real. A scratching outside the crypt.

Carmela leapt to her feet, screaming at the top of her lungs. "Help! I'm inside! Please get me out!"

"Carmela?" came a very faint voice.

I know that voice!

"Shamus?" she screamed at the top of her lungs. "Shamus!" Her words reverberated inside the crypt.

"Hang on, honey," came his faint reply. "I'll go get help!"

"Wait, Shamus!" shrieked Carmela. "I'm going to try to pass a key out to you!"

"You've got a key?" came his muffled but surprised answer. "Where the hell did you get a key?"

But Carmela was already on her hands and knees, scrambling to shove the hard-won little key through the crack under the door, pushing with the tips of her fingers until they felt numb.

And then the key disappeared. Under the door and . . . she wasn't sure where.

Until there was a sharp crack and a sudden *whoosh* as the wooden door creaked open.

Then she was flying into Shamus's arms, listening to him croon her name over and over again, faintly aware of excited barks and yips.

"Don't ever let go," she told him.

"I'll never let you go," he promised, holding her tight. "But for God sakes, honey, who did this to you?"

"Jamie Redmond had a brother. Jud."

"You're kidding," murmured Shamus, stroking her hair.

"And he murdered Jamie," sobbed Carmela. "His own brother."

"Shh," said Shamus, kissing the top of her head, her eyebrow, her cheek.

"Ouch."

Shamus raised an eyebrow. "Ouch?"

"I got smacked hard in the jaw," she told him.

"Oh, my God!" said Shamus, his eyes filled with concern. "We're going straight to the emergency room." Shamus had suddenly assumed the take-charge attitude Carmela had always admired.

"Wait a minute, wait a minute," she cried. The adrenaline was really kicking in now, making her feel schitzy and a little hyper. "How on earth did you find me?" She clung to Shamus like he was her one, single lifeline.

"I went to your shop, looking for you," explained Shamus. "And that weird St. Roch Chapel photo was propped up in the middle of the table. For some reason, I had a hunch . . . you never could keep your nose out of trouble. Anyway, I drove over here and then, of course, spotted your car." Shamus stopped and suddenly held her at arm's length. "But I didn't find you," he said. "Poobah did."

Carmela gazed down at the little brown and white dog with the torn ear. He'd been milling about their knees anxiously.

"Poobah tracked you here," explained Shamus. "He just picked up your scent and dragged me over here." Shamus smiled. "Poobah remembered you. He's the one who really saved the day!"

Carmela knelt down gingerly. "Come here, boy." She held out her hand.

Tentatively, Poobah crept toward Carmela. He stretched out his nose for a sniff, unsure what to do, but anxious for her approval. Then Carmela was gathering him into her arms. Cradling the little dog, hugging him, her tears dampening his furry coat.

"Good boy, Poobah," she told him. "Good boy."

Chapter 26

"THEY got him," Shamus told her as he hung up the phone.

Carmela was home in bed, cozied up under a down comforter, holding an ice pack to her aching jaw. Boo and Poobah were snuggled at her feet. There had been no mention of fleas.

The doctor in the emergency room at St. Ignatius had taken x-rays and assured Carmela her jaw wasn't broken, but urged her to come back tomorrow to see a specialist. An orthopod. Just because the bone bruise was so severe.

She blinked slowly and turned to stare at Shamus. "They got Jud Redmond?" said Carmela. "Are you serious?"

Shamus nodded, looking pleased. "With major help from you, of course. You gave the police very credible information. A good physical description of Jud Redmond and, of course, the tip on the blue car. And you were dead right about him high-tailing it down to Boothville. They apprehended him on Highway 23, just south of Ironton."

While Carmela was being checked out in the emergency room, Shamus had hastily summoned the state police. Laying on the gurney, feeling tight-jawed and clutching Shamus's hand, Carmela had recounted her abbreviated and somewhat sketchy story, but the police had seemingly jumped on her information.

Carmela shifted the ice pack from her jaw to her cheek, wincing at the cold.

"Call Wren," she told Shamus, her voice a hoarse whisper.

He bent down, frowned slightly. "Now?"

Carmela nodded. "Before she reads something in the newspaper tomorrow or sees it on TV. Before the rumor mill starts cranking out misinformation." She grabbed for his hand. "Please? It's important."

Shamus nodded. "Okay. But you stay here, awright? Tucked in tight."

Carmela gave a faint wave with her hand. She was

deliriously content to remain in bed, being ministered to by a very solicitous Shamus. A Shamus who still seemed enormously shaken by her encounter with the dangerous and nasty Jud Redmond.

And, truth be told, Carmela rather liked this subdued Shamus. He reminded her of the Shamus she'd married not so long ago.

Closing her eyes, Carmela wiggled her toes, felt one of the dogs shift slightly. She knew that tomorrow she'd have to fill everybody in. Ava, Gabby, Tandy, Baby—they'd all been part of this, they all had a stake in it.

But for now, she was quite content to lay in her own bed where it was clean and safe and warm. Carmela could hear Shamus on the phone, but couldn't quite make out any words. Oh well . . . he'd be in later to tell her, she decided, as she slid into a light slumber.

"Wren wanted to hurry right over," said Shamus, breezing into Carmela's bedroom some ten minutes later. "But I told her to hold off until morning. Wait until you're feeling better."

"I'm feeling better now," Carmela croaked. Her voice sounded so bad even she had to laugh. "So how was Wren? How did she take it?"

"She was absolutely stunned," said Shamus. "Had no idea there was a doppelganger brother hanging around. And, of course, she was terribly upset. And I think she felt responsible for what happened to you tonight. But in the end she was mostly grateful. Grateful that Jamie

291

wasn't really a forger or counterfeiter or whatever. Grateful that you stumbled upon his parents' grave, even though the circumstances were certainly not the best."

"Everything turned out okay," murmured Carmela.

"Oh, and she had some good news she wanted to share with you," said Shamus.

"What's that?" asked Carmela. She was starting to yawn now. To feel uncontrollably sleepy again.

"Apparently, in her frenzy of conducting an inventory at the bookstore, Wren stumbled across some sort of Mark Twain book. Not a manuscript per se, but a type of pre-publication edition. Jekyl thought it might be worth seventy, eighty grand."

There it is, thought Carmela. *The money Wren needs to pay off Dunbar DesLauriers. The money that will make her home-free and clear. And even help pay back part of that Preservation Foundation grant, if need be.*

"So it's been a night of surprises," said Shamus, exhaling. "One hell of a night."

"I'm still stunned the state police caught up with Jud so fast," Carmela told him. She couldn't believe her misadventure at St. Rochs had wound down so quickly.

"For one thing, it's Federal," Shamus explained to Carmela. "Anything to do with counterfeiting almost always brings in the Secret Service." He shook out a pain pill from the little bottle the hospital pharmacy had given them, then handed her a glass of water. "And it didn't hurt that you were part of the Crescent City Bank Meechums."

"Am I really?" she asked him. "Am I still?"

Shamus sat down on the bed next to her. "Don't you want to be?" he whispered softly.

Carmela nodded her head. Slowly, so her jaw wouldn't hurt any more than it already did. "I do," she said.

"No," said Shamus, tilting her chin up oh-so-gently. "*I* do."

Her eyes locked onto his. "You said those words once before," she reminded him.

Shamus met her gaze with fierce intensity. "This time I sincerely mean them."

Carmela lifted the covers, let him crawl into bed with her. "What were you so fired up about?" she asked as he eased himself down next to her. "When you called me earlier, you said there was something you had to tell me."

They snuggled together, Carmela suddenly feeling happier and content and more hopeful than she had in so many months.

"I want us to move back in together," Shamus whispered in her ear. "Into our old house."

"I thought your cousin was living in that house."

"Not anymore." Shamus reached up and snapped off the bedside lamp. "Real estate being what it is, there's been a sudden vacancy."

Carmela let the icepack plop to the floor as her hands sought him out. *This is it,* she thought. *We've reconciled before, but this is for real. The third time's the charm!*

293

Scrapbook, Stamping, and
Craft Tips from Laura Childs

A Different Kind of Stamping
Colorful postage stamps also look great on scrapbook pages. The U.S. Post Office has issued thousands of colorful and sometimes crazy stamps. Check out Bugs Bunny, Daffy Duck, Elvis, sea turtles, sports stars, even big-eyed cartoon pets.

Scrapbook the Holidays
Why not create a special Holiday Scrapbook every year? Gather cards, photos, bits of gift wrap, menus from holiday dinners, and favorite recipes for party treats. And be sure to have family and guests pen a few lines or recall a favored tradition!

Takin' Care of Business Scrapbooks
If you or someone in your family has a small business that could benefit from a scrapbook, why not create a "commercial scrapbook" just like Carmela does? Florists, caterers, wedding planners, interior designers, landscapers, restaurants, and lots more businesses could benefit from displaying their talents and finished products in a beautifully done scrapbook.

Design Your Own Gift Coupons
The same papers, press type, stamps, and stencils you use to create scrapbook pages and cards can be used to

create special "gift coupons." Give your husband or special fella a coupon that entitles him to One Free Foot-Rub or a Game Day Snack Extravaganza! Kids love Zoo Day or Pizza Party coupons.

Designer Candles

It's easy to turn ordinary, inexpensive pillar candles into designer candles. To decorate a six-inch pillar candle, cut a two-inch high strip of paper or card stock to wrap completely around it. Gold emboss the edges and stamp designs in the center of the strip. Wrap the strip around the candle and glue the ends together, then tie a gold cord or ribbon around the candle to finish it off. Crinkle paper also looks surprisingly elegant when wrapped around candles and embellished!

Creativity Cubed

You can use your rubber stamps and colored pens to turn ordinary white cubes of note paper into fun desk items. Wrap paper cube with a rubber band to keep paper together, then stamp your favorite motifs on the sides and fill in with colored pens. Four beads hot-glued to the bottom as feet complete your memo cube.

Jump-start Creativity

Ever get "creative block" when it comes to designing new scrapbook pages? You can find fresh ideas in all sorts of places. Art books, graphic design books, and fashion magazines all offer fresh takes on typography and layout.

Favorite New Orleans Recipes

Bon Tiempe's Bell Peppers Stuffed With Rice and Shrimp

4 bell peppers
1 lb. shrimp (small to medium-sized)
1 medium onion, chopped
1/2 clove garlic, chopped
2 tbsp. butter
1 small can tomato sauce
1 cup cooked rice
3 bay leaves
1/4 cup parsley, chopped
1 egg
1/2 cup bread crumbs

Cut tops off bell peppers and clean, then set aside. Sauté shrimp, onion, and garlic in butter until cooked. Add tomato sauce and simmer for 10 minutes. Fold in rice, bay leaves, parsley, egg, and bread crumbs. Gently spoon mixture into peppers and place peppers in baking dish with 1 inch of water in bottom. Bake at 350 degrees for 25 to 30 minutes.

Ava's Dirty Martini

1 1/2 oz. vodka (or gin)
1/4 tsp. dry vermouth
2 oz. olive juice
olives for garnish

Pour vodka, vermouth, and olive juice into a martini shaker half-filled with ice. Shake quickly, then strain into martini glass. Garnish with 2 olives.

Mississippi Mud Cake

1 cup butter
2 cups sugar
1/2 cup unsweetened cocoa
1/8 tsp. salt
2 tsp. vanilla
1 1/2 cups chopped peanuts
17 oz. jar of marshmallow cream

Cream butter and sugar until fluffy. Mix in cocoa and salt, then sift flower into creamed mixture. Mix well and add vanilla and peanuts. Pour into greased and floured 9" x 13" pan and bake at 300 degrees for 35 to 40 minutes. Remove from oven and immediately spread marshmallow cream over top of cake. When cake has cooled, cut into squares and place on dessert plates, top with brandy sauce.

Brandy Sauce

1 stick butter
1/2 cup sugar
2 egg yolks
1/2 cup heavy cream
1/4 cup brandy

Melt butter, then add sugar and egg yolks. Cook over medium heat, whisking constantly for 3 to 4 minutes until sugar dissolves and mixture forms a thick sauce. Remove from heat and add cream and brandy, then continue stirring until mixture is creamy.

Carmela's Big Easy Chocolate Chip
Peanut Butter Cookies

2 sticks butter
1 cup sugar
1 cup brown sugar
1 cup peanut butter
2 eggs
1 tsp. baking powder
1 1/2 tsp. baking soda
1/4 tsp. salt
1/2 tsp. vanilla
2 1/2 cups flour
1 cup chocolate chips
1 cup peanut butter chips

Melt butter in microwave, then place in mixing bowl with sugar, brown sugar, and peanut butter. Mix on medium speed until blended. Add eggs and beat mixture for 2 minutes. Reduce speed to low and add baking powder, baking soda, salt, and vanilla. Add the flour, a little at a time, until blended. Add the chocolate chips and peanut butter chips and stir in by hand. Place 1-inch balls of cookie dough on greased cookie sheet. Bake at 350 degrees for 10 minutes or until lightly browned. Yields 4 dozen cookies.

Momma's Pumpkin Muffins

2 cups pumpkin (canned)
1 tsp. vanilla
4 large eggs
1 cup oil
1 1/2 cups sugar
3 1/2 cups flour
1 tsp. baking powder
1 tsp. baking soda
2 tsp. cinnamon
1/2 tsp. salt
1 cup raisins

Combine pumpkin, vanilla, eggs, oil, and sugar in a bowl, then set aside. Sift flour and combine with baking powder, baking soda, cinnamon, and salt. Combine wet and dry ingredients and beat until batter is smooth. Add raisins. Pour batter into greased muffin tin, filling each cup 2/3 full. Bake for 30 minutes at 350 degrees until lightly browned.

Cream Cheese Frosting

1 3-ounce package cream cheese
1 tsp. vanilla
2 cups sifted powdered sugar
1/2 cup butter or margarine

Combine all ingredients and mix at medium speed until smooth. Frost pumpkin muffins when cool.

Big Eye Louie's Crawfish Gumbo
(Less adventuresome eaters can substitute crab meat!)

1 lb. crawfish (or crab meat)
2 tbs. butter
1 large onion, chopped
2 cloves garlic, chopped
1/2 cup celery, chopped
1/2 cup carrots, chopped
3 tomatoes, chopped
1/4 cup flour
5 cups chicken broth
10 oz. okra (fresh or canned, sliced in rounds)
1/4 cup parsley, chopped

Melt butter in sauce pan, then add onion, garlic,

celery, carrots, and tomatoes. Simmer gently and stir occasionally until vegetables are tender. Sprinkle flour over mixture and blend well. Gradually add in chicken broth, okra, and parsley. Bring to boil, stirring occasionally, then lower heat and simmer for five minutes. Add crawfish (or crab) and simmer 5 or 6 minutes longer. Season with salt and pepper to taste.

Ava's Bubbling Brown Sugar Hot Chocolate

3 oz. unsweetened chocolate
1/3 cup water
4 cups milk
3/4 cup brown sugar (packed)
1/8 tsp. salt

Stir chocolate and water in saucepan over low heat until chocolate melts and mixture thickens. Gradually whisk in milk, then add sugar and salt until blended and bubbly. To serve, pour into mugs, reheating in microwave if necessary. Garnish with peppermint sticks or whipped cream. Yields 4 servings.

Bon Tiempe's Sea Bass with Mango Salsa

2 mangos
4 tbsp minced cilantro
4 tsp. olive oil
2 lemons, juiced
1/2 red pepper, diced
1/2 cup green pepper, diced
4–6 oz. filets of sea bass
1 cup barbecue sauce

MANGO SALSA (Can be prepared one day ahead)
Peel and dice 2 ripe mangos. In mixing bowl, combine mango with cilantro, 2 tsp. olive oil, lemon juice, red pepper, and green pepper.

SEA BASS
Sear sea bass in 2 tsp. olive oil over high heat until lightly browned. Brush each filet with barbecue sauce and transfer to roasting pan. Roast in a 400 degree oven for 5 minutes. Carefully transfer sea bass to serving plates and garnish with mango salsa. Yields 4 servings.

Find out more about the
Scrapbook Mystery series
and the Tea Shop Mystery series
at www.laurachilds.com

Center Point Publishing
600 Brooks Road • PO Box 1
Thorndike ME 04986-0001 USA

(207) 568-3717

US & Canada:
1 800 929-9108

COMPAGNIE GÉNÉRALE
TRANSATLANTIQUE

PAQUEBOTS·POSTE FRANÇAIS

LIGNE DU HAVRE A NEW-YORK
TOUS LES SAMEDIS DÉPARTS DIRECTS DU HAVRE POUR NEW-YORK

LIGNES DES ANTILLES
DE SAINT-NAZAIRE	le 6 de chaque mois pour: ANTILLES FRANÇAISES · VENEZUELA · COLOMBIE & PACIFIQUE le 21 de chaque mois pour: ANTILLES · MEXIQUE & GUYANES ·
DU HAVRE le 21 & DE BORDEAUX	le 25 de chaque mois pour: ANTILLES · VENEZUELA · COLOMBIE & PACIFIQUE ·

LIGNES DE LA MÉDITERRANÉE
DE MARSEILLE, départs quotidiens pour: ALGÉRIE · TUNISIE · CORSE · ITALIE · MALTE · TRIPOLI · MAROC · ESPAGNE ·
DE PORT-VENDRES & DE CETTE, chaque semaine pour: ALGER & ORAN ·
BILLETS DIRECTS de PARIS pour: ALGÉRIE · TUNISIE · CORSE · MALTE ·

VOYAGES CIRCULAIRES DANS LA MÉDITERRANÉE
AU DÉPART DE PARIS, LONDRES & BORDEAUX
combinés avec les chemins de fer
PARIS · LYON · MÉDITERRANÉE · MIDI · NORD · OUEST · ORLÉANS ·
ANWABD · TRAVERS · ESPAGNOLS · ALGÉRIENS · P.L.M · BÖNE · GUELMA · EST · ALGÉRIEN

S'adresser A PARIS
DIRECTION : 6, RUE AUBER.
PASSAGES : 12, BOULEVARD DES CAPUCINES (GRAND HÔTEL)
FRET : 108, RUE DU FAUBOURG St DENIS.

Cⁱᵉ Gⁱᵉ
TRANSATLANTIQUE

HAVRE · NEW · YORK
LA PROVENCE
LA LORRAINE
LA SAVOIE
LA TOURAINE

F. Le Quesne

SERVICES CONTRACTUELS
DES
ESSAGERIES MARITIMES

LEVANT, EGYPT
EAST AFRICA
FAR EAST

N OFFICES
FENCHURCH ST.E.C
PALL MALL .S.W.

PARIS.HAVRE.NEW YORK

French Line C.G.T.

CHAMPLAIN

LAFAYETTE

ECONOMY - SHIPS THAT SET A STANDARD
"PARIS"
"LAFAYETTE" TO NEW YORK
"CHAMPLAIN"

French Line C.G.T.

SOUTHAMPTON TO NEW YORK

EXPRESS LUXURY SERVICE

NORMANDIE

Cⁱᵉ Gˡᵉ TRANSATLANTIQUE

French Line

N é en 1934 au Havre,
descendant d'une
famille de marins, lui-
même ancien de la
Marine marchande
devenu journaliste,
Pierre-Henri Marin a
conservé un profond
attachement au monde
maritime auquel il a
consacré articles et
émissions de radio. En
qualité de journaliste,
il a vécu le retour des
paquebots de l'après-
guerre et notamment
le dossier du *France*,
de sa construction à
son départ. Passionné
d'histoire maritime,
il a publié plusieurs
ouvrages dont
*Les Hirondelles
de la Manche, pilotes
du Havre* (Gallimard).

Ce livre a été réalisé
en collaboration avec
la Compagnie Générale
Maritime, qui a bien
voulu mettre ses
archives à la disposition
de Découvertes
Gallimard, et a bénéficié
des conseils de Jean-Paul
Herbert, responsable des
Archives au Havre.

*Tous droits de traduction
et d'adaptation réservés
pour tous pays
© Gallimard 1989*

*Dépôt légal : Décembre 1989
Numéro d'édition : 48133
ISBN : 2-07-053095-7
Imprimerie Kapp Lahure
Jombart à Evreux*

LES PAQUEBOTS
AMBASSADEURS DES MERS

Pierre-Henri Marin

DÉCOUVERTES GALLIMARD
TECHNIQUES

Cinq générations de marins, six cents navires, des milliers de traversées… Du «Washington», qui le premier se lance dans l'aventure océane, au «France», qui tourne définitivement la page, c'est toute l'histoire de la Transat. Née d'un modeste armement de pêche à la morue, cette compagnie inventera la French Line et transportera par-delà l'océan le Gotha international.

CHAPITRE PREMIER
VERS LE NOUVEAU MONDE, LES TRANSATLANTIQUES

En six images, la marche inéluctable du progrès technique. Sur mer, la vapeur a vaincu la voile après cinq siècles de suprématie. Sur terre, les chevaux de la diligence s'inclinent devant le cheval de fer de la locomotive. Enfin, la fée Electricité remplace le gaz, qui avait lui-même détrôné la lampe à pétrole.

Au milieu du XIXe siècle, la voile règne encore sur les mers

Pendant cinq siècles, elle est restée le seul moyen de traverser les océans. A son apogée, les clippers, ces fins voiliers à l'étrave en lame de couteau construits par les Anglais et les Américains pour la course au thé, filent 17 nœuds, comme le *Cutty Sark*, et abattent 300 milles par jour, des performances que les vapeurs ne semblent pas prêts d'égaler.

Entre 1850 et 1870, Le Havre est à la tête de 20 lignes régulières de voiliers, dont ceux de la Compagnie Barbey qui en arme plus d'une centaine. La vapeur ne prendra que très tardivement l'avantage, et il faudra attendre 1885 pour voir le tonnage mondial des navires à vapeur atteindre celui des voiliers.

«Tournebroches» contre clippers

Les traversées en voiliers sont soumises aux aléas des vents, le confort y est relatif, le nombre de passagers limité. Le rôle de ces navires est surtout de transporter des marchandises et le nombre des cabines est réduit. Ainsi le *France-II*, le plus grand cinq-mâts jamais réalisé, ne peut-il embarquer que sept passagers dans des conditions d'agrément rarement connues sur des voiliers.

Il faut trente jours pour aller de New York au Havre et quarante dans le sens contraire, en raison des

Depuis 1823, Le Havre n'est plus un port de guerre. L'essor de la vapeur nécessite des bassins et des écluses de plus en plus grands. En 1844, des travaux de creusement de darses, d'amélioration des accès et de protection de l'avant-port sont entrepris. En 1870, le port compte sept bassins à flot, dont le bassin de Leure qui peut accueillir les plus grands bateaux du temps. On l'appellera le bassin des Transatlantiques.

Jusqu'au milieu du XIXe siècle, la plupart des navires sont encore construits en bois par une véritable armée de charpentiers, menuisiers, scieurs de long, chauffeurs de brai, calfateurs, apprentis, si nombreux qu'il n'est pas rare de voir travailler jusqu'à 2 000 ouvriers en même temps.

vents. Pour améliorer la vitesse, des voiliers de plus en plus grands sont construits en France et en Allemagne, les cinq-mâts. Mais ces géants nécessitent un équipage important pour manœuvrer une voilure qui peut déployer, comme sur le *France*, jusqu'à 6 300 mètres carrés avec un grand mât culminant à 64 mètres.

La polémique est grande entre tenants de la voile et de la vapeur. Les marins de la voile, fiers de leurs beaux et fins clippers, se moquent de ces bateaux à roues balourds, crachant une abondante fumée noire, qu'ils appellent les «tournebroches». Dans le même

L e *Great Western* (en haut), navire de 72 mètres, n'a rien de commun avec son frère géant, le *Great Eastern* (en bas). Celui-ci, en fer, avec cinq mâts et cinq cheminées, une propulsion à roues et à hélice, est si long qu'il a fallu le construire sur des berceaux spéciaux (ci-contre) et le lancer sur le côté.

temps, des voix s'élèvent contre la voile, qui «gaspille les hommes alors que la vapeur permet de les ménager». Le commerce des Etats-Unis avec l'Europe s'intensifie. On souhaite de plus en plus utiliser le navire à vapeur qui assure avec ponctualité le transport des hommes, des marchandises et du courrier entre les deux continents.

La France est en retard dans la course à la vapeur

Le *Savannah*, le premier vapeur qui a traversé l'Atlantique en 1819, est américain. Les Anglais, qui se sont très tôt tournés vers la vapeur et alimentent les chaudières avec le charbon de Cardiff, ont déjà une avance indéniable. Dès 1838, ils établissent sur l'Atlantique un service régulier avec deux steamers à roues, le *Sirius* et le *Great Western*.

La technique française a pourtant été très présente dans cette évolution. Le *Great Western* ainsi que le géant le *Great Eastern* (qui, avec ses 210 mètres de long, inspira Jules Verne pour *Une ville flottante*) ont été construits par l'ingénieur d'origine française Isambard Brunel. La machine à vapeur avait été inventée par Denis Papin en 1690, et c'est à Paris que Robert Fulton présenta dans l'indifférence son «chariot d'eau mû par le feu» en 1803. C'est encore un Français, Frédéric Sauvage, qui fit des essais d'hélice concluants aux Chantiers Augustin Normand du Havre.

Robert Fulton (1765-1815), mécanicien américain, construit le premier sous-marin à hélice, le *Nautilus*. Déçu par l'accueil des Français, il retourne dans son pays mettre au point le premier navire à vapeur (1807).

Mais les faits sont là : en 1835, la France possède 82 navires à propulsion mécanique alors que l'Angleterre en a déjà 500! En 1840, les Britanniques occupent toujours le premier rang avec The British North American Royal Mail Steam Packet, compagnie qui deviendra célèbre sous le nom de son directeur Samuel Cunard.

Pour pallier cette carence, le gouvernement décide la création d'un service postal entre la France et le continent américain

Deux armateurs havrais, Hérout et Handel, fondent en 1847 la Compagnie générale des paquebots transatlantiques avec quatre frégates. Le mauvais temps sur l'Atlantique Nord et la concurrence effrénée des Britanniques eurent raison en six mois de cette première tentative. La traversée de *L'Union* dure quinze jours, celle du *Missouri* se poursuit à la voile, faute de charbon. Les frégates, trop lourdes

S amuel Cunard, fils d'un marchand de Philadelphie et simple agent de la Compagnie des Indes orientales à Halifax, va devenir le premier armateur anglais.

et trop lentes, sont inadaptées aux services demandés. C'est l'échec.

Juin 1855, naissance de la Compagnie générale maritime

Le gouvernement est conscient de la pénurie de navires (à laquelle il a été confronté lors de la guerre de Crimée) et estime qu'il est urgent de rapporter en Europe les matières premières nécessaires au développement de la révolution industrielle. La marine marchande française, supplantée par les Etats-Unis, a perdu sa seconde place. L'intérêt et l'honneur national exigent l'intervention de l'Etat.

   Celui-ci reprend les projets avortés et recherche d'autres armateurs. Il va les trouver en la personne des banquiers Emile et Isaac Péreire, convaincus que les lignes maritimes transatlantiques sont les compléments du rail dont ils ont été les premiers promoteurs en France.

L a Compagnie générale maritime est constituée le 24 février 1855, avec un capital de 6 millions de francs. La moitié est assurée par la Société générale de crédit mobilier et le reste par une cinquantaine de souscripteurs de Paris, Lyon et Mulhouse. 12 000 actions de 500 francs de valeur nominale sont émises. Elles se négocient avant même la signature du décret d'autorisation de la Compagnie. Dès le lendemain, elles s'enlèvent à 595 francs et, en juillet suivant, à 625 francs.

C i-contre, arrivée d'un paquebot français à New York au milieu d'une foule de bateaux en tout genre, selon une aquarelle de Lebreton, datant du XIXe siècle. Il s'agit très certainement d'une des frégates de Hérout et Handel qui tentèrent la première aventure transatlantique.

Les deux frères possèdent leur propre organisme de crédit, la Société générale de crédit mobilier fondée en 1852, qui va souscrire plus de la moitié du capital de la Compagnie générale maritime. La société s'installe place Vendôme à Paris et affiche un programme éclectique et ambitieux : opérations d'armement, de constructions et d'affrètement des navires, créations de lignes maritimes, mais aussi pêche à la morue, fondation de fermes d'élevage à La Plata et production de conserves et de cuirs.

Les Péreire signent en 1860 leur première convention postale avec l'Etat et constituent leur flotte

La Compagnie générale maritime pourra desservir pendant vingt ans les lignes transatlantiques du Havre à New York, avec escale à Brest, et de Saint-Nazaire aux Antilles et au Mexique, avec escales à Cuba, Tampico et Cayenne. L'Etat accorde une subvention annuelle de 9 300 000 francs et avance deux annuités. De son côté, la Compagnie s'engage à construire dans les trois ans les 14 paquebots nécessaires à l'exploitation des lignes postales.

Emile (en haut) et Isaac (en bas) Péreire, les deux frères fondateurs de la Transat, photographiés par Nadar.

Devenue Compagnie générale transatlantique en 1861, elle passe commande de trois paquebots pour la ligne de New York aux Chantiers John Scott de Greenock en Ecosse : le *Washington*, le *Lafayette* et l'*Europe* coûteront chacun 3 200 000 francs.

Les Péreire se sont engagés à faire construire en France la moitié de leur flotte. Effarés par les prix que mentionnent les devis des chantiers français interrogés, ils créent leur propre chantier à Penhoët, près de Saint-Nazaire. Celui-ci ne fabrique que les coques des navires : l'outillage est importé d'Angleterre, les tôles sont commandées en France à Commentry et les machines à vapeur au Creusot.

Le 15 juin 1864, salué par des salves d'artillerie, le «Washington» quitte Le Havre à destination de New York

Cette ouverture de la ligne de New York a lieu deux ans après celle des Antilles, desservie en priorité en raison de la guerre du Mexique pour assurer le ravitaillement des troupes et leur liaison constante avec la métropole.

Le *Washington*, construit en fer, mesure 105 mètres de long. Il est propulsé par une machine à vapeur de 850 CV entraînant deux roues à aubes et peut atteindre 12 nœuds. Par sécurité, cependant, il reste gréé en brick avec 885 mètres carrés de voilure. Prévu

Pour le premier départ du Havre du *Washington* (page de gauche), le vent est portant et incite le commandant à hisser foc et huniers, tandis que le pilote qui a assuré cette sortie regagne le port.

L'embarquement sur les premiers transatlantiques se fait sur le pont. Le commissaire vérifie sur sa liste l'identité de chaque passager et lui désigne sa cabine pour le voyage, tandis qu'un matelot hisse à bord les bagages que leurs propriétaires cherchent à reconnaître. Les grands halls d'accueil n'apparaîtront que plus tard.

pour 400 passagers, il n'embarque pour ce premier
voyage que 67 personnes, dont l'ambassadeur de
France, M. de la Roncière, qui rejoint son poste à
Washington. La traversée dure treize jours et demi
sans incident.

La ligne de New York connaît très vite un grand succès

A la suite de la guerre de Sécession, la marine
américaine est exsangue et ne se relèvera pas avant
un demi-siècle. La «Transat», comme on l'appelle
déjà, a le champ libre.

Grâce à des paquebots modernes et rapides, comme
le *Péreire*, le *Napoléon-III* ou le *Ville-de-Paris*, elle
va effectuer des liaisons d'une rapidité et d'une

régularité exceptionnelles, le meilleur moyen pour
s'assurer la fidélité d'une clientèle d'élite que toutes
les lignes se disputent. Dès 1866, en effet, la
traversée est réduite à un peu moins de neuf jours,
un record pour l'époque.

Le service, au début bimensuel, est doublé par
une ligne destinée aux passagers les plus modestes :
les émigrants qui vont peupler le Nouveau Monde.
La Compagnie est prospère, mais des nuages
apparaissent à l'horizon.

L e *Péreire* (en bas,
page de droite),
d'une puissance de
1 000 CV, lancé en
1866, atteint la vitesse
de 13,6 nœuds. Il
consomme 1 000
tonnes de charbon par
voyage, mais peut en
embarquer seulement
1 100. Par sécurité, il
reste gréé en trois-mâts
barque. En 1872, il
reçoit une deuxième
cheminée et ses
machines sont
modernisées. Ci-contre
à gauche, les banquises,
un des multiples
dangers de la ligne de
New York.

Catastrophes financières...

En 1866, les paquebots français assurent 26 départs sur New York; quelques années plus tard, on en compte 130, dont 104 sous pavillons étrangers. Car l'Empereur est libre-échangiste et, bien sûr, son libéralisme s'applique aussi à la législation maritime. Le droit de jauge de 4,50 francs par tonneau qui frappait les navires étrangers est aboli. La mer est libre, les ports sont ouverts et la concurrence se développe, en particulier celle des Allemands qui viennent compléter leur fret et le nombre de leurs passagers en France. De plus, la ligne du Mexique est touchée par l'arrêt des opérations militaires et les désastres naturels. Les recettes et les bénéfices diminuent. Les Péreire font d'abord face.

Cette coupe du *Ville-de-Saint-Nazaire* (en haut) montre la disposition des différents ponts, la machine alimentée par trois chaudières et l'éperon sous-marin dont il est doté.

Mais la crise économique et la guerre implacable
menée par les Rothschild, leurs adversaires depuis
vingt ans, amènent le Crédit mobilier à déposer son
bilan. C'est une curée impitoyable contre les deux
frères, qui démissionnent le 23 juin 1868.

... et maritimes

Cinq ans plus tard, un nouveau coup est porté à la
Compagnie. En novembre 1873, à 1 800 milles des
côtes, le *Ville-du-Havre* est abordé par le *Loch Earn*,

Le 10 avril 1874, malgré une mer très forte et grâce au dévouement des officiers, l'évacuation de l'*Europe* s'effectue en bon ordre. Les trois canots du bord s'éloignent vers le navire anglais *Greece*, qui a répondu immédiatement aux signaux de détresse. Les 218 passagers sont sauvés. Le commandant, reconnaissable à ses galons, quitte son navire le dernier, selon la tradition, avec à la main une petite mallette renfermant sans doute les papiers du bord. La Transat a transporté jusqu'ici 160000 passagers sans incident et l'on se demande si l'allongement des coques des navires n'a pas affaibli leur résistance.

un grand voilier en fer. Le paquebot coule en douze minutes, faisant 236 victimes. C'est le premier accident de la Transat en dix-huit ans de navigation.

Le sort s'acharne. L'année suivante, l'*Europe* est abandonné avec 6 mètres d'eau dans ses cales, heureusement sans pertes humaines. Douze jours plus tard, l'*Amérique*, pris dans le gros temps, est évacué au large

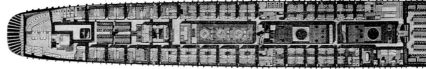

d'Ouessant. Le paquebot ne coule pas et, remorqué par deux navires anglais, il est conduit à Plymouth. C'est le déchaînement contre les états-majors et les équipages de la Compagnie. La clientèle déserte les paquebots. Et l'œuvre accomplie avec bonheur par les Péreire semble gravement remise en cause.

Pour relancer la Compagnie, il faut regagner la confiance des passagers...

Emile Péreire est mort en 1875. Isaac, son frère, prépare la revanche et fait entrer la Compagnie dans le patrimoine familial. Son fils aîné Eugène devient président en 1887.

Coupe longitudinale et transversale de *La Champagne*, prototype d'une série de quatre paquebots alliant pour la première fois rapidité et confort. Ci-dessous, le conseil d'administration de la Transat réuni au grand complet.

Pour ramener les passagers sur la ligne, une propagande bien orchestrée annonce l'amélioration des conditions de sécurité à bord des navires. On embarque des pigeons voyageurs pour rester en liaison avec la terre. Les paquebots sont équipés de fanaux de position éclairant à longue distance et le feu blanc réglementaire est remplacé par un phare portant à 10 milles.

En mars 1876, l'*Amérique* fait une entrée remarquée à Plymouth et son phare, symbole de la renaissance et de la prospérité retrouvées, éclipse ceux des navires présents au port.

Vue des chantiers de Penhoët réorganisés, agrandis et modernisés, en 1886. Au second plan, sur cales, on aperçoit *La Bretagne* et *La Champagne* en construction, tandis que deux autres paquebots sont en achèvement au quai d'armement.

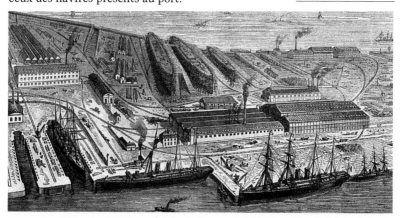

… et renouveler la flotte

Sans être certaine de
la reconduction de sa
convention postale,
la Compagnie ne peut
cependant aller trop loin ;
elle ne commande qu'un seul
paquebot jusqu'en 1885,
La Normandie, qui lui coûte
6 millions de francs. La
nouvelle concession postale
est finalement accordée pour
la ligne de New York, celles des Antilles et de la
Méditerranée. Avec les primes de vitesse, la
Compagnie reçoit 12 430 000 francs, soit le double
du coût de *La Normandie*.

Cependant, le cahier des charges impose la
construction de quatre paquebots dans un délai
de trois ans et porte la vitesse à 15 nœuds.
La Champagne, La Bourgogne, La Bretagne et
La Gascogne mesurent 155 mètres ; la vitesse aux
essais atteint 18,85 nœuds pour le plus rapide.
Ils peuvent embarquer 1 200 passagers dont

A l'Exposition
de 1889, près de
2 millions de visiteurs
découvrent *La
Touraine*, dont les
coursives, les salons,
la salle à manger et le
fumoir ont été
reconstitués sur deux
niveaux. Parvenus sur
la passerelle, les
visiteurs peuvent
admirer, grâce à un
diorama peint en
trompe l'œil, toute la
rade du Havre avec les
70 navires de la Transat
au mouillage. Faisant
également partie du
diorama, cette esquisse
de Poilpot montre
l'arrivée du train
transatlantique et
l'embarquement à bord
de *La Normandie*. Page
de droite, le paquebot
quitte Le Havre,
acclamé par la foule
des amis et des
curieux.

900 émigrants et, pour la première fois, il y a l'eau courante dans les cabines. Impressionnées par ces résultats, les postes américaines confient aux navires français leurs malles à destination de l'Europe.

Les lignes des Antilles et de l'Amérique centrale sont prospères, mais celle de New York reste l'artère essentielle de l'Atlantique.

La mise en service de *La Lorraine* et de *La Savoie* ainsi que l'Exposition universelle de 1889 marquent une étape dans la vie de la Compagnie qui est alors à son apogée.

La concurrence farouche entre les nations se traduit par la course au gigantisme et à la vitesse

En plus des Anglais de la Cunard et de la White Star, la Transat doit aussi se mesurer avec les Allemands, les Italiens, les Américains et même, plus tard, les Italiens. On compte 150 paquebots sur New York, appartenant à 17 lignes différentes, et trois départs par jour dans les deux sens.

L'émulation est vive. La White Star a en chantier le *Majestic*, long de 172 mètres; la Hamburg Amerika se prépare à mettre en ligne le *Prinz*, qui doit dépasser les 20 nœuds. Pour faire face, *La Touraine* est lancé,

❝ L'immense paquebot, traîné par un puissant remorqueur qui avait l'air, devant lui, d'une chenille, sortait lentement et royalement du port. Et le peuple havrais, massé sur les môles, sur la plage, aux fenêtres, emporté par un soudain élan patriotique, se mit à crier "Vive *La Lorraine!*" acclamant et applaudissant ce départ magnifique, cet enfantement d'une grande ville maritime qui donnait à la mer sa plus belle fille. ❞

Guy de Maupassant,
Pierre et Jean

avec ses 157 mètres, ses 12 000 CV et ses deux hélices. Il dépasse les 20 nœuds et traverse l'Atlantique en moins de sept jours.

La vitesse devient une hantise, et les compagnies tentent de s'attacher la riche clientèle américaine grâce à cet argument. A la fin du siècle, on dépasse les 23 nœuds, la traversée dure moins de six jours. C'est la surenchère d'unités de plus en plus rapides.

Le Ruban bleu récompense le navire ayant effectué la traversée la plus rapide de Bishop à Ambrose

Une étroite flamme bleue, aussi longue que la vitesse réalisée en nœuds, est hissée en tête de mât du vainqueur. Dans cette compétition, il faut reconnaître la suprématie des Anglais. Ils s'octroient le Ruban bleu les premiers dès 1838, avec 6,92 nœuds d'est en ouest. Il faudra près de cinquante ans pour atteindre les 20 nœuds, avec le *City of Paris*, qui parcourt 20,2 nœuds en 1889. Mais le record appartient au *Mauretania* de la Cunard, qui va détenir le trophée pendant vingt ans avec plus de 25 nœuds, avant de se le faire souffler, en 1929, par le paquebot allemand le *Bremen*, avec 27,92 nœuds.

Les Allemands, avec quatre paquebots, se classent deuxièmes, notamment avec le *Deutschland*, qui remporte deux fois le titre, le *Bremen* et le *Kaiser Wilhelm der Grosse*. Troisièmes devant la France : les Américains avec l'*America* en 1850 et 1852, puis soixante-huit ans plus tard avec l'*United States*, à 35,59 nœuds, la vitesse la plus élevée jamais enregistrée.

En 1933, le Ruban bleu deviendra italien, grâce au *Rex*, dépossédé de son titre deux ans plus tard par le *Normandie* lors de son voyage inaugural, avec 30,31 nœuds. Puis le *Queen Mary* et le *Normandie* se disputeront alternativement la victoire.

La Touraine emporte le Ruban bleu en 1891, avec 21,20 nœuds, mais son record ne sera jamais enregistré. En 1906, *La Provence* s'oppose pendant toute une traversée au *Deutschland.* Sur chaque bateau, les milliardaires comme Rockefeller et Vanderbilt engagent des paris. C'est finalement le français qui l'emportera de quatre heures, mais sans faire tomber le record de son adversaire. Ci-dessus, de gauche à droite : l'*Aquitania*, le *Deutschland,* l'*Arcadia* et *La Touraine.* Ci-contre, une passagère du *Bremen* salue le *Norddeutscher.*

Séries noires

L'épidémie de choléra et le protectionnisme
américain font s'effriter les recettes, la crise s'installe.
Des catastrophes maritimes vont la précipiter.

En 1897, le paquebot le *Ville-de-Saint-Nazaire* est
abandonné en mer. Pendant une semaine, passagers
et équipage vont s'affronter dans les canots de
sauvetage. Il y aura 65 morts.

Plus grave, en juillet 1898, *La Bourgogne* est abordé
par le voilier anglais le *Cromartyshire*. Le
commandant Deloncle tente d'échouer son navire sur
l'île du Sable, au large de la Nouvelle-Ecosse. En vain.
Il coule avec 568 passagers. L'héroïsme du
commandant et de ses officiers qui se laissent
engloutir ne servira à rien. Une campagne de presse
anglo-saxonne reprise en France dénonce le naufrage
comme étant la conséquence de l'usure des paquebots
de la Transat et de la lâcheté des marins français.
Quarante ans plus tard, il reste encore quelque chose
de cette calomnie et les passagers continuent de
bouder les navires de la Transat.

En juin 1907, les
grévistes assis sur
les chaînes du pont
tournant empêchent
la sortie des bateaux.

Grèves et lois sociales

La Compagnie occupe plus de 10 000 personnes, dont 6 000 officiers et marins de tous grades. Elle n'échappe pas aux crises sociales de l'époque. Les grèves touchent successivement tous les ports et toutes les catégories de personnel : travailleurs des quais, dockers, chargeurs, équipages, et même officiers. Elles sont largement suivies et la Compagnie ne connaît aucune année de calme complet, mais plutôt des périodes de paroxysme de 1904 à 1909, puis en 1912 et en 1923. Les mouvements aboutissent à la libéralisation des règlements.

Confort, table et service : les nouvelles armes de la French Line

Le président Charles-Roux, qui a remplacé Eugène Péreire en 1904, est opposé à la folie de la vitesse. Il décide, pour lutter contre la concurrence, de privilégier la qualité de la vie à bord. *La Provence,*

Nouvel atout pour la sécurité, la TSF est aussi un objet de curiosité pour les passagers.

en 1906, atteint 23 nœuds et se classe parmi les cinq navires les plus rapides du monde. Mais c'est aussi le premier paquebot muni de la télégraphie sans fil, permettant aux passagers de lire chaque jour *L'Atlantique,* journal imprimé à bord. Le *France,* le deuxième du nom, offre à ses 1 500 passagers une vitesse de 23 nœuds et… reçoit les milliardaires américains dans les meubles de Louis XIV. Dans ce «Versailles de l'Atlantique», toute la décoration rappelle le Grand Siècle.

Le premier conflit mondial va causer la perte de près du tiers de la flotte

La plupart des paquebots rapides sont «mobilisés» et transformés en croiseurs auxiliaires, transports de troupes ou navires-hôpitaux. La guerre sous-marine fait des ravages. Le 26 février 1916, sur la route de Salonique, *La Provence* est coulé en dix-sept minutes avec 1 693 hommes du IIIe régiment colonial.

En 1918, la France a gagné la guerre au prix de millions de morts. Le quart du tonnage français est

Avec ses quatre cheminées, ses quatre hélices mues par 45 000 CV et ses 217 mètres de long, le *France-II* est le plus grand paquebot français de l'époque. Il rallie New York en cinq jours et dix-neuf heures, alliant l'attrait de la vitesse au charme de sa décoration et à la qualité de sa table. Ses cabines de luxe sont si prisées qu'elles seront vendues aux enchères.

coulé. Les pertes sont difficiles à remplacer, car les chantiers sont débordés. Il faut acheter ou affréter.

L'«Ile-de-France», symbole de la reconstruction

Les paquebots, démobilisés les uns après les autres, reprennent leur service, comme le *Lafayette*, livré en 1915, qui n'a connu que la guerre. Le partage des paquebots allemands n'est pas très favorable à la Transat. Il lui faut attendre 1921 pour recevoir le *Paris*, le plus grand paquebot jamais construit en France (234 mètres de long avec 11 étages de ponts), qui emporte ses 3 246 passagers à la vitesse de 22 nœuds. Pour son voyage inaugural, le *Paris* transporte le maréchal Foch, très populaire aux Etats-Unis. Le *De Grasse* rajeunit un peu la flotte vieillissante des 11 navires qui desservent alors New York.

Commandé en 1924 pour remplacer *La Lorraine* et *La Touraine*, le T5, qui ne s'appelle pas encore *Ile-de-France*, est construit en trente-trois mois par les chantiers de Penhoët. Pour son lancement, le 14 mars 1926, aucune personnalité de premier plan n'a été invitée et c'est Mme Fould, épouse du président du chantier, qui brise la bouteille de champagne après qu'un prêtre précédé d'enfants de chœur a fait le tour du navire pour le bénir. Quelques années plus tard, l'*Ile-de-France* inaugure un nouveau service régulier de poste aérienne et transatlantique en catapultant, à 500 milles des côtes, un biplan Lioré et Olivier de 3 tonnes avec un moteur de 480 CV.

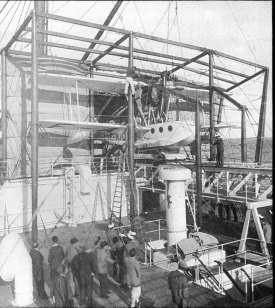

Mais le véritable renouveau est apporté en 1927 avec l'*Ile-de-France*, le plus grand paquebot français de l'époque, qui a droit à trois ministres pour son lancement, prélude à une carrière qui sera l'une des plus riches de la Compagnie. Long de 241 mètres, il file 23 nœuds grâce aux 64 000 CV de sa machine. Ses 1 500 passagers sont logés dans des cabines spacieuses et confortables, la plupart avec salle de bains.

L'année suivante, l'*Ile-de-France* inaugurera un service d'hydravion, catapulté depuis sa plage arrière, afin de faire gagner une journée à l'acheminement du courrier.

Comme dans la Royale, les matelots de la Transat portent autour de leur béret des rubans aux noms de leurs navires : *Ile-de-France, Lafayette, Paris...* Le *Paris*, avec son pont promenade de 130 mètres et sa salle à manger de 540 couverts, devient l'un des plus populaires ainsi que l'*Ile-de-France*. A l'époque où la Prohibition sévit aux Etats-Unis, le bar abondamment pourvu de ces navires, considérés comme territoire français, contribue à leur succès...

Au sortir de la crise de 1929, le «Normandie» est le porte-drapeau de la technologie et du luxe français

La crise a affecté les échanges commerciaux : le taux de fret est en chute libre, la diminution des passagers se fait sentir en toutes classes, les matières premières sont en hausse. La Transat en subit le contrecoup comme tout l'armement maritime.

Le *Normandie*, premier navire de plus de 300 mètres, mis à l'eau en 1935, est tourné vers l'avenir. Tous les superlatifs lui sont attribués : le plus grand, le plus rapide – près de 30 nœuds et le Ruban bleu à son premier voyage –, le plus beau aussi, un vrai palace flottant, «une cathédrale, un acte de foi», comme le dit Georges Croisile, jeune lieutenant sur le *Normandie* au côté du commandant Thoreux et futur commandant du *France*, qui poursuit : «Non seulement un chef-d'œuvre technologique avec les premiers compas gyroscopiques et l'ancêtre du radar, mais un éblouissement de luxe où rien n'était trop beau.»

En 1942, l'étincelle d'un chalumeau mettra fin à la carrière du paquebot qui,

L' arrivée triomphale du *Normandie*, escorté par les bateaux-pompes dans la baie de l'Hudson.

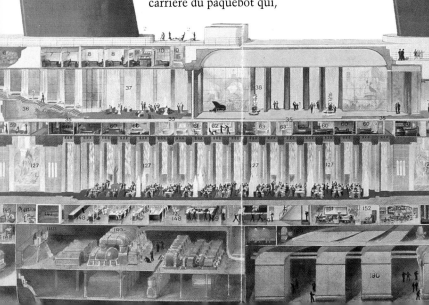

surchargé d'eau par les pompiers, coulera dans le port de New York, terminant sa trop courte carrière à la ferraille...

A la Libération, la situation de la flotte de l'Atlantique Nord est catastrophique

Le *Lafayette* et le *Paris* ont brûlé dans le port du Havre deux ans avant la guerre; le *Normandie* a fini tragiquement à New York; le *Champlain* a sauté sur une mine devant La Pallice en 1940; enfin le *De Grasse*, sabordé en septembre 1944, gît toujours dans les eaux de la Gironde. Quant à l'*Ile-de-France*, le seul paquebot encore en état en dépit de ses dix-huit ans de carrière, il n'est pas encore démobilisé. Rallié aux Forces navales françaises libres dès 1940 à Singapour, il a transporté plus de 300 000 militaires parcourant 500 000 milles à travers les océans. Attitude qui lui vaudra croix de guerre et Légion d'honneur, fait rare pour un navire.

Du pont promenade à la salle des machines, cette coupe du paquebot *Normandie* donne une parfaite idée des proportions de ce géant, avec notamment l'immense salle à manger des premières classes (127). On peut admirer aussi la perspective menant du grand escalier du fumoir jusqu'à la salle de spectacle (37 à 41) qui s'étend sur 110 mètres, la piscine intérieure (156), ainsi que l'immensité des cuisines et de l'office (148 à 150).

COUPE LONGITUDINALE
DU PAQUEBOT
NORMANDIE

CUNARD
WHITE STAR

A l'assaut de New York

L es paquebots ont inspiré les peintres de marines, comme Marin-Marie qui réalise cette affiche du *Normandie* quittant New York pour Le Havre. Les compagnies confient le soin de créer leurs images publicitaires à des artistes de talent tels que Cassandre, Wuilguir (brochure sur le *Normandie*, ci-dessus) ou Roquin, qui représente pour la Cunard le *Queen Mary* et le *Queen Elizabeth* de part et d'autre de l'Empi State Building

Les Anglais ont eu plus de chance en retrouvant intacts le *Queen Mary* et le *Queen Elizabeth*, tandis que les Américains ont repris la ligne où le trafic est très intense en ce lendemain de guerre avec l'*America* et le *Washington*.

Il faut réorganiser la flotte, d'abord avec des navires de charge et l'apport des liberty-ships, puis avec la remise en service en 1947 du paquebot le *De Grasse*, renfloué et rénové en un temps record. Mais cette année-là, malgré le retour émouvant des passagers fidèles, la Transat ne transporte que 10000 voyageurs sur les 650000 de la ligne. En 1948, pour noircir encore le tableau, un nouveau concurrent apparaît : le *New Amsterdam* de la Holland America Line.

Le 30 juin 1949, un concert de sirènes et d'acclamations salue le retour de l'«Ile-de-France» enfin rénové

Le paquebot a perdu sa troisième cheminée et rajeuni sa silhouette. Il est méconnaissable. Après dix ans d'absence, il franchit les digues, acclamé par les Havrais venus par milliers assister au retour de l'enfant prodigue dans leur port qui se relève de ses ruines.

L e *Queen Mary*, que les Anglais chérissent, est le grand rival du *Normandie*. Légèrement plus petit que celui-ci, cela ne l'empêchera pas de ravir deux fois le Ruban bleu.

Le premier départ de l'après-guerre a lieu neuf jours plus tard, avec 862 passagers. A New York, l'*Ile-de-France* reçoit tout au long de la remontée de l'Hudson le second accueil à l'américaine de sa carrière, avec cortège de bateaux-pompes, remorqueurs, avions, concert de sirènes de tous les bateaux présents au port, mouchoirs aux fenêtres de Manhattan, banderoles de bienvenue. Ce navire exceptionnel connaît une troisième fois cet accueil en ramenant à New York en juillet 1956 les 754 passagers et marins de l'*Andrea Doria*, abordé par le *Stockholm* qu'il a secouru en plein Atlantique.

Les médailles du «saint-bernard de l'Atlantique»

A cette occasion, l'*Ile-de-France* reçoit le Gallant Ship Award, une haute distinction américaine remise pour la première fois à un navire étranger. Pour ce sauvetage et celui du *Greenville*, accompli trois ans plus tôt, pour sa conduite héroïque pendant la guerre, l'*Ile-de-France* reçoit le Mérite maritime, la médaille de sauvetage et la croix d'officier de la Légion d'honneur. En octobre, c'est le gouvernement italien qui l'honore à son tour. C'est le navire le plus décoré au monde. Ces événements se répercutent

Les *piers* de New York, ces quais perpendiculaires à la rivière Hudson, sont à la dimension de la ville et de ses gratte-ciel qui se dressent au bord même des quais. Construits à la grande époque des paquebots, ils sont réservés à chaque compagnie; celui de la Transat porte le numéro 88, deux chiffres associés à l'existence de la French Line et au *Normandie*, pour lequel ce quai de 1 000 pieds (330 mètres) a été spécialement conçu. Sur cette photo, on reconnaît le *Liberté* au premier plan.

évidemment sur la fréquentation de la ligne qui atteint 36 000 passagers cette année-là. Trois ans plus tard, l'annonce de l'envoi à la casse du paquebot soulève dans le monde un torrent de protestations. Mais si dur que cela puisse paraître, la démolition est la seule issue possible.

Le «Liberté» et les derniers beaux jours

Dans les années cinquante, les Boeing-707 ne sont pas nés. Les avions mettent encore quinze à vingt heures pour se rendre à New York.

En août 1950, au titre des dommages de guerre, la Transat reçoit le *Liberté*, ex-*Europa*, paquebot allemand datant de 1930, d'une capacité de 1 500 passagers. Un appoint de taille auquel s'ajoute la construction des paquebots *Flandre*, pour la ligne de New York, et *Antilles*. Le *Liberté* commence une carrière très honorable et transportera près de un million de passagers, dont tout le Gotha de l'époque, tout au long des 120 tours de la terre accomplis.

Préparer l'avenir sans nostalgie

Les dirigeants des compagnies mesurent l'importance des pertes provoquées par la concurrence du transport aérien, et commencent progressivement la reconversion gigantesque de leurs unités : les paquebots doivent céder le pas aux navires de charges.

La flotte de la Transat est atteinte par la limite d'âge, et la construction d'un nouveau paquebot s'impose. Dès la mise sur cale du *Normandie*, les services techniques préparaient les plans d'un super-*Normandie* avec, comme hypothèse de travail, une traversée en six jours à 25 nœuds pour 1 300 passagers ou en cinq jours à 31 nœuds avec 2 000 passagers. Ce dossier, appelé alors T6, est celui du futur paquebot *France*.

Le *Liberté* aurait dû s'appeler *Lorraine*, un nom dans la tradition de la Transat, mais Jules Moch, ministre des Transports de l'époque, propose de le nommer *Liberté* pour effacer le souvenir de la domination nazie sur l'Europe qu'évoquait son patronyme d'origine.

Parmi les fidèles de l'*Ile-de-France* : Kirk Douglas, John Ford, John Wayne, Dean Martin, Bing Crosby, Humphrey Bogart et Lauren Bacall (ci-dessous).

S i Le Havre et la Transat ont ouvert largement la porte océane, Marseille et les Messageries maritimes misent sur l'Orient. D'un côté des traversées transatlantiques de plus en plus rapides, de l'autre des voyages au long cours au hasard des escales et des typhons dans un parfum d'exotisme et d'aventures cher à Monfreid, à Loti ou à Claude Farrère qui empruntèrent ces lignes.

CHAPITRE II
LA PORTE DE L'ORIENT

L es compagnies ont pris naissance grâce aux conventions postales signées avec l'Etat, qui confie à des entreprises privées le soin d'assurer le service postal maritime et lui fait obligation, en contrepartie d'une subvention, de disposer des navires nécessaires pour accomplir un nombre de voyages annuels fixé à l'avance, à une vitesse déterminée.

Une navigation née des impératifs politiques et liée à l'histoire coloniale et militaire de la France

Dès 1836, le gouvernement, soucieux de maintenir son influence en Algérie et d'affirmer sa présence dans le bassin méditerranéen, arme une flotte de 10 navires-poste pour relier Marseille avec les principaux ports de ce que certains n'hésitent pas à appeler le «lac français».

Mais les résultats financiers sont décevants et l'administration décide de faire appel à une compagnie privée, les Messageries nationales, qui depuis 1790 assurent des services de diligences entre les principales villes de France.

Le 6 août 1851, la Compagnie des services maritimes des Messageries nationales est créée et se donne comme objectifs de favoriser le développement de l'industrie et des échanges et de faire flotter le pavillon français sur toutes les mers du globe. Un vœu qui se réalisera au-delà des espérances des signataires : le pavillon à coins rouges des Messageries sera présent au cœur des guerres de Crimée et d'Italie, des expéditions de Chine et de Syrie, de la conquête de Madagascar et de l'Indochine, des guerres de 1870, de 1914-1918, de 1939-1945, d'Indochine, de Corée et de l'évacuation de l'Algérie.

Le *Périclès*, lancé en 1852, est le modeste ancêtre de toute une lignée de paquebots.

Le 8 septembre 1851, l'«Hellespont», premier vapeur de la Compagnie, quitte Marseille pour Civitavecchia

Il navigue sous les ordres du commandant Caboufigue qui, «superbe dans sa redingote bleue galonnée d'or, couvrant au-dessus des genoux un pantalon de toile d'une blancheur éclatante, recevait à la coupée, la casquette à la main. Il s'inclinait devant les dames quelque peu anxieuses de se retrouver sur l'élément liquide en demandant à chacune d'elle "Madame est sans doute une de nos passagères?" avec un rire si encourageant, si persuasif, qu'elles se trouvaient rassurées».

Lorsque l'*Hellespont* prend la mer, la flotte des Messageries se compose déjà de 16 navires. 13 d'entre eux viennent de l'administration des Postes et sont construits en bois. Les trois autres, plus récents et en fer, ont été rachetés à la Compagnie Bruno Rostand. Cette flotte d'occasion n'est pas très adaptée aux besoins; aussi, dès 1852, commence la réalisation d'un programme naval avec le lancement du *Périclès*, un modeste paquebot à aubes de 486 mètres!

La colonisation de l'Algérie fournit une clientèle fidèle aux lignes de l'Afrique du Nord et assure un bon coefficient de remplissage des cabines de troisième classe des paquebots. Ces «rationnaires», dont l'État paie les frais de voyage, se composent de militaires ou de fonctionnaires regagnant leurs postes, d'honnêtes et laborieux artisans et de pauvres cultivateurs quittant le sol natal, heureux d'avoir obtenu une concession de terre en Algérie.

Méditerranée et mer Noire, les berceaux de l'expansion

Depuis 1853, la Compagnie s'appelle, politique oblige, Messageries impériales.

C'est en Méditerranée que les Messageries vont débuter avec la concession des lignes postales sur l'Algérie et la Tunisie dès 1854, puis vers la mer Noire et le Proche-Orient.

Suivant un schéma presque identique à celui de la Transat, les Messageries rachètent le chantier de La Ciotat pour y faire construire ses propres bateaux.

Un ingénieur de grand talent, Henry Dupuy de Lôme – disciple de Brunel et de Russel qui conçurent le fameux *Great Eastern* –, leur apporte une collaboration précieuse. Rendu célèbre avec le *Napoléon*, premier vaisseau de guerre à vapeur et à hélice, il applique sa technique pour dessiner le *Danube*, premier vapeur à hélice des Messageries.

Henry Dupuy de Lôme (1816-1855) va assurer la construction des nouveaux navires des Messageries pendant seize ans.

L'expansion dans la guerre

En 1854, la guerre russo-turque entraîne l'intervention de la France, de la Grande-Bretagne et du Piémont en Crimée. Devant Sébastopol, 200 000 hommes à 3 000 kilomètres de leurs bases (soit dix-neuf jours de mer) ont besoin de vivres, de munitions, de chevaux. Il faut ramener les blessés et les prisonniers. Les quais de Marseille sont transformés en camp militaire où se croisent les uniformes colorés de la garde, de l'armée d'Afrique, zouaves en turban et pantalon bouffant, chasseurs en dolman bleu

Long de 49 mètres, l'*Osiris* fait partie des paquebots en bois rachetés à l'Etat en 1851. Construit en 1843, il peut embarquer 26 passagers. Sur cette peinture, on le voit quittant La Joliette par fort mistral.

et culotte rouge. Les 25 navires des Messageries transporteront des milliers d'hommes couvrant pour cette seule année 770000 milles marins.

A la même époque, Napoléon III intervient au côté de Cavour pour défendre le Risorgimento italien de la menace austro-hongroise. Une navette quotidienne est établie entre les ports de Marseille et de Gênes pour transporter les troupes et le matériel de guerre. La Compagnie profitera largement de ces expéditions pour développer son activité en mer Noire et en Méditerranée orientale.

En 1857, les Messageries obtiennent la concession des services postaux de l'Amérique du Sud

L'Etat a décidé d'organiser et de répartir les services maritimes postaux dans le monde. Ceux de l'Atlantique, New York et Mexique, sont confiés à la Compagnie générale maritime, devenue

Scènes de joie et de fraternité sur les quais de Toulon où débarquent des soldats ayant échappé à la guerre de Crimée. C'est pendant ce conflit particulièrement sanglant et meurtrier que Florence Nightingale organise des hôpitaux militaires de campagne afin de soigner les blessés sur les champs de bataille. Son action entraînera la création de la Croix-rouge.

la Transat, alors que l'Amérique du Sud est attribuée aux Messageries impériales pour une ligne Bordeaux-Rio de Janeiro via Lisbonne, Gorée et Bahia. Le voyage inaugural est assuré par la *Guienne*, premier paquebot construit dans des chantiers français.

En 1861, avec ses lignes sur la Méditerranée, sur la mer Noire et sur l'Amérique du Sud, dix ans

En 1840, les passagers d'un vapeur à aubes débarquent dans le port de Canton (page de droite).

après la fondation de la Compagnie, la flotte comprend 52 unités récentes parcourant plus de un million de milles marins par an. Et pourtant, l'expansion ne fait que commencer.

La porte de l'Orient

Le 31 janvier 1861, une indiscrétion du *Sémaphore* révèle qu'un service régulier va être établi en direction de la Chine avec transbordement à Suez (l'isthme n'est pas encore percé) et qu'il sera confié au paquebot l'*Impératrice*, mis récemment à l'eau à La Ciotat en présence des souverains. En effet, pour assurer le développement de ses industries, la France est tributaire des Indes et de la Chine (en particulier pour la soie). En créant un service régulier entre la France et la Chine, l'Etat veut tirer avantage de son établissement en Cochinchine et rouvrir l'ancienne route française des Indes.

Les Messageries ont trois ans pour organiser ce nouveau service (avec un départ mensuel d'Aden vers Saigon et un relais par navire annexe jusqu'à

Le *Mekong*, construit en 1870, est affecté à la ligne d'Extrême-Orient. En 1877, il fait naufrage sur le cap Gardafui. Les passagers, sauvés par un vapeur anglais, devront faire 15 kilomètres dans les sables mouvants et l'on déplorera quatre morts.

Hong Kong) concédé pour vingt ans. La subvention de 60 francs par lieue marine (5,5 kilomètres) et un prêt de 12 millions sans intérêts sur douze ans doivent permettre de construire les navires, d'installer les agences et les bases nécessaires à l'entretien ou aux réparations. Avec une ligne annexe sur la Réunion et l'île Maurice, l'océan Indien s'ouvre devant les étraves de la Compagnie.

L'ouverture du canal de Suez rapproche l'Orient de l'Occident

En 1854, le *Lycurgue* avait conduit Ferdinand de Lesseps à Alexandrie pour rencontrer le vice-roi Mohammed Saad et vraisemblablement obtenir l'accord de construire le canal, qui contribuera à l'expansion des échanges commerciaux à travers le monde et à celle des Messageries.

Le 17 novembre 1869, le canal de Suez est inauguré par 78 navires rassemblés à Alexandrie. Le *Péluse* des Messageries impériales occupe la huitième place dans ce convoi. Il est le premier navire «au commerce» à franchir l'isthme.

Le percement du canal en 1869 rapproche de 3 000 lieues (16 000 kilomètres) l'Orient de l'Occident. A bord du yacht *L'Aigle*, suivi de navires français, anglais et autrichiens, l'impératrice Eugénie inaugure la traversée de l'isthme, le 17 novembre 1869, dans la liesse générale. A partir du printemps 1870, la ligne principale d'Extrême-Orient emprunte directement cette nouvelle voie. Mais le canal n'est accessible qu'aux vapeurs, et son ouverture sonne le glas des paquebots à voile.

Parallèlement, les progrès techniques améliorent la vitesse et la sécurité des navires. L'acier permet l'allongement des paquebots en réduisant leur poids, l'hélice remplace la roue à aubes, l'électricité est désormais produite à bord des navires et la TSF les sort de leur isolement. L'*Atlantique* sera le premier à être doté d'un Marconi de 1,5 kilomètre de portée !

A bord du yacht impérial, l'impératrice Eugénie note ses impressions dans son journal : «L'instant le plus émouvant fut pour moi celui où *L'Aigle* prit la tête de cet étonnant défilé pour pénétrer dans la nouvelle grande voie maritime vers l'Extrême-Orient. Mais le plus étonnant était ces Bédouins venus en foule sur les deux rives du canal, qui avaient transformé 140 kilomètres de désert en un immense campement oriental.»

Au départ de Marseille, avec les Messageries maritimes, on rejoint l'Australie et Nouméa par Suez ou par Panama

La guerre du Tonkin, la conquête de Madagascar, où le *Yang-Tsé* conduira Gallieni pour déposer la reine Ranavalona III, n'altéreront en rien l'expansion des Messageries : l'Australie, la Nouvelle-Calédonie, les Nouvelles-Hébrides sont désormais reliées à Marseille dans des conditions de rapidité rarement atteintes ; ainsi, le *Polynésien* effectue en 1896 une traversée à 17 nœuds de moyenne.

En 1901, la Compagnie assure au départ de Marseille une ligne hebdomadaire sur Constantinople via Alexandrie et Beyrouth, un départ chaque samedi vers Constantinople et la mer Noire, une ligne postale sur l'Inde, l'Indochine et le Japon, tous les mois un service postal sur l'Australie via les Indes prolongé à Sydney par une ligne annexe sur la Nouvelle-Calédonie, Nouméa et les Nouvelles-Hébrides, deux départs par mois sur Madagascar, la Réunion et Maurice via les Seychelles, un service commercial (libre) sur Londres via Le Havre. Un départ tous les quinze jours est assuré de Bordeaux vers l'Amérique du Sud via Dakar. L'ensemble de ces services représente un million de lieues marines (5,5 millions de kilomètres), 60 navires pour 241 500 tonneaux.

En 1914, les Messageries mettent à nouveau leur flotte au service du pays : rapatriement des troupes d'outre-mer, opération des Dardanelles, convois de ravitaillement, paquebots transformés

En 1897, Ranavalona III, reine de Madagascar, est déposée par la France sur l'initiative de Gallieni et exilée en Algérie, qu'elle rejoint sur l'un des paquebots des Messageries.

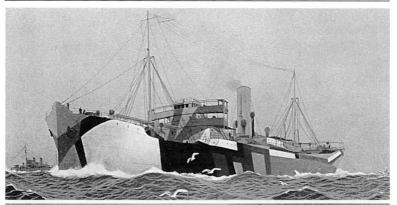

en navires-hôpitaux. A la fin du conflit, 22 navires ont été perdus et 428 marins et militaires ne sont pas revenus. En leur hommage, la Compagnie puisera dans son martyrologue les noms de nouveaux navires.

En 1919, le *El Kantara*, qui ramène dans leurs foyers les vétérans de Nouvelle-Calédonie, inaugure la ligne autour du monde de la Compagnie en empruntant pour la première fois le canal de Panama.

La création du tourisme en Afrique du Nord

A la suite du percement de l'isthme de Suez, les Messageries ont abandonné l'exploitation des lignes de l'Afrique du Nord qui sont reprises et développées dès 1879 par la Compagnie transatlantique.

Pendant la Première Guerre mondiale, les navires sont mobilisés. Ils sont soit camouflés comme le *Lieutenant-de-Missiessy* (en haut), soit transformés en navire-hôpital comme le *Portugal*, premier paquebot en acier et destiné à la ligne d'Amérique du Sud. Mis à la disposition du gouvernement russe, il sera torpillé en rade de Batoum en 1916 (ci-dessus).

L' année 1879 marque dans l'histoire de la Transat la prise de possession d'un nouveau domaine commercial : celui d'Afrique du Nord, qu'elle va contribuer à mettre en valeur. Les conditions d'exploitation sont très différentes de celles de l'Atlantique Nord, avec une concurrence étrangère faible mais avec une multiplicité d'intérêts à travers les ports desservis : Oran, Alger et Tunis. Privilégiant la vitesse comme sur l'Atlantique, la Compagnie met en service en 1884 le *Ville-de-Tunis* qui relie Marseille à Alger en vingt-sept heures et inaugure la première ligne dite rapide. En vingt ans, la Transat s'assure un rôle prédominant dans le bassin occidental de la Méditerranée. Ci-contre, à Alger, une scène d'embarquement sur l'un des nombreux paquebots de la Transat qui desservent l'Afrique du Nord. Au moment des adieux sur le pont promenade, les riches indigènes en burnous et turban d'apparat se mêlent aux enfants et aux passagères en robe longue.

Elle dessert Alger, Philippeville, Bône, Oran et Tunis. Mais surtout, en accord avec les réseaux ferroviaires français, anglais, espagnols et italiens, la Transat organise le tourisme nord-africain. Elle crée toute une infrastructure d'accueil et d'animation avec les Grands Hôtels nord-africains et le service des Auto-Circuits nord-africains. En 1929, 44 hôtels fonctionnent et 288 véhicules parcourent l'Afrique du Nord, avec plus de 5 000 touristes.

Progrès techniques et luxe à bord

Pour satisfaire la clientèle, les compagnies rivalisent de luxe et de confort, offrant aux passagers les services d'une «abbaye de Thélème sur la mer». Certains paquebots des Messageries, comme le Mariette-Pacha, le Félix-Roussel ou le Maréchal-Joffre, sont des palais flottants dont la décoration obéit souvent à l'art des pays desservis : celui de la Haute-Egypte sur le Mariette-Pacha ou un décor khmer sur le Félix-Roussel.

Pour prolonger le bénéfice de ses lignes, la Transat devient dès 1920 «tour operator» et organise au départ de Marseille un premier circuit touristique en Afrique du Nord. A Fez, accueillant les premiers invités du circuit, le résident général Lyautey exalte «l'exemple d'une initiative privée qui ouvre au grand tourisme les beautés et les charmes secrets du Maroc».

La puissance des navires est évoquée par la taille et le nombre des cheminées, dont certaines sont d'ailleurs postiches. Les Messageries se placent résolument à contre-courant en dessinant des cheminées très basses en forme de tables carrées aux rebords arrondis permettant de reconnaître immédiatement leurs paquebots. Dès 1921, l'*Angkor*, ex-*Amérique*, reçoit la chauffe au mazout, progrès énorme qui relègue au magasin des souvenirs l'image des chauffeurs à demi nus, ruisselants de sueur et jetant leurs pelletées de charbon dans la gueule des chaudières. Ces bateaux qui prennent le curieux nom de nautonaphtes annoncent déjà la marine moderne. Le *Georges-Philippar*, qui porte

> " Le navire, noble et beau avec toutes ses richesses précieuses, prend le large, brillant et sûr. "
>
> Walt Whitman

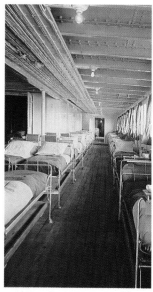

le nom d'un président de la Compagnie, est l'un de ceux-là, mais c'est le mystère entourant son dramatique incendie en mai 1932 qui le livrera à la postérité. Soixante ans après, certains s'interrogent encore sur les causes de sa disparition : court-circuit ou attentat ? Il est vrai que la personnalité du journaliste Albert Londres, qui périt dans les flammes avec 40 passagers, n'était pas étrangère à ces rumeurs.

Les ravages de la crise et de la guerre

La crise de 1929 secoue le monde maritime. Alors que la Transat passe sous le contrôle de l'Etat, les Messageries réussissent à

Des navires qui s'adaptent aux conflits et aux événements politiques : ci-contre à gauche, le pont du *Sphinx* transformé en navire-hôpital. Page de droite, un membre d'une délégation de l'Afrique-Occidentale Française se rendant en métropole.

surmonter ce cap difficile juste au moment où éclate de nouveau la guerre. La flotte réquisitionnée au côté des Alliés est durement éprouvée. Plus de la moitié des navires disparaît, et il ne reste que 22 bateaux représentant 177 000 tonneaux. A la Libération, il importe de reconstituer la flotte : les navires de charge reçoivent un appui avec l'attribution de 15 liberty-ships, et il faut reconvertir

Les menaces proférées avant le départ à l'encontre du *Georges-Philippar* (ci-dessous à quai à Saigon), diverses anomalies au cours du voyage, la propagation très rapide de l'incendie et la présence d'Albert Londres à bord ont alimenté la thèse de l'incendie criminel lors de la disparition du navire en mai 1932.

les 12 paquebots restants qui ont servi de troopers. Seul *La Marseillaise*, ex-*Maréchal-Pétain*, lancé le 8 juin 1944, est un bateau neuf. Premier navire de l'après-guerre, il peut embarquer 416 passagers et file 20,5 nœuds. Mis en service en juillet 1949, *La Marseillaise* reprend la ligne d'Extrême-Orient.

La fusion avec la Transat

Le *Champollion*, le *Félix-Roussel* et le *Maréchal-Joffre* sont reconvertis, tandis que sept paquebots nouveaux sont construits. Une fois de plus, les Messageries participent à une guerre, celle d'Indochine.

En 1962, à la demande du gouvernement, la Compagnie reprend quatre paquebots des Chargeurs réunis de la série des savants, le *Lavoisier*, le *Laennec*, le *Louis-Lumière* et le *Charles-Tellier*, pour ne pas fermer la ligne d'Amérique du Sud.

Remarquablement décorée et aménagée, *La Marseillaise*, à laquelle sa coque blanche (comme celle de tous les paquebots des Messageries sur les lignes d'Orient après la guerre) confère une allure de yacht de milliardaire, est ici représentée par le peintre Albert Brenet dans le cadre des mers de Chine qu'elle sillonnera pendant vingt ans.

La ligne du Pacifique s'enrichit de deux unités nouvelles, le *Calédonien* et le *Tahitien*. Ce dernier sera victime d'un grave incendie à 600 milles de Balboa en 1969 avec 273 passagers à bord, mais le sang-froid de l'équipage assisté des passagers évitera cette fois le pire. Le *Pasteur*, connu sous le nom d'*Australien*, sera le dernier paquebot lancé pour le compte des Messageries en 1966 pour la ligne d'Amérique du Sud, qu'il assurera jusqu'à la fermeture définitive en 1972.

Deux ans plus tard, la fusion avec la Transat fait disparaître des mers le pavillon à coins rouges au profit de celui de la Compagnie générale maritime, nom sous lequel la Transat avait vu le jour en 1855.

Au moment de la fusion avec la Transat, l'emblème de la Licorne disparaît des mers. Ce symbole rappelait le passé des Messageries, c'est-à-dire le cheval des diligences, tout en lui donnant un caractère maritime avec la corne du narval.

De 1820 à 1920, 72 millions d'Européens quittent leur pays en quête d'une nouvelle patrie. 34 millions d'entre eux embarquent à destination des Etats-Unis, espérant y trouver la liberté de travailler, de penser, de gouverner ou de prier. L'émigration fera la fortune des compagnies maritimes, qui se partagent l'Europe des proscrits économiques, politiques ou religieux.

CHAPITRE III

DANS L'ENTREPONT, LES ÉMIGRANTS

Qu'ils soient Italiens, comme ce groupe d'hommes et de femmes attendant le moment de l'embarquement à Gênes, ou Anglais, tel ce couple peint par F.-M. Brown, les émigrants ont tous le même regard où se mêlent l'espoir et l'anxiété, le déchirement ou la nostalgie.

Le fret humain

Pour les compagnies maritimes, les émigrants sont un fret comme un autre, qui possède toutefois sur les marchandises l'immense avantage de débarquer seul. Pour les attirer, elles vont se livrer une concurrence et une guerre des tarifs telles qu'il sera nécessaire en 1892 de créer un pool de l'émigration pour moraliser ce commerce.

Les Anglais ont sous la main les Irlandais, qui choisissent en masse le Nouveau Monde. L'Allemagne, qui rassemble tous les candidats au départ d'Europe centrale, est au cœur de cette émigration massive passant par Hambourg et Brême à destination de New York en criant : «Quelle est la patrie allemande? L'Amérique.» Entre 1851 et 1860, un million d'Allemands traverseront ainsi l'Atlantique; la France tentera de les détourner vers l'Algérie mais sans succès.

Les Français s'expatrient peu, et la Compagnie générale transatlantique, moins bien placée géographiquement, va devoir s'organiser pour profiter elle aussi de cette manne extraordinaire.

Les premières vagues d'émigration sont en majorité anglaises. Viennent ensuite les Irlandais, les Allemands et les Scandinaves puis, dans la dernière décennie du XIXe siècle, les Italiens, les Russes, les Slaves et les Hongrois.

C'est la liberté religieuse et politique que recherchent les premiers émigrants, alors que ceux qui vont les suivre embarquent pour le Nouveau Monde afin de sortir de la misère. A l'instant de monter à bord,

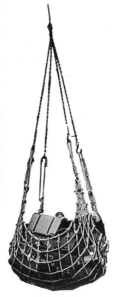

chacun rassemble son maigre bien, ici un matelas, là un baluchon, avant de se présenter à la passerelle pour gagner l'entrepont, tandis que les bagages chargés dans un filet sont hissés à bord sans précautions.

La chasse aux émigrants et l'organisation des trains spéciaux

La Transat ne néglige rien pour prendre sa part de trafic. Elle implante des agences de recrutement en Autriche, en Italie, dans les pays des Balkans, et même au Proche-Orient pour «ratisser» large. A Marseille, des paquebots de la Compagnie Frayssinet vont chercher des Napolitains, acheminés ensuite jusqu'au Havre par trains spéciaux de 400 à 600 personnes.

Car la Compagnie a décidé d'affréter des trains spéciaux qui conduisent directement les émigrants en gare du Havre. Elle obtient des tarifs réduits similaires à ceux pratiqués en Allemagne vers Brême et Hambourg. Elle réussit surtout à faire établir des trains directs mieux équipés et plus confortables que ceux de troisième classe, sortes de caisses percées d'une fenêtre unique, avec éclairage à huile, sans toilettes et livrées aux courants d'air.

Eugène Péreire commande des voitures de 40 ou 80 places, avec des banquettes larges et rembourrées, des berceaux pour les enfants, un W.-C. avec lavabo à une extrémité et un coin pour le chauffage. Dans le wagon buffet, les émigrants trouvent au prix coûtant vivres et boissons. Le café est distribué gratuitement deux fois par jour et le lait à discrétion pour les enfants. Dans les années qui suivent la mise en service de ces voitures, la Transat enregistre 30 000 à 40 000 passagers supplémentaires.

Le voyage dure vingt et une heures de Bâle au Havre; les trains, composés de cinq voitures et de quatre fourgons pour les bagages, s'arrêtent devant la tente Transatlantique qui va devenir la gare maritime. Là, les émigrants reçoivent un repas et

Comme les compagnies maritimes, les différents Etats américains se disputent les émigrants. Ci-contre, un document émanant de la Commission de l'émigration, créée par l'Etat de Californie pour leur venir en aide.

❝ Toujours situé au-dessus des vibrations des machines, il est bercé par le vacarme saccadé de la ferraille en mouvement et le grincement des amarres. On y accède par un escalier étroit, aux marches visqueuses et glissantes. Une masse humaine, des couchettes nauséabondes, des toilettes rebutantes : tel est l'entrepont. C'est aussi un assemblage suspect d'odeurs hétéroclites : pelures d'oranges, tabac, ail et désinfectant. [...] Une nourriture médiocre, apportée dans d'énormes bidons, est servie dans des gamelles fournies par la Compagnie. Au moment de la distribution, c'est à qui jouera des coudes. ❞

Edward Steiner
On the Trail of the Emigrant, 1906

passent une visite médicale, avant d'embarquer aussitôt dans l'entrepont. Cet examen sera reconduit à Ellis Island aux Etats-Unis avec, à la clé, une longue quarantaine ou le rapatriement.

Des conditions de traversée précaires

Des dortoirs sont aménagés dans l'entrepont avec des couchettes superposées sans draps, car l'on craint que les émigrants n'en fassent des chemises. La plupart dorment d'ailleurs tout habillés, sans même ôter leurs bottes. Ils mangent au pied des lits sur des tables en bois, garnies d'un pot à eau, d'une bassine, de gamelles et d'assiettes en fer.

TO IMMIGRANTS

The State of California Commission of Immigration and Housing is created to protect and aid immigrants in California

PER GLI EMIGRANTI
КЪ ЭММИГРАНТАМЪ
A LOS INMIGRANTES | DO EMIGRACJI
PARA EMIGRANTES | DOSELJENICIMA
A BEVÁNDORLOKHOZ | PRISTEHOVALCÙM
ΠΡΟΣ ΤΟΥΣ ΜΕΤΑΝΑΣΤΑΣ

«Paquebots démocratiques, paquebots du progrès»

1907 est une grande année, avec 107 000 émigrants transportés. La Transat décide de mettre en ligne, en 1908 et en 1911, deux paquebots à classe unique, le *Chicago* et le *Rochambeau*.

Les installations réservées aux émigrants ne cesseront de s'améliorer, notamment à la demande des autorités américaines qui exigent plus d'espace et d'hygiène pour chaque passager.

La guerre va tarir ce flot qui reprendra en 1920. 69 voyages postaux et supplémentaires sont effectués, et 55 000 émigrants sont encore embarqués. L'année suivante voit le nombre de traversées monter à 91, un chiffre record qui ne sera jamais plus égalé.

En 1921, l'Amérique établit des quotas d'émigration qui raniment la concurrence entre les compagnies

Dès 1918, un mouvement d'hostilité à l'émigration se dessine et se renforce en 1920, quand le pays entre dans la crise économique avec 3 millions de chômeurs. Des mesures sont prises pour contrôler le flot de l'émigration. Elles limitent à 357 000 le nombre des entrées annuelles, soit le quart de ce qui existait auparavant. En 1924, la restriction

En 1880, le peintre James Tissot transpose dans le monde contemporain la parabole de l'enfant prodigue, parti pour un pays lointain et revenu sans fortune. A gauche, *Le Départ* : le fils, assis sur la table d'un intérieur bourgeois d'où l'on aperçoit des mâtures de navires, affiche morgue et arrogance, tandis que le père tente de le dissuader de partir. A droite, *Le Retour* : débarqué d'un navire modeste, comme l'attestent les animaux de basse-cour, le fils, vêtu de haillons, pieds nus, misérable, se jette à genoux aux pieds du père pour implorer son pardon sous les regards choqués d'un couple symbolisant l'opinion.

s'accentue encore et le nombre des Européens admis annuellement est réduit à 161 500. Les candidats restants vont être l'objet de toutes les sollicitudes. Tous les moyens sont bons, tous les coups sont permis. Une compagnie accepte le paiement des places en monnaies dévaluées, une autre obtient de ses chemins de fer des rabais énormes. Les Irlandais, qui constituent déjà une force politique aux Etats-Unis, favorisent l'entrée de leurs compatriotes. Aussitôt, les compagnies font escale à Queenstown, au sud de l'Irlande.

A la gare Saint-Lazare en 1920, ces émigrants attendent le départ du train transatlantique qui les conduira jusqu'au Havre, où ils entameront le grand voyage.

   D'autres astuces sont déployées pour tourner les
rigueurs de la loi américaine qui a établi des quotas
mensuels. Les horaires des navires sont calculés pour
arriver à New York le premier de chaque mois à
0 heure 1. Ce n'est plus la course à la vitesse mais
celle au débarquement. Car si un concurrent s'est
présenté avant, il peut avoir épuisé tout le quota du
mois. On assiste alors aux scènes déchirantes du
refoulement et du retour vers l'Europe.

Le mouvement East Bound

Beaucoup d'Italiens, d'Autrichiens et de Galiciens
embauchés pour des travaux saisonniers trouvent
moins onéreux de revenir en Europe pendant la morte-

L e rêve écroulé!
  Refoulés des Etats-
Unis après la visite de
quarantaine d'Ellis
Island, la dernière et
redoutable épreuve
avant de mettre le pied
en Amérique, ces
émigrants allemands
repartent à bord du
Kaiser Wilhelm II.
Pour éviter les
exclusions à l'arrivée,
les consuls des Etats-
Unis dans certains
pays européens sont
habilités à délivrer des
visas aux émigrants.
Des amendes frappent
les compagnies qui
transportent des
passagers n'ayant pas
obtenu ce visa.

saison que de rester aux Etats-Unis. Ce reflux, appelé East Bound, augmenté par l'apport des victimes du mal du pays ou de la crise, assure aux compagnies près de la moitié des passages de troisième classe.

A partir de 1923, l'émigration ne fait plus recette

La restriction américaine s'accentue encore, et les quotas défavorisent en particulier les candidats originaires d'Europe méridionale et orientale.

Les chiffres de 1923 montrent l'évolution de ce trafic d'hommes : les recettes de la Transat passent de 235 millions de francs en 1920 à seulement 87 millions trois ans plus tard. Il faut alors démonter les installations de l'entrepont où s'étaient entassés des milliers de pauvres bougres venus chercher, et parfois trouver, fortune au Nouveau Monde.

Heureusement, le niveau de vie américain s'est élevé, faisant apparaître une importante classe moyenne qui vient en Europe pour affaires ou pour jouer au touriste. Les compagnies arment des navires à classe unique, tandis que dans les grands paquebots apparaît la classe touriste.

Pour ces Italiens qui viennent de débarquer du paquebot, c'est l'espoir. Seules ces grilles cadenassées les séparent encore du Nouveau Monde. Leur ouverture, dans quelques instants ou quelques heures, les récompensera enfin des mois d'efforts et de sacrifices imposés pour ce voyage de la dernière chance, car pour eux devenir Américain, «c'était manger et boire comme un chrétien»...

« Le transatlantique ne fait pas partie de notre univers, c'est nous qui participons au sien. On se sent comme un membre de sa caste, investi d'un rôle à jouer. Cette traversée de cinq jours ressemble à un bal masqué, gigantesque et grandiose, où chaque homme est un gentleman, chaque femme une lady, où le reste ne compte pas. »

CHAPITRE IV
À BORD, OUBLIER LA MER

La Transatlantique, un mode de transport, un style de vie, qui évoquent le luxe et le plaisir.

Etat Major   Équipage
& Personnel de l'Hôtel ___   812
Nombre de Personnes à Bord ___ 2450

D'un quai à l'autre, une semaine de gala

La fête permanente, c'est le maître mot des
compagnies pour assurer la réussite des traversées.
Les activités, les distractions et les spectacles s'y
succèdent en un rituel attendu de tous.

   Les clients sont rois et ne doivent avoir aucun
souci. Du commissaire au groom en passant par les
maîtres d'hôtel, cuisiniers, sommeliers, garçons de
cabine, femmes de chambre, serveurs, coiffeurs,
masseurs, lingères et beaucoup d'autres, chacun
prend en charge les passagers pendant toute la
durée du voyage : une personne pour deux
passagers ; de quoi être libéré de tout tracas,
comme en témoigne le récit suivant qui
évoque les moments les plus agréables
d'une journée à bord du *Normandie*.

P aris-New York :
les deux extrémités
de «la plus grande
passerelle du monde»,
symbolisées sur cet
éventail.

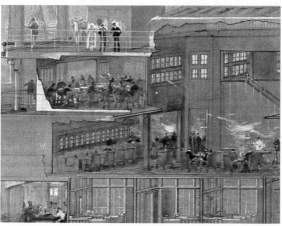

Cette gouache
d'Albert Sébille,
représentant la coupe
longitudinale de l'*Ile-
de-France*, mesure 4
mètres de long et a été
réalisée pour le
dépliant remis aux
passagers. Elle montre
l'immensité de cette
ville flottante et les
différents niveaux
d'occupation où se
trouvent passagers et
équipage en action,
résumant ainsi le
déroulement d'une
journée à bord (ci-
dessus, détail ci-contre
et pages suivantes).

«Dès le réveil, le garçon de cabine vous a apporté un merveilleux petit déjeuner»

Il faut s'en arracher «pour descendre à la salle de gymnastique, où se pratiquent escrime, ballon, haltères, boxe, etc., puis vite le bain de vapeur avant de sauter dans la piscine pour un 25 mètres. Après le massage, il faut s'habiller en tenue sportive pour aller pratiquer le deck-tennis, le golf ou le shuffle-board sur le sundeck. Peu avant 11 heures, c'est le moment de faire ses 3 kilomètres de marche en dix tours de pont promenade où le tout-Normandie se rencontre. Mais déjà *L'Atlantique*, le journal du bord, vient de sortir des presses avec les toutes dernières nouvelles grâce à la

Parmi les activités sportives proposées aux passagers : tennis, tir aux pigeons d'argile, volley-ball, anneaux, bowling et palets (ci-contre).

Déplacement ___ 41.518 T ˢ
Jauge Brute Totale 42053 T ˣ
Puissance ___ 55000 C.V.

TSF. On s'allonge sur des transats, sur le pont promenade où les grooms vous servent un consommé chaud que les mauvaises langues surnomment le bouillon d'onze heures».

«Il est temps de passer une tenue de ville pour se rendre à la salle à manger avec un appétit aiguisé par l'air du large»

«Il est de bon ton de ne pas choisir un des 75 plats figurant sur la carte du jour, même si l'un d'eux

Sur le pont supérieur, le visage caressé par l'air du large, certains préfèrent paresser, allongés dans un transat et choyés par le personnel du bord.

Sur le sundeck, entre les immenses cheminées, des emplacements de plus de 500 m² sont réservés aux jeux et aux sports de plein air. Nombreux en sont les adeptes, soucieux d'achever au grand air l'entraînement poursuivi chaque jour dans la salle de culture physique. Le sundeck, un des coins les plus agréables et les plus populaires du bord.

retenait votre gourmandise. On le demandera demain quand il n'y figurera plus. Mais le maître d'hôtel, qui connaît son monde transatlantique lui aussi, vous met au défi de commander un plat ou un mets qui ne puisse être servi. Après ce déjeuner qui doit rester léger, courte sieste avant d'aller tirer quelques pigeons d'argile, et c'est déjà l'heure du cinéma. Aujourd'hui, on donne *Les Trois Lanciers du Bengale*. Ce n'est pas mal, car le *Normandie*, qui consomme 144 films pour 40 traversées, ne possède évidemment pas que des chefs-d'œuvre. Après avoir jeté un œil distrait à la finale de ping-pong, il faut choisir entre le thé dansant et le bridge. Le rendez-vous pour le dîner est à 20 heures 30 et il reste un quart d'heure pour passer son smoking.»

«Dîner de gala avec le commandant Thoreux qui recevra à sa table une quinzaine de privilégiés»

«Par le grand escalier, les passagères en robe longue font des entrées très étudiées avant de gagner leur table sous la conduite d'un maître d'hôtel digne comme un archevêque (celui du *France*, Olivier Naffrechoux, qui avait 750 traversées à son actif, était même surnommé Monseigneur). Le dîner commence par le caviar, suivi au choix d'un consommé de tortue

Autre type de compétition, celle de l'élégance qui s'exprime tout au long de la journée et surtout lors des dîners et des soirées. Le décor des paquebots se prête d'ailleurs admirablement aux défilés de mannequins.

ou de la crème Reine Margot. Poisson ensuite avec suprêmes de sole Païva. En entrée, une noisette d'agneau Richelieu, puis volaille avec un dindonneau poêlé Ile-de-France. Quelques haricots verts pour reprendre haleine et voici le caneton grillé et le contrefilet à l'anglaise. Un cœur de laitue pour se rafraîchir. Ce sont alors les desserts, une pièce montée, le gâteau Succès, puis la glace et les petits fours, et quelques fruits pour terminer. Le tout arrosé de vins fins ou maison puisque la Transat possédait ses propres vignobles.»

L a carte du sommelier ne compte pas moins de 1 000 crus afin de soutenir la réputation de haute gastronomie des paquebots français.

«Le théâtre, qui fait relâche ce soir, est remplacé par un spectacle au grand salon»

«Le speaker improvisé Charles Boyer présente une gamme d'artistes, passagers, prêts à donner gracieusement leur concours. C'est ensuite le défilé des mannequins d'une maison de couture, suivi de

la musique du VIIe régiment Lafayette de New York, qui défile en fanfare à travers les salons! Enfin, l'orchestre du bord paraît et, sur la piste lumineuse, les couples se mettent à danser. A 2 heures du matin, pour resserrer les rangs, l'orchestre monte au grill, où il est temps de se faire servir un petit souper. Seules l'aube et la bordée de nettoyage font fuir les derniers couples qui, sur le pont promenade, vont découvrir que la mer est toujours là…» Un programme copieux qui fait dire à Henri Bordeaux : «Il y a vingt ans, on pouvait, à bord, méditer, mener une vie contemplative en oubliant la terre; aujourd'hui, on oublie la mer et la terre vous poursuit.»

Le dépaysement est de rigueur lors des escales qui jalonnent les lignes d'Extrême-Orient. A Djibouti, les négrillons montés à bord plongent dans les eaux du port pour repêcher les piécettes que leur jettent des passagers coiffés du casque colonial traditionnel.

Sur la ligne d'Orient, un parfum d'aventure et d'exotisme

Sur les paquebots des Messageries, où les voyages vers l'Extrême-Orient durent plusieurs semaines, la vie à bord est plus conviviale et surtout ponctuée par les escales : Aden, Ceylan, la Chine, Tahiti, des noms qui font rêver et des moments précieux qui inspireront Dekobra, Morand, Kessel ou Farrère. C'est la rencontre de paysages, de civilisations et d'hommes hors du commun. «On ne sait plus si on vit ou si on rêve!»

Ce paquebot remonte la rivière de Saigon au grand dam des occupants du sampang pris dans les remous du sillage.

A Colombo, un marchand ambulant propose des bijoux de pacotille aux passagères installées sur le pont.

C'est ce qu'écrit, dans son journal, Mme Durand-Fardel qui se rend à Shanghai sur l'*Hoogly* en compagnie de son mari. A Aden, la voyageuse visite l'agence de la Compagnie dont «le jardin de 4 mètres carrés est fait avec de la terre rapportée de Marseille par de gracieux officiers à qui les filles de l'agent précédent demandaient toujours en cadeau un sac de terre de France!» Le paquebot fait escale à Ceylan. Le commandant Gauvain, toujours galant, invite une trentaine de passagers à déjeuner dans une propriété qu'il a achetée dans l'intérieur.

«De Saigon à Hong Kong, nous entrons dans la queue d'un typhon. Le commandant ne s'est pas couché pendant cinq nuits. Le paquebot dansait des cachucas désordonnées, la vaisselle se cassait pendant la nuit avec grand fracas et nous réveillait en sursaut.» A Hong Kong, avec deux jours de retard sur l'horaire à cause de ce mauvais temps, les Durand-Fardel embarquent sur l'*Iraouaddy* qui les conduira à Shanghai retrouver leur fille.

C es étiquettes multicolores sont destinées aux bagages à main que les passagers conservent avec eux dans le train transatlantique jusqu'à l'embarquement. Les malles-cabines, elles, sont acheminées directement à bord.

T out ce que le monde rassemble de talent, de classe et de puissance succombe aux charmes de la French Line. A bord de ces ambassades du luxe et du savoir-vivre français, cette élite participe à une sorte de théâtre vivant et affirme son appartenance à une nouvelle caste, celle de la *ship society*.

«High society», «ship society» et système des castes

A bord, les lignes de démarcation sont nettes. Le capitaine, les officiers et l'équipage constituent la bureaucratie, les passagers de première classe forment l'aristocratie; ceux de seconde classe, la bourgeoisie et ceux de l'entrepont, le prolétariat.

Les passagers des premières se recrutent parmi l'élite, celle conférée par la naissance ou par la réussite personnelle, habituée à ce qui existe de mieux en matière de service, de confort et de table.

Aristocrates, vrais ou faux princes, magnats des finances et de l'industrie, artistes et hommes politiques, débutantes ou vedettes confirmées font partie des habitués de la French Line parmi lesquels on reconnaît aussi bien Vanderbilt, Rockefeller, Toscanini, Maurice Chevalier, Jules Romains, Hemingway, Marlene Dietrich, le sultan de Tahore ou le comte de Warwick. Cette clientèle ne représente en fait que 200 à 300 personnes sur les 2 000 qui voyagent.

Les anonymes de la classe touriste (ci-dessous) côtoient, sans vraiment le rencontrer, le monde des milliardaires et des célébrités (ici, Fernandel à la barre du *Liberté*). Car les compagnies veillent jalousement au respect des frontières imposées par les classes.

Passagers anonymes et classe touriste

Le boom économique et la nécessité pour les compagnies de trouver une formule de remplacement au transport des émigrants amènent une nouvelle clientèle sur les paquebots. C'est la création des paquebots à classe unique et des classes touristes, formule fourre-tout qui permet de satisfaire cette *middle class* dont parfois les ancêtres avaient voyagé dans l'entrepont des émigrants : chefs d'entreprise, médecins, avocats, architectes, professeurs, commerçants et groupes divers, qui allient le plus souvent travail et tourisme, côtoient les aristocrates et les millionnaires.

Patriotisme et couleur locale

Sur les lignes d'Orient, on voyage souvent par obligation et les paquebots transportent les militaires, fonctionnaires ou colons qui rejoignent les lointaines colonies françaises.

Le transport des passagers des lignes régulières d'Afrique du Nord et des pèlerins vers La Mecque justifie une organisation libérale pour l'époque, permettant l'installation de tentes sur le pont arrière pour abriter les harems et les femmes arabes avec des «charniers» (sorte de tonneaux) renfermant de l'eau pour les ablutions rituelles. Le respect de l'Islam inspire aussi les instructions de la Compagnie à ses commandants : «Les voyageurs doivent obtenir tous les égards qui leur sont dus. Ils ne doivent être ni rudoyés, ni tournés en ridicule. Que les femmes surtout ne fassent pas l'objet d'une curiosité indiscrète.»

Seul moyen de transport pour relier bon nombre de pays, on trouve sur ces lignes des personnalités et des célébrités. Gauguin effectuera deux traversées sur la ligne d'Australie et de Nouvelle-Calédonie qui passe par Tahiti. Malade, Arthur Rimbaud, le poète devenu

Les indigènes, qui emmènent femmes, enfants, animaux et objets hétéroclites, transforment parfois le pont en véritable souk. Ci-dessus, le pont de *La Seyne*, au cours d'un voyage vers la Syrie.

À bord du *Liberté* (page de droite en haut), le standard téléphonique permet d'entrer en relation avec n'importe quel point du globe alors que le bateau se trouve en haute mer.

aventurier, se fait rapatrier sur le *Melbourne*. Loti et Claude Farrère, tous deux officiers de Marine, embarquent sur des paquebots de ces lignes, comme beaucoup plus tard, en 1929, le commandant Charles de Gaulle qui rejoint son poste à Beyrouth. Sur ces lignes, on côtoie aussi bien Henri de Monfreid, l'aventurier de la mer Rouge, que le père Teilhard de Chardin revenant de Chine.

Un millier d'hommes et de femmes chargés du bon déroulement de la vie à bord

Au sommet de la hiérarchie se trouve le commandant, le «maître après Dieu», une responsabilité écrasante qui fait de beaucoup de commandants des solitaires. Mais le maître de maison est le commissaire principal qui doit avoir l'œil à tout, garder le sourire en toutes circonstances et surtout être fin diplomate. Ce devait être le cas de celui qui dut consoler cette passagère américaine se plaignant qu'on ait jeté à la mer les cendres de son défunt mari.

Pour son premier voyage, le *Normandie* est confié au commandant René Pugnet (à droite). Son adjoint Pierre Thoreux (à gauche) lui succédera en 1936.

La réputation du paquebot et de la Compagnie repose sur le talent du chef cuisinier. Le chef Lindauer, le premier, donne ses lettres de noblesse à la cuisine en mer. Une tradition qui ne se démentit pas, puisque sur le *France,* dernier du nom, il y a sous les ordres du chef Grangier 160 cuisiniers, 18 pâtissiers, 8 boulangers, 8 bouchers et 11 cuisiniers de buffet, tandis que le chef sommelier veille sur 1 000 bouteilles. Les membres du service hôtelier sont en contact permanent avec la clientèle. Un garçon de cabine a en charge 20 passagers en première classe et 30 en classe touriste.

A 10 mètres sous la flottaison, le personnel des machines vit dans des conditions difficiles, dans une ambiance surchauffée. Des salaires plus élevés que ceux versés pour les mêmes professsions à terre compensent ces difficultés et expliquent qu'il y ait eu de véritables dynasties familiales de Bretons et de Normands se succédant sur les mêmes navires.

On naît, on vit et on meurt dans les villes flottantes

Les mariages religieux ont lieu dans les chapelles des paquebots, transformables selon les cultes représentés à bord, tandis que le commandant fait office de maire de la ville. Le commandant de l'*Ile-de-France* unit en 1928 Robert Esnault-Pelterie et Carmen Bernaldo de Quiros. Comme à terre, la vie et la mort se côtoient parfois. En juillet 1960, sur le *Liberté*, le photographe des stars Teddy Piaz décède brutalement au Café de l'Atlantique à l'instant même où le jeune Jean-Claude Campellonne, tremblant d'émotion, tient dans ses mains la barre du grand bateau où il était né neuf ans plus tôt…

Tous les paquebots ont au moins un médecin et une infirmerie pour les soins les plus urgents.

Apprentissage de l'anglais pour les grooms et sortie des chiens par le spécialiste chargé de leur bien-être. Sur le *France*, ils ont même droit à un menu à leur intention.

Certains ont de véritables salles d'opérations avec une équipe médicale. Les opérations les plus fréquentes sont bien sur les appendicites de passagers ou de membres de l'équipage, ou même de marins de navires croisés en mer. Le *France* est le premier paquebot, en 1965, à pouvoir transmettre, grâce au satellite relayé par Pleumeur Bodou, les électrocardiogrammes réalisés à bord. Le docteur Monnier, qui est à l'origine de cette innovation, travaille d'un côté de l'Atlantique avec le professeur Lenègre de l'hôpital Boucicaut à Paris et de l'autre avec le professeur Wright de la Cornell University de New York.

Les fortunes de mer

Conditions de navigation difficiles ou erreurs humaines, tempêtes de l'Atlantique Nord ou typhons de l'océan Indien, les naufrages sont une réalité que toutes les compagnies voudraient bien gommer de leur histoire.

Erreur pour le *Drummond Castle*, dont le commandant confond, en 1896, les phares de Ouessant et ceux de Molène et qui vient se jeter sur les rochers des Pierres vertes avec ses 250 passagers. A Beyrouth en 1952, erreur fatale aussi pour le *Champollion*, non informé de l'installation du nouveau feu de l'aéroport.

Les navires sont aussi menacés par la brume, l'abordage et les incendies. C'est le cas du *Ville-du-*

En 1928, les nouveaux mariés sont salués par une haie de mousses de sonnerie.

Les cuisines sont à la dimension des paquebots. Celles du *Normandie* ont 60 mètres de long et les trois fourneaux fonctionnant à l'électricité mesurent 17 mètres. Chaque jour, 76 chefs et une centaine de garçons de cuisine y préparent 4000 repas.

Havre touché par le *Loch Earn* en 1873, qui coule en dix minutes, entraînant 226 personnes dans la mort.

Mais les paquebots déjouent parfois les catastrophes. Ainsi, en septembre 1923, l'*André-Lebon* est à Yokohama, chaudières éteintes et guindeau démonté, quand à 1 heure 55 la terre tremble. En une minute, Tokyo et Yokohama n'existent plus. Dans des conditions périlleuses, le commandant Cousin parvient à accueillir à bord 1 500 réfugiés, dont l'ambassadeur Paul Claudel. Toute la journée, en jouant sur ses amarres, il réussit à écarter son navire de la ville en feu et des brûlots qui dérivent, évitant les navires aux amarres rompues.

Louis-Joseph-André Delacour, sauveteur havrais de soixante-quatorze ans, a réalisé 23 sauvetages et arraché 46 personnes à la mort.

Entrés dans la légende, les naufrages du «Titanic» et du «Lusitania»

Le navire géant de la White Star, pourtant réputé insubmersible, heurte un iceberg au cours de son voyage inaugural sur New York le 4 mai 1912. La mer s'engouffre brutalement dans la brèche longue de 80 mètres qui défigure la coque. Cassé en deux, le *Titanic* s'enfonce avec 1 600 passagers qui n'ont pas trouvé place dans les canots de sauvetage, tandis que l'orchestre du bord entonne le cantique «Plus près de toi mon Dieu».

Deux naufrages sans rescapés : à gauche, celui du *Liban* en 1903 qui, éventré par l'*Insulaire*, coule à une heure du port de Marseille; ci-dessous, le *Lusitania* torpillé par les Allemands.

L'émotion est à peine apaisée que l'on apprend le naufrage du *Lusitania*, coulé sans sommation par un sous-marin allemand, le 7 mai 1915, au large de l'Irlande. Là encore, les canots de sauvetage sont en nombre insuffisants, et l'on déplore 1 200 victimes dont 124 citoyens américains, ce qui déterminera les Etats-Unis à entrer en guerre.

L'indignation de l'opinion publique face à ces catastrophes oblige les compagnies maritimes à réviser les conditions de sécurité. Le nombre des canots est désormais doublé pour permettre de sauver à la fois passagers et équipage avec ceux d'un seul bord.

C e croquis, commencé dans un canot par un des naufragés et terminé sur le *Carpathia,* montre les différentes phases de l'engloutissement du *Titanic* (de gauche à droite et de haut en bas). 11 heures 45 : collision avec l'iceberg. 0 heure 5 : le *Titanic* fait eau, on descend les chaloupes. 1 heure 40 : il s'enfonce par l'avant. 1 heure 50 : le bâtiment se brise par le milieu et l'avant coule. 2 heures : le gaillard d'arrière pivote. 2 heures 5 : l'arrière reste planté verticalement pendant cinq minutes puis disparaît. 868 rescapés, essentiellement des femmes et des enfants entassés dans des canots en nombre insuffisant, sont recueillis par le *Carpathia* qui, à 5 heures du matin, est le premier à arriver sur les lieux de la catastrophe. Ci-contre, l'un de ces canots photographié par un passager du *Carpathia.*

De génération en génération de paquebots, la demande de sécurité, de rapidité et de confort se transforme en un besoin de splendeur et de théâtralité croissantes. Le luxe se déchaîne. Vitrine des tendances décoratives d'une époque et reflet de l'éthique sociale, le style transatlantique atteint son apogée au moment même où les paquebots semblent voués à la disparition.

CHAPITRE V

STYLE ET LUXE EN MER

Les panneaux de laques sculptées de Dunand ornent le fumoir des premières classes que chacun traverse pour se rendre du grand salon au café-grill. Ces laques représentent la Conquête du cheval (ci-contre), la Pêche, les Vendanges et la Danse.

Architecture domestique et confort bourgeois

Pour transformer l'épreuve de la traversée en plaisir de naviguer, les premiers paquebots à vapeur vont s'attacher à offrir un confort inconnu jusque-là sur l'Atlantique, en reconstituant l'atmosphère des maisons bourgeoises cossues. Les compagnies allemandes et Johannes Poppe donnent le ton avec le *Lahn*, puis avec le *Kaiser Wilhelm der Grosse.* Toutes les nations vont suivre ce mouvement dans une surenchère à l'opulence, à la surcharge. Alors qu'à bord du *Viceroy of India* le fumoir évoque irrésistiblement les châteaux écossais, avec sa cheminée, ses armoiries et ses épées fixées à la cloison, le *Winchester Castle* suggère la chaleur d'un intérieur hollandais, avec une imposante cheminée surmontée d'une galerie avec balcons en fer forgé et poutres apparentes.

Le *Washington*, premier paquebot français qui se lance dans l'aventure océane, n'est pas en reste, comme en témoigne ce récit de voyage :

Pour lutter contre le roulis, des ingénieurs anglais imaginent en 1874 des salons montés sur un système à cardans qui maintiennent une parfaite horizontalité quel que soit l'état de la mer.

«Le *Washington* est confortablement aménagé et la vie en mer présente maintenant autant d'agréments qu'un séjour dans une station balnéaire. Le salon des passagers de première classe est blanc et or, fort bien meublé de sièges rembourrés, de lampes de cuivre et de plantes vertes, dans le dernier goût de la capitale. [...] En dessous des gaillards, à l'arrière, se trouve une salle à manger de 168 couverts. Son décor traditionnel de bois d'acajou est du meilleur goût. Il y a deux salons pour les dames à l'avant, ils sont très fréquentés et certainement les plus agréables et les plus délicatement décorés du navire avec leurs poufs de soieries bleu roi, leurs cuivres, leur bois d'acajou et leurs fleurs.»

Plus tard, sur *La Bourgogne, La Champagne* ou *La Touraine,* le décor est somptueux, mais reste lourd, avec ses tentures de satin ornées de glands, de pompons et de franges qui dissimulent fenêtres et ouvertures de ces locaux rutilants où l'air et la lumière ne pénètrent que difficilement. Les bois précieux ornés de marqueterie, les panneaux d'onyx gravé constituent l'une des bases de cette décoration fin de siècle.

Dans le salon du paquebot allemand, le *Kronprinzessin Cecilie,* la décoration est surchargée de colonnades, de plafonds à caissons et de balustrades en fer forgé, accumulant les matériaux les plus riches et les tissus les plus lourds. Elle reflète les habitudes de luxe cossu des classes aisées qui, seules, empruntent les paquebots. Page de gauche et en haut, on retrouve les mêmes tendances dans le salon de *La Lorraine.*

Ce soir, on dîne au Ritz : le triomphe de l'«hôtelisme»

Il faut satisfaire une clientèle qui exige de plus en plus de trouver en mer le luxe et le confort dont elle jouit sur terre. Pour cela, les paquebots vont essayer de ressembler aux grands hôtels européens qui font leur apparition, comme le Savoy ou le Ritz.

Sous l'influence d'Albert Ballin, président de la Hamburg Amerika, les paquebots deviennent des palaces flottants, avec leurs salles à usages multiples – salon de lecture, de correspondance, salle de bal – et leur inévitable jardin de palmiers.

Avec le «France», première incarnation du musée national flottant, la Transat fait appel à l'histoire

La clientèle américaine d'hommes d'affaires, financiers, écrivains ou jeunes gens fortunés vient découvrir dans la vieille Europe ce qui lui manque le plus : un passé et une culture. Le *France-II*, le «Versailles de l'Atlantique», rappelle à tous que sur le plan historique et culturel la France donne le ton. Ce paquebot crée un style national, où se mêle l'héritage de l'élégance royale et quelques éléments contemporains. Incrustations dorées et marbres pyrénéens y évoquent la demeure du Roi-Soleil avec copies de fauteuils et bergères d'époque, que les malheureux mousses déménagent chaque fois que l'on fait du cinéma parlant, tandis que l'on tend un écran devant la copie du portrait de Louis XIV par Rigaud.

Le *Paris* hésite, dans sa première version, entre la pesanteur historique de ses prédécesseurs et les lignes pures ou brisées du nouveau style : retour au XIXe siècle et au fer forgé dans la salle à manger, émergence de l'Art nouveau dans les suites luxueuses.

Après avoir franchi la passerelle, les passagers du *France* pénètrent dans un hall de réception en rotonde, éclairé par un dôme cristallin qui projette la lumière sur un sol en dalles de caoutchouc imitant le marbre (ci-contre).

Surmontée d'un dauphin, une des premières représentations du sigle de la Compagnie transatlantique qui, en fonction des modes, évoluera vers des formes de plus en plus simplifiées. Entre 1870 et 1935, il fera l'objet d'une vingtaine d'interprétations avant de se fixer à la création réalisée pour le *Normandie.*

Un dôme central lumineux, une enfilade de colonnes corinthiennes ponctuées à chaque extrémité par un portrait du Roi-Soleil, des fresques de Boucher, des fauteuils copiés du mobilier national, tel est le grand salon du *France* (ci-dessus). Malgré la surabondance des styles exclusivement français représentés sur ce paquebot, les décorateurs atteignent une cohérence esthétique rare.

Les escaliers monumentaux, orgueil des paquebots

Sous les voûtes dorées de la salle à manger Louis XIV du *France*, les architectes introduisent pour la première fois ce qui deviendra le trait distinctif des bateaux de la Transat : la grande descente.

Les escaliers monumentaux des grands paquebots témoignent du génie des constructeurs, car cette trouée verticale dans un navire ne doit pas en compromettre la rigidité. Celui du *France*, qui occupe trois entreponts et a une hauteur de 8 mètres sous plafond, est une copie de l'escalier réalisé par Robert

L e soir des dîners de gala, les grandes descentes donnent aux passagères l'occasion attendue et redoutée de faire admirer leurs toilettes à tous les dîneurs déjà attablés.

S ur le *France* (ci-dessus), le grand escalier est orné de scènes empruntées à l'école de Watteau. Ci-contre, la grande descente du *Président-Charles-Roux*.

de Cotte pour l'hôtel du comte de Toulouse. A double volée sur *La Bourgogne*, triomphe de la ferronnerie avec balustres et balcons sur le *Paris*, ornés de figures allégoriques sur *La Provence*, se développant sur trois ponts en fer forgé noir, marbre jaune et pierre grise sur l'*Ile-de-France*, les escaliers deviennent une manifestation d'art.

L'«Ile-de-France», émissaire naval des temps modernes, inaugure le style paquebot

Selon la volonté du président Dal Piaz, un paquebot doit être une création, et non une copie ou une anthologie flottante des styles et reliques de l'histoire.

Ce projet de Bouwens Van der Boijen pour la grande descente du *Paris* montre la prédilection du modern style pour les ferronneries, les galeries et les balcons. Il sera quelque peu simplifié au moment de la réalisation du paquebot dans sa première version.

Dans la grande salle
à manger de l'*Ile-de-France*, l'architecte Pierre Patout a souligné audacieusement l'ossature du navire par 112 motifs lumineux, en verre moulé de Lalique, qui répandent une lumière douce sur les parois en marbre des Pyrénées de trois tonalités de gris. Deux pilastres carrés de marbre blanc de 8,50 mètres encadrent le grand escalier.

Avec l'*Ile-de-France*, les paquebots s'ouvrent aux manifestations de leur époque. Les ornements superflus – sculptures, corniches, frontons – sont supprimés au profit de formes simples, de grandes surfaces lisses à angles droits où la pierre de Lunel grise s'allie aux marbres jaunes gravés de fleurs.

Essences exotiques en ébénisterie, incrustation de nacre, d'écaille, d'ivoire confèrent une grande beauté aux salons, galeries et appartements inspirés de l'exposition Arts déco de 1925.

L'architecte Bouwens Van der Boijen signe une grande part de ces aménagements. Les suites de grand luxe portant des noms de châteaux sont confiées à des artistes de renom comme Tardif et Bruyer, Eric Bagge, Martine et Poiret, et même à de jeunes élèves de l'école Boulle qui peuvent donner libre cours à leur imagination. Il n'existe pas deux décors semblables parmi les 139 cabines de première classe, les 10 suites de luxe ou les 4 appartements de grand luxe.

L'*Ile-de-France* est aussi le premier paquebot à posséder une chapelle. Due à l'architecte Danis, elle comporte deux étages sur une hauteur de 6 mètres et est ornée d'une croix lumineuse en verre, dans le style de l'époque cher aux Gallé et Lalique. L'atmosphère de luxe et de raffinement de l'*Ile-de-France* lui vaudra le surnom de « Rue de la Paix de l'Atlantique », et le style paquebot sera bientôt adopté sur les bateaux anglais, allemands, italiens, et même à terre.

Sue et Mare, chargés de décorer le grand salon de l'*Ile-de-France*, respectent l'immense espace de cette salle de 24 mètres sur 18 de long, de 5 mètres de haut, avec un plafond de 432 mètres carrés d'une seule portée. Ils reportent sur le pourtour de la pièce leur architecture de colonnes, rétablissant ainsi l'équilibre entre ses trois dimensions. En revanche, le compartimentage du plafond en caissons lumineux et dorés, avec des coupoles surbaissées aux quatre angles, divise l'espace pour la satisfaction des yeux.

«La rue de la Paix de l'Atlantique»

La grande descente est le cœur de l'*Ile-de-France*, le lieu de toutes les rencontres. A double révolution et construite sur trois niveaux, elle débouche sur le foyer, véritable grand-place du paquebot. C'est là qu'aboutissent les galeries d'accès aux salons et aux cabines, les ascenseurs desservant les différents ponts et que s'ouvrent les bureaux du commissaire, du médecin. C'est là aussi que chacun peut découvrir les boutiques, une succursale du Bon Marché, les salons de coiffure et l'entrée de la chapelle.

«Normandie», la grande salle à manger

Cette pièce immense, œuvre de Patout et Pacon, s'ouvre sur une perspective de 86 mètres de longueur et 8,50 mètres de hauteur. 38 appliques, dont chacune émet un rayon de 5 mètres de haut, servent de fond aux 12 colonnes de Lalique. Un champ lumineux rectangulaire où rien n'arrête le regard. Au bout de la pièce, par-delà l'alignement des tables aux nappages soigneusement dressés, chargées de cristaux de Daum et d'argenterie de Christofle, une immense statue par Dejean, représentant la France pacifique, préside à l'entrée des passagers.

Quatre couples de colonnes séparent la nef des bas-côtés de ce «salon-église-galerie».

Glaces et panneaux muraux, dorés ou argentés, de Jean Dupas ornent les quatre angles du grand salon du *Normandie.* Ils mesurent chacun 6 mètres de haut sur 15 de large et représentent les mythes grecs.

Le style transatlantique atteint son apogée avec le «Normandie»

«Ce n'est plus une ville flottante, titre un journal, c'est une capitale.» Le *Normandie* mérite bien son surnom de «vaisseau de lumière» : tout est en verre.

Une volière fleurie, dans le jardin d'hiver planté par Vilmorin et réalisé par Ruhlmann (ci-dessous).

La salle à manger, plus longue que la galerie des Glaces du château de Versailles, est entièrement décorée de dalles de verre moulées, gravées, ciselées et signées Lalique et Laouret. Des perspectives grandioses sont dessinées dans les lieux de réception. Celle du pont principal, œuvre de Patout et Pacon, va de la chapelle à la salle à manger en passant par le grand hall. Au pont supérieur, Bouwens Van der Boijen et Expert réalisent une enfilade unique : théâtre, galerie, salon, fumoir, restaurant-grill où, par-delà les baies, la vue se prolonge jusqu'à l'horizon. La lumière est une des plus subtiles parures dans le

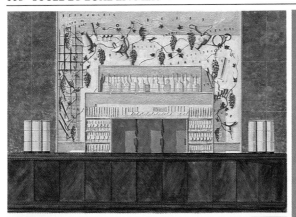

Une simplicité qui se revêt de somptuosité; c'est ce qu'évoquent ces esquisses d'**Expert** pour le bar (en haut, à gauche), le grill (ci-contre) et l'escalier du fumoir des premières classes du *Normandie* (ci-dessus).

Détail du *Char de l'aurore* (en bas, à droite), l'un des panneaux de laque de Dunand qui associent l'art raffiné des Orientaux à celui des bas-reliefs antiques.

grand hall pourvu de caissons lumineux et dans les coursives où les corniches la projettent vers les plafonds à profil courbe qui la reflètent. Elle contribue à l'atmosphère douillette du jardin d'hiver.

Tapisseries d'Aubusson de Gaudissart, dont un tapis de 8 mètres sur 12, glaces peintes à profusion, laques aux couleurs vives dorées à la feuille, tel le panneau *La Pêche* signé Dunand, piano à queue dessiné par Ruhlmann : c'est le luxe pour le luxe, une vitrine de l'art français qui, dans l'exhubérante vanité de ses réalisations, est l'image fidèle des tendances complexes de l'époque. Plus jamais on ne construira de paquebot qui surpasse, ou même approche, la

splendeur et la puissance du *Normandie* et de ses
homologues britanniques, le *Queen Mary* et le
Queen Elizabeth.

Le «France», la fin de la légende

La succession est difficile, pour ne pas
dire impossible, à assumer pour le
France, le paquebot démocratique des
années soixante. Il a la même taille, mais
plus les mêmes impératifs. Le *France*
n'est pas né d'un souci de prestige, c'est
avant tout un navire agréable et
fonctionnel. Après la guerre, les passagers
recherchent d'abord un moyen de
transport peu coûteux·

   A cause des risques d'incendie, le bois
est proscrit au profit de matériaux
nouveaux incombustibles, comme
l'aluminium, le verre, les matières
plastiques, les textiles synthétiques.
Les longues enfilades, les plafonds
démesurés à colonnades ne sont plus de
mise. A terre, d'ailleurs, les palaces ont
aussi resserré les cloisons et abaissé les

plafonds. Toutes ces règles draconiennes handicapent certainement les décorateurs. Ils réussissent cependant à faire de ce dernier paquebot un hôtel flottant confortable, offrant un moment privilégié de détente, de vacances.

Le fumoir des premières classes sur le pont véranda est en prise directe avec la mer, ce qui est nouveau. Il est décoré d'une très belle tapisserie de 17 mètres de Picart Le Doux. Deux salles de spectacle, dont un théâtre de 665 places décoré par Peynet, un salon de bridge et de lecture et une bibliothèque signés du décorateur Leleu, la prestigieuse suite Normandie ornée de toiles du peintre Hambourg montrent la large place accordée à la représentation contemporaine.

Jugé trop audacieux pour les uns, pas assez moderne pour les autres, il fut cependant plébiscité pendant treize ans par l'ensemble de ses passagers. Une fois de plus, l'évolution de la société avait donné le ton au style des grands paquebots.

Sur le *France*, la décoration est résolument gaie et fonctionnelle.

Dans le fumoir des premières, une tapisserie de 17 mètres de long de Picart Le Doux (ci-dessous).

LE HAVRE / SOUTHAMPTON / NEW YORK

Cⁱᵉ Gˡᵉ **TRANSATLANTIQUE**

French Line

FRANCE | NORMANDIE

le Havre

« Que ce navire aille vers sa destinée. Porter des hommes vers des hommes! Qu'il aille vers l'océan pour y voguer et y servir!» Mais l'avenir du «France» ne sera pas aussi brillant que celui tracé par le général de Gaulle lors du lancement en 1960. Treize ans plus tard, un siècle d'aventure transatlantique s'achève. Le «France», désarmé, quitte Le Havre pour vivre une seconde destinée sous le nom de «Norway».

CHAPITRE VI
«FRANCE», LA FIN DE L'ÉPOPÉE

Le France (315 mètres de long, 30 nœuds de vitesse) est la quarante et unième unité d'une prestigieuse lignée de paquebots. Les ailerons révolutionnaires de ses cheminées ont fait deux fois le tour du monde.

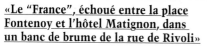

«Le "France", échoué entre la place Fontenoy et l'hôtel Matignon, dans un banc de brume de la rue de Rivoli»

De 1946 à 1956, le trafic maritime progresse, atteignant le million de passagers, tandis que le trafic aérien passe de 530 000 passagers en 1953 à 835 000 en 1956. Cette accélération ne semble pas encore inquiétante. Les Américains ne viennent-ils pas en 1952 de mettre en ligne l'*United States*? L'élection à la présidence de la République du Havrais René Coty paraît aussi de bon augure pour le futur *France*, paquebot de 55 000 tonneaux. Il faudra pourtant trois ans de discussions au Parlement et au Sénat, de réunions interministérielles pour aboutir à une décision.

Le 20 juin 1956 enfin, l'heureuse nouvelle est annoncée : le *France* sera construit. Il coûtera 273,6 millions de francs. L'Etat apportera au chantier de Penhoët une aide de 76,6 millions pour compenser la différence avec le prix offert par les chantiers étrangers. Le 25 juillet, la commande est signée. Mais trois années ont été perdues, dont on ne mesure pas encore les

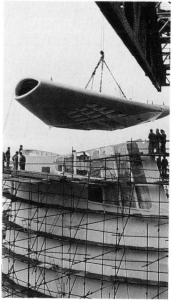

En juin 1961, l'un des ailerons de cheminée en forme de chapeau de carabinier espagnol est mis en place sur le paquebot.

Trente-sept mois et le travail de 1 300 ouvriers ont été nécessaires pour construire le *France*, sur la cale du *Normandie*. Page de gauche, la partie inférieure de la coque atteint déjà le pont A, soit la hauteur d'un immeuble de quatre étages (janvier 1959). A côté, un élément préfabriqué est assemblé sur cale. Ci-dessus, en mars 1960, le *France* reçoit sa première couche de peinture.

La bouteille de champagne lancée par Mme de Gaulle éclate sur la coque. Peu après, le général de Gaulle s'écrie : «Le bateau *France* est lancé, il a épousé la mer! Vive la France!»

redoutables conséquences pour l'avenir.

Le *France* est lancé le 11 mai 1960. L'année suivante, il atteint 35 nœuds aux essais avant de rallier Le Havre, sous la conduite du commandant Croisile le 23 novembre, où il est accueilli triomphalement par 100 000 personnes en liesse.

Le 8 février 1962, le «France» arrive à New York après une remontée triomphale de l'Hudson

Fêtes et réceptions marquent ce premier voyage, avec 2 000 passagers, et les suivants. En avril, on vend aux enchères pour une œuvre de bienfaisance le goulot du magnum qui servit au baptême… Le 23 novembre, pour la première fois, le *Queen Elizabeth* est dépassé par le *France,* qui file plus de 30 nœuds; les deux paquebots se saluent en illuminant leurs cheminées. Le 14 décembre, une passagère embarque sous une importante surveillance policière. De tout le voyage, elle ne sortira pas de sa cabine, la M 79! Il s'agit de *La Joconde,* prêtée aux Etats-Unis pour quelques semaines.

En treize ans, le *France* accomplit 377 traversées avec 588024 passagers sur la ligne de New York et fait 93 croisières avec 113682 personnes. 1 800 000 milles ont été parcourus sans la moindre avarie grave, ce qui prouve la qualité de la construction et de l'entretien. Mais ces passagers coûtent cher à la collectivité, car remplissage n'est pas synonyme de rentabilité.

La Transat et les Messageries ont contribué au développement du transport aérien. Dès 1937, la compagnie Air France-Transatlantique est fondée, qui étudie tous les itinéraires possibles entre les Etats-Unis, les Antilles et l'Europe du Sud-Ouest. Mais en 1945, l'Etat nationalise Air France et lui concède tout le transport aérien. Cependant, la Transat gardera l'exploitation des lignes sur l'Algérie jusqu'en 1962.

Au terme de cette première année d'exploitation, le *France* a effectué 22 rotations, deux croisières et transporté 65 300 passagers.

Avec les premiers Boeing-707 sortis en 1960, les jours des paquebots sont comptés

Les 338 000 passagers transportés en 1969 (on est loin du million des années cinquante) tombent à 132 000 en 1973. Dans le même temps, le trafic aérien atteint 12 millions de passagers. Pour pallier cette récession prévisible, l'armement multiplie les croisières et effectue deux tours du monde. Celui de 1972 est bénéficiaire ; par contre, celui de 1974 perd 28 millions de francs. Le premier choc pétrolier est passé par là, multipliant par quatre le coût du mazout, et il faut 600 tonnes par jour pour alimenter les 160 000 CV du *France*. Les dépenses d'équipage ont augmenté de 25 %, ce qui n'empêche ni grèves, ni retards à l'appareillage, ni les exigences du personnel civil et de la CGT qui s'opposent à toute modification ou diminution de l'effectif. Les premiers craquements se font entendre.

> " La mission de *France* sera de transporter d'un bord à l'autre de l'Atlantique des hommes, c'est-à-dire des pensées et des activités, des pages de connaissances et des sommes de travail, de l'art et de la richesse. "
> Général de Gaulle

L'heure des bilans et de la révolte

En fait, le *France* était condamné dès sa mise en service. En 1974, le déficit d'exploitation atteint 100 millions de francs; le 9 juillet, le gouvernement décide de ne plus subventionner le paquebot. La Transat riposte en annonçant que dans ces conditions elle va le désarmer.

Le compte à rebours est entamé. Les retards à l'appareillage se multiplient lors de chaque voyage. Le 11 septembre, à 22 heures, c'est le coup de force. Quelques membres d'équipage contraignent le commandant Pettré à mouiller dans le chenal. En réalité, le port du Havre ne sera pas bloqué. Mais pendant treize jours, le *France* est immobilisé en rade du Havre.

Occupation du "France" par les ouvriers C.G.T. du "Parisien libéré" et de la presse parisienne du 18 au 23 mars 1976

Quai de l'oubli

Dans un climat social et politique très flou, personne ne prend de responsabilités pour la survie de ce symbole du prestige national. Le 24 septembre, la tempête l'oblige à aller se réfugier à l'abri du Cotentin, devant Saint-Vaast-La-Hougue. Au terme de longues tractations avec les syndicats, le *France* ne revient au

Quai de l'Oubli où il reste cinq ans, le *France* va servir de tribune politique à plusieurs reprises, comme ici aux ouvriers du livre CGT, en mars 1976.

Havre que pour s'amarrer au quai de l'Oubli dans la zone industrielle où il va rester cinq ans, peu à peu abandonné de tous. Rien ne bougera jusqu'au coup de théâtre du milliardaire saoudien Akram Ojjeh, qui le rachète en 1977 80 millions de francs pour en faire un musée flottant témoin du patrimoine français. Pendant deux ans, il ne trouve pas de port d'attache pour abriter son projet et revend le paquebot 77 millions à l'armateur norvégien Knut Kloster.

Décembre 1989 : pour dix jours, le *Norway* est redevenu *France* le temps d'une croisière en mer des Caraïbes, preuve que la Compagnie générale maritime est fière de son passé.

Le «France», devenu «Norway», quitte le Havre

La Norwegian Caribean Lines décide de réduire la vitesse, donc la consommation, d'abandonner le luxe au profit de la classe unique et de diminuer les frais de personnel en utilisant pour le service hôtelier une main-d'œuvre d'origine asiatique.

Les transformations du *France* représentent un million d'heures de travail que l'armateur norvégien veut effectuer en Allemagne. Un nouveau conflit éclate, la CGT exigeant que le paquebot soit transformé en France. Pour ce dernier baroud d'honneur, elle bloque pendant trois jours l'écluse François-Ier, passage obligé pour la sortie du paquebot. Après l'intervention des forces de police, le 19 août à l'aube, le *France*, devenu le *Norway*, quitte enfin le port, assisté de remorqueurs français et hollandais.

Une nouvelle vie pour les paquebots?

La Transat transforme ses activités. Elle ne transportera plus de passagers mais uniquement du fret. Elle adaptera ses moyens matériels et humains, son image à cet objectif.

De son côté, le *Norway* fait le bonheur des touristes dans les Antilles, tandis que les Chantiers de l'Atlantique construisent un super-paquebot, le *Sovereign of the Seas*, et en ont un second sur cale. Au Havre, des paquebots à voiles à quatre et cinq mâts voient le jour avec succès.

TÉMOIGNAGES
ET DOCUMENTS

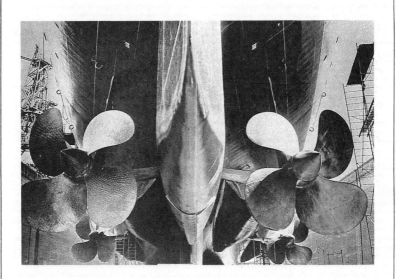

Les paquebots de l'émigration

Pour atteindre l'Amérique 40 millions d'émigrants en l'espace d'un siècle ont traversé l'Atlantique dans des conditions souvent difficiles. D'abord sauvage, l'émigration est bientôt réglementée. Des lois améliorent l'hygiène et la salubrité à bord tandis que les compagnies maritimes s'organisent.

Les conditions de vie à bord

Jusque vers 1850, les immigrants n'étaient, pour les armateurs, qu'un simple fret de retour. Les bateaux ne leur étaient pas destinés et leur aménagement était très variable, mais le plus souvent sommaire. [...]

Dès que les passagers étaient en nombre, les conditions de traversée étaient pénibles, surtout par gros temps. Un jeune Norvégien écrit en 1853 à sa famille : « La traversée a été terrible. Trois jours après avoir quitté la terre, nous avons eu une terrible tempête et pendant la nuit nous avons perdu le grand mât et le mât de misaine. [...] Beaucoup de provisions ont été gâtées et des vêtements ont été endommagés par l'eau. Cette tempête a duré deux jours et deux nuits et, pendant ce temps-là, nous sommes restés sans boire ni manger car nous ne pouvions rien préparer dans la cuisine où chacun devait faire cuire sa nourriture. Nous n'avions pas non plus d'eau potable.

Dans la cuisine, il y avait une grande cuisinière, mais comme il y avait toujours beaucoup de monde à vouloir l'utiliser, la seule loi était la loi de la jungle. Les plus forts et les plus agressifs arrivaient toujours à se faire cuire quelque chose, quoique avec difficulté, mais les plus faibles et les plus timides devaient se contenter de rester à l'arrière de la queue, au risque de voir leur gamelle chassée du feu, la nourriture à moitié cuite, par un plus fort qu'eux.

Les querelles et les bagarres étaient quotidiennes... » [...]

Si les hommes souffraient surtout de la faim, c'est la promiscuité et la saleté qui restaient le plus longtemps dans le souvenir des femmes : ainsi, cette émigrante italienne, voyageant en 1884 au départ du Havre, se remémorait trente ans après : « Nous tous, les pauvres gens, nous devions descendre par un trou au fond du bateau. Il y avait une grande pièce sombre avec des rangées d'étagères en bois tout autour où nous allions dormir — les Italiens, les Allemands, les Polonais, les Suédois, les Français — tous les genres. Et à ce moment-là, la troisième classe n'était pas comme maintenant : les filles, les femmes et les hommes dormaient tous dans la même pièce. Les hommes et les filles couchaient dans le même lit avec seulement des demi-planches de séparation pour que nous ne tombions pas tous les uns sur les autres. Mais j'ai eu de la chance : à côté de moi il y avait deux filles. »

La réglementation de l'immigration

Vers le milieu du XIXᵉ siècle, l'immigration aux Etats-Unis apparut enfin aux yeux des gouvernements et des opinions publiques comme un phénomène de masse qu'il fallait réglementer. En Grande-Bretagne, aux Etats-Unis, des lois furent votées pour assurer un minimum d'honnêteté, d'hygiène et de régularité dans le grand commerce qu'était le transport des immigrants. Entre 1842 et 1855 des lois anglaises prescrirent l'enregistrement et le cautionnement des agents des compagnies maritimes et de leurs « rabatteurs ». Un *Passenger Act* de 1842, un autre en 1855 prescrivaient une inspection des navires, des normes de cubage d'air, d'hygiène et de nourriture. Il y aurait désormais un rapport fixe entre le tonnage des navires et le nombre de passagers (deux passagers pour cinq tonnes). Il était prévu deux lieux d'aisance pour cent passagers. Les rations alimentaires étaient déterminées précisément. A partir de cent passagers, le navire devait avoir à son bord un cuisinier. Après 1847, l'année terrible, un médecin doit embarquer sur presque tous les navires. A peu près aux mêmes dates, des lois américaines équivalentes prenaient effet.

L'émigration irlandaise de 1847 est une tragédie de la misère, du laisser-faire, de la sous-administration volontaire anglaise et américaine. Cette année-là, environ 150 000 Irlandais, chassés par la « famine de la pomme de terre », s'embarquèrent pour l'Amérique du Nord. En temps normal, New York ou Boston auraient été les points de destination de ces émigrants peu soucieux de retrouver outre-Atlantique une autre Angleterre. Mais les Etats-Unis venaient d'adopter un *Passenger Act* plus sévère, et les Etats de New York et du Massachusetts adoptèrent, pour barrer l'entrée à l'afflux prévisible des Irlandais, des lois prévoyant des amendes pour les compagnies de navigation qui feraient venir des immigrants susceptibles de tomber à la charge du public. C'est donc vers Québec que fut détournée la plus grande partie de cette vague d'immigration. Affaiblis par la misère, la faim, stupéfiés par la promiscuité, le mal de mer, les émigrants furent frappés par des épidémies, surtout de typhus. William Smith, un tisserand, a raconté son voyage sur le navire *India* entre Liverpool et New York, l'hiver 1847-1848. 26 passagers et le capitaine étaient morts de la fièvre. A l'arrivée, 122 émigrants furent hospitalisés : « Quotidiennement je voyais des scènes horribles. Les cris des femmes perdant leur mari, les souffrances des hommes devant le cadavre de leur femme... Souvent les matelots ne pouvaient retenir leurs larmes. » [...]

Au fur et à mesure que d'autres pays d'Europe entraient dans le circuit de l'émigration de masse, l'arsenal législatif s'étoffait. La loi la plus complète fut celle adoptée par l'Italie en 1901 ; un médecin avec des pouvoirs très étendus d'inspection, le *commissario regio,* devait prendre place sur tous les bateaux en partance d'Italie et faire appliquer les normes d'hygiène strictes.

Toutes ces lois bien intentionnées ne réussirent pas à éliminer le très grand inconfort, et les difficultés de la traversée que le gros temps faisait tourner au tragique. Certains bateaux étaient très vétustes et certains capitaines particulièrement peu soucieux de leurs responsabilités. Dans l'ensemble, l'équipage des bateaux de ligne réservait son attention aux passagers de la première classe. [...]

Les médecins du bord, de l'avis général, n'étaient pas les sujets les plus brillants de leur profession. Pourtant, la mortalité à bord baissa : autour de 1 %

vers 1850, elle était de 0,06 % en 1880. Le raccourcissement du trajet y était pour beaucoup. [...]

Les dangers du voyage

Après 1850, des sociétés d'entraide se créent pour chaque nationalité : *Hibernian Society* pour les Ecossais, *Irish Immigrant Society* pour les Irlandais, *Bethel Ship* pour les Scandinaves. Particulièrement bien organisées étaient la *German Society* et la *Hebrew Sheltering and Immigrant Aid Society*, fédération des agences juives de charité (1909). A New York, l'organisation du débarquement à Castle Garden, puis à partir de 1892 à Ellis Island, limitait aussi les abus, sans arriver jamais à les supprimer.

Surtout, l'afflux des immigrants entraîna des efforts d'organisation de la part des compagnies de navigation. [...] Tous les bateaux d'émigrants n'étaient pas des vaisseaux de ligne : c'étaient très souvent des cargos non spécialisés de tonnages variables (environ 1 000 tonnes).

L'entrepont des émigrants sur *La Provence.*

Des émigrants à bord du *France* en 1913.

Les pires étaient ceux qui partaient directement d'Irlande, enregistrés à la seconde classe de Lloyds comme impropres au transport de chargements secs mais parfaitement aptes au transport, sur n'importe quelle distance, de chargement que leur nature ne rend pas sensibles aux dommages de l'eau de mer. De toute façon, même dans les vaisseaux de ligne, la traversée dans la cale était une dure épreuve qui dépendait beaucoup du capitaine et de l'équipage. Les brutalités étaient fréquentes. Au total : « Au bout d'une semaine en mer l'émigrant n'est plus le même homme. Comment en serait-il autrement ? Des centaines de personnes, hommes, femmes et enfants de tous âges, du vieillard gâteux de 90 ans jusqu'au nouveau-né, sont entassés sans lumière, sans air, marinant dans la saleté et respirant une atmosphère fétide, malades de corps et découragés de cœur... » Telle était l'expérience de Stephen de Vere, un philanthrope irlandais qui fit la traversée en 1847 dans la cale.

Dans la deuxième moitié du XIXe siècle, de grandes compagnies, la White Star, la Cunard, la Hamburg-Amerika, la North German Lloyd, ont des bateaux mieux agencés, mieux inspectés, mieux aérés. La revue médicale anglaise, *The Lancet* fit une enquête en 1873. L'un des enquêteurs concluait : « Le traitement est généralement bon si l'on s'en tient à la notion commune de ce qui est dû aux classes pauvres et ignorantes en retour de leur paiement. » Surtout, les compagnies de navigation contrôlaient désormais les pensions de famille et les hôtels pour émigrants, assurant une standardisation des services offerts et limitant les occasions de fraude et de vol. L'exemple le plus remarquable était celui de la compagnie Hamburg-Amerika qui avait créé un véritable village d'émigrants à Hambourg, où les voyageurs pouvaient se loger et se nourrir à un prix raisonnable, et où les Juifs religieux venus de Russie ou de Pologne pouvaient trouver de la nourriture cascher.

America ! America !
ouvrage collectif,
Gallimard/Julliard, 1980

La propulsion turbo-électrique du « Normandie »

Vitesse et régularité des arrivées sont deux objectifs vitaux pour les géants des mers qui rivalisent de puissance. Pour propulser la masse énorme du « Normandie » à la vitesse de 30 nœuds, c'est-à-dire à 55,56 kilomètres à l'heure, seule l'installation de turbines à vapeur offre la possibilité d'obtenir les 160 000 chevaux nécessaires.

Les quatre hélices avant le montage.

Choix de l'appareil propulsif

Depuis la mise au point par l'Anglais Parsons des turbines à vapeur, un problème s'était constamment posé. Pour qu'une turbine ait un bon rendement, il faut qu'elle tourne vite ou que la vitesse circonférencielle des étages d'ailettes soit grande, c'est-à-dire que la vapeur rencontre sur son chemin le plus possible d'ailettes. Les hélices, au contraire, doivent tourner le plus lentement possible car, au-delà d'une certaine vitesse, il se forme autour des pales de l'hélice une poche d'air et de vapeur mélangés qui diminue considérablement le rendement et provoque une détérioration rapide de l'hélice elle-même. Ce phénomène s'appelle cavitation.

Pour résoudre ce problème, il existait trois solutions à l'époque de la conception de *Normandie* :

1. Le branchement direct des arbres d'hélices sur les turbines qui imposait d'avoir des turbines de très grand diamètre pour que la vitesse circonférencielle soit suffisante.

2. Une réduction de la vitesse entre les turbines et les hélices par un jeu d'engrenages.

3. Une réduction électrique obtenue en utilisant d'un côté des alternateurs entraînés en prise directe par les turbines, et de l'autre des moteurs de propulsion entraînant les arbres d'hélices. Les alternateurs étant pourvus d'un nombre de pôles beaucoup plus réduit que les moteurs auxquels ils fournissent le courant, la réduction est d'autant plus importante entre alternateurs et moteurs que le nombre de pôles est différent entre chacun de ces deux groupes d'appareils.

La première solution qui avait été adoptée sur tous les grands paquebots transatlantiques français jusqu'à *Ile-de-*

France inclus (1927) fut tout de suite écartée pour *Normandie* car, compte tenu de la puissance à développer, soit 40 000 chevaux sur chacune des quatre lignes d'arbre, il aurait fallu des turbines gigantesques qui eussent été beaucoup trop encombrantes.

La seconde solution, celle des réducteurs à engrenages, était apparemment la plus simple et avait été adoptée sur les plus grandes et les plus récentes unités étrangères, essentiellement les paquebots allemands *Bremen* et *Europa*, et les paquebots italiens *Rex* et *Conte di Savoia*. Elle offrait l'avantage d'un rendement élevé (entre 97 et 98 % d'énergie transmise entre la turbine et l'hélice) mais était grevée de certains défauts : les turbines tournant par définition toujours dans le même sens, il était nécessaire d'avoir des turbines annexes moins puissantes pour effectuer les marches arrière, et d'autre part la réduction par engrenages présentait encore à l'époque des inconvénients tels que le bruit et les vibrations.

Il restait la troisième solution, celle de la propulsion turbo-électrique. Son rendement était un peu moins bon (environ 96 %) et elle présentait aussi l'inconvénient d'imposer des hélices plus rapides car la réduction était limitée par l'encombrement des moteurs qui ne pouvait dépasser certaines normes. Par contre, la présence de deux entrefers entre les turbines et les hélices conférait une extraordinaire souplesse aux machines et permettait des changements d'allure très brutaux sans risque d'avarie. Et surtout, il était possible d'obtenir la même puissance en marche arrière qu'en marche avant par simple inversion de l'arrivée du courant dans les moteurs. Si les turbines à réduction

Embarquement d'un organe de moteur.

mécanique permettaient d'économiser un peu de combustible lors de la marche à toute puissance, la propulsion turbo-électrique offrait en revanche la possibilité de diminuer très fortement la consommation en alimentant les 4 moteurs de propulsion avec 2 alternateurs seulement ; lorsque le navire serait appelé, certains mois de l'année, à fonctionner très en dessous de sa puissance maximale, les conditions d'exploitation deviendraient ainsi très avantageuses car, comme la puissance propulsive augmente approximativement selon le cube de la vitesse du bateau, une réduction de moitié de la puissance propulsive selon le procédé décrit ci-dessus ne correspondrait qu'à une réduction de 20 % seulement de la vitesse.

Enfin, si la propulsion turbo-

Un des quatre moteurs électriques de propulsion de 40 000 CV.

électrique était un peu plus lourde et encombrante que les turbines à réduction mécanique, elle ne pouvait occasionner ni bruit ni vibration. C'est pourquoi elle fut adoptée pour *Normandie* en dépit de sa complexité. Elle constituait une hardiesse exceptionnelle si l'on songe que ce type de propulsion n'avait jamais été adopté que pour des bâtiments ne disposant même pas du quart des 160 000 chevaux prévus. Elle fut réalisée par Alsthom.

Les 4 alternateurs avaient chacun une puissance maximale de principe de 33 400 kilowatts (soit 45 411, 308 chevaux) à 2 430 tours/minute. Ils produisaient du courant triphasé atteignant 81 périodes à l'allure maximale, sous une tension de 5 500 à 6 000 volts. Ils comportaient 4 pôles.

Les 4 moteurs de propulsion avaient chacun une puissance maximale de principe de 40 000 chevaux et comportaient 40 pôles. Ces moteurs étant synchrones, sauf pendant les manœuvres de démarrage, d'arrêt et d'inversion de marche, la réduction obtenue par la différence du nombre de pôles entre alternateurs et moteurs était donc de 10 à 1.

Il convient de préciser que cet appareil propulsif avait été largement surdimensionné de manière à pouvoir fournir la puissance de 160 000 chevaux avec une vitesse de rotation des hélices nettement plus réduite que l'allure maximum de 243 tours/minute, donc avec un couple résistant plus important. D'autre part, l'appareil propulsif pouvait fournir à son régime maximum une puissance supérieure de

138

Le *Normandie* dans sa forme à Saint-Nazaire.

25 % aux 160 000 chevaux prévus ; autrement dit, les moteurs étaient capables de développer environ 50 000 chevaux par ligne d'arbre soit au total 200 000 chevaux torsiométriques en super-surcharge (160 000 chevaux étant considérés comme puissance de surcharge permanente et 130 000 chevaux comme puissance de marche économique). Dans ce but, et en tenant compte d'une perte de 2 % dans les moteurs, les alternateurs furent calculés pour pouvoir développer chacun au moins 37 600 kilowatts (51 122

chevaux). Cette possibilité de marche en super-surcharge ne fut pas révélée au public, car il avait été décidé de n'en pas faire usage durant la première année d'exploitation.

Production auxiliaire d'électricité

Pour éclairer et chauffer le navire, assurer la ventilation, pour faire fonctionner de très nombreux appareils annexes, il était nécessaire de disposer d'une autre source de courant que les alternateurs exclusivement affectés à la propulsion. Ce courant était fourni par 6 turbo-dynamos alimentées par l'une des 29 chaudières principales. Chacune de ces turbo-dynamos avait une puissance normale de 2 200 kilowatts, soit au total 13 200 kilowatts. En surcharge, cet appareillage pouvait fournir une puissance supérieure de 25 %, soit 16 500 kilowatts. Le courant produit était continu sous 220 volts de tension. On peut avoir une idée de l'importance de ces génératrices si l'on se remémore la puissance électrique de *Conte di Savoia*, paquebot le plus électrifié avant *Normandie*, qui ne dépassait pas 5 100 kilowatts, et celle de *Queen Mary* entré en service un an après *Normandie*, qui était de 9 100 kilowatts en fonctionnement normal. Sans parler de la propulsion, *Normandie* était donc de très loin le paquebot le plus électrifié de son temps. Les groupes turbo-dynamos étaient complétés par 2 génératrices diesel de secours développant chacune 150 kilowatts en marche normale et 187 kilowatts en surcharge.

En totalisant la puissance de l'appareil propulsif turbo-électrique et celle des génératrices en état de fonctionnement normal, on obtient

Le tableau principal de distribution électrique, long de 27 mètres.

une puissance globale de 146 800 kilowatts. Avec tous les appareils en surcharge, y compris les génératrices de secours, cette puissance pouvait atteindre 167 274 kilowatts. L'ensemble du réseau métropolitain de Paris n'absorbait pas 120 000 kilowatts à l'époque de la mise en service de *Normandie*. D'ailleurs cette puissance électrique impressionnante faisait de *Normandie* la quatrième centrale thermique d'Europe en 1935, les trois autres étant bien entendu terrestres. La production de courant à bord eut suffi pour alimenter $1/25^e$ de la France !

Jean-Pierre Mazeirat,
in « *Normandie* »,
l'épopée du géant des mers,
Editions Herscher, 1985

Arrivée ponctuelle du *Normandie* au *pier* 88 à New York grâce à la puissance de ses moteurs.

Le paquebot, star de l'écran

Le mythe du paquebot et de la traversée transatlantique, l'histoire de l'émigration et celle des naufrages ne pouvaient qu'inspirer le septième art. Depuis le cinéma muet, le paquebot a été le théâtre ou la vedette de nombreux films.

Emigration, exode

Julien Duvivier, *Pépé le Moko*, 1937 (page de gauche, en haut).
Elia Kazan, *America, America,* 1964 (ci-dessus).

Charlie Chaplin, *L'Emigrant,* 1917 (page de gauche, en bas).
Otto Preminger, *Exodus,* 1961 (ci-dessous).

Comédies américaines

Irving Rapper, *Now, Voyager*, 1942
(ci-dessous).

Leo McCarey, *Elle et lui*, 1957 (ci-dessous).

George Stevens, *Swing time*, 1936
(ci-dessus, à droite).

George Stevens, *Swing time,* 1936 (ci-dessus, à droite).
Mark Sandrich, *L'Entreprenant M. Petrov,* 1937 (ci-dessous).

Howard Hawks, *Les hommes préfèrent les blondes*, 1952 (ci-dessus, à gauche).

Les Marx Brothers à bord

Sam Wood, *Une nuit à l'opéra*, 1935
(ci-dessous).

Norman Z. McLeod, *Monkey Business*, 1931
(ci-dessus et ci-contre).

Naufrages et catastrophes

Ronald Neame, *L'Aventure du Poséidon*, 1972 (en haut, à droite).
Atlantique Latitude 41 (ci-dessus).

SOS Titanic (en haut à gauche et ci-contre).

Jean Negulesco, *Titanic*, 1953 (ci-dessus).
Sauvez le Neptune (ci-contre, à droite).

Mythes et parodies

Federico Fellini, *Et vogue le navire*, 1983.

Tournés sur le « France »

Les Amoureux du France (à gauche).
Gérard Oury, *Le Cerveau,* 1968 (à droite).

BIBLIOGRAPHIE

Robert D. Ballard, *La Découverte du « Titanic »*, Glénat 1987.

Marthe Barbance, *Histoire de la Compagnie Générale Transatlantique*, Arts et Métiers graphiques Editeur 1955.

John Malcolm Brinnin et Kenneth Gaulin, *Style et luxe en mer*, Robert Laffont 1989.

Roger Carour, *Sur les routes de la mer avec les Messageries Maritimes*, Editions André Bonne 1968.

Michel Eloy, *Le Havre de 1517 à 1966*, Ancienne Imprimerie Etaix 1967.

Jean Hazard et Maurice Coquin, *Atlantique Nord, dix mètres sous la ligne de flottaison*, Editions Louis Soulanges 1969.

Commandant Lanfant, *Historique de la flotte des Messageries Maritimes de 1851 à 1975*, Grafic Foto Dunkerque 1979.

Edmond Lanier, *Compagnie Générale Transatlantique, de la pêche à la morue au « France »*, Plon 1962.

René Laurent, *Evolution chronologique de la Compagnie Générale Transatlantique*, Editions de l'Atlantique 1959.

Louis Le Cunff, *SOS Atlantique*, Editions André Bonne 1956.

Jean Legoy, Philippe Manneville, Jean-Pierre Robichon, Erik Levilly, *Les Havrais et la mer*, Editions du Petit Normand 1987.

Otto Mielke, *Les Grandes Catastrophes maritimes*, Denoël 1958.

Michel Mohrt et Guy Feinstein, *Paquebots, le temps des traversées*, Editions Maritimes et d'outre-mer 1980.

Charles Offrey, *Terminé pour la machine*, Presses de la Cité 1974.

Commandant Pettré, *Splendeur et rouille, « France »*, Editions du Pen Duick 1978.

Roger Regondy, *Quand le « Norway » s'appelait « France »*, Editions René Pacaut 1980.

François Robichon, *« Normandie », l'épopée du géant des mers*, Editions Herscher 1985.

Serge Sautreau, *Les Rituels du naufrage*, Editions Hier et Demain 1977.

Jules Verne, *Une ville flottante*, Editions Jean de Bonnot.

TABLE DES ILLUSTRATIONS

INDEX

CRÉDITS PHOTOGRAPHIQUES

COLLABORATEURS EXTÉRIEURS

Michèle Decré a été responsable de la rédaction et de la coordination de cet ouvrage. Manne Héron a réalisé la maquette des Témoignages et Documents.

REMERCIEMENTS

L'auteur et les Editions Gallimard remercient : M. Jean-Paul Herbert, responsable des Archives de la Compagnie Générale Maritime au Havre ; MM. Guy Mercier et Georges Krumeich de l'Association havraise des Amis des paquebots ; M. Patrick Cornet, chargé des Relations publiques du Port autonome du Havre ; Mme Christiane Mauban, conservateur des Musées du Havre ; M. Wagner, directeur du Musée maritime et portuaire du Havre.
Les éditions Gallimard remercient plus particulièrement Frédéric Morvan et Pierre Pitrou pour l'aide précieuse qu'ils ont apportée à la réalisation de cet ouvrage.

Table des matières